Giants, Devas

and other stories

Francis Oeser, born 1936 in St. Andrews, Scotland, grew up in Australia, returning to UK in 1967, now lives on Aigina island in Greece.

He has collaborated with artists and musicians as poet and librettist, publishing since 1983 a score of books, poetry and prose.

WORK IN PROGRESS:

Changes 1-5 a novel, *Seasons, Shakespeare's Songs, O for Love 2, Aspects of Eden, Time & Memory, The Language of Social Dreaming.*

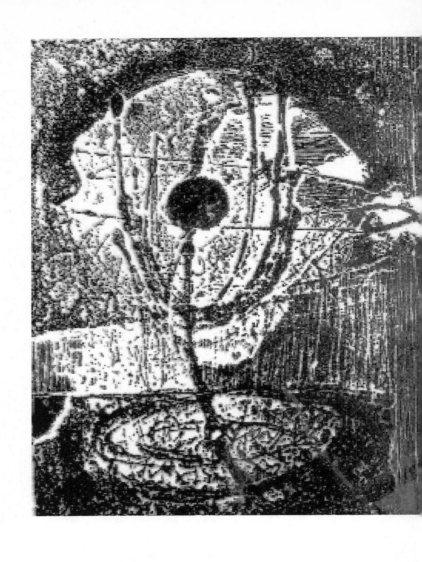

Giants, Devas

and other stories

by **Francis Oeser**

Sicnarf Press

London, Melbourne, Ithaca : 2009

Also by F.Oeser & The Sicnarf Press:

Orchestra 2008
Reflections 2008
Outrageous Fortune 2007
Loukoumia 2006
Africa Sung to 2005
After you've Brushed your Teeth (Bunyip Stories) 2005
48 Evening Ragas 2003
Your Whispered Name (with Ann Dowker) 2003
Eyeland (with Akiko Fujikawa) 1997
Scenes from Childhood 1997
But (with Akiko Fujikawa) 1996
Persephone 1996
O for Love (with G. Wickham) 1994
You, Me, We 1993
Social Dreaming & Shakespeare 1992
Bay Break 1991
Africa Sung (1). 1987
Seasons End 1984
Black Notes 1983

British Library cataloguing-in-publication data.
A catalogue record for this book is available from the British Library.

© The Sicnarf Press 2009:
122 Dartmouth Park Hill, London N19 5HT, UK.
Box 708, Aigina Port, Aigina 18010, Greece.
francisoeser@hotmail.com.
Readings, PO Box 1066 Carlton Victoria, Australia.
Bookery, de Witt Mall, 215 N.Cayuga Street Ithaca, 14850 NY, USA

ISBN: 978-0-9552974-3-4

Printed & bound in UK by CPI-Antony Rowe, Eastbourne, East Sussex
on paper from FSC (renewable) forests.

Contents

Acknowledgements

Thank you, Yaeko Ueno for your care and advice about Japanese religion in *Giants*; thanks too for shrewd comments from Don Maclennan on *Stampede* and *Choices*, Marius Bukauskas for help with Chinese in *Circles of Repair*. However, errors remain mine.

FO - Aigina 2008

Circles of Repair

SYDNEY AT LAST. Below, a glimpse of the nesting sails of the Opera House as the plane banked over the Pacific, down through empty sky, skimming beaches and roofs, landing on a sizzling summer runway.

On a carefree visit to friends and old haunts, the man strode into the terminal thronging with queues, police, machines and dogs. "Welcome to Australia" a sign belied the atmosphere of threat. Sure, travelling was dangerous; was his arrival in this "sunburned country"?

'Just come from Asia? Wait there, Mate.' an officer drawled. 'Photos fingerprinting, x-rays and drug checks, passenger identification.'

'I've an Aussie passport.'

'So 'av I. It's quicker with us. Y' know, we 'avta watch-out.'

'Keep Australia squeaky white and all that?'

'Sure thing, Mate. The White Australia policy is a bit tarnished these days, know what I mean, 'Nam cafes, Thai restaurants, Satay shops, curry houses, and the Chinese bin here for ever. All bloody rabbits. This government's tough. It's best for the country.'

'It's no welcome.' The man pointed at the brazen sign.

'No one has t' come. Go back where you're from, I say.' said the officer winking and moving off towards the inspection booths smugly slapping his revolver.

Waiting, waiting. The queues grew ragged. Children whimpered, the elderly desperately sought resting places, the able-bodied fretted.

'We treat criminals like this.' a woman said.

A student nodded. 'We're all criminals here.'

The man looked gloomily along the unmoving line. 'Their past has caught up with them. Well, I'm not becoming a jail bird. I'll go back.' He trudged across the concourse, found a ticket office and bought a single to Kuala Lumpur. 'So, where should I wait?'

The girl blinked. 'Through the Domestic Terminal, follow the signs, then go straight on to gate Four.'

'I don't want to enter the country, only leave.'

The girl busied herself on the telephone. An officer arrived and escorted the passenger to a distant police office. The Chief wagged his head. 'I see you've just arrived. Goin' so soon?'

'I refuse to be subjected to criminal handling; fingerprinting, dogs, forms, questions and x-rays. I carry a national passport. Presumably checks were made. It's scandalous, for the few days. I'll return to Malasia. The flight leaves shortly. Please let me through.'

'Av t' check your documents. Wait here.'

Half an hour later the man fossicked in his bag for his other passport and, unattended, slipped away into the departure lounge, boarded an aircraft and flew off.

The day was waning as the plane touched down. The man finished his champagne and danced into Arrivals. After passports he noticed in the knot of waiting men, a pair with a card headed by the Australian coat of arms crowning his badly printed name. He walked on. After greeting his hotel taxi he was whisked away through the throttling city over clogged canals, seething tenements, footpaths, forests of palms and out into the country to the *Golden Sands Hotel* rearing above a beach faintly reminiscent of its name.

After supper he ventured onto the day-warm sand before ambling to his room. Through his open window the ocean gently grated on the shore accompanied by the sough of wind in tall palm trees. His sleep was filled with freedom and glee.

In the morning everything gleamed. He bounded to a late breakfast in an empty dining room, attended on by gentle smiling boys and girls, 'Straight out of Eden.' He muttered smiling back at them.

'It's some distance to Eden. You *are* Doctor Cunningham, sir?' The two he'd noticed at the airport had caught up with him.

'A beady-eyed serpent would know.' he said selecting an apple from the fruit dish because it reminded him of home.

'We waited for you.'

'I know.'

'Finding you was hardly a trouble, sir.'

'Good for you.'

'The Ambassador has your documents. He was wondering how

you travelled without them.'

'A fig leaf is all that's required, don't you know?'

'Eden? Adam and Eve, yes. Not you, sir. It's illegal to have two Australian passports.'

'My *only one* was claimed in Sydney. This is Eden, so bugger off.'

One of the men laid an envelope on the table. 'From His Excellency. A car will pick you up tomorrow evening at six. Dress informal. It's Australia Day. He'll deal with the matter then.'

The envelope held an invitation. 'Invited onto Aussie soil here and prohibited to step onto the real thing.' The man sighed. He fondly watched the gracious dance of the young sarong-clad staff around the dining room. 'This happens in Eden.' A doe-eyed girl cleared his table watching his frown vanish as his eyes swept her body.

She was shyly attentive. 'Another coffee, mister?'

'I'd love a long glass of tropical juice. May I?'

'I will see for you.'

She slipped away. He turned and gazed out to sea through thin elephantine palm trunks. There, some fishing boats lay, gulls greedily swooping overhead. The beach flowered: bright umbrellas unfurled. The sea gleamed.

'Someone's added milk to it.' he murmured.

'It's the coral reef.' The girl laughed lightly, setting a tall frosted glass on his table.

'Really?' the man grinned. 'I thought it was the magic milk making you bloom.' He searched the deeps of her hazel eyes, silenced. Such freshness should never be tampered with, he thought.

'Do you like it here?' she said.

'The raggedness and the beauty are spectacular.'

'Am I untidy? I'm sorry.'

'The ragged palms, hay-rick rooves, dusty tracks, the ruffled edge of the sea, the frothy clouds. No straight lines. The hairy swell of coconuts, the delicacy of exotic flowers, children playing. You, untidy? Not at all. A gentle beauty from the milky sea transforms you all into fruits of this ragged Eden. Thanks for the drink.' He wandered to the edge of the terrace overlooking the garden pool, and sat sipping reflectively.

'The ice at my centre is melting. It's the warmth of Eden here.'

The man closed his eyes. When he looked again, the fishing boats had gone. Gulls still hovered and the umbrella flowers shivered in a teasing breeze. He smiled at the bright-eyed birds seeking crumbs at his feet who scattered when he stirred, rose and strolled up to his room. He worked with his computer, dozed and worked again. Nothing disturbed him all that day, or the next.

At six o'clock he waited in the lobby. A long black car bedecked with an Australian flag whispered to the hotel entrance. Wide-eyed staff thronged as one of them opened the doors. The man was ushered out. Many bowed and waved. It might have been the TV news.

The embassy party was run of the mill. Men in creased tropical suits, women in cool crushed dresses. Only the staff in black pants and crisp white shirts looked fresh. The man wore a dun coloured cotton jacket, matching trousers and an open necked gold silk shirt showing a sliver of his chest sporting a gold emblem awarded him by the Danish Academy of Science (more important to him than the military decorations sported by other guests).

Standing alone he viewed the embassy garden beyond the window, turning to accept a passing glass or snack. He watched dusk infiltrating, saw the party gradually reflected in the dusk-backed glass. Knew His Excellency was drifting over to assail him.

'Doctor Cunningham, I presume?'

'Mister Stanley.'

'Blair Grant.'

'Representing van Diemens land?'

'Van? Oh yes. Australia. I do apologize for the mix-up at Sydney. Our new regulations caused undue, um .'

'Anger, Mr Grant. And distaste.'

'Officers were doing their best. You can't know what consternation your disappearance caused. Security wants to know how you managed to get here. It shook them. By the way, we kept your documents in our safe. I'll give them to you.'

'No need, Ambassador. I'll manage. Didn't your men report my comment that fig leaves help one get around Eden? They signify the Fall, don't you know. After eating Eve's fruit, understanding good and evil, Adam donned a fig leaf to face his wrathful maker, wore it when trumpeted out into the wilderness. I missed trumpeters in Sydney.'

'I've tried to explain.'

'It was a private visit, there'll be no official complaint.

I appreciate this hospitality. Thank you.'

'Glad to have you with us.'

'Lovely people.'

'You know many of our guests?'

'The gentle Malasians.'

'Oh? Don't know what a distinguished scientist like you has in common with our dusky brothers.'

'Or what any of us do?'

'Well, you're frank.'

'Mr Grant, I've always preferred Eden.' The man lifted an arm and waved to a drink waiter. The ambassador caught a glint from his gold medal. The calls from Sydney and Canberra were strictures. He'd tried to calm things. Cunningham was prickly and obscure. Luckily he was smiling. Blair Grant took a slim passport from his pocket and held it out. 'Doctor Cunningham, how?'

'I hold dual nationality. I won't need it again. Thank you.'

'It's in our safe.' The ambassador retreated.

By now, the garden was dark. The mirror, brilliant, the wish to go, clear. His elbow was nudged by a slight greying Chinese man. 'May I trouble you. Are you not Colin Cunninham?'

The man nodded.

'I am Charles Chua, your university college neighbour. So many years ago. This *is* a treat.'

They found a couch, perched and gossiped like undergraduates. The staff stood about until there was no one else. Carefully they rose and wandered to the entrance agreeing to rendezvous shortly in Malacca, Charles' home town.

'You'll stay with me for a long time. We must catch-up.' Charles said warmly. 'We'll find a way of pub crawling although we don't have them or darts. Terrible. But you'll not be bored or lonely, I promise.' Charles regarded the tense face, sensed a troublesome life he'd never wished on his friend. 'Of course you can work. Freely. I enjoy your brand of sharing and being alone. It always reminds me of swimming: coming up out of the watery silence for air, shouting, and diving back to depths. You must come, CC.'

The pleasures of the reception returned with him. The hotel felt easier. Colin meandered through the lobby. Going outside, looking for a chair, he was greeted by his favorite waitress offering drinks.

'Tropical, as yesterday. Do you like it too? Yes? Then bring two and put them on my bill.' He sat back enjoying the aftermath of champagne and the prospect of visiting Charles Chua. He knew the girl had returned by the clink of the glass she set down. She hovered. Enjoying her succulence, he nodded her to a nearby chair.

'Can I ask you?' She sat quite still. He grinned encouragingly. 'I want to visit my brother in Australia, can you help me? I don't understand how.'

'Me?'

'The embassy take you in a limo. They listen to you. There, I wait and wait. They give me many papers. I don't know what to do with them.'

'Do you have them here?'

'Yes.'

'Get them. We'll fill them in together.'

'Now?'

'Of course. Go.'

The girl slipped away.

'It's her, mixing with champagne.' he muttered trying to still his longing to abandon wilderness and home in her arms. He shifted sideways into half the capacious chair, pulled the table round in front, set his glass on the pavement and waited. Pulling her unresisting into the chair, as warm and fragile as a bird, together they managed every form.

She sighed, torn about intimately tending him as thanks and a wish for simpler things. 'Tomorrow I'm not here.'

'Day off?' She nodded. 'Let's go in to the embassy. My time's limited.' What he specially liked was reading her thoughts. He saw her inner battle shuffling all tomorrow's arrangements, watched her dusky face cleared by a winning smile, felt her relax against him. As she would after love, he thought, ashamed how simple she was, how gross his desire, and, by the flicker of distress in her face, that she understood how his help might be repaid.

Yet she remained beside him, quietly watching his relaxing face until his big hand released hers so the papers blew around.

He delighted in her dance to recapture them. 'Taxi, here, tomorrow after breakfast? Good. We'll go together. You're very beautiful. I won't hurt you. Eve is safe in Eden. Good night.' Waiting for the lift, he turned for another look. The chairs were in order. One was nudging a bare table. The two glasses, the girl, the papers had vanished.

Then he was leaving for Malacca. The girl's uncle took him to the airport. The family was very grateful for a proper visa, with time enough to help with the birth of her brother's first child and (never ever admitted) time to illegally work there while her sister-in-law was confined.

Her uncle chuckled. 'She likes you. She's never invited anyone home. We're not allowed to mix with hotel guests. No one admits what happens under the palms or inspects the babies. By the way, the family all enjoyed your visit. The boys are still boasting about their football game. It's easier for boys; girls are caught-up in their own contradictions. Yet her mother forgave her working at the hotel. Tell me, did you like her?'

'A lot. She belongs in this unspoilt place.'

'Unspoilt, you say? You should've seen it before the hotels ravaged it. Life was better then.'

'Humanity has lost contact with the earth. We don't know how to live anymore. There are remnants here. Treasure them as your children and your dreams. Most of us are out of touch with such wisdom.'

'You care. That's a form of wisdom. Please do come back to us. You're part of the family now.'

'Yes. Thank you.' He belonged; it warmed him all day.

Charles met him. His chauffeur, Darus, drove them through Malacca to a neat walled compound on its outskirts. The buildings were snug inside high perimeter walls. The main house stood at the middle of the block facing an airy garden. Kitchen, stores and servants' rooms were behind off a smaller courtyard. Colin was deposited in the guest house separating the garden from the street. It had been Charles' space until his mother died when he moved back into the main house.

Charles' sallow face broke into grins. 'Dear friend, you are a part yet separate. Come and go as you wish. Meals are eaten in the main house. Please come over often and chat. I miss long talks, the quiet of listening to music, the delights of a lively house, don't you agree? I took a small cache of books to your room. Browse every where. Washing and room cleaning is done by Rantun. She and Koki look after us here. Come and meet them.'

The two men drifted into the kitchen. They were greeted by two voluptuous young women. Koki respectfully shook hands with a ravishing smile. Her elder sister, Rantun, half-turned away busied with pots and jugs, pulled a scarf round her face and nodded, murmuring in a mellifluous voice, '*Také*. You are welcome, *Tuan*. *

Charles smiled happily. 'I told them you were my other brother from distant times. They honour and love you as such. Now, Rantun, tea for us. Bring the English biscuits for Colin. That's what you should call him. He's your brother too.'

As Rantun turned away to tend the kettle Koki seized a garish biscuit tin to fill an elegant porcelain bowl, gripped the tea pot and, with a winning smile, ferried everything into the lounge. She poured the men tea and stood savouring their talk uncovering memory and friendship, glad Tuan Charles was happy.

Rantun's voice from the kitchen, 'Koki, come along my dear. Chores before rest.'

The girl nodded and skipped happily away.

Charles appraised her as he would a butterfly. 'They care for everything. I've promised them they may remain as long as they wish. Silence haunts the house but nowadays it comforts me.'

'Such gentle beauty.' Colin sighed. 'We've mislaid such delight.'

Charles patted his knee. 'Look inside your heart, you'll find it. I did. Now, arrangements: I've taken the rest of the week off from work to show you around. Then I'll leave you to Rantun and Koki, and the breathing silence of our house. Work and play. Visit the villages beyond. Much is unspoiled and worth a stroll. You've met Darus, my driver. He'll ferry you anywhere you wish. Tomorrow I'd like to show you my home town, if you'd agree?'

'Thank you, Charles. Are those two really sisters? Koki is so warm and cheerful, Rantun resentful.'

'Ah, yes. But don't be mislead by appearances. Rantun's life toughened her exterior. Inside she's soft and unquenchable. She prepared your room. Understand its welcome as representing hers. The source of the pleasing calm here is Rantun, you'll discover.'

Charles slowly got to his feet. 'This is my time of rest. Let's have tea or something stronger in the cool of late afternoon? Believe me, all of us regard your visit with delight.' He rose and padded away. Colin sat watching the supple back of Koki outside as she tended an untidy spray of frangipani before she too vanished.

---

* *Také* is a Malay greeting.
  Tuan is Malay for lord, sir, master.

The garden wilted in the midday heat. Colin peeled his sweaty shirt off the chair back-cushion, stepped into the empty garden and sauntered towards his room. He clambered up onto the verandah as the shrouded figure of Rantun was gliding away.

His case had been positioned on a low stool inviting unpacking. A small vase with a spray of orchids graced his bedside table. A frosted glass of juice sweated nearby. Indoor slippers stood sentinel on the floor. He sniffed the flowers. The only scent was tropical fruits.

'How did she know it was my favorite drink?' Colin murmured. He found drawers and hanging space for his meagre possessions, a table and chair for his computer, a shelf in the bathroom for his sponge bag.

He pulled off his clothes and fell contentedly onto the bed burying his nose in its fresh sunny tang. He dreamed hands caressed him. Then, hands eased his creased brow, soothed his aching legs. Innocence faded as his ejaculation woke him.

At once he knew someone had been there. The shutters had been drawn, the bedside table pushed closer, a mosquito net unravelled around his bed.

'She watched my wet dream.' he said softly, untroubled by surprise. 'So, what's her secret? She sees, remaining unseen. Visible, but not a part of the world.' He groaned. 'An inside-out me. My shadow glimmering in the deeply polished floor, unable to get out into the breathing world?'

Colin showered then made his way through the dusky garden to the main house where Koki stood waiting. She bowed him in grinning with such a mischievous smile, Colin decided she was the spy. This dream taunted him.

Charles graciously poured him a beer, putting a wooden plate of Chinese crackly cookies at hands' reach. They talked mainly about the past, the early years after they graduated, going their separate ways, easing into familiarity until Koki, carrying a steaming pot of clear soup, announced supper. Deftly she served, delighting in her two mens' satisfaction. She nudged close to Colin demonstrating an effective hold of his chopsticks which slipped frequently from his hand, 'They want me to be thinner.' he said.

Koki laughed gently. 'No, no. *Tuan* Colin must not starve, must he *Tuan* Charles?'

Charles grinned. 'Bone is slippery. Do we have bamboo ones?'

'Rantun's in the cook house.' Koki slipped away.

They feasted on laughter and Chinese delicacies ending with smooth, creamy lychees. Then Charles suggested listening to some Vivaldi concertos before bed.

When Colin returned to his room, a soft lamp had been lit, the bed turned down, pyjamas nestled under his pillow and the tropical juice replenished. He sat momentarily before his computer unwilling to wake it, invaded by the care-touched room. His sense of belonging in that morning's taxi ride now returned. He undressed and donned pyjamas, tip toed to the outer door and looked out. A new moon rocked over the house gilding its roof tiles, glancing into the garden, the only visible light. Colin's wishes flew up into the night.

'How peaceful it is.' He bowed and blew kisses to the skewed bone-coloured smile in its vast velvety face.

Soon he was asleep. Deep, repairing, soothing him all night.

Enjoyable rambling days followed, enjoyed by Charles as much as Colin who became one of the household easily, only marred by his perplexity over Rantun's off-handedness.

'Maybe the sisters represent good and bad.' he wondered. 'The beast glowering in the one, goodness and joy radiating from the other.' In confusion about the buxom pair Colin consulted Charles.

They stood in the garden feeding plump carp in a round pond.

Charles broke a withered frond from water lilies and looked fondly at his old friend. 'Rantun and you are strangers. Like a wild animal, her trust takes time to grow. Koki's love is instantaneous, as you've seen.'

'She cleans my room lovingly.'

'Koki only tends this house and the garden.'

'Are you saying Rantun looks after me?'

'I am. Believe me. So, go now and ask her.'

Colin walked hesitantly through the house and into the kitchen. Rantun was alone, humming to herself, sculpting vegetables into exotic flowers, adding them to a picturesque display on a broad ceramic plate. She turned expectantly, her head scarf falling from her face revealing a livid birth mark branding one side and down her neck. Rantun gave a stifled cry and hid her face.

Her fear and distress brought tears to his eyes. 'My dear, I'm so sorry. No one told me. I didn't understand. I thought I displeased you.' Trembling, she shook her head. 'Since I arrived you've been here yet not here. Doing invisible good turns, bringing good dreams, calming the beast inside.'

She looked at him in wonder and gathered a tear from his cheek. He gathered her lusciousness into his arms and held her until her trembling ceased. He relinquished her. 'Thank you'. Shaking her head she faintly smiled.

She bent over her flowers. 'Now you know, *Tuan*.'

It was an easier silence. He watched her deft fingers cut and shape carrots, tomatoes and radishes. She sat like a masked puppet dancer in an ancient ritual whose meaning escaped him yet stirred him so deeply it hurt. Without another word he went away through the house and into the garden. Charles had gone. The carp were nosing the surface and chewing as they flicked round and round. 'My thoughts are carp'. he whispered. 'Round and round with no resolution. So are my feelings. I might swim the primal river again, finding a way to the open sea.'

But bad voices plagued him: 'They care this way for everyone. It's not because I'm special.'

He fought back: 'It's their thought and conviction, and because it's me.'

Circles within fiery circles piloted him into restless sleep.

He awoke suddenly and hurried out making for the kitchen. No one there. He looked out the door into the service courtyard. At the bottom of the steps Koki was showering. Cheeky water tongues caressed her honeyed flesh enhancing its nakedness. Her smile beguiled him utterly. There was a slight movement under a tree by the far wall. Rantun. Blazing with confusion Colin fled back into the house. He played a CD of Chinese music, every clash and shriek an echo of his desire. During supper Koki's coquettish smile confirmed his wild dreams. He knew she'd come to him; it was only a matter of time.

Days passed. He was in the river, hardly swimming, relishing waiting. Charles dropped ice into Colin's glass of whisky one evening. 'I'm so glad you're settling in. Rantun tells me you're going to market with her tomorrow morning.' He smiled. 'Improve your appetite. The dazzling array of colour and shape, multitudinous scents, the garrulous throng, the songs of children playing, working, larking, mimicking us - the small sprites in charge of laughter - make a rich prelude to dining on pleasures fresh from the bountiful earth.

'Such connections are represented by the Chinese circle. A

symbol of completeness, of perfection, the centered calm we Chinese seek.' He drained his glass. 'Don't hurry. Let the great circle close. That's all.'

'I'll swim to a crawl.' Colin laughed.

'Sounds fishy.'

'Oh, it is.'

'Colin, you're sounding better, looking better. I am relieved it's turning out to be great fun.'

'Charles, you have no idea . . .'

'Dear friend, of course I do. We all do. That's why I suggested you stay for a long while. We've found a centre here and want to share it.' Charles turned on the ceiling fan. 'I was so troubled at University. Alone in so strange a place. Your friendship steadied me. You didn't know? Now I can tell you, I'm forever grateful.'

'I was thinking today: feelings are like the wind. They're unseen but have awesome effect.'

'Ignoring invisibles, we're overwhelmed by the seen. We must learn to linger, as I told you, in order to experience the still centre.'

'I will linger tomorrow, blind-eyed.'

They left for the market very early. But already the streets were filled with people, with weaving bicycles, carts brim-full of produce, and scantily clad children cheerfully dodging the throng. As Rantun stepped from the entry gate she wrapped her scarf around her face. Colin took her arm as she expertly threaded through the bustle. Initially he attended on her as she bargained and chatted and handed over coins for fruit and vegetables still shining from the earth, all stored in her woven grass carriers.

At a spice stall she ordered and left him to collect the many small parcels of earth-coloured powders and fragrant seeds. Then he explored, charmed by smiles and unintelligible talk friendly with curiosity. Later, footsore, he found her. He took some of her bulky carriers and together they wended through the edge of the market to quieter realms where Colin spied a tea stall.

'Rantun, lets have tea.'

'We'll have better at home.'

'I'd like to sit down . .'

'Of course.'

'. . With you.'

'Me? What can I say?' Rantun put bags down.

'Is it a matter of words?'

'No.'

They sat at a bench under a leafy tree sipping bitter-sweet tea from small glasses. Rantun pushed her veil away and studied his face. 'You desire women?'

Colin nodded. 'I need to be inside.'

'You find Koki attractive?'

'Yes, with the beauty of paradise.'

'Playing with paradise?'

'More than that.'

'Your eyes tell me everything.'

'I couldn't hurt her.'

'I know. What stops you?'

'The gulf between inside and out, the contradiction between seeing and feeling. Old scars. It must be joyful as well as safe.'

'Risking joy?'

'I learned to stifle longing.'

'So, you stay outside?'

'Rantun, you understand.'

She nodded. A tear coursed down her unblemished cheek. She gripped the table. 'Yet it *is* a matter of words. Breaking silence is crossing a bridge, the first risk?' She watched a fly jog round the lip of her cup. It stopped now and again to lick its sugary feet and wiggle its furry abdomen. 'Perhaps shyness prevents you taking what you need?'

'Brutality.'

'Of course. The oldest dragon.' Her smile lit him.

Colin stood. Placed coins beside their empty glasses, taking his share of the bulky bundles, waiting. She pulled her clothes about her and sheepishly stepped from the tea house into the thronging street. He followed her home.

Colin tiredly ate a light lunch on his own. Charles was at work. The women ate in the kitchen as usual. Afterwards he retired, showered and fell asleep on his bed. He dreamed of being with a small joyful boy, gambolling through breasty mountains of fragrant spices and the fresh colours of exotic fruits, daring to explore everywhere. He woke smiling.

Someone had left a vase with a fresh spray of flowers, a cool drink and a well-turned bowl with red spiky lychees. He looked down his naked body. Had Koki inspected his equipment? Would she come tonight? he wondered. Suddenly he realized the fruit represented Rantun: the red of her livid birth mark enclosing luscious white syrupy fruit within. Charles had rightly counselled him about the connections leading to perfection. It had been an inspiring day.

Colin dressed and ventured out. He walked far into more open farming land intruded upon by houses crowned by ragged rooves of palm, grass and corrugated iron. Unkempt dogs lifted lazy heads and sniffed at him. The ubiquitous children played and danced. Women almost completely covered by their massive loads trudged back from the fields. Wispy grey haired grandparents sat patiently against walls, chewing smoking and talking in intrusive tones. Only the children seemed to notice him. 'It's like my dream.' he muttered.

He found an itinerant *satay* stall. Sat, ordered beers and a dozen sticks set about a small bowl of peanut sauce. He studied the antics of the crowd. No one minded. Alcoholic happiness coursed through him.

When he returned the house was in darkness. He stumbled to bed. Swimming through the circles of carp and lychees and small brown bodies, he slept.

Colin, heavy with beer and peanuts, woke in blackest night, swung groggily out of bed and padded to the darkened bathroom. Returning he stumbled on a body sleeping on the floor beside the bed. In a trance he pulled the woman up and into his bed. Warmth overwhelmed him. He opened her sarong and grazed her succulent breasts. She moaned, arching in longing. Colin caressed her firm thighs. His fingers creeping around and into her lush patch of pubic hair until he could wait no longer. He felt Koki shiver as he plunged in. Deeper, deeper. They thrashed. In an ecstasy of delight they fell into one another, falling, falling into sleep, the circles complete.

He woke to find her gone. He lay shot-through by inner laughter, lust shimmering with thoughts of feasting on Koki's perfection. He showered, wrapped a sarong round his waist and bounded to breakfast. She was waiting. Her smile banished what inner shadows remained. Ah, such grace!

Suddenly he wanted for nothing.

Weeks passed. Colin glowed with pleasure. Days of calm enjoyment. Nights of uninhibited passion. The burrs grating inside him diminished. The greying world burst with colour and throbbed with life.

One day, a problem - failure of the electricity supply - made irrelevant when he abandoned his computer and set out to explore.

That evening they all dined by candle light, the house lit by the same soft glow he held inside.

She came to him in the dark of night as usual. He took her gently and filled her with softness until sighing they slept in deeps where words couldn't articulate unity or separate reality from dream.

Colin was woken by a glare in his eyes. The lights had come back on cutting the night in half. Koki lay curled up her lovely back facing him, hair cascading down her neck onto the sheet, her bovine hip shielding her sex. Hungrily Colin stretched a leg over her and followed seeking embrace, seeking, seeking her riches. She lay open before him. All her perfection seen for the first time. He gasped. Her face, half masked by the livid red of lychees accused him, accused them both. He collapsed on his side watching Rantun sleep.

The glare woke her. She stretched, smiling through sleep, saw his pensive face in the accusing light. With a terrible wounded cry she cringed, struggled off the bed, snatched up her sarong and fled.

Colin spent the rest of the night in wretched sleeplessness, saw dawn lighten the sky and then the garden. He groped for clothes and heavily went through the garden, through the service courtyard and into the quiet kitchen. Rantun was bending over a sickly flame fluttering from charcoal over which she would braise a duck. Stricken, she turned away. He put out his hands and carefully turned her face to his, seeing a haze of red he kissed along its edge, from forehead to neck to forehead, clinging to the shoreline of an island of peace and generosity protected from drowning. Her tears saved them, and his desire for comfort and release pushing against her flimsy sarong. Her trembling hand parted his sarong, found his phallus. She bent down and kissed it again and again holding it until its velvet spurted and his silent cries, and hers, stilled.

There was movement at the house door. Hurriedly she rose and pushed him outside and down the steps tenderly wiping her sticky hand across his lips in farewell and welcome.

Koki had watched. She was shocked by the passion of her dear ugly sister and this fascinating man. She too ached, fumbling for a dream in the growing light.

The day became routine. Colin drifted to his room after lunch. He found Rantun brushing the verandah and humming.

'What are you singing? It's lovely.'

Rantun looked up at him. 'I'm glad you like it. This traditional

Malay song tells us many things which are still new:

> When the civet cat is blinded
> the chickens strut lighthearted.

> When pussy grows toothless
> the mice become fearless. *

Rantun smiled. 'It tells me you took the teeth out of the light and your kiss made me fearless.'

Colin grinned. '*R a n t u n* in ancient Malay must mean cat. You are my own dearest cat, and not only in the night.'

'What rubbish. But I agree.'

'Rantun, why do you love me?'

'Because.' she looked far away. 'I don't know.' she saw a smile flit across his face. 'On your first day I watched you sleep. I'd never been close to a man. You were strong and complete yet there was a scar between your legs, something extra, as if at the beginning, when everything was pushed into men, there was too much, so something slipped out and flopped about. You hid your scar as I did. But until this morning I thought only yours was magic.'

'My scars are invisible yet you saw them.'

'Everyone has scars. You deny yours.'

'And everyone has a cock.'

'Yours speaks rather then bruises. Your gentleness fills me with dreams.'

'I love you Rantun.'

'That's best of all. Dear *Tuan* Colin, Koki is upset. I promised to go to her. Can you sleep?'

'If Pussy brings me a mouse tonight.'

'Will a drink do?'

'Of course, of course, of course' his grin proclaimed. She tossed her head as if shaking free and glided away.

Peace prevailed. Chickens strutted, mice danced fearlessly and days passed gently with a growing sense of permanence. Charles announced the Chinese New Year would be celebrated in a few days time, that he and Colin would see the parade in the Chinese quarter. Darus

---

* see: *A House in Bali* by Colin McPhee, Singapore: OUP, 1991, p60.

would drive, wait and return them to the house.

'A men's night on the town.' Charles crowed. 'To celebrate our busy family.'

The din swamped them when they stepped from the car in a deserted back street. They were soon confronted by the acrid smell of fireworks and a multitude of lanterns. People thronged the narrow streets, filled the shops and stalls, adding to the cacophony. Fireworks crackled and jumped announcing the procession led by a long leering paper dragon held aloft by scores of grinning youths, and swaying above the heads of the crowd. It was fun. Noisy. Endless. Charles drew Colin along a side alley to a neat wooden door to a tea house with ranks of cubicals tended by winningly clad girls. The receptionist waved them in. Two smiling girls brought tea and cookies pulled across a privacy curtain and sat with them.

Charles got to his feet.' I'm going upstairs. The girls are for our pleasure. It's good for a man. Colin, follow if you like yours.'

Colin looked doubtful.

'The cover price is added to my bill. No? I won't be long.'

Alone, Colin's girl nuzzled into him, lay on his unresponsive lap looking into his averted face. He slid a hand through the parting of her silken gown and pressed her small soft breast. A racing heart didn't pound under his fingers, flesh didn't simmer with passion. The girl was an object unable to join with him. Unable to love. He bent and kissed her. 'I'm sorry.'

'No matter. You pay anyway'. She was gone.

Colin recalled his many nights with Rantun. Their dark passions overwhelming words and images until the world vibrated with meaning. It was the real thing. Nothing else mattered now, he knew.

When Charles returned Colin couldn't explain, only shake his head over questions of morality and gayness, and haltingly admit how perfect life had become in Charles's serene house.

'Dear friend, I never thought you monkish. However, we hope you'll stay. It's a joy having you.'

Colin started. 'It's my joy too. But I want to tell you the Institute has summonsed me. There is work to be finished, so I must go soon. I hope - no long - for you to invite me back. I must tell you this has become home in every sense. I can't explain, only say you all matter to me so very very much.' His cheek quivered.

'Colin. Go if you must. Then come back to us. We're comfortable together. All of us.'

'It's enough for me. Is it enough for you?'

Charles nodded slightly. 'Sometimes, perhaps, there's something missing. Nothing much, really.'

'You should marry.'

'I don't need a wife.'

'Living here, I understand.'

'Have you told Rantun?'

'Why?'

'She dotes on you.'

'It's for a few months. Until I extricate myself.'

'Ah, a short absence. Good for you.'

Colin vanished into his distant world. Over four years later Charles met his plane. Darus packed Colin's many bags in the boot and filled the back seat. They drove home. Rantun was out. Colin's room shone with welcome. They piled his bags up in the corner and went for tea in the house, served by a local girl who replaced Koki now married and moved away. Then Colin rested.

He slept deeply. Woke with a start only to fall delightedly back remembering where he was. He struggled up rubbing his eyes, then padded across the floor, leaned against the door, intently viewing the garden. Abandoned in a corner lay a bright plastic tricycle, a ball nearby. A small boy regarded him quizzically from the edge of the verandah.

'*Také Tuan.*'

The bell like voice charmed Colin. 'Well now, who are you?'

'My name is Lin.'

'Where do you live?'

'Here.'

'With?'

'Mummy.'

'And Daddy?'

'Daddy's away.'

'For a day or so?'

'No. Mummy says he'll come when he's ready.'

'Will he?'

'Yes, of course.' The boy smiled. 'You're *Tuan* Charles's best friend. Come and feed his carp!'

Colin went with the boy, watched him stretch out on tip toe, like a dancer, and spill grains onto the pond. The boy grinned; the surface of the water boiled as red, gold and white scaled sides broke the surface.

'They're fat and greedy. Pussy watches and thinks of breakfast.'

'So, Pussy has teeth?'

'And three kittens. Not like the song.'

'Three blind mice?'

'Fearless anyway.' The boy stepped back, fell into the pond. Colin grabbed him and also slipped. He retrieved the dowsed muddy bundle and staggered back to dry land.

'Oo, we're muddy.'

Colin carried the giggling boy into his bathroom, stripped the scant shorts off, then his own clothes, and showered them both down. The boy, shining dry stood admiring the big *tuan*, high as a door, strong limbed and with a tool far mightier than his wee spout.

Colin wrapped a towel round his own waist and followed the naked sprite who turned and grinned. 'Now tell me a story!' They huddled happily on the bed.

Once there was a boy who had many friends. A cat with three kittens, a dozen carp, many song birds and a cricket which lived under his verandah and sang to him.

'How did you know that?'

'Some stories are true.'

'Well, go on then!'

The cat loved him and tickled his bare legs with her tail. Her kittens purred when he held them gently. The song birds sang of his beauty and skill, riding his bike around the garden, or making sure the greedy carp each had a morsel. They said nothing. It's hard speaking under water. You try it!

'How do you know these things?'

'I'm a teller of tales: cats' and birds' and fish' and boys' and kite's tails.'

'They have long tails like, um, men.'

'Boys' tails grow into big hairy ones. That's why kites are envious, theirs never get any longer, so, they dive and pull, to get away from growing boys.'

'Yours and mine.' the boy whispered. 'Go on!'

The boy enjoyed songs, particularly the songs of the cricket.
He used to sit nearby. One day Cricket said, 'I know when it's going
to rain. I'll tell you. So listen. I have two types of song: a purring
sleepy sort about sunshine and snoozing. The other, a rain song,
skirls and trills excitedly. Listen, so you'll know when it'll rain.
Then, you can easily wash off mud when you fall into the pond.'

'Did you know it wouldn't rain?'
'I was too busy trying to catch you to consider.'
'So was I. Go on!'

One fine day Uncle Charles put his fine straw hat out to refresh it,
Mummy hung out the laundered clothes, and Aunt Koki aired all the
bedding. The boy sat in the shade listening to Cricket singing. He
crooked his head intently. 'Isn't that a rain song?' he said as a tiny
trilling skirl hung in the air. 'Oo, yes it is.' He jumped up and ran
to Uncle Charles. 'Tuan, your hat will get wet and floppy.'
Charles chuckled. 'Nonsense dear one. The sun's shining.'
The boy ran to Mummy. 'Take the clothes in, they'll get wet.'
Mummy laughed. 'Darling one, the sky's as clear as an empty bottle.'
He found Koki in the kitchen. 'It's going to rain. Save our bedding.'
Koki grinned and kissed him. 'You little scamp, telling me stories. Go
and play. I'm busy just now.'
The boy took his tricycle onto the verandah (to keep it dry). Moodily
he said to it, 'No one believes me or cricket, we're too small.'

The sky darkened. Thunder crashed and rain spattered down
drenching the garden, the hat, the washing and all the bedding.
Everyone ran about slipping and shouting taking soggy bundles
inside. But it was a passing shower. Soon the sun came out and every
thing steamed, including the hat, bedding and clothes.

The boy crouched down and complained to cricket who stopped
singing his lazy purring sun-filled song to reply. 'It's a pity little
things are overlooked, for without them no big things could happen.'
The boy rode his sparkling dry cycle round the muddy garden and
stopped at cricket's house. 'Will it rain? My bike needs a wash.'

Cricket's song was full of sun. Birds were singing. He left his bike and went to feed the carp who didn't care whether it rained or not.

The boy nodded to himself. 'It's true about little things. And, words - like tale - mean other things like tail. And I have one which grows unlike kites; no wonder they pull away. I'm glad I'm not a carp and I know about rain.' He grinned. 'That was a great story.' He wriggled on the bed like a contented fish.

Someone was coming:

'Colin, Lin, my two dear green men.* Oh.' Rantun fell against the door, joy entwining pain, the day become a dream. 'Colin, Colin you've come.' She dropped everything as he came to her.

'Mummy we fell in the pool. Our clothes got shitty. Will you wash them? It's not going to rain.'

The boy was startled by the intensity of their embrace. 'Mummy, CoLin is my Dad's name.'

'My little green darling, he is your daddy. He's come home.'

'You said he would, "in his own time." Is that now?'

'Rantun looked deep into Colin's eyes. Luxuriating against his yearning she said, 'Is it?'

Colin nodded.

The naked boy on the bed rolled off and ran into their embrace. 'It's our time too. And Pussy and the birds, and Cricket and the silly carp.' He snuggled in Daddy's strong arms squealing from Mummy's wild kisses up and down his tummy until Cricket and the birds fell silent in envious wonder. For surely this was the very best story of all.

*

---

* *Lin*, in Chinese means variously, a grove of trees, jade, a long spell of rain (making things green); also, a mythic female unicorn, or a jem. Here, it may be understood as a diminutive of Colin, a little green jem.

Beyond the Shadows

FILMS FASCINATED ME from early on. So I was very excited to be chosen for the cast of *Lord of the Flies* offering an escape from throttling boyhood. It was a perfect location. A froth of palm trees, a gentle lagoon, waves lapping golden sand. Beyond, scrub from which a jumble of rocky hills emerged under a sky vaster than the ocean with its own flecks of untidy white. Lashings of scrub for filming our fights, chases and hunting. Best of all it was a tropical island. We didn't get chilly waiting for shoots, the times in between filled with a riot of swimming and mooning about in sunny holiday mood.

We boys had two sets of clothes. For the beginning and the ending of the film. One, well tailored, the other, ragged (with some of us, in next to nothing). This chimed with a suspicion we were making two films. One, properly dressed for parents and the cinema, the other ragged and risky suiting our wildness, and beyond judgmental rules.

The official film, *Lord of the Flies,* about boys marooned and destructive, was scripted. We were told the action and given outlines for speech. There was a timetable: rehearsals, discussions, and meetings for crew, actors and minders. The other film was darker, acted without script, with promptings to behave unconventionally, a script far less clear to all of us . Was it a grown-ups' war? It focussed on our bodies, our nakedness and on all sorts of unrest.

In retrospect this other film touched some of the dark and hidden themes in the main film, expression of what could not be said in an official version. Things which we boys (and probably most of the film crew) did not quite understand.

The crew loved Ralph's bits. They filmed him often, and for long takes. They sat him under a palm and shot his shadow-graced face and torso, sometimes getting a group of us in-shot, dressed or undressed. They took him bathing. For the first scene, undressing on an empty beach (with Piggy teetering) galloping into the sea in flimsy underpants; then later, naked with Douglas in a water ballet before racing out, pulling clothes over wet bodies, to scramble up the rocks searching the sky for the speck of a plane. This scene was filmed two or three times until the sun was right, water gleaming off his torso and dripping through his pubic hair and down his slender willy.

'It looks like the lead from your pencil' a camera man joked. Ralph blushed. Getting hard-ons lying about naked, he too was glad of his shorts in other scenes.

They practised the last hunt a few times, later ripping his clothes into shreds. They anointed his visible skin with cream and streaks of make-up.

'We don't want you looking gorgeous.' they joked.

'I'm running away.' Ralph said.

'And no wonder.' they chortled.

His face burned. Desire is as discomforting as flight.

Innuendo whispered throughout another scene in which Ralph and Piggy were joined by the completely naked Sam and Eric and later, George. The boys sat beside Ralph who didn't look at them. The rehearsals and the actual take were filmed until the boys sauntered, sat, rolled over unembarrassed about showing everything.

'Be like lovers in paradise.' someone prompted. 'It's how things should be.' they murmured. 'Nude, intimate innocence - how the young are if left alone.'

The boys' discussion was not so much about eating of the succulent fruit of the knowledge of good and evil, as digesting the sour fruit of action in retrieving Piggy's spectacles from Jack's hellish savages.

'Too long.' the producer said.

The director shook his head. 'Shows too much.'

The official version displayed discreet flanks, back views and pensive faces. The other version shimmered with boyish flesh and sexual bits in a breath-held paradise of sand, tousled hair and shadows.

The second pig hunt ended with Charles yelling. 'I stuck [my stick] right up its arse.' It wasn't scripted. They liked that, extending the theme into a trial scene in the savages' rock castle. Held naked across a rock, Robin was caned. He was told to cringe in pain and cry out. (In the third run through, he was hurt). Then, in front of a crowd of curious boys, he was banished into a shadowy grotto, completely bare. Robin felt bad, the spectacle of his bottom being wounded like the pig or a girl was distressing. In spite of the praises of the film crew, he wouldn't swim in the nuddy from then on. The murders of Simon and Piggy were grim. Some of the eight year olds, weepy after doing those bits, were gladdened remembering it was only a game. It was reassuring to see those two at meal times. They were missed on the set. We all felt vulnerable with nothing on. Clothes are armor to hide in. Proof against bullets and contempt, deflecting blame. Robin felt wounded inside and on his bum. No wonder he kept something on.

Roger and I enjoyed exploring beyond the location. One afternoon we crouched in thick scrub, hearing muted voices. We wriggled closer. A voice gasped. 'Yes. Deeper. More. Yes, more!'

Two of our crew, the nicer ones, were having it off. I was shocked. I liked them. They were completely gay, doing it like dogs. Roger and I froze. We crept close spying. Denis was kneeling, Phillip poking into him. As he jerked in and in Denis was gasping.

'Den, all right?'

'It hurts like shit. Yes. Fill me, Phil. All of it!'

Denis sprawled wide open. Phillip thrashed and froze with a muted groan, and fiddled between Denis' legs until he weed slime. Wilting, they embraced as breathing settled. (I didn't mind that). They lay on their backs holding hands looking into the face of the sky.

It was terrible watching so much agony. (A twelve year old's view). Roger (ten) was clutching his willy. I shared his distress, and sweated with excited alarm. Men being animals; what they wanted us boys to become? I never thought about death or about using my body in that way. Were these unspeakable things demonstrated in the unofficial film? Did my clothes and skin hide a similar brute as well as a boy? I'd been called a monster. Was it true? Or half-true?

A beast in Phillip made his stiff, made him push till it hurt them both. Did the beast in Denis open its mouth and suck Phillip's and chew it until it shrank? Did I have a beast stiffening mine and lying in wait in my bottom, shitting and sucking, wanting the impossible, the unthinkable? It's true, sometimes I bubbled with a beastly rage clamouring to destroy everything. Another certainty was my stiffening. At those times I enjoyed the beast, never dreaming I'd ever want to rut like a loony dog.

The question haunted me, and tainted our (other) film as the dark cave had confronted Robin. I tucked my shirt in and, taking Roger's trembling arm, slithered away.

'That's the most disgusting thing I've ever seen.' Roger

whispered. His gentle face broke with distress. 'This *is* the monster in our film. It's real.'

I nodded. 'They enjoyed hurting one another.'

'I won't ever let anyone in.' Roger whispered.

I recalled the calm afterwards. 'Maybe we don't understand.'

'Who wants to know anything as horrible?'

'Afterwards the Beast rested.' I stammered. I lay on my back next to Roger feeling sick. The sky was far away. His warmth invaded me. Comforted me. I turned and, resting on an elbow, carefully wiped away his tears with tentative fingers. Here, alone in the brush, we could cry.

Roger sniffed. 'I'm glad it's you. We'd never hurt each other like that. Never.'

We lay for ages, becoming ourselves. Then we sneaked away and rejoined the others for afternoon tea. Everything was unchanged. We said nothing. No one noticed. Nothing had to be explained. Although the gang's usual evening skinny dip was a bit discomforting. It's difficult to be oneself on a crowded beach.

Next day we rehearsed the final scene of Ralph fleeing savages and driven by fire. We all lost our way, blinded in the end from the confusions of smoke and burning, we stumbled weepy-eyed onto the beach to face the pristine white orderly naval officers and a horizon interrupted by a grey corvette.

The official film was concocted from these clips. Our film, showing the shadows in shadows, contained other bits abandoned on the editing floor.

Denis directed a scene, an echo of what I'd seen in the brush. 'They're practising the same shitty thing.' I told Roger who refused to sit it out. George and Charles leaped about like silly puppies frothing the water. Then, laughing, bounded up the beach hand in hand. They tumbled about a bit in the sand sliding on top of each other and recovered lying side by side looking at the sky just as Phillip and Denis had. No wonder George's stiffened. Charles rolled over showing his sandy bottom (hiding his). Shadows danced over their bare bodies. Phillip said. 'Like sun writing.' 'Love letters.' Denis said. The others tittered. I found it exciting and disgusting having seen the real thing.

In another scene in the brush, Simon and Harold painted each other everywhere with white splodges and red and black lines making rib patterns, circles marking tummy and buttocks, and a line along the willy to the navel. Harold got excited. No one minded. They waited a little and finished the scene with Harold's dick intruding as 'A trainee pig-sticker.' Roger muttered.

Then they persuaded Jack and Ralph to stage another fight, pulling and pushing, tearing off clothes falling on one another until Jack grabbed his pole and brutally speared down between Ralph's open legs near his crotch echoing the beastliness I'd seen in the brush.

'Now fall on Ralph.' someone shouted. The two lay face to face panting straining and sweating until Ralph wriggled free calling a halt. 'You two were tussling with the beast.' someone said. I knew what that meant now.

There was another short bit when Douglas pulled Bill to him and they kissed. No one was supposed to watch. I heard about it. Phillip said it represented tenderness. He and Denis didn't know much about that I thought. Roger decided Doug and Bill did it as part of a game. He was confident they'd never go further.

Our crew wanted other pairs, twins like Eric and Sam, Ralph and Jack, Bill and Douglas, George and Charles. 'They told us, 'twins' were mirrors but I knew differently. Sam and Eric finally agreed to spend time naked.

'So you're natural during the shoot.' their minders argued. The producer agreed.

Then Sam had a tantrum because some of the boys sniggered. So those hanging around were ordered to strip. Everyone fooled about on the beach, in the water and around our sleeping tents located away from the film set. Sam and Eric relaxed and gradually naturalized.

'They're gorgeous.' someone whispered. 'Lovely little sausages, I could eat them.' I think most of us secretly wanted to be eaten.

We practised the scene of seeing the aeroplane until Denis was satisfied. He wanted all of us to be naked on the beach, firstly swimming. Then we had to scramble out of the water and run up the beach with our backs to the camera. We had to pick up our ragged shorts and only then, turn round and show ourselves. 'Running up the beach you're neither boys nor girls. We find out when you turn round. Initially, you represent girls too.' Phillip said. The big boys were upset. 'We're not bloody girls. How could we be?' They strutted about showing off, hanging towels on their hard-ons and jerking their hips provocatively. But we saw the truth in the rushes, us gambolling up the sand showing lots of untidy hair and genderless backsides. It was a surprise when we flashed our willies and pulled our shorts on.

Running around wearing nothing made us wild. It's what the crew lapped up. By the end, being admired caressed and keenly watched was fun, although having an inkling of what they wanted but never stated (except secretly in the brush) disturbed me. Roger said they wanted us to do sex. That's why we held hands, swam and lay together. And kissed. Would it lead to our hurting each other as well?

After the flight home, Roger's parents dropped me on a bus route to my house. Roger and I sorted my luggage out of the boot and placed it on the footpath. We stood smiling, sad the fun was over, contented being together. I reached out, nervously clasped his bottom, drew him close and lightly kissed him.

      Roger flushed. 'We had a great time, Woodrow.'

      'I didn't want to come back here.'

      'You are staying with me after the film premier.'

      'Roger, you didn't mind?'

      'Nope. It's ending our weird desert island games.'

      I waved as the car drove away, wondering whether our kiss was an ending, and if it were only a game.

All that was years ago. Recently I read the Book[*] which says if it were not for law and order we'd be savages. But we are. Under our designer clothes we're *all* ragged little boys (and girls) playing adult games, without adult skills. It's little wonder we fuff about beating each other up. Maybe sex calms you down. Sex with a woman places the Beast beyond by containing it in the mystery of the other, a Beast falling between two stools (cock and cunt), a scenario not as rampant or stoked by the loneliness hidden in sameness?

      Lord of the Flies ended with Ralph escaping to the beach and colliding with a white clad god whose presence ended the chase and the fantasies driving it. We are all man-handled from birth by godlike adults with godly power. After realizing our loneliness our second lesson is being the smallest losers. Hungry puppies haunting a feast, the fight over scraps driving our lives until death. We appraise external scraps but overlook internal hunger. By so doing, we also ignore hope, desire, respect, imagination, terror, joy, hunger, love . . . associated mysteries in

---

[*]   This is a tribute to William Golding's book, *Lord of the Flies* and to the film (1963) directed by Peter Brook.

the darkling pit, each with its particular significance.

During the unofficial filming, we broke conventional rules and experienced darker drives; shadowed territory stumbled upon? Naturally. The new territory necessary for managing ourselves in so careless a world. The Beast, experienced and understood, becomes a sibling, a shadow in the shadows with others such as hope terror and love; all are vital life resources if carefully tackled. In our naked games we found and explored these shadows.

Our last film-set meal was candle-lit (replacing the burned-out generator). Soft light, bright eyes, mops of hair, velvet skin and fresh voices. We were stars enmeshed in shadows: in our dusky tents, in the breathing bush and deep in adult eyes, caressed by unbidden messages, sometimes haltingly read. A gleam of achievement reflected our success. It was more than doing only what we were told. The film crew had hunted us. Peeling off our reserve with our clothes, struggling to get inside and finger every privacy. Mixing our secrets with theirs. Now I understand. They were hunting bear, sandy pigs foraging in mud, spearing, fighting for scraps!

We were driven to the edge of a pit. Two or three older boys fell in (there were whispers of immorality or reprisals, so Denis and Phillip were not alone). The rest of us teetered on the brink wrapped in our childhood with a dawning awareness of yawning depths and of our vulnerability. Looking into the pit we faced an awesome seething darkness of towering cocks, and we lost ourselves in the maelstrom of flesh and dreams.

Ralph never quite lost himself, even naked. He also wanted everything. Wanted to be immersed in nakedness yet holding it as shyly as he displayed his nascent pubic hair. "Holding" at arm's length rather than in a trusting hug. He was the star again that flickering half-regretful triumphant evening. Everyone perved on Ralph, dreaming of sharing his shining centre whilst searching for a way through the deathly pit.

The film crew made us play their sex games. We were boy soldiers struggling with weapons too heavy for us, imaginary weapons as threatening as the Beast. As uncontrollable as the signature of our civilization, a mushroom cloud. I see the 'other' film in the scenes enacted that wild pleasurable summer. A film involving more of us than being merely children.

*

Giants

for Aiya, Eri and Kóta who know the true story:

A MOTLEY ASSORTMENT of people attended the honouring of a memorial to an old postman in the cemetery beyond a group of shrines nestling between steep wooded hills high above the city.

'Probably all his old clients.' the duty policeman murmured. The black robed priest nodded, aware how small the mourners seemed. 'Death shrinks us all.' he said regarding the high slender bamboo crowding the sturdy towering cedars clothing the steep sides of the ravine beyond the clearing made for graves and stone shrines edged by a vibrant blue of massed hydrangeas. 'But then, nature and the *kami* (deities) tower over everything.' he said softly as if the truth were appropriate *soto voce*. 'Katsuki *san** was an unusual man.' he added in explanation of the special memorial plus the diversity of mourners - from farming families to dignitaries from cities, and others such as Nosé *san* builder, woodworker and water wheel maker. The priest sighed. 'So many!' He paused. 'For nowadays, everyone gets letters, I've had a couple myself.' He brushed dust off his robe. 'In the old days everyone knew the priest. Now I suppose it's the postman.' He watched small, long-tailed white and brown birds glide from the dense green forest to forage for insects in the recently turned earth under the hydrangeas whose myriad blue eyes softened the extremities of mourning and prayer.

The mourners drifted away until only Katsuki *oxan**, clinging to her children, remained; thin, bent with grief, as fragile as a dry twig. The priest knew her well. She had attended this shrine all her married years, daily during pregnancy and her husband's recent illness. She seemed unaware of his approach as she spoke to her youngest daughter. 'Aiya, he's gone. In the emptiness I am confounded by the house filled with his

---

*   *san* = The Honourable, Japanese near-equivalent to Mr. or Mrs.
  oxan = wife.
  chan - an informality only allowed children: they say 'Oba chan' to
      Grandmother instead of 'Oba san'. (see page 42).

work leaving no place for me.'

'Mother, you should stay.'

'A child grows up and moves on. His big baby has taken us over.'

'Don't worry Mother. I'm sure that architect will help. Look, here's the priest!'

'Aiya is right.' said the priest. 'It is time to move on. Let him rest in the Dark Land [of the dead].' Nodding to her family, he handed the old lady a *mamori* charm, and gently guided them down the path threading through shrines and memorials. Under the stone *torii* (gate) he bowed them from the sacred realm of the *kami* onwards into the mortal world. He watched them, shrouded in loneliness, tip toe down the steep road into the clutter of the town. He thought, Why is it we cling to the familiar? Liberation attends on change. Death is liberation; a change to be welcomed. History is but a story about life's old threadbare coat. Children, so wide-eyed and joyous, see only the future, the newness in the world, its sacred promise. What they soon overlook is the most precious: embracing invisibles makes for a rich life. He turned and walked resolutely to the main altar to complete his *norito*, prayers honouring Katsuki *san*, blessed now in unseen places the realm of *Amaterasu* the most glorious goddess of the sun.

Aiya was right. The architect, after examining the dusty boxes of photographs, sheets of measured drawings, study sketches of old village buildings and bric a brac collected over fifty years consisting of wooden mill belt wheels, stone troughs and grind-stones, tools and utensils, proclaimed it an invaluable record of the past. The architect, Yura *sensei*,[*] had taught and practised in Kyushu for most of his life. Offended by the brash tatty modernity springing up everywhere, he had retreated into traditional ways, becoming a conservationist as well as a committed Modern Architecture practitioner; believing in the best of both worlds, a profound way of thought seldom understood or achieved. His decision about Katsuki *san's* work was shrewd and crucial. Most of the buildings recorded had, by now, vanished, and with them the skills that fashioned them.

Losing its past, Japan is shorn of traditions, invisible perhaps, yet an irrecoverable loss. Alarmingly, few are aware of this gradual decay.

*

---

[*] *sensei* = teacher. A term of great respect in Japan.

37

Norio Katsuki turned eighteen just after the war finished. As a boy he had experienced hunger and terror, seen his village become ruinous, the prefecture gutted, then watched the tall hairy invaders ruling his shattered and cowed country.

Not far from his aunt's house - where his family had sought refuge during the war - was an intimate garden, once part of a grand house now gone. The owner, an elderly gentleman, tended it daily. Its tranquillity, a comfort to many, delighted the boy.

In one corner water gushed from between two large rugged stones falling onto a miniature water wheel with bells which tinkled when it turned making the boy's eyes twinkle. Birds graced this watery corner, swooping to drink, staying to fossick and squabble over worms and seeds and pecking orders. The boy lingered, eventually sharing tending and tidying with the old man. The work centred him, calming his torrential adolescence in a beleaguered world.

The man talked about his early life as a carpenter making wooden structures such as houses and looms and water wheels. The boy was entranced by the complexity and power in combining water with wood. The man's words took the place of the story books missing in the youngster's life; words creating a vibrant reality which shielded him from wartime horrors.

When the war ended his family moved away. Slowly normal life returned. But the boy was too old to go back to school so joined the post office with its secure career structure. He was swept into the rigours of rates, regulations, the geography of deliveries and the social complexity of a national organisation. None of which compensated for an intangible lack of something in his life keeping him restless.

One day, dawdling back to the post office, Norio Katsuki stopped beside a rushing mountain stream. On the opposite bank on a wide shelf stood an assortment of buildings sheltered by trees. Below one of them water gushed from a cleft fashioned in the rock. Birds playfully darted through the trees singing and feeding. A derelict and charmed air pervaded the scene. An unruly forest greened the slopes behind. Where did the gush of water come from, and why? Were the buildings a sort of gateway to the green dark mystery rising beyond?

In a trance he hop, stepped and jumped over the stream and clambered up rough steps hewn in a rock wall. Arriving panting at the top he saw a huge wheel turning in its gloomy cavity, heard the plash of water and rumble of a host of belts and pulleys and the rhythmic drumming of heavy wooden plungers falling and pulverising a mess of cedar leaves, making the fragrant dust on incense sticks. Water was the sole power, relinquishing strength absorbed from the mountainous landscape.

Katsuki *san* was astonished. This was no boyish dream. He sneezed and grinned. He was so happy he blushed. He would study and map everything, aware there must be other water-wheel buildings, knowing, as postmen do, he could deliver his letters of joy, his dreams, to each rare address up the valleys throughout the prefecture. Letters to *Kappa* the busy water imp, to monster arthritic wood spirits, even the birds. People, surely, would have to listen?

He left, his heart dancing with his feet, his eyes twinkling, laughing in chorus with the stream unaware it would be more than a lifetime's work. A lively vision of repairing the damaged world stayed him. Much later, others would regard him as a conservationist.

Norio Katsuki found a larger truth: that life in tandem with the natural world gained both meaning and longevity. In re-connecting to the tranquil garden of his childhood his life was enriched.

Ancient places, as well as that small garden, are havens in a grim world, enlivening and bringing hope. Preserving *minkas* (old thatched farm houses) or water wheels or traditional crafts, healed the world, healing ourselves. Far more vital than blindly resisting the new or wanting Japan to be a museum, it represented a life-line to the past which carried an internal prosperity threatened by modern life.

No wonder Norio Katsuki skipped across the raging stream and blindly biked down the twisting track to the plain beyond and on to his office. A window had opened. He glimpsed a dream, felt renewed. Whether craggy mountains or a couple of rocks, a trickle or a torrent, he didn't care. It was all one and quite wonderful!

However, over the next few years, recording moldering bits of tradition, Katsuki *san* grew aware of the destruction of everyday life, not only craftsmen but families and, as he was to discover, complete villages. The phalanxes of skill and power changing Japan were mainly interested in cost and objects, not the invisibles underpinning life which engaged priests and poets.

The Egawa Dam project mooted in the late 1960's highlighted the disastrous collision of old and new. The Koshiwara river ran down a steep sinuous valley between precipitous mountains densely clad in cedar and bamboo. Numerous settlements dotted its course, sites probably older than a neighbouring valley containing the castle town of Akizuki at least 800 years old. The largest dam in the prefecture was to be set half way down flooding the upper valley. The development raised the intractable issue: the pride of the prefecture versus protection of a thousand years of human settlement.

Katsuki *san* began painstakingly recording the string of villages. The joyous arrival of Aiya, his third child was a reminder of thousands of years of parenting and nurture. The demise of the Koshiwara villages was as invisible to others as the advent of this child. It remained to be seen if she too were doomed. Surely the magic in her curled fingers and toes and her throaty gargles of pleasure would protect her?

Fierce opposition was helpless in the face of the Water Company's and Prefecture's well rehearsed claims the dam would benefit thousands in and beyond the valley by controlling flooding and providing water for agriculture and town use.

Norio Katsuki said on many occasions, 'People have lived here for a thousand years. Surely we're not frightened to occasionally get our feet wet?'

The problem centred on the large village of Egawa intricately knitted into a tapestry of irrigated fields set cheek by jowl along the water course.

'Moving folk will involve the destruction of an ancient way of life of farming, crops and livestock, forestry, of summer sports, winter snow-balling and sledging on fields, of water power and all the traditions of a settled community - schools, temples, festivals, water highjinks and land rights, thatching, weaving, pottery, folk songs, a sense of history and of place. It's chopping off the nose in case it gets sunburnt.' Katsuki *san* said bitterly watching bulldozers at work.

'What's to become of us?' many villagers said. 'This is home. We grew up here with our children. And parents and grandparents - countless generations, making the peace of our valley.'

The children were excited by the flow of strangers. Dignitaries tempted them with novelty and promises of all sorts matching "The biggest dam in the prefecture." 'We'll all be rich.' they chortled to the school master who (with private doubts) had, as an official, to support the dam publicly. The school master enjoyed the company of Katsuki *san* and accepted that folk hereabouts had a rare robustness which he sometimes needed to temper in his young charges. 'Yes. It is a cheery village I'm pleased to say. You listen because you care. Do you know, the old people say their *Kappa* has driven off the dour water spirits which haunt other mountain villages.' He refilled Katsuki *san's* tea cup. 'I tend to agree with you and the old folk, we are destroying paradise in order to keep our feet dry. But, what is one village compared to the thousands who will benefit?' He sighed. Hadn't the Buddha said, "The nail of the little finger is as vital as the hand, arm, torso. Wholeness is all"? The Koshiwara valley is equivalent to a torso. Not to be sneezed at, he thought. Blushing with a mixture of metaphors he'd not allow in class, adding, 'I hope the children will be happy.'

His disquiet was allayed by Katsuki *san's* work. 'It's as if you are collecting the robustness gifted by their *Kappa*.' he murmured, inspecting the drawings of *minkas*, the photographs and sketches, much he had never clearly acknowledged which, surely, contributed to village life? 'Ah, such memories.' the schoolmaster said. 'So much in the village: traditions - like a fishing line with hooks - snagging our thoughts beyond memory to lives on which ours is based.'

Norio Katsuki nodded. 'The umbilical cord joining us to beginnings real if unremembered.'

The school master sipped his tea. 'Are we not ready for birth, the start of life's adventures?'

'When we bear the scars of our origins, when the past is as active as it is here in Egawa, then we're ready.' Katsuki *san* said. 'A man can only be a man when the boy in him lives.'

The school master blinked. The Buddha had said something along the lines of "the inner navel" through which we must venture in order to find enlightenment. 'So, objects such as houses, wells, bridges, utensils carry us back.'

'Yes. And the river, the fields, the clouds in the sky which exist before and beyond us. They can feed us after we're separated, "born" as you put it.'

The school master beamed. 'It makes sense. Better than the many speeches and company promises. Reliable. Real. Solid. Comprised of good *and* bad, a totality. Yes, yes, all the village; its reality, traditions and dreams. My word, your work is important, I see that now. It's better than nothing. Ah, but what will become of us?'

He watched a fly exploring the rim of his tea cup its feet wet with bitter green tea, shaking its head in disbelief and flying off. It was then he determined to retire further up the valley to one of the potters' villages beyond the flooding where traditions were embraced in a present seamlessly joined to the past and the future. 'Minds are cleaned by dirty hands.' he said watching the fly vanish into thin air. 'At least the potters remain at the top of the valley. It's not the end of our steep winding road.'

For four years Norio Katsuki determinedly mapped Egawa village. Often shadowed by children struck by his quiet concentration. In due course they shyly confided their secrets, fears and dreams through the games they played nearby as he sat and sketched, or in moments of reflection when he seemed receptive to chat.

Only certain rocks on worn paths, certain gnarled trees in the forest, only the multitude of gilded straws at the eaves of old thatched roofs and certain wormy wooden beams in familiar barns and houses were party to their talk.

The children saw Katsuki *san* was recording everything in his notebooks and sketch pads so wanted to help. One of his little shadows, Kaoru, whom he nicknamed *Kokeshi chan* (doll) proffered apples saying, '*Oba chan* sent them. She told me that at the beginning, our valley had giants who made huge steps so they could easily go from the river to the woods. In each step her great great great grandparents had made a field for rice or vegetables, positioning the houses in between so they wouldn't be stepped on. But the giants went away through the woods to another place. *Oba chan* says they will come back and defend our valley if rice doesn't grow, when there are no more apples or children. Daddy says that's silly. Do you think so?'.

Katsuki *san* shook his head. 'No, I do not. But the giants, needed everywhere, may forget Egawa.'

Kaoru nodded and smiled. 'Is that why you're saving things on all that paper?'

'Yes. To remind us, and the giants.'

'Please take my picture so the giants will know me?'

'Of course. Stand, there. The edge of village behind. One day a giant you will understand how sacred the ordinary can be.'

'What does irretrievable mean?'

'Ask *Oba san* I must get on, to be away before sundown.'

Katsuki *san* ambled down the hill to the majestic thatched house he was measuring. It's fit for giants, he thought eyeing the regal areas of tatami floor. At dusk he collected his notes, filled his heavy bag and sighed. 'Dark already. I'll be late home again. Aiya, Kota and Eri will chide me in the morning. Maybe Gran's apples will mollify them.'

He stepped out into the courtyard. A cow lowed in the barn

where hens were sleepily cooing. A feather-light evening breeze cuffed his face. He smiled. 'Goodnight my beauties. See you all tomorrow.' he said softly. Something stirred in the shadows. The giant slept on as Katsuki *san* purred away on his small red post office motorbike.

The apples were well received. *Oba san's* ministrations usually were. Katsuki *san* chuckled recalling their first meeting on being shrilly chided, as all the men were, by her remonstrations over the roof.

43

The three thatchers had arrived, a dozen neighbours and friends followed. *Oba san* had smiled conspiritorially when Kaoru looked shocked, saying 'Of course thatching is thirsty work but it needs to be done quickly. Unless we women scream at them, the men simply turn it into a party, so need someone to remind them of the work, bless 'em.'

'So many big men.' Kaoru sang.

'Oh yes. It's giant's work.' *Oba chan* retorted.

'A giants work party.' the youngster murmured.

'Yes, my pet.' her granny said. 'Will you carry out the *saké* cups? I'll bring the flask. And remind me to get a demijohn more to soak the indigo leaves for dyeing.'

'It allows blue in the sky to creep into the vat.'

'It does, little one. Just as it allows the red of sunset to creep into the faces of our giants.'

'Oo, I'll remind you. Will you get blue hands again? Carry all the cups? Of course I can.' Kaoru grinned.

'Careful my child. Hear the roof sighing with pleasure at its new hat. We'll all sleep better now.'

'There's spare straw for the bed of the cow. And the hens.'

'Yes, them too. And, snug and full of their good food, you'll sleep like a little lamb, I promise.'

'And you?'

Grandmother nodded. 'We all will, in spite of my son's, your father's, *saké* snores.'

'Thunder in our house.'

'Reminding Roof it's needed even more.'

'Doesn't it sleep, *Oba chan*?'

'It spreads its wings and watches over us my child.'

The little girl confided all this to Katsuki *san* in a quiet moment. 'No wonder I feel safe here.' she said ' O f course you do.' he said grimly considering the asphyxiating depth of water soon to fill the valley.

The dam was opened with a flourish displacing doubts and regret. 'We are better served now.' the head of the prefecture said. 'Modern Japan involves good management of people and resources.'

However, serene though the vast new lake was, a soulless silence settled on the valley. Yet somehow life continued. Katsuki *san* sadly worked on elsewhere.

The war Norio Katsuki experienced as a boy had shown him terror and destruction undreamed of. Yet the small garden made visible by the collapse of the mansion became a deep comfort to him. An inspiration.

What had its owner once said? "When you can see that rock as a cloud-capped mountain and the trickle of water as a raging torrent, then you will have found tranquillity." It had become his quest ever since. Now it was time to go.

He reached up. The great water wheel slowly lifted him up towards mountain peaks. Water gushed round him singing and soothing as he reached the clouds. There was bird song and the throbbing croak of a multitude of frogs. Children's voices, a farmer urging on his stolid water buffalo, directing the shapely plough through lines of delicate rice. Thatchers were joking as they bundled and tied golden sheaves onto an ancient beamed roof. There, the dry notes of a *koto*. He knew this was his garden by the mountain and the torrent, knew the great water wheel of life had returned his dream to him.

Norio Katsuki was still smiling when they vainly tried to wake him.

Norio Katsuki 1927-2006

Stampede

I TURNED AWAY FROM THE SEA towards a greater barrier (reef), the Queensland wilderness, which lay inland to the west. It was soon after dawn. The light streamed with an ocean shimmer as I drove out of Townsville, picking up the Overlander's Way, slipping through a gap in Leichardt's Range beside the Mount Isa railway, breakfasting and re-fuelling in Charters Towers which I'd known as a boy.

It was already hot. Mirages shimmered along the road; the window sill almost too warm to rest an arm on; the dun coloured ground cooking the blue sky a dirty cream where it touched the horizon; the tangy scent of eucalyptus, the after-sun smell of rare stands of trees where sometimes I tarried in a cloud of flies, opened the car bonnet, snacked and swigged from a water bottle. Ah, memories of thirsting and space.

What a vast landscape! Almost untouched: a few place names, a raw track or two, occasional groups of cattle and nothing else but solitude in ancient grandeur. There was little sign of man. No grey concrete, no paint, no gleaming metal. Only silvered wooden fence posts, warm rusting wire, the soft ochres or reds of earth and rock, the dun green leaves and creamy tree trunks, the occasional glimpse of yellow crested cockatoos, the multi coloured flash of small gouldians and the nipple pink of rakish galahs. My creamy Australian Geographic map blended. It was vague about water courses (had they mapped in the summer?).But I think I dowsed myself in the Campaspe and later, the Flinders River. But enjoyment doesn't depend on names. It spurred me on, for I knew where I was going.

The landscape flattened out, grew stony and treeless, vanishing into a distant hazy "dead heart" whose life, measured in millennium heart beats, seemed lifeless and unaware of the minute thumping of mine. No wonder the road south from Hughenden is named Dinosaur Way.

The relentless light drove me into the Stanford Road-House for cool beers, and again, for a gossip, at Corfield (neither ford nor field in sight), the one house town I remembered, where I was advised to stick to the bitumen and arrive in Belmont territory, rather than get bushed (there wasn't much of that) on a faint rough track about 50km further on, to the left.

The woman chuckled. 'Believe me, it's tough. If you meet Jim Bell get him to show you his dinosaurs. He's been collectin' them for ages. Great finds, too. Old timers get kinda stony round these parts. Watch out if they stare at you, it's stone feet you'll be havin'.'

'Looks a bit dry for dinosaurs.' I countered.

'All this,' she gestured vaguely towards the horizon, 'was a pond once. A bit before my time.'

'Before all of us, even Dreamtime.' I said.[*]

'Sure thing. Before rules. Before love even.' she said.

'They probably loved one another. Otherwise they'd've died out.'

'They did. Some Tyranosaurus Rex outlawed love.'

'But he couldn't control what happened at night in the shallows.'

She laughed. 'You're right. "Boys will be boys".'

'It's an urge stronger than war.'

'Y' reckon?'

'In animals certainly, and dinosaurs. Not man.'

'Maybe you're right. Guess we'll know in a hundred million years.' She shook her head. 'Listen Mate, you'll get on with the Bells. They warm to barmy folks like you. Their Tim's a cheeky young bugger. Salt of the earth, a post with a dinkum smile, if you get my meaning. You'll find he belongs here. That's why he came back after finishin' at his fancy college on the coast. Heart here. Feet in the dirt. Born and bred, not like most of us. He's a great kid.'

'He's lucky he could return. My dad bankrupted here when I was a lad and we left. Never came back. It broke his heart. Mine too. Too late to come back now. Listen, I'd best be off.'

'Yer. Hope it brings good memories. Mind how y'go.'

'I'll take it easy, that track sounds challenging.'

'Goin' to try it, eh? Get them to ring me when you arrive. Otherwise I'll send out a search party. It's no place to be alone. Good to see a city slicker takin' risks. Sometimes, even them bred here, falter. But that's how we gets on out here. Y' see, takin' risks stops us fossilizing. Cheery-o.'

---

[*]   100 million years. 'Dreamtime' is Aboriginals' Creation myth.

The side track was really too rough for the car (luckily, it was hired). I painstakingly drove through the featureless land, relieved when, in the middle of nowhere, a voluminous blue tent and a battered truck hove into view. The truck had a barrel perched on the back with a big tap.

I washed my head and cooled my arms as a youngster idled up. He was tall and slim ("Thin as a post") with a beguiling smile making his elegant eyebrows rise up like wings on his gentle face.

I shook my dripping head. 'Tim?'

'Um, yes. Who'd'y'want?'

'Howdy, I'm Ric. Come from the coast. Born here yonks ago. I'm chasing fossils and memories. I was hoping you'd show me around. They tell me you know what's what.'

'Me?' the boy smiled.

'Do you live here?' Ric pointed at the tent.

'No. Over there.' Tim pointed with a dusty hand to a distant windmill floating above the haze.

Ric, brushing clay dust off the boy's cheek, felt him shiver. Ric rested a reassuring hand on his bony shoulder. A flicker of passion flashed between them.

All the minutiae of Ric's journey fell away before the boy's sigh which could have been his own. Signifying a longing to combat the depthless loneliness in this vast stony landscape. Both guessed such emotions had no place in the ordinary world, and no words. But the meaning was uncomplicated and urgent, fading.

'Let me wash your face, Tim.'

The boy stood, eyes half shut against the glare of realization that a stranger cared for him; a stranger, yet oddly not a stranger. It was a comfort. They hugged lightly. But the boy didn't retreat. Rather, he snuggled, savoring nearness, unembarassed. Ric held him, a precious breathing thing in this wilderness of stone and light, the shadowy dream embedded in all of his life.

'Better?'

'Sometimes it gets to you.'

'Sure does. It's a harshness lodging deep and forever.'

'You too?'

'Sure. I grew up here, many years ago.'

'I've always liked it. But now it's not enough.'

'You want to share?'

'Everything. Sometimes.'

'When you smile, Tim, you shine.'

'She tells me that.'

'She?'

'A, um, a friend.'

'Girl friend?'

'It's not, um, like official, Ric.'

'But you share with her?'

'Mm, have. For ages.'

'How long?'

'I was fourteen when we started.'

'And she was?'

'Um. Just a girl. No one knows'

'Local girl?'

'Sort of. Look, it kinda happened. And took off from there.'

'Your dark secret.'

'Yes, she's black. So what.'

'So, you love her.'

'She, um. She says *she* does.'

'You're such a lovely young man, no wonder. I mentioned "love",
because it matters. You see, love grows if allowed room. There's a gentleness and courage in you, something to love, I felt at once. No wonder she
loves you. Aren't you drawn to her? Isn't that why you share? Fourteen.
Wow. What a great start.'

'She knew I needed help.'

'And gave herself to you, Tim?'

'Suppose so. Yes. But it's not that often now, with me been away
so much and,' He shivered. 'No one must know.'

'I understand. A love with no name.'

'No one. There'd be a storm.'

'Is secrecy an answer?'

'I guess so Ric.' He sighed. 'Yer, Mum'd go spare.'

'Even in this vastness we are not supposed to share our bodies.
Such a tiny shiver of lust in the blinding light, but censure creeps in and
ruins love.' Ric looked far away. 'I've learned to stifle my want. You're
wonderfully expressive seeking comfort.'

'I don't know why I told you.'

'Less secrets? It felt like a kind of welcome. Can I pitch my tent
somewhere, Tim?'

'Come home. You can kip there. We've a guest room at the far end of the back verandah. It's bright and clean.'

'Are you sure?'

'Yes.'

'I don't need much.'

'There's not much here.'

'I do remember that, in spite of the years away.'

'Some call it desert. It's home to me.'

'It feels home. Will you show me around?'

'All my shadow secrets?'

'Everything, Tim.'

'It'll take time.'

'Then, let's go walkabout. Will *she* know?'

'Probably. The blacks have a way with invisibles.'

'Tell her I'm passing through. I'll not harm you.'

'Why should you?'

'Envy. But I'll not break your heart or drag you away.'

'She knows that.' Tim crammed a wide brimmed bush hat on his coarse mop of hair and strode off through the sunlight to collect his tools.

Ric fondly watched him withdraw. 'What an extraordinarily eloquent boy. I feel I've known him all my life.' he said under his breath.

The barren landscape glowed, enhanced by the beauty of the lean boy anointed by its yellow dust enlivening his body. It was as if the stones were singing for the mirages' dance.

The Bell Homestead, marked by the rusting skeletal windmill, included a clutter of high barns and an assortment of lesser out-buildings. A couple of elevated water tanks flanked the back door. The yard was littered with bits of machinery, coils of pipe and wire, drums and derelict carts and wire storage boxes, the bric-a-brac of outback farming. A few gaunt trees proclaiming water and settlement provided a shifty shade for dog kennels and some hens.

Jim and Mary Bell were glad of company. Pleased their Tim was attentive to the stranger, and approving of the plan for their shy son to play host to him for several days.

After supper they all sat on the verandah. Jim turned off the house lights so they could view the stars emerging before the moon dimmed them. A warm breath brushed their cheeks as the evening wind gently died away and a vast canopy of silence engulfed them.

Jim pushed his chair back. 'Think I'll hit the sack. G-night all.'

Mary scrambled up and followed him into the house.

Ric touched Tim's arm. 'Let's walk for a bit?'

They ambled through the yard until stopped by a fence. Beyond, firelight faintly winked.

'Aboriginals, Ric.'

'Your girl, Tim?'

'Yep.'

'Do you want her tonight?'

'Always.'

'Your dreams'll have to do.'

'Suppose so.'

'Second best, better than nothing, eh?'

'Guess so.'

Ric, standing behind the boy, hugged him, slipping one hand under his shirt onto his warm chest. They stood stock still, the evening breathing around them.

Tim stirred. 'It's as if I've known you all my life.'

'I feel the same.'

'It must be us both growing up here.'

'It lasts. I've never been back, and here we are.'

'It's the space. It settles inside.'

'A love of grandeur and mystery.'

'Cassara says the mystery breaths in us.'

'Cassara, it's a strong name. Like the ancient Greek princess, Cassandra whom no one believed. Tell me Tim, do you, er, go all the way with her?'

'Yep. From the first. I had to.'

'I sensed that imperative in you.'

'It puts most off. Not such a bad thing, people scare me.'

'Didn't she scare you?'

'She simply let me in.'

'Was she scared?'

'Hungry. Willing. Fearless.'

'I'd like to be friends that way.'

'No bullshit?'

'I mean it.' Then Ric whispered, 'You mean a lot to me, Tim.'

Nervously eager, the boy flushed. They stood, a single shadow filling with old old dreams. The landscape waited as it had for millions of years for fear to be ruled by curiosity or lead to flight.

A softer acceptance seeped into Tim. 'I'd like to tell you my ideas for farming here - to coexist puts it better - with the land and its people. A combination of our ways with their Dreamtime wisdom. I know you won't think me daft. But now, let's hit the sack.'

They meandered through the moonlit yard. Lights blazed momentarily. Then, silence reigned.

Ric was stilled by the soothing chirruping of crickets and a sense of being at home. He slept deeply.

Just before dawn he was woken by Tim gingerly sitting on the end of his bed. His top was bare. He wore long striped pyjama pants gaping at the fly.

Ric blinked. 'Underpants too?'

'I've always slept in them.'

'Your balls'll get too hot.'

'Need em up for riding.'

'Not at night. Must be air-cooled, like a two-stroke engine, keeps seed spunky. One day you'll want kids so you got to stay fertile.'

'Don't like flopping in boxers.'

'Try nothing. You must! Off with them. There we are. Isn't that all right?'

'It's rather unpredictable.' Tim lay on his stomach.

'You must fly the flag sometimes when Cassara's absent. No shame in that.' Ric laughed, rolled over and straddled him, playfully bouncing so both rocked at sea.

Tim groaned. 'I told you.' He blushed at the spotted sheets.

Ric grinned. 'Feeling better?'

Tim nodded uneasily. 'It leaked out.'

'We must wet the land sometimes.'

'I'm not gay, if that's what you . . .'

'I don't mind what you are. We're friends, whatever. I meant it last night.'

'I've never let a bloke . . . not since school. I, um, just burst. I'd better get dressed.'

'Tim, your body's talking. Wild and wilful. It's saying, "give, give, everything you've got. Then you can live with-out secrets, sharing emptiness and love." - stones, light, your woman.'

'It doesn't disgust you?'

'Sacred signs?'

Tim was confused. He grinned. 'OK. You lie in if you want. I'll come back for you later.' He galloped off down the verandah like a frisky brumby. Ric shook his head, brushed the dampness lightly with the backs of his fingers, pulled up his sheet and slept.

He dreamed of galloping in parched ochreous spaces shimmering with caressing hands and a warm deep homecoming which engulfed him. He flew like a bird, sailing in trembling space. He came, aware in his dream he'd ejaculated and woken still dreaming. Strangled by his roomy tee shirt rucked up round his neck, he rolled onto his back. Day bore down on him. A dream butterfly hovered. Ric slowly opened his eyes. A black girl clad in a light cotton dress, holding Tim's underpants stood up from sniffing the bed. Her deep brown eyes held his, neither raking his naked form nor darting about. Reading his thoughts, taking in the scents and signs of debauchery. He rummaged for the illusive sheet, pulling it over him, covering the damp spots. Felled by her curiosity he lay aware she knew.

She nosed the grubby underpants and very slightly nodded.

'Cassara?'

She bent her head in assent.

'I'm Ric. Sorry. Men sometimes boil over.'

'Men are hungry, the Tim, always bin hungry.'

'He told me your secret. How he needs you, how much you give,'

'He's my man.'

'Among others?'

'Only him.'

'Really?'

'Him.'

'For six years?'

'For looong time.'

'I'll never tell.'

'Because you trust him.'

'Whatever. But I'm not staying long.'

'I don't mind.'

'That he's a . . .'

'He honours everything. Rocks and trees, men, me. He special.'

'He really is. And you knew. Is that why you . . .?'

'Him a proper man.'

53

'After this? Though it's not what you think.'

'He's wild. Like rocks and trees. Free as water, hungry as the earth. He's wind, making clouds burst, bringer of serpents and rain.'

Ric savored her full perfect breasts. 'And babies?'

Cassara was startled. 'Oh. Him proper man.'

'Does he know?'

She shook her head. 'That one not only mine. We went away, then I give to Mother.'

'So, he doesn't know.'

'That way best.'

'He'd want to help you.'

'You can't hold water in the hand or own rocks or trees or move clouds. He stays here now. That is help. That matters. Makes milk and tribe strong.'

'Did you know that suckling stops another baby? You don't have to stay away from him while you're feeding. Other times, kiss it or do it the back way.'

'I come to him when I can.'

'Do you want to always stay with him?'

'My tribe his tribe bring bad spirits. This way only way.'

'He's desperate to share. He wants you in his bed, his house, his whole life. His longing is strong and insistent. You and I know that. There must be another way. Let's see now: You can hold water in cupped hands; you can live with rocks and trees and marvel at the clouds and serpents chasing dreams over the ground. Are you scared to try?'

'With him, nothing scare. But him need white girl to share proper dream-time.'

'When he comes home afterwards?'

'I don't mind.'

'If his love is strong.'

'*That* matters.'

'Cassara, no one will believe you. We must make him see the truth you speak. I don't want to leave him alone, as I am. It's not an answer, and it's not his own dream. Perhaps his serpent is too strong to listen, but I'll try. Because he's very special, and because you have been his fantastic shadow all the growing years and because of the rocks and trees and clouds and misty dreams of this ancient place. Let me talk to him, then I'll send him to you and you can decide.' Ric struggled up.

'Time to shower.'

'All go away. Your food on table. You take bush shower outside.' She reached for a towel and led him out and into the strong sunlight.

A large shower rose projected from the wall of the house. Cassara hung the towel on one of the nearby pegs and turned the tap. Ric undressed and, soap in hand, stepped into the warm shower. As he soaped himself the water chilled until his skin tingled.

She stood idly by watching as he capered and snorted. 'Sun warms pipes.'

'Not for long. Cassara, would you scrub my back?'

She grinned at skin familiarly pale, and was drenched.

Ric cheerfully watched as her form showed through the flimsy cotton dress. He chuckled and deftly pulled it off. He looked in wonder at her succulent young body.

With lusty giggles, they soaped each other; he thoroughly soaped her mop of hair and, lathering her thighs, slipped wriggling fingers into her vagina; she knelt and bathed his legs, straying into his crotch so that he guided her hand around his erection.

She timidly pushed back the foreskin. 'You and him, proper men.'

He winced with pleasure. 'Knives are for eating peas, not cutting boys' cocks.'

'Neat and real.' she murmured and disengaged. 'We just friends, stop now before trouble.'

They dried each other. She shimmeyed into her sodden dress and tossed her fluffed hair. 'No matter. Dress soon dry like head.'

He wrapped himself in the wringing towel and went looking for clothes.

She set out his meal on the kitchen table, made tea and grinned. 'I wash seed off your legs, now do pants and sheet so all seed gone into earth. After, no one know how many clouds burst last night. I finish cleaning, I go; very clean person like you. Remember, you promise to send him in time in time. But what we do? I think and think. Maybe Elders speak wise plans. Maybe I ask Billy.' She brightened. 'My piccaninny will be 'Ric' because he loves him. He, our first rainbow. You make another for us.' she said earnestly.

'I'll try.' Ric said. "I'll try." It hung in the quiet air, beginning another rainbow.

After breakfast Ric examined the silent house. He found Tim's room containing records of his life. Walls a mosaic of outings on the property, group pictures from boarding school (his sweet face unchanging). There were pictures from his Agricultural College of ploughing, fencing, shearing, horse gymnastics and prize giving. There was a large poster of Mickey Mouse, a *Space Wars* fighter zooming towards a crusty planet, a print of a painting *Gums at High Noon,* and large prints of Uluru rock at sunset, and the variety of dinosaurs.

Ric lay on the boy's bed sniffing as Cassara had, finding his faint tang of stock and tree bark and, was it musty oranges? When the boy had sheltered in his arms, he'd learned more from their embrace than from the room. Ric remembered their first touch: evocative, direct and needy, its longing as absent from Tim's room as from his bed clothes or social demenour. Cassara knew. The only one who understood? Why does everyday life smother drives and dreams, ignoring our deepest wishes?

Ric glowed from the company of this boy and his woman. It felt like thanks. What had he done? What the 'thanks' represented would need defending. For whatever they had shared belonged with the rocks and trees, the slow boiling clouds, the searing blue sky, the laughter and sadness of the many who had striven to be part of this ancient place of dinosaurs and dreams and dryness.

Ric was unsure how to explain to Tim he'd actually stumbled on a solution when a mere fourteen, and denying it would loose him everything that mattered. 'We know so much, yet understand precious little. It's what's inside, the spirit of things, we must connect to.' he said to himself as he went out nearly blinded by the harsh light, started up his car and went in search of the spirit in his own dream.

Ric found Tim in a distant paddock, an indistinct blob against the sky, precariously perched at the top of the light steel tower of a windmill which fed stock water troughs. At first it was hard to be sure. Yet the slanting shoulders, the slim form and an elegant pair of legs of nomadic slenderness suggested, and when, tool box in hand, he stepped carefully down a rather rickety ladder and jumped to the ground, his smile confirmed everything.

'Did you bring me a drink?'

'No. Sorry.'

'Mine's warm. Let's have that.' Tim wiped his greasy hands, swigged from a bottle and offered it to Ric.

'You have it, Tim. Cassara made me tea.'

'Oh, you met her then?'

'She was cleaning. Found your underpants and saw the messed sheets. She knows and doesn't mind. She washed everything so nobody would guess. You didn't tell me how very beautiful she was.'

'I told you she'd find out.'

'How right you were. She says you're a "proper man", the only one. Her love of you is remarkable. Like love should be but seldom is. Because you and I are friends, I'm also her friend *not* a competitor. I get the impression she readily accepts all the other bits of your life (all your loyalties) because some of you is in hers.'

'I feel whole with her.'

'So do I. Isn't she what you're searching for?'

'Yes.' Tim swigged from the bottle and wiped a sticky arm over his sweating brow. 'To me she is this place.'

'You were right to come back after college.'

'But it's hard to know what to do.'

'You want to farm here?'

'Yes.'

'Cultivate, plough, water, discover, renew, harvest?'

'All that.'

'You went to college to learn about the land. Now, look into your heart and ask: how can I cultivate, water, protect, harvest, discover Cassara?'

'Be with her. Come home to her. That's impossible.'

'It's a big country. Take her somewhere else. She'd go with you. She wants you to come home to her, wants your seed in her soil. I don't know how, yet this land is a land of dreams. *If* you want her it can happen, with all the love and pain, certitude and doubt. Deep inside, listen to the whispers. The message is already there.'

Tim's cheek trembled. He looked away. 'There's a bit of fence mending.' He pointed into the haze. 'Come if you like. Leave your car here. We'll pick it up on the way back.'

His drawn face distressed Ric. 'I'd like that.' He tentatively put an arm round Tim's waist.

Tim relaxed yet pulled away. 'I can't take more just now. But I'd be glad of company.'

Without another word they set off.

The blazing light cut them down to stick figures. They toiled with rigid wire. Sagging lengths of fence were tightened and twanged like a huge harp, their tasks generating the only talk.

Tim grinned. 'The final twang. Thanks mate.'

'Once, I did a bit of fencing, working as a young jackaroo for vacation money.'

'Elephants never forget.'

'It was fun with you, Tim.'

'Let's go out for a couple of days. Work, camp, sleep in your tent, swim water holes. Would you like that?'

'More than anything.'

'You'll see more of the country.'

'Explore my dreamscape.'

'Mine too. Come on let's get back.'

They turned tail, picked up the car and headed back to the homestead. The plan was approved by Jim and Mary. The LandRover filled with fuel, equipment and a couple of *Eskys* to cool food and drink. Jim kitted Ric out with tough shorts, boots and a big bush hat. Mary, worrying about the heat, advised lots of drinks and sunscreen, 'And don't work Ric too hard, Son.'

Tim grinned. 'Old jackaroos don't work hard, Mum.'

Jim was circumspect. 'Any problems, sit tight. I'll come after you with Billy and the lads in three days if you've not returned. Stay with the vehicle, it's the only safe shade, and our beacon.'

'Aw, Mum and Dad, you sound as if I've never done this before. *You* sit tight if the house burns down, and Billy and the boys and I'll build you a new one.'

After supper the two ambled to the kennels in the yard with scraps for the dogs to quieten them. They drifted through a snuffling night gazing at the stars, seeing the glow of aboriginal fires through the trees. Tim avoided contact, aware of his lower unaccustomed nakedness. A freedom of sorts, but his unbridled excitement needed curbing. Wide eyed from star gazing, they parted on the verandah and slipped to their beds.

Ric ached. Ruefully he admitted many years had elapsed since his last fencing spree. He slept so deeply too tired to dream. Tim roused him as dawn was breaking.

On the way out, they drove along the crusty verge of a small lake. Two naked boys, about thirteen, and five, were gambolling in the shallows the morning light enhancing their gleaming skin. They jumped up like startled birds and cheerfully waved.

Tim flashed an arm out the window. 'That's Micky and his little brother, Cassara's brothers. I occasionally take Micky to the highway for the school bus. Great kids. Bright and eager.'

Ric caught a glimpse of one stolid and one sylphlike body, wondering if "the little pole" was Tim's son. He decided to ask Cassara sometime.

Tim turned on him. 'Hey, what a wild look. Do you want to eat them?'

'They're perfectly beautiful, Tim.'

'The real thing. Make us look anemic. Cassara says we whites had the colour stripped off - we're a circumcised race.'

'Not complete.'

'That's right.'

'What lustrous varnish they were dipped in.'

Tim nodded. 'By the way, the boys'll tell the others where we're going - our safety net.'

'I feel quite safe.'

'This is not easy country.'

'I don't take it or you lightly. But I trust you both.'

Tim coughed. 'Thanks for the calming stroll last night. Supper was a trial. They badger me. I get in a bit of a state.'

'Family life's like that. I thought you coped well. Anyway, thanks aren't needed. I enjoy your company, working or walking.'

'Me too. It was a long day. Don't do too much. Keep something back for yourself otherwise the land'll drain you.'

'Dry, parched and barren.'

'That's it.'

'I guess we all need watering and tending.'

Tim sniffed. 'No one understands deserts.'

'If you find someone who does, cling to them.'

'Cassara? Her folks'd spear me. Mine'd go mental.'

'So, do nothing.'

'Heck Man, what can I do?'

'Take the risk.'

'I don't know how.' Tim moaned.

'Tell someone, explain your need. Tell *her* what you've got isn't good enough. (She'll agree). The two of you are formidable. Something *will* happen. Tim, you can't nurse that ache for much longer. It'll cripple you.'

'I wanted to get away from all that.'

'Shit! I'm sorry. Really sorry, Tim. I'm a blundering fool. I'll shut up. I long for these two days in the open, feeding off the spirit of the place, being as carefree as those angelic boys back there. You're right: it's the best medicine. Let's work the desert, splash in billabongs and sing to the stars. They're always twinkling with laughter. Let's twinkle a bit too.'

Tim, shaking his head, pulled up. He gazed at Ric and said slowly. 'I'm comfortable with you and I trust this country. That's why I wanted you here. By the way, I thought the stars were naked jewels. Let's be opals and twinkle. If there's going to be a fight I need a bit of twinkling first.'

They bumped along an almost invisible track following silver shimmering mirages, tending fences, checking drinking troughs, watching huge lumpen cattle move ponderously through stony space, smiling with sweat and emptiness and Tim's promise of a water hole camp site, where, mid afternoon, they halted.

They set up camp near the dam. Several tent pegs were bent pounding them into the barren ground. Leaving the billy to boil they stripped and ventured through its muddy margin into brown calm refreshing water.

Suddenly they were boys again. Larking about, silly as puppies. And no one to scold them. Tim seldom showed off, and (he thought) was seldom admired. Now he basked in Ric's admiration in rare feelings of beauty and promise. Confidence blossomed.

He lolled about watching Ric prepare the meal, admiring the deft way he dealt with vegetables and sauces. He was intrigued when Ric laced cling peaches in whisky he'd taken from his suitcase. Heating them until they caught alight was tantalizing but a mushroom sauce lubricated with whisky, well peppered and poured over steaks quenched his hunger.

After eating they cleaned and washed up, carried the remaining food to the LandRover, beyond night creatures' temptation, and as the first stars pricked the darkening sky, scrambled into the tent and sprawled on mattresses of quilts and sleeping bags snug from the chilly dew.

Both basked more brightly, talked and exchanged dreams. They eventually lay with the majesty of the heavens' benediction until first light.

Tim was tending the sluggish fire when a lean aboriginal padded up.

'Billy. What's up, cobber? Here sit down and have a cuppa.'

'Nothin Boss. Wanted words.'

'Tell me, Billy. Here's your tea. LOTS of sugar.'

'Good tucker, Boss. Can I have more sugar? Y'see, I bin thinkin, time for you belonga me. You, my family. My skin sign.' We all one tribe, eh?'

Tim frowned. 'You run all this way to tell me this?'

Billy looked away squinting into the distance beyond them, and slowly nodded.

Ric whistled. 'Billy, you want him part of your tribe?'

'Yes Mister. That way we all goannas. He bin proper man.'

Ric looked at Tim. 'Billy is asking you to join his tribe. It's fanbloodytastic.'

'I don't understand either of you.'

Ric grinned. 'It's Cassara, yes?' (Billy nodded). 'Don't you see Tim, if you share their skin sign, you and your children are tribe members in a new family if you loose yours. You'll be as part of this land as they are, as lizards are. You, your woman, your child belonging with rocks and trees. Isn't that what you want?'

'Me, my "woman and child" what are you saying?'

'You said they'd spear you, Tim. But they're welcoming you.'

'Fuck. Are they? You want me, Billy?'

'Yes Boss.'

Tim was near to tears. The others smiled and looked away, watching the light imperceptibly fill every nook and stony cranny until he understood.

'Billy, you old bugger. You came all this way?'

'Sure Boss. Make time to think. You must talk Cassara out, "in time in time", she reckons. So, need to think. She say your piccaninny also called Ric. He rainbow child.'

Ric gasped. 'Billy, did that little rainbow boy tell you we were here?'

'Yes, him and Micky tell us you goin' places.'

Ric put a reassuring arm round his trembling friend. 'That small black angel we saw swimming is your son, Tim. She was going to tell you, but now it's out, eh Billy?'

'My son?'

'Yes Boss.'

'No one ever told me. It can't be.'

Ric grinned. 'You can't hump a woman for over six years without consequences. Not even a cocky young stud with the tightest underpants in the Outback.'

'You knew.'

'I guessed.'

'I, I wondered about her milk.'

'It's the flavour of love. Shall I make us porridge? You'll stay and have some, Billy? Good. LOTS of sugar. For all of us. Sugar makes you twinkle y' know. Come on Tim, you're a father now, gotta learn how to make a family breakfast. Cheer up, it's the wonderful mess you told me of last night. See, it's not only me worrying about you.'

Billy looked from one to the other. 'You best friend, Mister Ric. You bring him home in time in time. Big future waiting. We all there, you tell 'im.'

They ate porridge in silence. Drank tea. Then Ric and Tim struck the tent and stowed everything in the LandRover. They returned to the fire. Billy had vanished.

Tim nodded. 'Went before it hots up. Ric, this eclipses yesterday. Does that sound ungrateful?'

'No Tim. Sounds like the truth.'

'You could've told me.'

'I was going to.'

'Listen man, twinkling was fun.'

'Tim, the bad news is it's late. The good, that we've got one more glorious day.'

A smooth area where the tent had stood and a few sticks of charcoal were the only sign remaining as they headed off. Again, they crawled over stony rises, skirted silted water courses checking fences and watering, looking for dinosaur remains and evidence of native creatures. By early afternoon their arms and legs blazed from exposure to the fierce sunshine. A few straggling trees enticed them, with a water hole close by. They erected the tent and lolled on the shady side of the LandRover pouring cool beers down their dusty throats.

With a contented sigh, Tim pulled off his sweaty clothes and, in unlaced boots, stumbled to the water.

Ric savored his trim body flexing and gleaming in the slanting light. 'I don't know why I'm so enamoured.' he murmured. 'He's lovely. Deep. Unspoiled. Rough like the land, as captivating and mysterious. God, it's been hard work. But elating sharing it, tracking the wilderness until submerged by it. I've never been so happy. Now I see it's what I've missed ever since Dad took us away. Too late to change my life now. But imagine, doing nothing in nothingness with a no-body, becoming such perfection. This arid place is Eden. This boy, the first Adam. We are little children crawling on the hide of this rugged land, feeling like gods. It's heady stuff. And he knows it. A wild animal in its wilderness - the Great Mother. He's in love with her and enabled to love anyone in a strange incoherent way. Who's taming whom? What was it Cassara had said? "Washing his seed into the ground"? Having been 'washed' herself does she think other life, like her son, will emerge? Right now I believe other life is being gestated. It doesn't make sense. But nor do our feelings which bind us tempting me with visions of making life. Not babies or creatures, something else. Alive, active, new, effective, long lasting. The new Australia. What a crazy idea. The Dead Heart beginning to beat, this ancient moribund continent breathing once more while the rest of the world founders, too young to save itself. Too busy. Too venal.

'I see a dream beginning to happen. Right now it's wallowing in water. Tonight we'll dream again before returning. To what? The making of another dream? A rude awakening back to the madness of the every-day? Back to solitude and fear?

'That boy doesn't know what a burden he carries. Nor do I. Maybe he'll hold the world up like Atlas. Maybe it's another chance for everlasting tranquillity, at least for him and his tribe.'

Ric pulled off his clothes, stepped bare into his boots and shuffled to the bronze water rippled by a naked body smiling and splashing as if nothing else mattered.

Again, they ate well. Finishing off all the beer and the whisky. Lying giggling on their backs they saw the stars dance and the world whirl round and round.

Ric tried to sing. After a muddle of sound he hiccuped. 'I'm squiffy.'

Tim guffawed. 'I'm bloody fucking drunk. Never been so boozed up. Come on let's sing a sroper pong.'

But they lay mesmerized by spinning stars, reduced to croaking and laughing. On and on and on.

The fire died. Suddenly it was dark and cold.

'Time for shut eye Rici. Time for brown eyes and mud pies, starry skies and all that.' Tim struggled to his feet, pulled his shorts down and pissed on the fire. The acrid steam roused Ric who followed suit and staggered after him to the tent. They fumbled with clothes and bedding and, drunkenly, almost hugged. Then, falling into a black hole of sleep, everything was freed.

The morning light was cruel. Ric half-sleepwalked to make them tea. Tim groaned at the thought of moving anything.

'Poor old Tim the hangover kid. Drink up, it's the best cure, I promise. Lots of liquid to swill out the poison, a gentle swim, then a light breakfast you'll not throw up, before we make any plans. Oh, Tim, you were a buffoon. An unruly opera singer, a conductor of star ballet, my dear, lovely . . .' Ric couldn't go on. His feelings spun like stars. facing going home tore his guts.

Tim read distress. 'Ric, I fucked up. You wanted so much and I must've passed out. Oh, I'm . . . SHIT what a waste of our last night. I lost everything. Never been drunk like that. Needed a mate to lean on and a lot of understanding. Glad it was here with you. You must hate me. Sorry.'

'Tim, I think you hauled me to bed through a cyclonic cloud till I passed out beside you. Hey, it was wild and crazy. The usual hard work keeping up with you. I didn't care. Being with you was fun. Wow, you country bumkins can sink a bathtub of booze and still piss straight.'

'Ric, the night before was sensational. Real talk for a change. I wanted to take it further, didn't you?'

'Dear Tim. Perhaps we kinda knew we couldn't cap it so we manufactured another sort of event. It was meant to be. The whole trip has been perfect.'

'Another secret shared.'

'Crossing the last frontier.'

'Ric.' Tim giggled. 'Remember what you said? "You are Atlas (whoever he is) holding up the world, too busy to pull his pants up or scratch his arse". Then you offered to hold the world for a while so I could pull my pants up and scratch my arse and pour you another drink. What bollocks. But it sounded fine last night. Did Atlas wear pants?'

'No.'

'Well, there you are: bollocks. Can I have another mug of your nectar? My throat's like a rasp.'

'I'll get you one. You look better already.'

'Feel like shit. I must take a piss.' Tim shambled to a tree, leant his head on the rutted trunk and wet its roots.

Ric watched him shake out the last drips like an ancient rainmaker. His chest tightened. It was too beautiful to be mundane, strangely reminiscent of every ordinary stone between here and home.

They made a beeline for the homestead. Jim and Mary welcomed them with questions and comments until Tim grew impatient, 'Yes, we did everything and a bit more. The two of us, and Billy, well, for as long as it takes to eat and drink.'

After lunching there, Tim pottered about under Jim's curious eyes, and unpacked the LandRover. After showering, Ric drove into Winton, the nearest town. Supper was hurried as Jim and Mary were expecting a couple of neighbours to drop in for cards. Ric and Tim demurred, wearily going to bed.

Sometime in the pristine quiet of night Ric felt the bed sag. Tim demure in his pyjama pants shook him. 'I woke up, thinking of what we said. You were away. I wanted to talk like the other night in the tent.'

Ric told him about visiting the bank in Winton where he'd set up an account. Tim agreed to go in the morning and sign the forms. He was disbelieving, 'A hundred thousand dollars? It's a fortune.'

'My export business won't even be dented, and it's a tax dodge. Your fund is an amount plus the cost of a house for your family and shelter for the tribe, to begin your own life, to make it work.'

'You beat Father Christmas. A shack with extra external covered space? Isn't it too much?'

'No, it's nothing. I visited a barn specialist on the edge of town. He's got a huge galvanized iron building with a roof like two open wings. I thought you could fit in a house at the centre leaving one side for Cassara's folks, the other for machinery, gear and vehicles.'

'Us, flanked by machines and people. Proper cockies.'

'If the barn's insulated, living under it should be comfortable. In fact, I saw a little pre-fab house. They'll do it without a roof and it'll fit in snugly. Two bedrooms and an ample living/dining/kitchen, a shower, a store and loo.'

'We only need one bedroom.'

'Having a five year old in with you and Cassara will cramp your style, worse than tight underpants.'

'Oh, I forgot about kids.'

'Typical.'

'Ric, what did you mean the other night after I'd said I wanted to live with Cassara and fuck the consequences, and you talked of holding up the world?'

'This one's doomed unless we change our ways. You follow your heart, love the land and its people, and live and work simply. It's a way forward. Changing the rules, changing the culture of greed and prejudice. You and Cassara and her folk are holding each other, holding the land. For me that's "holding the world". See what I mean, Tim?'

'Doing it different? Like I want?'

'Of course.'

'Lots of kids, my big tribe sharing the land?'

'All that.'

'Why are you doing all this?'

'You deserve it.'

'Deserve?'

'Something like that. It's my way of belonging here.'

'We're proper mates, aren't we.'

'Sure thing.'

'It's strange being so close. Like boys.'

'Strange your loving a black girl, acres of stony nothing, loving a dream of riches which no bank could quantify. It takes determination tackling everything beyond mirages. It's raw strong and undeniable. I wish I'd had a bit more in my life. Doing it your way makes you freer of rules, busy with hope. You and Cassara. And the others.'

Ric dozed off unaware Tim had lain down, also stricken by tiredness.

Ric was woken by the dawn light. He watched Tim sleep. Mouth slightly open, eyebrows flying below his forehead, one hand clenched, the other open - was his dream a tussle of contradictions, fear and success, clenched war and relaxed love? Lying akimbo on the bed, he had the same youthfulness as in the school photos in his room. Sleeping, his beauty is not masked in shyness nor is his strength, Ric mused.

He pushed a finger into the fist. It was damp and gripped him. Tim smiled and opened his eyes. 'Gotya. Let's play hide and seek. I'll close my eyes. You hide. I'll find you within a minute, OK? Ready steady, go!'

Ric slipped off the bed and hid in the wardrobe. Tim found him in no time. They changed places. It took Ric a little longer to spy him balancing on a chair behind the curtains which billowed as he frantically tried to stop his pants slipping to his ankles. Grinning, he kicked them away, lay face up on the bed, eyes tight shut. Ric silently rolled under the bed. In the stillness the door opened. It was Tim's mother.

'So, there you are. What *are* you doing, and naked?'

'Hello Mum.' Tim rolled onto his stomach. 'Playing hide and seek.'

'Grown men can't behave like this. You used to play with school friends, but never undressed.' She bent and picked up his pyjamas and threw them onto the bed. 'Make yourself decent. I don't know what your father will say.' She stormed out.

Ric emerged from beneath the bed as he was dressing. Tim angrily shook his head. 'She's always been prim. Never liked bare flesh. She made me wear the underpants: boys had to be properly dressed even under their shorts.'

'Otherwise, it might pop out and lead to fornication.'

'She's too frightened to know anything. I'm sure she kept her nighty on when Dad made me.'

'No wonder you're shy.'

'Usually I can be her "good boy". Sometimes I burst. And I hate skulking in the dark.'

'Or with Cassara.'

'She'll go blotto when she learns about my little Ric. It'll be my "unbridled lust, her sluttishness, the shame of it all". Ric, what's wrong with openness, lust, love, children and laughter?'

'They'll fill your own house. It's your life now. Buck up Tim. Breakfast and then we're off to town. You knew it'd be a battle.' He almost smiled. 'Strange she doesn't hear the energy or the longing bubbling in you. It's all there. Few notice. Typical. It's a shame.'

'Cassara listens, her folks too.'

'Yes, she does. It's a caring gift.'

'It's as if they know what you're thinking.'

'They watch keenly and listen. We do express our feelings. If someone would only listen.'

'It's being straight too. Saying what things are, not beating about the bush, like Mum.'

'It's nice to think that those with so little have so much besides.'

Tim nodded and smiled. He checked the coast was clear and

hugged Ric. It soothed them both.

The row continued over breakfast until Ric said, 'I get the message. I'll leave this morning. I was going anyway.'

Tim's face blazed. 'I'm coming with you. Can't take any more. I'm off.'

Jim blenched. 'You can't just walk out.'

Tim choked. Ric put a calming hand on his arm. 'Leave it, Mate.'

Tim shook. 'No one tells me what to do.'

'Leave it, Mate.' Ric eyed Jim and Mary. 'Don't worry, I promise we won't go far.'

Tim leapt up in fury. Without a word he stalked to his room, filled a bag and went to Ric's car. Waiting in the sunshine drew some of his anger off. He kicked at stones and glowered at the dogs who'd come from their kennels licking his hand expecting an outing. He crouched on his haunches and took a furry head on his bare legs. 'I'll come back for you Blackie. I promise.' The dog eyed him growling in dismay. Ric appeared lugging his case. Soon they were off. A cloud of dust hung over the yard like a frown. It dispersed into emptiness.

There was a lot to do in town. Ric dispatched all the business quickly. Tim was impressed. He wondered how much his status as a $100,000 man keened the bank, solicitor and the companies supplying barns and pre-fabs. It was fun making old inchoate dreams real. Until he remembered his intractable parents. But Ric's playfulness was infectious. It grew into a day of exploration of dreams and countryside. Ric waved a pamphlet he'd picked up at the bank. 'Let's go to Lark Quarry Park and see the oldest news report in the world.'

'Y' mean the stampede. Never seen it.'

'It says a hundred million years ago scores of foraging chicken-sized coelurosaurs and ornithopods were disturbed by a giant carnivourous theropod and fled along the muddy shore. The tracks, some three thousand footprints, were overlaid and eventually fossilized. Similar to chicken-hearted folk's prints running away from the obvious such as living within our means, or conservation, or the truth dreams tell, or feelings and intuition - as if they'll trample and kill. The history of mankind has been one stampede after another, false prophets masking greed with defense against (and flight from) theropods; or sabre toothed tigers, the enemy over the hill, witches, communists, revisionists, refugees . . . the list is endless. Tim, you've broken with the ancient shackles of superstition by wanting to speak plainly and mixing thought and feelings as you and Cassara wonderfully manage in the face of stampeding relatives. To some it's breaking the rules. You know better. It's living in harmony with the cosmos. I absolutely know you're right.'

'Quite a lecture.'

'Tim, you must hold onto your dream (whatever it is). Don't be steered by this morning's anger or old wounds or others' rules.' Ric sighed. 'I think you love this place and Cassara with it. You want to bring up your kids and make the place flourish in all manner of ways. Tell me, is that correct?'

'Maybe it's time to ditch dreams.'

'Or time to implement them.'

'How?'

'Ask yourself, Cassara (me if you want). But first consider the dream, and only then ask, "How". Am I right?'

'You know you are. We've talked and talked.'

'That's fine. Now for the "How". First, you must clarify your plans about managing the property. Face your parents with an ultimatum: either they agree or you'll vamoose. You know their involvement is diminishing. Who else is there to take over? After that, I'm not sure. I'd advise "suck it and see". But know, the house, the barn, equipment and all the rest merely have to be ordered and delivered so you can start. Oh yes, another first (there are always a couple you know): talk and talk, make love with Cassara, and don't hide anything to shield her. That way she'll be an effective partner. Working together, your own rules will firm-up. Coupled with all your love and skill and passion, you'll avoid the stampede. You will find your dream again by making it.'

'If only it were that easy.'

'Only the best generals hazard "all or nothing". As *you* must. Focus. Then you'll remember it's worth the fight.'

'Something for my son. The tribe.'

'For the land.'

'All those things.'

'With a past *and* a future.'

'Will you help, Ric?'

'Only to get you home. Then I must go through to Adelaide and Melbourne, returning in three months to find what you've done.'

'You must?'

'Yes Tim.'

'Mm. You'll come back?'
'I promise.'

The rest of the day was spent holidaying. They booked a twin room in a small motel on the Matilda Highway before taking the bitumen road to Opalton, then a dusty drive to Lark Quarry Park which housed the dinosaur stampede tracks. The road, smoking behind them, led back to the Highway, then a cafe where they wolfed steak, eggs and numerous cups of tea before returning to the motel.

Ric took a shower. Tim sprawled on his bed. The door flew open. Jim and a couple of his mates burst in. He pulled Tim up. 'Come on son, I want a word with you.' And pushed him outside.

The others threateningly confronted Ric. 'Thought you'd scarper, eh?'

Ric took a deep breath. 'Easy fellahs. We're not going anywhere.'
'Too right.'

'We've been pottering around the country. I told Jim and Mary we wouldn't go far.'

'And the motel told us you was holed-up here.'

'Fellahs, you got it wrong. This is Tim's country. He loves it here. Wants to stay. He's got plans, big plans. He's no fool. Won't be pushed around. Would you?' They glowered in unwilling assent.

'He told Jim and Mary he'd go if they don't let him get on with it. You know he can work anywhere - well trained, great background. He will unless you all back off. You must know that?' They nodded grudgingly.

'He needs tonight to calm down and think, then I'll deliver him to Belmont to reach a deal with his parents. We're not going anywhere. Take my car keys. But unless you take Jim home right now you may as well forget a future here with Tim. He'll not stay. I know, spent the day trying to get him to see sense. He's as pig headed as his dad. Listen fellahs, Tim's a fantastic bloke. Born and bred here. Don't drive him away. He's irreplaceable. You know that. You look as if you've broken horses? Well, it's a matter of little by little *and* very gently. Don't harry him, he'll gallop off. Gentle handling will work combined with his love of this stony place and its people. And a little time.'

The two men nodded. 'The lad's one of the best. Keep your keys. Do your bit and we'll do ours.' They left without another word.

Tim returned bemused. He sat heavily on the bed. 'Ric, I blew it.

Told Dad the lot: the new house, little Rici, Cassara, plans for working the property with the blacks as partners (and relatives), conservation, water, stock management . . . the lot. He was gob smacked. All he said was "OK, OK, I'll speak to your mum." The others dragged him away and here I am.' He looked crestfallen.

Ric drew him into an admiring hug. 'Well done. Our talk, your planning. So the ball's in their court. Tim, that's wonderful.' He pushed him to arms length. 'You smell. Have a shower and we'll play hide and seek.'

The game didn't even begin. There was little more to say before a deep sleep. It was a short drive home in the morning where agreement was reached. The parents' disbelief their boy had become a man was, by and large, tinged with pleasure. Ric was plied with conciliatory tea in a muted celebration that the bridge of dread had been negotiated, to every-one's' relief.

Tim came out to see him off and polished the dusty head and tail lights of Ric's grimy car with a pair of underpants and a broad grin. 'Cassara's never liked them either.' he said tossing them into the boot. 'Thanks, Mate. You were dead right. See you in three months.'

Tim, spanners in hand at the top of a shining windmill supplying water to his new house, saw Ric's car stop at the distant highway gate. He shouted down to the children gambolling below. 'He's here. Tell Cassara.'

A scurrying hoard descended on the house, delighted message bearers, now adding a welcome to their games. For had not Billy told them the stranger was a proper fellah (nearly a goanna). Of course there was time for hugs and smiles with little Rici's mum, time for cool drinks, time to jig and canter off along the track through the trees and out into the glare where they'd meet him.

The car had a passenger. Mickey. He'd clambered in at the gate after being dropped by the school bus. Mickey's grin confirmed how special the visit was. A small knot of kids stood open mouthed across the track. 'We know you.' someone murmured as the car rolled to a stop. Mickey leant out and yelled. 'Rici. Come on! It's Uncle Ric.'

A small boy nimbly climbed onto Mickey's knee and serenely gazed out over the sea of excited faces, absorbing the ambience of his name emanating from the white man. Then Daddy was there, striding to the other door. Big Ric and he, embracing and kissing (only real big men did that). Beyond, Mummy waving from the shade, taking in all the excitement, mystery, dreams. All the spirits jostling to share in the celebration.

All the other children squeezed into the back. Luckily it was a short distance. But for years later they recalled a luscious, long journey over rocks and through airy shadows to the expectant house.

The stranger was so hot, everyone had a bush shower with him beneath the spinning windmill. Shorts and dresses piled on the verandah. Lots of ebony fish gleaming and jumping, wet bellies, buttocks shining like their eyes, pink and brown soles and palms, and shouts of pleasure.

The stranger was pale, paler than little Rici, and *much* bigger. Sharing a shower game with a huge hairy man, they stood tall. It was not shrinking water, but, magic tall-making stuff running all over them and into their mouths and eyes. Some of the children suddenly felt bigger and stronger. They were unusually glad. No wonder the elders were gathering to welcome this white man and his spirits.

After drying off, everyone donned a bright tee shirt from a roomy cardboard box from the boot of the car. Mickey had a special *Mickey Mouse* tee shirt. Cassara laughed. 'You can't be that Mickey, your ears are too small.' Everyone sniggered. But Mickey was too delighted to care.

Little Rici had smaller shorts matching his "brother's", and a cream tee shirt, matching his skin, with an eloquent drawing by a San bushman from South Africa, of a man with a bow and arrows.

'Is it magic?' whispered the boy.

'It's a hunter's story' Ric said quietly. 'It tells of hunting skills: a keen eye, a steady hand and an awareness of the animal spirit which will accept the arrow and provide food for his tribe.'

Tim guffawed. 'To remind you to hold your willy with a "steady hand", a "keen eye" and not wet your toes.'

The wee lad, lost in clouds of mirth, looked down at his demure tail and finally grinned. 'Anyway, my feet get hot.'

All the naked tails and vaginas and bottoms, crowned in brightly coloured shirts, jigged up and down in glee. It didn't matter, yet it mattered. It was such fun.

After a cuppa, Tim took Ric over to meet the elders, many of whom still lived in their traditional mia mias under the bark-stripped trees beyond the new building. They were uncomfortable in the yawning roofed space, in spite of being open on three sides, where most of the others had moved. Billy had wisely remarked, "Now we have a choice. Here or there" (for dry or wet weather).

Ric presented them with some thick grass mats woven by women in Arnhem Land. 'To soften the stony ground and ease aches and pains.' he said. He proffered a set of five litre acrylic paints in shades matching the natural hues of the land and sky, suggesting they begin to paint Dream Time stories on the high wall of their new space. 'Use white man's paint and brushes but tell your very own sacred stories. Other tribes have natural caves for their books. Maybe this new "cave" could substitute.'

The elders at first looked doubtful. Struggling with memories of proper ancient rituals, they reluctantly concluded these new-fangled things might be useful. The women wailed with excitement. They better understood the awkward partnership of old and new.

When Tim remarked it was making their new home into a sort of story-church, with images blessing them all, many nodded. Perhaps there were ways of holding the world in spite of and because of white culture.

'It's hard to kill us goannas.' an old man said shaking Ric's hand.

Ric nodded. 'But its hard for a goanna to live long without its tail. The world is different now. It seems to me you must allow some whiteness into your blackness, in much the same way white men must acknowledge their feminine, and white women, their masculine aspects. It's an inner partnership underpinning survival.'

Billy looked severe. '*You* should also allow black men's ways. Too much beer, TV and pop songs no good.'

'Not good for anyone.' Ric said.

Billy sniffed. 'We must listen to the earth.'

'Maybe with black and white ears.'

Billy's eyes twinkled. 'We do that.'

'That's what I hoped to find. I'm delighted.' Ric said.

Billy smiled. 'The earth will sing again.'

'That's the best dream of all.'

Later Tim picked up his snuggling San-decorated son and carried him home. They ate as evening light streamed across the landscape softening and enhancing it, as their talk, tinged with gladness. Ric then took his sleepy little name-sake (godson, to us) to his bedroom, their bedroom he was sharing: sleeping in the empty bed which the boy had forsaken for the grounded comfort of the floor. The mite was a little overawed sharing his room. However, emboldened by the pleasures of the afternoon, he shyly asked his big name-sake for another hunting story. Cuddling his newly acquired teddy bear, he listened:

Once upon a time in a great wide bright place lived a tiny goanna
with no name and no tail. During the day he scuttled about over
stones which burned his feet; during the night he nosed under them for
snacks, enjoying the dew and the stars, playing with his many friends,
all of whom had lovely long names, and tails, and who assured
him that one day, if he kept hunting, he'd find his name under a
special stone.
So, the little goanna looked everywhere, usually finding mite, ant and
worm snacks making him fat which was also important, although he
didn't yet know why.
One day he was basking under a tree when a soft furry bear climbed
down and said. 'Let's be friends. I'll help you find your tail and your
name, if you like?'
'Oo, yes.' said the goanna.
So, they fossicked and roamed far, far over the hard dun-coloured
earth, far into rocky wastes shimmering in silver heat, way beyond
home. They found many worms and mites and beetles as they adven-
tured. With each gulp the little goanna grew heavier until it was
arduous dragging himself through the heat and dust. He was very
busy indeed snacking and looking for magic stones, and being aware
kites and eagles might snatch him up for lunch. However he kept on
hunting.
Time passed. He was unaware his tail was growing until a fly landed
nearby and, without a thought, he swatted it and grinned.
He and Teddy were terribly tired. Found a large decorative stone and
snuggled underneath for a rest. He was about to close his eyes when,
with a start, he saw the decoration on the stone. 'Look.' he whispered
to Teddy 'Doesn't that say something?'
'It's a bit back-to-front.' Teddy murmured. 'But it reads CIᴙ which
sort of spells CIR; that might be a name.'
'It looks backwards' muttered the goanna doubtfully.
'Who cares.' said Teddy shutting his eyes.
'It might be my stone.' breathed the little goanna swishing his tail.
'Your what?' said Teddy, angrily, his sleep disturbed.
'The stone with my name on it. Please Teddy, what word is there?'
'It's a silly old dinosaur fossil.' Teddy said tiredly.
'But it is a real word.' said the goanna.
'If it is backwards, then forwards it says RIC.'
The not so tiny goanna hummed happily. Yes, it was hot and stifling

like any other sunny day. But today was an extra special one. He was so happy he sang, and woke Teddy who glowered until his little friend cried gleefully, 'Today we found a magic stone, I grew a fine tail and (best of all) I got a name.' He hugged Teddy until his scowl became a smile and he muttered as he drifted into sleep, 'Hello, Ric. I'll be the first one to ever call you by your name. You're lucky. You've got a fine tail, much longer than mine.'

And that's the end of my tale about how a sweet tailless goanna found his tail and his name and lived happily ever after.

The little boy was solemn. 'That's a *real* story.'

Ric smiled. 'Yes it is. Teddy knows too.'

'Does Teddy know I got my name before before?'

'Yes. And he tells me you'll grow a long tail by-n-by.'

'Like Daddy?'

'Exactly.'

'Mummy blows farts there and it grows stiff.'

'It's looking around happily.'

'Um, yes.'

'You need sleep as well as running and eating to grow. Now I'll say goodnight. Teddy will keep a look out for kites and eagles, so Rici, sleep well.'

The boy reached up and hugged Ric. 'It's my first own story. I'll paint it for Mummy. She's got a baby inside, don't you know. I'll help him find his name.' He curled up and fell blissfully asleep.

Ric trembled at his beauty and trust, with an inkling it was going to be all right for everyone, better than his own boyhood. He tiptoed out and into the living space, his face relaying his thoughts to Cassara who blushed and smiled, took Tim's rough hand and squeezed it passionately.

Tim grinned. 'We're doing all right.' he said softly.

Ric nodded. 'I know.' was all he said.

In the morning Tim announced there would be an expedition to check a distant rickety windmill.

'We'll take tucker and a tent in case we stay out.'

Cassara, with some grace, said. 'Fix pump and fix your goodbyes.'

Tim coloured and nodded. As they drove away, waving to the

kids, he muttered. 'Glad she isn't jealous.'

Ric sighed. 'We all need need chalk and cheese.'

Tim grinned. 'She says "sometimes pickle too".'

'She's the queen of your house. You're lucky Tim.'

'Cassara's sweet, with the toughness of truth.'

'Perfect wife and mother to your kids.'

'"Kids"? You know.'

'Your Rici told me.'

'Shit, Ric, it was easy.'

'Fun?'

'Honeymoon time. Best night of my life.'

'So, you'll stay here with her?'

'For ever.'

'Then, I'll check you up in ten years.'

'Come and stay. It's your place too.'

'Ah, what a great dream.'

'We need dreamers here.'

'I'll be an old pensioner.'

'We'll build you a little old house. Kids'll help look after you, if you tell them *real* stories. Little Rici's over the moon about goanna tails and names and tales and making pictures about them. You're a wizard, he's in love with you. He's lucky to be a picanniny; love comes easier. Mine is a bit tortured, guess it's because of the Y-fronts.'

'Tim, we don't need to stay out.'

'I'd like a break. I put a crate of beer in. Thought we'd get gently drunk, watch the stars careering round like old times. Anyway, ten years is a long time.'

'Rici will be Mickey's age - gruff and hairy, beginning to discover men's dreams. Two great kids. Hey, they all are. You've a terrific tribe, Tim.'

'We've got to stay free. Keep the Native Affairs, the legislators and minions out. We must do it our own way, legal and illegal: transformations influenced by aboriginal lore and the modern needs of the land. Needs not defined by whitemens' law, regulation and commerce but decent science and long experience. Maybe it's impossible. I'd like to jaw with you over the camp fire; say goodbye, our way.'

'No stampede?'

'Absolutely not. Careful tracking using *their* ways.'

It was an uncomfortable ride. A tyre burst. Just as well, as the old

LandRover cooled while they changed wheels. They arrived to find half-empty troughs. The windmill couldn't supply sufficient water. Tim, tools in a haversack over his shoulder, climbed the rusted ladder and began to tinker behind the sails. Suddenly the fragile ladder fell away. Tim fell pulling ten meters of gossamer ladder with him into a tangled mess below. He lay as dead.

Ric's hellish panic lessened when Tim finally groaned. Ric's blind determination got Tim back into the LandRover. Then the appallingly rough journey home, marshalling many hands to transfer Tim to Ric's car, and then, accompanied by Cassara, Ric made for the hospital.

Tim was admitted immediately for observation. The white gowns firmly dismissed Cassara and Ric. Silent and grim faced they drove away.

'What if he'd been alone?' Cassara whispered.

'I was thinking that.' said Ric uneasily. 'We must do two things pronto: get two or three mobile phones, and teach you to drive. There's a phone shop near Tim's bank. Let's do that now with my credit card. When we get home, you, I and Mickey (if he's there) will have a driving lesson. He can ride a bike - most of the kids can. He's nearly old enough for the roads and is a fine back-up. Come on.'

It took their minds off graver matters.

'We need new windmills.' Cassara said firmly. 'Water is first, like hands.'

So, Ric and she visited a local supplier and arranged for a rep. to spend a day advising on replacement and locations. Shocked about Tim's accident, he promised a visit as soon as possible. (He knew Tim had a large bank balance, it was common knowledge; he was also curious to see what was happening at Belmont since Tim's stewardship had become the prime local gossip). Ric left him their mobile phone number.

Cassara judged this new fangled gimmick a vital addition. She realized she'd have to check all the white man's junk against their own needs. Safety and happiness had obvious dimensions to which phones and gas cylinders contributed. It was reason to clutter their lives with them. And driving - like a white woman - seemed essential. Other lives could be saved. She decided to learn as fast as Mickey who was already skilled with machines. It would be part of their plans. Some of her distress evaporated. The children in particular were heartened by the determination in her report that BossTim was going to be all right.

In spite of this news, the elders convened a corroboree and danced and sang the great spirits to Tim's bedside to shield him from harm. In their deliberations over changing life patterns it hadn't occurred to them Tim could go so soon. The spirits reassured them this was not the time. But the kinship they felt deepened to the extent they acknowledged he was a secondary chief. The mirages danced confirmation all the next day, the elders noted. Tim was one of their own now. They'd take care of him too.

Tim's wee boy was shaken. He'd never imagined losing his father so soon after finding him. Ric and Teddy comforted him as best they could until responding games and repairing sleep lent a hand.

Cassara cried a little. Her Rici was right, it was frighteningly early to lose Tim. Her mother and many of the women gathered on her verandah singing propitiatory songs, bringing the stars out winking support, easing the agony.

Ric agreed to stay until Tim came home. He sat withdrawn and sightless in the living space unable to deal with the gloom. His only gesture was the decision to fund a monthly payment for little Rici: money magic supporting his sweet life; ensuring his tail, his name and his father. When the women ceased singing he crept to bed where Teddy guarded the sleepers through the long quiet night.

Tim was allowed home three days later with a big box of pain killers and strict instructions to take it easy for several weeks.

The doctors were amazed no bones were broken, only painfully deep bruising and debilitating concussion which time would mend.

The elders of the tribe nodded conspiritorially. The great spirits watched over him. Always had. They placed signs of gratitude on ritual stones nearby and listened to Tim's ideas more carefully. Although goannas had tough skins, they needed 'stones' of plans and tribe to protect them. It was time to listen to wild ones like Billy. Perhaps the great ones spoke through him? Something had spoken. They felt stronger and more confident. Like snakes, they too could change their skins yet remain the same. That's what Billy observed. It sounded good sense.

Hugged and blessed, Ric eventually left, his car bursting with children who clamoured to farewell him at the distant gate. Their delight was infectious. It leavened his sadness driving north to Hughenden where he took the Overlander's Highway towards the coast.

Sadness halted him in a layby under majestic gums signalling the White Mountains National Park. His head on the steering wheel, he didn't see the policeman.

'Anything wrong, mate?'

'Oh, um, just resting. A long sticky drive after an emotional farewell.'

The policeman leaned nearer. 'You bin drinkin?'

'No.'

'OK. Your breath's clean. Love of yer life, eh? Yer, it's a wrench gettin away after.'

'Yes to that.'

'Goin to the coast?'

'Yes. Short holiday before going back to work.'

'Fishin, sailing, a nice easy time, good grub, dark nights, that what you have in mind?'

'Yes.'

'I know the perfect spot. Just beyond Ingham, off the highway. A backwater behind Hinchinbrook Island. Ask for Andy and May at *The Cockleshell*. All heart. No style. It's the place to unwind. Tell em, Cliff from Charters Towers sent you. Tell em I'll be down for fishin in six weeks so get the booze in and catch a few woppas.

'Listen Mate, it's like the Outback: simple and powerful. No bullshit. OK, not a wilderness like the centre, but not fucked over like the rest of the coast. You can dream there, get real, if you get my drift?' He winked and strode back to his panda car, waved and disappeared into the haze.

Ric sat for a long time considering. "You can dream there", Cliff had said. 'It's probably the only way I can let go.' he muttered. Tim was right, ten years was a long time to stay away.

He had changed. Not his skin. Something murmured much deeper. He'd touched the heights of a life-held dream. A tribe of eager children, plans, families, elders and the great spirits. He'd shared a precious love (his and theirs) and helped make a hope in them to hold onto the world - a marriage rather than an ending. In his own Bethlehem.

Ric sighed. 'I'm reminded of Judith Wright's vivid poem titled *Australia*. How does it go?

> *I praise the scoring drought, the flying dust*
> *the drying creek, the furious animal,*
> *that they oppose us still;*
> *that we are ruined by the thing we kill.*

Could it also mean: *We are revived by life we instill.* Can Tim with the others with the land, be revived?'

Ric drove through the afternoon, the sun blazing at his back, the road drumming out ruin and death until, below lay a long apron of greenish coast confronting a million square miles of ocean.

Somewhere to the left the haze hid Hinchinbrook Island, pushed against a meagre stretch of water (Vance Palmer's *Passage* perhaps?). A small pinched place of peace, loneliness and healing that Cliff the policeman had mentioned. 'If you're not already too ruined ruined ruined to recover' the car droned.

The policeman was right. *The Cock shell* certainly kept prudes away (*Cockleshell* only if you looked closely at the aged flaking paint) was an informal sprawling bungalow separated from the beach by an underused track, proclaimed by its profuse weeds.

Andy and May liked company, catching and cooking fish; and, yes, they had a room facing the water which I could have for a modest sum. 'We're not real smart like proper guest houses; lacking mod-cons such as phone or internet, but use our house phone.' drawled Andy as he helped me in with luggage. I moved the car so as not to interfere with the view.

The sea gently lapped a shallow beach intruded on by a tangle of mangroves. Across a narrow strip of water lay low wooded islands. A couple of miles away towered the granite peaks of Hinchinbrook Island, wooded to the water's edge. Somewhere beyond lay the Great Barrier Reef. To the right lay the passage south. To the left, a widening estuary joining reefs and islands to the north.

The only other house guest was a professor of music. Lanky, tall, straw-coloured hair, who looked more comfortable sitting. Standing up he stooped and sagged, his head too heavy for his small shoulders. He gestured gingerly as if a sudden movement might snap him in two. He played May's piano in the evenings. Usually gypsy music. Sometimes songs from the shows to which Andy sang along.

The Cockleshell looked just the place for me to unwind; it was a change from beer and beef where I might relax. Andy rang round finding a neighbour willing to hire me a small sailing boat for pottering along the coast. There was enough company to take my mind off all the tangled questions my visit to the centre had raised.

The professor was distracted and pleasant, a specialist on

Janacek, a Czech composer who annotated speech with musical notation because, as he had said, "I grasped the rise and fall of the notes in a conventional conversation, hearing inside himself, the person wept." and that "The melodies of speech are an expression of the comprehensive state of being." Or, as the professor put it, 'He peeled away the layers of song which conceal the soul itself as a preparation for the work of writing his opera *Jenufa* in which orchestral themes represent the cries of anguish and despair hidden in ordinary action.' [*]

The professor described Jenufa's house as representing a sealed room from where, finally, there is nowhere to go, where bad things happen that will never be spoken of, where two people can be separated by miles of isolation.

I was reminded of Tim and his parents (his mother in particular). Nowhere to go. Bad things. Folk miles apart. Ah, such bleakness.

I imagined Janacek's "soul music" through which Cassara and I (and her tribe) heard the cries in Tim's daily speech. By their keen perception of meaning behind ordinary words - perhaps sensing the voices of the great spirits? - the aboriginals allow soul music into ordinary life.

I once thought Cassara fearless and without guilt. Now I see, in touch with the soul, she saw differently, so responded with the soul's majesty. Majestic because we are bits of the huge soul of the world; her family connected through goannas to other creatures, also their habitat, their habits, rituals, visions and origins. No wonder they talked of a Dreamtime.

The Freudians might say this is consciously living with the unconscious. Music within speech and the anarchy and paradox in dreams are expressions of and acknowledgement of the unconscious.

However it is defined, I had been emersed in it all my stay, swept up and into passions so intense it hurt. So wild it was real. No wonder leaving had been a terrible wrench.

We were naked children, like the dark angels I'd seen swimming, or those later showering with me. No wonder Tim and I played hide and seek. Naked, unawares, engrossed in a soul search for ourselves in each other. Deep and vital as if feeding off one another. No wonder guilt disappeared. No wonder ecstasy reigned. It was a new sort of life. And

---

[*] see: G.O'Brien, *Nightmare on the Prairie - Jenufa*
      in New York Review of Books, September 21st, 2006. p35ff.

Cassara welcomed it.

From the old standpoint, their new life entailed less denial, more risk but far more wonder and joy. His mother, by hiding Tim's sexual organs behind layers of clothes hugged tight to his crotch, provided a life-long oppression which nearly broke him.

Cassara and I heard his longing, and responded in mentionable and unmentionable ways because of which he is forging a new life and (I hope) will find ways of holding the world. His pride and fecundity shine on his son, infect all his doings these days. The inner man (and boy) has a place in his life. He is not isolated by the tyranny of distance. Intimate listening is all.

One evening, watching the moon rise, I mentioned my time in the Outback to the professor, asking him if modern life was denying intimacy by replacing it with abstract thought.

He glanced away from the silver disk sheening the water fondling the beach in front of us. 'By intimacy, do you mean connections?'

I nodded. 'The idea of being joined, and the joining.'

He sighed. 'Janacek shows us intimacy overruled by judgement with little probability of happy endings. He doesn't specify a time. Rather, he seems to be saying human society has always been cruel, judgmental and insensitive.'

'Because we overlook "soul music"?'

'It's a spiral of carelessness leading to annihilation.'

'Like the end of the dinosaurs.'

'No, worse. The end of us *and* the world as we know it. Your descriptions of a new life in the outback are fanciful, according to Janacek (and I agree with him). There is no hope. Neither your thoughts nor Janacek's extraordinary music have a place here.[*]

'There is no soul to find, or nurture. Dead Heart equals dead soul. It's a projection of Australian life: greedy pointless exploitation, unconnected people and separated from place as rootless as gypsies.'

'I can't accept we're doomed.'

'Of course you can't. You know, and do something about it. But it will take such a vast change in society, culture and belief, that it's impossible for your way or Cassara's to ever be adopted.' He blinked.

---

[*] see: *Intimate Letters* in *Outrageous Fortune* by F. Oeser, London: Sicnarf Press. 2007, p172ff.

'We can't save ourselves or the world. Greedy and fearful we'll go down fighting to the end. We made the barren space, to inhabit.' He sadly shook his head. 'There is a special irony on this continent. Humans have lived in harmony here for fifty thousand years. We, in two hundred, will destroy it.'

The moon was balancing on the outline of Hinchinbrook Island whose black form faced us across the glimmering water.

I pointed. 'It looks as formidable as in daylight.'

'My, doesn't it glower.'

'Only if you see it that way, Professor.'

'Shadows are frightening. Leos Janacek's eloquent music is filled with them. They're undeniable.'

'Is there no beauty of hope there, Professor?'

'It naturally occurs in music.'

'As well as in the soul. It is time to start listening.'

*

Holding hands

GULLS HERALDING SUMMER: sheets of folded paper swinging high in the air, white against grey clouds, grey stones, the grey gnarled chimneys and squat tiled rooves of a Scottish fishing town. Papers poised on a breeze moaning in corners, shaking climbing roses on walls, tugging coats, bending swirling smoke to chimney pots, freshening the grey sea with multitudinous white grins.

In a crib placed within a frame of metal window bars bulging out below the eaves lies an infant, a well wrapped bundle of warmth, wide eyed, its face brushed by the busy wind. Its swaddling, the gulls' colours whose rawkous cries draw tiny moans from the bairn making one wind-swept song. Floating in air everything joins. Everything sings. Taut, tiny and white, held by grey vastness in one flying world.

Three summers pass. The wee boy having stretched skyward from crawling, now firm on balancing feet, felt but did not understand his lessening as the complexity of the world grew. A world he no longer contained. A world containing him; and another, his sister, proclaiming he was no longer Baby. No longer stuck to crib or pram or floor. Free (but not free) to explore, to fly like the gulls in raucous air stretching beyond the busy sea (perhaps to kindlier realms?).

Contented, he sat on the edge of his sand pit making smooth tracks for ants. 'Do they know? I'm so big, like the wild wind which whips the fishing boats and slaps my cheeks.' he murmured. 'They're too busy to know it's me. They're like everyone else.' He sighed in the silence. After finishing the ant highway, and quite alone, he then made for himself an inseparable friend.

'My name's Gull' the boy said, 'yours is Mousy Doggy.'

Mousy Doggy chuckled. 'I'm so glad we're friends. Let's adventure. And, I'll tell the silly ants who we are. You know, most people don't see the things in front of their noses.'

'There's a lot to see.'

'So what? Everything has a name. You only have to ask.'

The rough stone wall growled. 'Remember, I keep the naughty wind away from you and the ants. No one thanks me.'

Mousy Doggy, Gull beside him, scrambled to his feet. 'We were just about to, before you interrupted us.'

Gull whispered. 'We love your crown of thorns. Can you tell the sun to lick your face more often? We like that too.'

'Sun has a mind of its own. No one tells him. He has his own plan to light and warm us. He'd like thanks.'

'One day I'll fly to him.'

Mousy Doggy looked skeptical. The clouds get in the way.'

Gull giggled. 'Shifty clouds. No brains, like my sweet nursemaid, Mitzi. Some days she leaves things lying around. When she trips over the broom or bucket she scolds me. And gets cross when I laugh. Even Erasmus grins. But then, cats see everything.'

Wall grunted. 'They slouch along knocking rose petals off my coping.'

Mousy Doggy nodded. 'Like panthers hunting in Africa where Daddy comes from.'

Gull, jigged for attention. 'The knee grows in Africa, Mitzi says, as black as panthers or night or loneliness. One day we'll go there.'

Mousy Doggy hung his head. 'Not if it's dark.'

Wall sighed. 'Stay here with me away from African fierceness.'

Gull nudged Mousy Doggy. 'The gulls will tell us if Wind goes there. Like Ocean it comes from far away. I'm thirsty. Let's go up. The nursery window looks to sea. You ask the gulls. They don't talk to me.'

Mousy Doggy looked severe. 'You like cats.'

'No I don't. Yes I do. Mummy says I'm as quiet as a mouse. I'm Mousy Cat. Hunting, I crouch thrashing my tail, slope like a shadow, spring like a falling star green eyes blazing. My paws are scratchy-velvet. Birds are my brothers, truly!' The boy gambolled up the stairs. 'You're Mousy Doggy. I'm Mousy Cat. We're different and the same; just as birds and cats are brothers, like me.'

Mousy Doggy shook his head. 'I'll tell the gulls.'

'Let's have a drink first. Lap it up like cats.'

'Or dogs.'

'Or panthers.'

'Our heads back gargling like thirsty birds.'

Gull whooped. 'All brothers. Like you and me.'

A door opened. Mummy emerged. "SHSHSH, Baby's sleeping.'

The boy danced on. 'Quiet as a mouse, Mummy.'

'And wipe your feet. There's sand on the stairs.'

'Oh, that's Mousy Doggy. He's not house-trained like Erasmus. I'll tell him after we've drunk. Come on, messy boots.'

One morning, Mummy came down and sat on the grass watching her achingly precious boy playing around the sand pit. 'My poppet, you've wet your pants.'

'Mousy Doggy wet the path. Look there's the mark.'

'Darling, come here.'

The boy sidled over. His mother felt the springy wet bulge in his knitted rompers.

He wriggled. 'It's not that, Mummy. It's water. I was teaching the ants to swim. It spilled from my can.'

'From your neat little tail, I'll be bound.' She bent and sniffed. His crotch smelled sweet. 'I'll take them off to dry. No one'll see you.' She appraised his pert bottom and tiny sex (a miniature of his dad's). Mummy was smiling.

The boy gambolled back to the sand pit to show the ants how he made rain. He whispered to Mousy Doggy, 'Wall's grumpy because he can't rain like us.'

'Rubbish.' Wall growled. 'I'm stopping all those pryers and peepers, and just as well. They'd snatch your crown.'

Mousy Doggy touched his friend's glinting hair. 'Good Wall. Anyway, they'd be found out. The gulls would get it back.'

'Unruly scavengers, they'd bake a bird-pie and eat it.'

The boy filled his bucket, patted the sand and upended it He rolled Mousy Doggy over and flopped down. It was hot. He pulled off his top and admired his castle. 'You're the rascal.' he sang. 'The blackbirds will peck off your nose.'

Wall grunted. Mousy Doggy looked scared.

Mummy collected his clothes and rescued her little prince. 'All that sand, and I must go off to work.'

'Mousy Doggy said we should have a sand bath.' the boy murmured as she lovingly brushed him down before dressing him.

Her hands tingled with his velvet softness as she led him into the house. He brings a bloom to everything, she delightedly thought, closing the front door, mounting her bicycle, on an errand in town.

Sometimes Mummy, proudly wheeling the pram with his sister, took him through the crooked streets with a whiff of fish, and filled with Wall's "pryers and peepers".

'They're like big dressed ants.' the boy confided to Mousy Doggy, silenced by the throng.

'So much to see.' Mousy Doggy whispered.

At home again, the boy was crestfallen. 'I've lost bits of my crown.'

His sister had thrown his toys out of the pram.

'I suppose she needed the space.' Mousy Doggy said. 'Anyway, your real crown still shines.'

The boy sighed. 'Tell me Wall, do my hair and thoughts shine?'

'Real things last.' Wall growled.

Mousy Doggy jigged up and down in the sandpit. 'Let them go. Just say goodbye.'

'Goodbye Teddy. Goodbye Mouse. Goodbye rubber ring, goose feather and little red stick.' The boy dug a hole in the sand and buried some coloured blocks. 'Come on Mousy Doggy, let's tell the flowers to guard the blocks. Maybe the gulls took our toys to their nests far over the sea. But they should've asked first.'

After withering, summer bloomed again. The wee boy trotted beside the pram nodding to his sister as the family ambled to the sea shore. The wind rested. Waves licked grey shingle. The tufted grass on banks behind the beach stood sentinel against the sky. Only gulls were busy, swooping and calling, prancing along the margin of the sea as decorative as spume or clouds. But hungrier.

Soon the children were fossicking, teetering at the brink of the licky sea, stumbling over the rolling shingle with shells, crab's claws and drift twigs collected for Daddy who was going overseas for business until next year ("a long time", Mummy said). The boy collected smooth important stones, filling his bucket with wealth. Mousy Doggy guffawed. 'Weighting's nothing. Precious things such as gulls, wind, or clouds, are as light as feathers.'

'Or laughter.' the boy whispered.

As the shadows lengthened the family walked back past the ancient castle glowering brokenly over the sea.

Daddy held the boy's hand and pointed through a blasted gothic opening. 'In the old days a look-out was kept for Vikings who pillaged and burned and stole our boats, crops and women.'

The boy felt safe. 'Mousy Doggy, don't you agree these castle walls aren't as happy as our Wall because pryers are easier to deal with than warriors?'

Mousy Doggy nodded and grinned.

But not long after Daddy returned, war droned over the sea engulfing smiles and lights and plenty. The house was packed up, entombing all their treasures. Erasmus was taken away. Mousy Doggy went to live in safety with a policeman.

The family sat sooty-eyed in a big rumbling train roaring on and on to a huge port seething with crowds, bulky crates hanging from cranes and the sad toots of ships' whistles. The boy climbed into the mountainous ship with Mummy and his sister. Holding his sister's hand was a mite of comfort. They waved to a tiny Daddy on the wharf below. His was a terrible farewell, heavier than a bucket of Mummy's tears.

At sea, on the poop deck, the boy blinked as Wind boxed his face. 'I'm engulfed: war, flight, ship, sea, sky.' he whispered to a gull leaning on the billowing breeze as his friends did at home. The gull was hoping for a feed in the disturbed sea. Both cried.

This is not cradle rocking, thought the boy, who longed to fly this emptiness, fly to his sturdy wind-hugged nest, to Mousy Doggy's breathing world.

The ship wallowed half way round the world under strange stars to an alien Australian shore. The children's new land was a bad dream. Taut strangers, blinding light, places stretching beyond walking or sight into mirages of war and silence. A silence, about belief, about contradiction and dream, his "real things", not from a deadened heart. Far from the sea and gulls. Nothing under the sun not even a bucket of pebbles.

The children were delivered like sacks to primary school. Then, the boy went to boys only schools hard as nails, competitive without comfort or songs or pity where plans usurped dreams and fists determined plans.

Father's absences had bonded mother and son. Following on the long fearful war-separation the bond became a shackle as war came home. The reunited parents engaging in brutal rows used the children as excuses, targets or allies. Wounded they huddled together seeking safety. The boy, cowering in hazy distant dreams, escaped into his inner cosmos, cloaked in the stupidity of despair and an avoidance of competition with his awesome father, cankers which haunted him thereafter. He was a tragic, discomforting fool. Lurking within his silence lay fury and lusty dreams of a loving world, responses to the ravages of home, school and a heedless society. All these hells flickered around him, scorching the floundering inner gull.

Marking his demise, hairs colonized the boy's limbs, his high treble sank. The mob intruded. His crotch was mauled now he bore the boy-club semen insignia. It was a fresh link to a wild whirling world of peepers and pryers. With it, he demurely sought the comfort of intimacy, harking far back found a mate, a mirror of himself, handsome, shameless and shy. Their untutored bodies merged until shame prevailed. Inner judges howled, 'Your union is impossible.' For a second time Mousy Cat and Mousy Doggy separated, abandoning comfort for the Real World.

There were many better-half echoes later, in work, in love. Close, non combative relationships, shared achievement, the same sorrows. A variety of places. Friends judged his, an enviable life. Yet the boy - now man - yearned in vain for a holding hand. And withered. Lonely in a brutal world, he quietly cowered.

Finally, he dreamed of flying through damp grey clouds, he and his shadow, one gleeful ball of song. The wind was laughing too, and blew clouds off the smiling sun and off a confusing world. Everything sparkled - eyes, knees, lips, rivers, pools and stones. He sparkled inside. He blew up. He and everything rained and reigned. Happily he fell, down, down into feather-down, baked in a pie, pecked. Home at last.

Divas

LIKE NEW YORK CITY, the Metropolitan Opera House is busy much of the day and night. Either enlivened by music, the antics of Divas, or the hum of administration trying to keep up.

A handsome slightly greying man fronted the box office counter deliberating over seats, a comfortable drink period before a performance. The young man behind the bullet proof glass was patient, pointing out, if the patron really wanted to be at the front, that Row A had vacancies. They smiled as the transaction, approved by some distant computer, spewed out a ticket and credit card receipt.

'Enjoy the show.' the young man said graciously.

'Well, thank you. The enjoyment's started.' the man replied slipping his card in its leather pouch and backing away looking for the bar. He stopped and looked intently back. 'I mean it. You are charming.' He turned and wended through the throng of patrons.

Frederick didn't need a programme. He knew Verdi's *Macbeth* well. Because his back was playing up he'd decided to rest it with a little help from the witches hoping the spectacle would take his mind off pain. He finished his drink, meandered through the foyer and into the auditorium, finding A21 and settling down. The orchestra was nearly in place, warming up. He watched the exchanges between players, the grimaces and smiles which buoyed them beforehand. He, and they were soon ready.

There was an expectant hum of voices. A bejeweled furred elderly woman, after making a flamboyant entrance, had stalked down the isle and tapped Frederick on the shoulder. 'For goodness sake, you're in my seat.' she snarled.

'A21, it's mine, surely?' he said showing her his ticket butt.

'Mine, on permanent reservation. It's outrageous.'

'Please take it.' Frederick said quietly. 'There're no bookings for Row A so I'll sit further along.'

'Of course there are. I have them all.'

'Here, take my seat. But the show's about to begin. No time to do anything more.' he said rising and moving. The first flute winked at him and pursed his lips in sympathy. The lights dimmed and a spot light carried the conductor to the podium, to applause drowned out by the overture. Frederick settled into his seat wondering, as he often did, if the Scots recognised anything of themselves in the colourful Mediterranean music. In the gloom an attendant tapped his arm. 'I'm terribly sorry, Sir, there has been a mistake in the booking. You can't sit here. Please come with me.'

Frederick followed her out, the stiff double beforehand dissolving his anger. Back at the box office the flustered senior clerk was adamant. 'So, so sorry. Our mistake.'

Frederick was grim. 'What a waste of time. Give me a refund and I'll go back to my hotel.'

'Another night? Discount rate, Sir? It's the least we can do.'

'I specially came tonight. I don't want another ticket.'

'Graham, who issued this, should've checked with me. The lady, our platinum patron, insists on occupying the whole centre row. I suppose she more than pays for it. Graham should've known after working here a year. It's most regrettable, most. Please wait in the bar and I'll arrange a refund. Oh dear, what a night. Oh, there you are Graham. Take this gentleman to the bar and get him a complementary drink. I'll send your credit slip out Sir, just as soon as we get clearance. Graham!'

The charming young man led Frederick to the empty bar and ordered him a double bourbon. 'Lots of ice and two glasses.' Frederick called. After the barman left the order, he slid some ice into the empty glass, added liquor and handed it to the bashful young man. 'This is a thank you of sorts. Graham? I'm Frederick. Yours was the best performance of the evening. I don't really need to stay. Certainly not with that platinum dragon. And I'd rather sit here with you for a moment, if you've time? and then take my aching back carefully to my hotel.'

Graham deftly drained his glass (without being spotted). The drink brought him courage. 'No problem. My shift's just finished.'

Frederick warmed to his shy smile. 'Let's have another, then share my taxi. I'll drop you off, wouldn't that be nice.' He raised his voice. 'Two doubles, barman, on me.'

Graham's face flushed with the booze. He settled into his chair and eyed the man with interest. 'Few ever see me, ever say thank you as you did. I should say thanks. You cheered me up. Funny, separated by glass is the loneliest feeling, being a desolate goldfish, round and round, dreary, endless circles. Here's to you.'

Frederick grinned. 'It's pretty dreary on the outside.'

'But you're not trapped.'

'That's true. Maybe the art in life is to find freedom.'

'Miracles seldom happen.'

'Make them.'

Graham sighed. 'Wish I could.'

A tight faced girl tapped Graham's shoulder, proffering a refund slip. 'Here's your clearance. Merv's spitting chips. But he'll forget by tomorrow. You'd best scarper.'

They talked while leisurely finishing their drinks. Frederick grimaced as he rose. Graham looked questioningly at him.

'Bit of back pain. Must've ricked it.'

'Let me see. Ah, the muscles are very tense. Maybe a massage would help.'

'I hoped it would clear up.'

'I trained as a masseur. I'll get my table. I have a room off Washington Square Mews, not far from your hotel in Chelsea. I could easily get it, and ease the muscles. Your shoulders are tight as well. A loosening up should be a comfort.'

Frederick pressed his arm. 'Have you time? I'd be very grateful. This sort of ache is debilitating.'

The *Chelsea Inn* receptionist shook his head over the seat muddle at the Met.

Frederick frowned. 'Never mind. I missed the three witches, escaped the dragon diva but found a masseur. Graham here has his table and has kindly offered to sort out my back. Could you send four rounds of sandwiches and a bowl of fruit to my room? My mini-bar has the stuff to wash them down.'

Graham smiled. 'And a light blanket, please.'

'In the closet, Sir. White or brown?'

'White.' Graham said.

'Two rounds of each.' Frederick called making for the lift.

A trolley of food soon arrived with extras, a big pot of coffee, a plate of pastries and the evening papers. They left it near the door giving Graham space around his table. Frederick, stripped to his underpants, lay face down, preoccupied about probing fingers and palm pressure. The attentions were comforting, he soon closed his eyes.

'Lower back and shoulders.' Graham murmured reaching for his bottle of oil. 'Let's have your pants off, unless you're shy or don't mind them oily.'

Frederick raised his hips, shivered and flushed as gentle hands undressed him. 'Nothing to hide.' He grinned, not sure it could remain so. Hands slipping over his skin, teasing out knots, warming, soothing. The firm caress stirred him deeply. Witches' "double, double, toil and trouble" hands. The boiling cauldron, with eye of newt, toads' entrails, a fenny snake, frog's toe, gall of goat, Jew's liver, Turk's nose, the finger of a strangled babe, yew, hemlock and baboon's blood, faded when he opened his eyes to a trim young man bewitching his body into letting go secrets, loneliness, despair and desire, all bubbling inside; dispelling his usual composure.

'Any better?'

Frederick winced. 'Oh dear, yes. It's wonderful.'

'Turn over and I'll loosen your legs and chest.'

Frederick watched Graham work. Head down, hair fallen like a tattered blind over his pensive face, the set of his shoulders supporting his palms as they ironed legs and torso. Then, straying fingers pressed into his groin; life blood flowed connecting his ossified legs to his awakened body; unbidden his penis stirred.

He shut his eyes. Images of a younger Graham, of both of them, boys playing in the trees, hair fluffed like wind-blown birds, naked shining, the world filling with cloudy laughter and brimming sky-blue eyes, with the unfocused ecstasy only children experience. He wept.

'I'm hurting you?'

'No. Banquo's ghost (in *Macbeth*) set me thinking.'

'Unhappy?'

'Less now. Thank you so much, Graham.'

'I am glad you feel better. A session tomorrow should do it.'

'I'd love that. Tell me, do you massage your boyfriend like this?'

'Used to. He grew aroused like you. Usually I avoid the groin. It has switches which light men up. I felt you needed it and could cope. Here, I'll cover you with the blanket. Lie for a moment. Stay with your body. I'll wash. Shall I bring you your bourbon?'

'Later.' Frederick lay luxuriating in warmth after such attention. He felt another drink would loosen his tongue, spoil everything.

Graham sat on the end of one of the beds, snacked and sipped.

'I tossed Philip out a few months ago. Found him on his back with a very girlish Puerto-Rican guy. I was demented.'

'Is your love so singular?'

'No. I didn't mind him cruising (most of us do). It was our bed. And he'd never ever let me poke him. It was a double betrayal.'

'You prefer the passive role?'

'It's the way I am.'

'For ever?'

'I was raped at twelve.'

'Got a taste for it?'

'I never forgot.'

'Your hands speak tenderness. Memory isn't everything.'

'It's deeper than in hands. Gut stuff.'

'Memory is only a part of you. The drive and tenderness are certainly not passive. Nor is your sense of loyalty.'

Graham shivered in this gentle admiration. 'You mentioned *Macbeth*. Isn't the story about murder?'

'Yes, and the ambition driving it. The Macbeths killed to advance themselves, driven by hallucinations of three witches and a carelessness about friendship and loyalty.'

Graham nodded. 'I could never kill to get what I want. Although there are a few I'd like to maim.'

Frederick looked fondly at his troubled face. 'You make love, not war, then?'

'Um. I suppose. Well, I don't want to hurt anyone.'

'That's what your hands say.' Frederick watched pain flit across the young face. 'Picasso once explained making, saying: "Before I make a dove [out of clay] first, I must wring its neck." He seems to be implying that birth grows out of death; the old must pass away before the new happens; in sculpture, in everything. So, maybe there's war in all creative acts.' He saw interest flicker across Graham's face.

'You've probably heard of "The Little Death", the orgasm ending mating. They're vivid, those "little deaths". Real too. Yet I feel (you too?) that having lost everything you are left freer and fuller than ever. Wrung out, the old you has been replaced by a new person. That's the mystery and wonder about making love.' He savoured Graham's bare arms.

'You should consider your hands. They're telling you the passive stance is only one part of loving. The battle starts in ourselves when the prick rises. It both conquers and enables, takes (as you've been taken) and gives (which you avoid doing). In that world of shadows, many shelter. You seem to be struggling out of such a darkness.'

Graham grimaced. 'You make it so grand. I just want to live: work, have friends, have fun.'

'To "live" involves trampling, conquering and effort, as well as gentleness and generosity. Can I get up now?'

Graham nodded, viewed the manly body, so recently in his charge. It thrilled him, or was it the talk of war? He didn't know. He flung the dregs of bourbon down his throat, poured them both another stiff measure and munched a sandwich. He was thrilled. Troubled too. This sexy man was looking into his soul, trampling on it; however rather than disintegrating it grew firmer. He was not sure this had ever happened before. He was rapt.

Graham packed his table up. 'It's late. Can I leave this here for tomorrow?'

Good idea. So, tell me, are you on the late shift at the Met. again tomorrow?'

'Yes.'

'Then why not keep your table company. There's a spare bed. I've a meeting at two. We could breakfast together before you go to The Lincoln Centre.'

'OK.'

'I think I'll turn in. Do you want a shower?'

'Um. Yes. Can I share your toothbrush?'

'Anything.'

Graham disappeared into the bathroom. Frederick donned pyjamas, slipped into bed and switched off the light bringing a flickering dusk to the room from the lights of the city. He lay, Verdi's music running through his head like the bourbon in his veins, glad of the company. A shaft of light cut the gloom as Graham, demure in only a tee shirt, emerged, cut the light and stumbled over to the empty bed. He sat for a moment, then made his way to the window and stood enjoying the tenth floor vista, wondering whether his hands did speak for him as Frederick had told him. Work was one thing, sex was entirely different; separate. That's how he experienced it. Perhaps the split can be mended, he thought as the promising vastness of the city infected him. He leaned his tipsy head on the glass longing for union.

He felt Frederick's erection first. Then his hands falling from his chest onto his bare thighs, searching his pubic hair sharing yearning and demands.

'I'm glad you want me.' he whispered turning into the chest he'd so recently explored. Nestling like a fragile bird he looked eagerly up.

'You looked sad.' Frederick murmured.

'It's what you said about my taking and not giving.'

'We don't have to do this.'

'I know.' Graham smiled winningly. He hurried to the bathroom and then to the bed. 'Here's your goo.' He pulled Frederick into bed impetuously offering his body. He was entered. Filled. The deep stroking intrusion pushed him further and further into himself until he was floating over the shimmering city in the thrall of its pulsing life. Imperatives took charge. He stiffened, clenched and climaxed; tantalising pain tore him apart as Frederick finished and lay panting on top of him.

Graham allowed himself to be drawn into a gentle embrace. He clung, sweaty, tingling and content. Seldom had he felt such harmony or been held so tenderly. Suddenly everything mattered. On a feather-soft cloud of bourbon he drifted away into sleep.

The orange sun, reflecting off myriad windows beyond, woke them early. They kissed and began a languorous inspection from heads to toes. It was gentle and lingering, only stayed when Graham, with a shiver of pleasure, erupted in Frederick's mouth, then tended the flesh which had strayed so deeply into him the night before, enjoying Frederick's rising tension and the eruption oozing down his tummy. Enmeshed, they slept again. Breakfast was eventually ordered and demurely eaten in separate beds, nudging lunchtime, hastening the flight to work and the meeting, and a dreamy wave on parting in the subway.

In the early evening Frederick returned. He lay on his bed, his lingering back pain overruled by his pleasure in the warmth and tenderness he felt and a keening longing for more.

'It had the vividness of something new.' he said to himself. 'Yet, something more. The lad has turned my life into a dream I never thought existed.'

That evening Frederick took Graham shopping. Nothing spectacular, a couple of tee shirts and stretch boxers, sox and a pale pink shirt to spruce up his image. Then they ate swapping secrets and life histories, consolidating what they knew, fleshing it out, as Frederick said laughing as they wended back to repeat the previous night. The massage was deep and relieving. They showered together and lay whispering close until Frederick begged Graham to push in and fill him. 'The rest of the massage.' he said softly. Graham's excitement was so intense it carried him through his reticence to a gasping climax. The power, hunger and loss were immense. In the caress afterwards, something deep consolidated. Suddenly Graham understood their talk about death. His killer-hunger had both usurped and reigned, rained a willfulness freeing him, joining him to this dear man who admired his nascent prowess. Graham glowed. But this time it was not with bourbon. Through sleepy lashes he watched Frederick. 'Are you asleep?' (No answer).

He stretched and brushed mute lips with his, whispering so no one could hear, 'We took everything. I love you.' He reached down and cupped the sleeping sex in one hand, (not impressive, he shyly admitted). But soft or hard demanding or giving, like his own whose grace couldn't be hidden any longer. Had the sleepy giant become a tiny child again snuggling into the shelter of the one he loved? The question shadowed his delight in feeling completely at home.

Two days breezed by during which they decided to sneak away together for a week. Graham negotiated time off with the Met; Frederick poured over maps of Maine. They flew there and took a bus to Camden, found an old sail loft overlooking a boat yard, not quite renovated, but with a skeleton kitchen and bathroom and a big bed with views of the ocean.

The landlord looked doubtfully at their smiling faces approving their love of wilderness. 'It's not quite shipshape, but all right if you like boats, the smell of tar and fish and the brightness of sky.' he said.

'That's what we're here for.' Graham said grinning.

'Will a camp bed suit you, young man?'

'Perfect.' Graham smirked. 'I'll have to lie still.'

'The loft doesn't pitch and toss, you'll not roll out.' the landlord said. 'Two nights? I'll get you a set of yard keys. It's off-season, so no one's about after six. By the way, I know a comfy crazy inn, called Palmer's Place, off a rocky cove down the coast at Woldoboro. Run by a couple of wildies. One's a fisherman, the other's a farmer. Can you cope with cats and dogs a loony parrot and raccoons? Yes? Then, you should look them up. It's a great place for a few days in the wilderness. I'll dig out their card if you're interested? Grand. I'll ring them.' He stamped down the steep stairs to the cobbled yard below.

Frederick gazed out. The sea was serene. Flights of gulls swirled around a fishing boat, a small tourist ferry rolled through the swell, clouds banked up like fantastic islands on the horizon, a group of kayaks slid into the narrowing harbour, children gambolled on the shore. Graham sidled up behind and put his arms round him. 'We must be good until six. Then you can thump the floor as much as you like.' he whispered.

'Touch me there.' Frederick breathed.

Graham held him and capped the mound. They stood awash with briny air and scents of desire. It was as simple as the heaving ocean, the steady shore, the floating gulls. 'Will you always want me like this?'

'Always.'

They donned their jackets and walked through town, found a bottle shop and returned for a pre-dinner drink. Their landlord met them shaking a bunch of ancient keys to the yard gate and their door. He grinned at the small bag of bottles and nodded approvingly. 'That'll keep the chill out, eh? By the way, the wife just rang. Our son's coming over with bucketfuls of lobsters and a pramload of monkeys we call grandchildren, care to join us? There's enough for a small army.'

Frederick laughed. 'Yes, if we're eating the monkeys.'

Graham sniggered. 'We're vegetarians, you see.'

The man roared with laughter. 'Lobsters and the pram, only. The monkeys need taming before roasting. I'll pick you up in a couple of hours.'

The family settled easily with the newcomers who acquiesced to the children's routine setting the timetable. They had been fed, bathed and made ready for bed (in Daddy's old room). But they lingered. The eldest child, Stanley, led his sister and brother in hugging everyone good night. Having taken a fancy to Graham he proprietarily settled on his lap and asked, 'Do you hug Frederick?'

'Of course.'

'Mummy says not to hug strangers.'

'You hugged us?'

'You are Grandad's friends.' whispered Stanley.

'We all have to be careful.' Graham murmured.

The boy's eyes shone. 'Why?'

'In case the hugging hurts.'

'He might put it into us, they said at Sunday school.'

'Like a joke, hugging can go wrong.'

'Inside?'

'And in the head.'

'Are you hurt?'

Graham blushed. 'A long time ago.'

'Are you better now?'

'Frederick is making me better.'

'By hugging you?'

'Yes, Stanley. He's not cruel, like some.'

'Look there! Grandad likes talking to him for ages on the deck.'

'They are both good men, Stanley.'

His mother intervened. 'Off to bed, darling. Say good night, now.'

The boy slithered off Graham's knee. 'Will you tell us a story?'

'Only if you're in bed.'

'Oo goody. Come on Cyril, Amelia. Story time!'

The mother nodded after them. 'My neighbour's child was molested last summer. We have to be careful. It's a pity to have to say such things, he's only eight. Sex shouldn't be interesting yet and with so much nature around him. Why does a man want to abuse such innocence? Oh, Stanley's upset you. He doesn't understand. I'm so sorry.'

'No problem. You're right. I've often wondered why. Some say it's to dominate.'

'Or is it sucking their sweet life out, like sucking the meat from a lobster claw?'

'Ugh, what a terrible idea.' Graham winced. 'It's debilitating. I'll make the story a short one, those salads look delicious.'

She looked after him. It was difficult to understand so nice a young man knowing about abuse. She daren't pursue it.

The children were waiting. Graham told them:

Once upon a time, there was a little red lobster who lived with his parents, his sixteen brothers and sisters, fifty fish and as many crabs. They played much of the time when the sunlight filtered down to the bottom of the sea, and slept when it got dark, like all good children. One day the little lobster was washed by a sudden current out into really deep water where the sunlight hardly reached. It was murky, mysterious. A host of strangers swam there and crawled about through the weed and rocky crevices. 'I'm glad I'm red.' the little lob ster said to himself. 'At least they can see me and will leave me alone. If only my Mummy and Daddy were here and my sixteen brothers and sisters, the fifty fish and as many crabs. Then, I'd feel all right and get home.'

Something slithered up to him. 'Hello, little red thing. Let me help you. I'm your friend. Come this way.' and led him into a gloomy cave filled with eyes and slithery things and jagged rock which trapped the lobster's claws.

He struggled to get free, and to escape the opening jaws of his 'friend' who was about to eat him.

With a mighty effort he turned tail and scrambled out into the clear deep water, saw a couple of friendly fish who led him back to safety in the shallows where his parents, his fourteen brothers and sisters (two had been eaten by a shark), the fifty fish and as many crabs, welcomed him and played with him all the time so he would never be separated from them again.

He knew now, never to get swept into deep water away from home, and never to trust a strange slithery thing which said it was your friend.

An old crusty great grandfather lobster nodded his bony head, saying. 'That's quite right. That's why I survived. Always treat the sea with respect and great care. Then playing here is fun for ever.'

The sinewy weed and the elegant starfish agreed. In fact, everyone did.

The two younger children's eyes soon closed. Only Stanley was peeping. He knew something of deep water and slithery things. He nodded. 'I agree too.' he whispered. 'I'm glad he got home.' He smiled rapturously and slept.

Eventually, Frederick and Graham clambered up the stair, slippery with dew, to their loft room, and into their roomy bed lit by a sliver of moonlight, an extension of the silver path on the ocean. Then Frederick held him close saying, 'I've the rest of the story for you:

Once upon a time, as the little red lobster grew up, it seemed to him that in play something now was missing. So one low tide, he slipped away from his twenty seven brothers and sisters (There had been additions over time), the fifty fish and as many crabs, and ventured out into the deeps. There, he felt, lay what he wanted.

Something slithered up to him, enticing him into a dusky cave filled with eyes, the soft fronds of sensuous weed, sponges and the ebb and flow of water, restless, caressing and holding.

Frederick shimmeyed close and eagerly pushed. Graham shivered with pleasure, reached out for him and pulled him in. Their sighs entwined. Gently pulsing, Frederick continued the story:

> It seemed, he was eaten. He wafted on sponges, caressed by strands of kissing weed, rocked by water, rocked, rocked in new ways. The slithery thing filled him and burst. Or, did he burst? It was impossible to differentiate.
> They lay in clouds of shimmering milk. The not so tiny lobster dreamed of flying up into the clear dry sunlight, wallowing on blushing clouds until a calm settled, he settled, transfixed by the riches in this new game which, wonderfully, joined him to the world-girding ocean where he swam forever.

With a start, Graham erupted as Frederick, with a final thrust burst and fell on him. They lay panting. Graham felt down and grasped the slithery penis. 'But it's not fair to tease a little boy with such dreams. Stanley will find out about deeps and flying in his own time.'

Frederick grunted. 'Have you found out? It's time to ditch the horror and the loss, time to face the deeps and swim forever.'

Graham breathed against his chest, thinking, I've been there with him, and doesn't he know it's my turn tomorrow? He drifted smiling into the deeps of sleep.

They simply pottered all the next day, enjoying the calm sunny break on a windy coast. Graham felt Frederick needed rest. So he didn't insist on a fishing boat tour, or kayaking or hiking in the Camden Hills State Park, although they did climb up the watch tower in the boat yard to see Mount Megunticook, without snow, in the Camden Hills, celebrating the clear weather.

There was only one bus the following day which meandered along the indented coast leisurely passing Rockland, Thomaston, and on to Woldoboro where they'd been told to alight one stop before the centre.

A very old Buick, its original dark blue paint visible under a spray of seagull droppings, was the only thing in sight. A lean bearded man hopped out and waved. 'Fred? Gray? I'm Vernon. Welcome. Let's go. All in front if you don't mind. The back seat's out so we can cart wine. There's lots of room. Hey, fellahs, it's great you're here. It's been quiet. This week no one. Palmer will fuss over you. You can tell him and Butch our diva parrot to push off. It's all they understand.' He laughed, went to the front and cranked. The engine roared with life. Soon they were off, wallowing on soft springs down rutted tracks towards the inlet off the main water lying like a bluish silver tongue to left and right of them.

The house squatted near a dry creek bed on a flat rich area of ground sloping to a beach in a small cove held by rough grey rock where a boat lay awkwardly on its side, stranded on the sand. Lobster pots, nets and odd bits of boats littered the grassy top of the beach in cheerful abandonment, or was it work in progress?

The house roofs were steep and tiled sprouting gothic dormer windows mostly shut against the usual breeze. A scatter of spruce and pine provided shelter. There was a garage, full of gear, they were told. At the back lay a large plot of cultivated land with fruit trees and vegetables. An old tractor stood silent against a fence taking a breather, more work in progress?

The peace was shattered by howls and barking as three solid hairy dogs rollicked out to greet the car. Vernon grinned. 'Harmless, but watch your crotch, they're mighty nosy.' He jumped out grabbed their bags and led them, and the throng, into the house where Palmer had prepared a tea party of welcome with home-made biscuits, scones and cream and a family sized tea pot; it had to be big, what with the dogs and four cats taking a keen interest, and Butch bobbing on her perch, conducting proceedings squawking 'Tea for cocky tea cock tea Butch'.

Graham smiled at Frederick. Their previous landlord had been right, it was nice and crazy! He blushed.' Um, what does your sign at the entrance, a pink 'H', mean?'

Palmer looked from one to the other, then nodded. 'It's a chain of gay-run houses in Maine. We take anyone, and don't sniff when same sex couples want a double room.'

Vernon watched them. 'We put you in a twin. OK?'

Graham shook. Now his love would be out. 'Um, yes but we sleep,' He looked through the salt pocked window hoping for salvation. 'We sleep,' It was hard to admit.

Vernon's smile warmed his speechlessness. 'We've just the room for you. At the top under the roof. A sort of honeymoon suite. It's ready. Views of the water and woods. We're still fit enough to bring breakfast in bed when you're feeling lazy.'

Frederick squeezed Graham's muscled arm. 'Perfect.'

No more was said. An easy silence punctuated by mews, growls and scuffles filled the room. It had seen better days, but Graham didn't mind. It smiled a welcome without fuss, radiating some of the freedom he craved. A space to discover his new self where he and Frederick could nest, absorb the pristine beauty seeping in from outside. He suddenly wanted to give everything; swimming forever, just as in Frederick's story.

After tea Frederick went up stairs to rest while Graham trekked outside with Vernon, helping him cut and stack firewood. Vernon protested it was not guest-work. But by Graham's grin of pleasure and his messed clothes, he saw it was too late. Anyway, the lad was good company: shy, willing and very handsome. Vernon was calm and grew intimate. They quickly exchanged life stories, pleased to realise each loved deeply. Their age difference didn't matter. "Alike as two peas" as someone had said.

Vernon dug out Graham's gruesome rape details, balancing it with an appaling gang rape in his own youth in California. 'So we share the same scars. But you're dealing with withdrawal better than I ever did.' He said.

Graham blinked. 'Am I? Frederick pushes me to be myself, to put the guilt behind me. It's hard.'

Vernon nodded. 'The disgust sticks, eh?'

Graham flushed. 'Yes. I never talk about it.'

'Nor do I.'

'Frederick knows.'

'I've never told Palmer. Though I fled here.' He smiled. 'Funny, I never thought I'd shack-up with him. Came for a week and stayed years. One night, we just finished up in bed. Me in love. It took him longer.'

'Much the same for us. I never dreamed Frederick could be so nice or available. I fell - he too. Amazing! It's the best week of my life. And being here. You and this place are, you know . . . It's like being naked and no one minds.'

'We like both of you. Glad you feel the same.'

The light streamed across the tongue of water beyond the cove and through the grove of trees where they worked, throwing lengthening shadows from rocks, buildings and landscape. Vernon picked up the saw, Graham an armful of logs. They returned to the house. Vernon wanted to set and light the fire. He grinned. 'We thought you'd like to eat intimate by firelight. First night of the honeymoon.'

Graham frowned slightly. 'Not all of us? Afternoon tea was fun. Let's eat together. Unless you want your own space.'

'Graham, dear, of course not. We've got the space of the night.

Palmer will be delighted. He's gregarious, like Butch. Talks the same sort of nonsense. Bless you. But shouldn't you ask Fred?'

'He's a talker too. And you're right about later. That is important. I mean, very.'

Vernon took him to a utility room off the kitchen. 'Here're a pair of my old shorts. Well shrunk yet tough. Suit you better than me. Give us your jeans and tee shirt, I'll wash them now.' He cheerfully appraised the slim body, approvingly smoothing the shorts which fitted snugly. 'There, you look fetching enough for candlelight. Come down anytime after six. It's a lobster paté starter with the last gallon of Napa Valley Reisling, followed by mixed fish salad, complements of my boat and Palmer's field, dressed in a V-Special sauce to keep your eyes bright and your legs slim. Graham, I suppose everyone says you're beautiful.'

'Only Frederick.'

'Believe him. And me. If I weren't a married man, I'd eat you. Fred's right: forget the rape, walk proud.'

Graham flooded with happiness. He hugged a startled Vernon and bounded up the stairs, where cuddles and caresses warmed him for the evening's feasting.

It was a lingering meal. Afterwards, Graham lay, his head on Frederick's lap his feet on Vernon's, listening first to Frederick's tales of travel, then the house dramas: love and games played out; seasons of banked snow, of fishing through ice, of long summer days of near perpetual light for bathing and larking around camp fires on the beach and drug related orgies long ago. His life seemed staid. He envied the colour of theirs.

Vernon brought his final offering, a pie with cranberries from the freezer, oven-warm and topped with cream (from a tin).

'We picked them last year.' Vernon said.

Graham, mimicking the lazy purring cats, stretched out well fed and content in the intimacy of firelight and serene faces. He reached up and stroked Frederick's cheek. Vernon sighed and felt for his bare thigh straying towards his crotch. Graham's erection grew in his shorts. He lay on his back shyly displaying ardour he'd hidden all his life secure in a blushing thought they admired him by displaying their own. For the very first time, he showed his conquering randy sex, not his placatory backside. The visible, he'd made invisible now rose triumphant. Smiling, he nearly cried.

Palmer, deep in an armchair near the fire grinned. 'That's something to be proud of.'

Frederick leaned forward and kissed Graham. 'I tell him every time.'

Vernon prayfully capped the bulge. 'Such true words help him escape his rape labyrinth.'

Palmer started. 'Him too?'

Vernon gasped. 'You knew?'

'Of course. Your nightmares wake me. You plead with them to stop, cry of shitting out your life blood, lost in wilderness. I comfort you and trail my fingers across your rectum saying, nothing's wrong, only sweetness and love and you sleep again remembering nothing in the morning. Of course I know. The evil bastards. But they drove you here, that's a lasting blessing, my dear.'

Vernon was near to tears. 'All these years!'

'All these years of your devotion.'

Graham sat up and shyly shook Vernon's arm. 'It was the best feast, ever.'

'Was it? Your firewood did the trick.' Vernon sniffed.

Frederick smiled. 'And Vernon stoking up a mighty erection.'

Palmer grinned. 'He's good at that. Graham, thank you for waving your wand. Its magic gave us a perfect evening.'

They sat quietly. The firelight flickered, repairing and enhancing. Palmer poured out the last of the Reisling. They drank. Frederick rose. 'Good night All. Come on Graham.' Upstairs, and down, feasting continued until the shivering house fell silent, basking in moonlight, licked by the gentlest breeze, unchanging through many years.

After breakfast Frederick and Graham took the rough path to the ocean, dawdled on the salt-strewn rocks taking nature pictures of each other, fossicked for shells in protected crevices before coming back for lunch: a simple affair, as Vernon was taking them out in the boat to check lobster pots, 'Collecting our supper.' as he put it.

Frederick, in long trousers, was installed on a for'ad seat. Graham, in his shorts, pushed off from the beach and jumped in while Vernon pulled the starter rope and they eased out into deep water. It was a still day. The sun shone to the weedy rock-strewn bottom. (The Deeps, in Graham's story). Vernon navigated from buoy to buoy. Most of the traps were empty, however three had large garish crayfish crouching and snapping their claws, tipped into a plastic tank of sea water in the centre of the boat. Then they drifted, shirts off (trousers too), still hot even in scanty underwear until Vernon suggested a swim, adding, 'It's easier to get into the water than get out. There are a number of blocks at the bow up which you can step into the boat. It's a bit chilly but very refreshing.'

Without more ado, Graham stripped and dived in, emerging with a shout. 'Brrr. You get used to it. Come on Frederick!'

Frederick soon followed. They weren't in for long, clambered inboard and stood dripping and smiling through goosepimples. Vernon was captivated by thoughts of their coupling. He gazed in admiration at the young body, in almost amusement at Frederick's shrunken member which, he knew, had stirring power. Delightedly he stripped and dived without a splash, down down into the depths, a creamy streamlined seal pushing through liquid glass, soon a beaming man riding the dripping nodding boat.

They looked at one another, wordless, joyful, free in the sheened wilderness, washed of pretensions. The fresh contented silence was broken by Vernon. 'Thanks for last night. We never talk like that. It was just as you said Graham, "being naked". No wonder you two radiate love. You work on it. It's the hardest thing, baring inner secrets, particularly in a world hostile to "nakedness".' His penis swelled. 'We found our love again. That's what I want to say. We all honeymooned last night. You shook the old house. Luckily it's used to it. We did our bit below. Found I was tender, sitting first thing this morning.'

Graham laughed. 'Us too.'

Frederick nodded. 'We ate like kings; it gave us giant appetites.'

Vernon flushed. 'Tried everything, like us?'

Graham giggled. 'Until we dropped.' He sobered. 'Last night was brilliant. When we met I was a mess of guilt and disgust. Frederick has been wonderful sorting it. It's funny, the more we struggle the better it gets.'

'So, there's reward for nakedness.'

Frederick gauged the rising and falling phallus. 'As in everything. You prepare the lobster traps, moor them, ride out again and again to be rewarded. Caring for the orchard rewards you with fruit. It's the natural order of love.'

Vernon, unabashed by his pulsing stalk, nodded. 'That's why I stayed. Palmer and this place make me happy.' He looked with consternation at the water building up in the boat; found a bailer and scooped. 'Shit, the leak's worse - that's why I beached her. She's sturdy clinker-built. One of the strakes must've come away. We'd best get back.

Graham bail while I steer? Fred, sit to that side. Yes. It keeps the leak above water.'

Frederick leaned over the side watching eddies. 'At least we can be giants tonight.'

'I was thinking of serving lobster thermidor. Is that all right?' Vernon said.

Graham nodded. 'Giants' food. Is it hot in the shell?'

'With a creamy cheese sauce to fill giants' pencils, Palmer's potatoes and sprouts, the rest of the cranberry pie and a local apricot liqueur. Palmer raided the cellar for some local white wine we put away last year. We try to please.' Vernon smiled.

Frederick trailed a finger in the running water. 'It will be hard tearing ourselves away tomorrow.'

Graham blenched. 'Could we come back on the way to the airport?'

'We'd miss a bit but the bus goes both ways.' Frederick said.

'Of course it does.' said Vernon steering into the beach and running the nose of the boat up the sand. 'I'll ring through for a timetable.'

Following afternoon tea, Frederick took Graham out onto the rocks defining the cove. They found a roomy cleft and lay together in sunshine talking about everything, sometimes caressing, sometimes lying still, silently watching the surface of the water wrinkle with breezes.

'It looks disdainful.' Frederick murmured.

Graham grinned. 'It's your sexy smell.'

'No, it's about what I want to say and can not.'

'You stumped for words?'

'Wondering how to say goodbye.'

'Today?'

'Before we have to part, before that agony.'

'Hey. You'll be back.'

'Of course.'

'Soon.'

Frederick sighed. 'If only. Work traps me.'

'But soon?'

'As soon as possible. Without you is unbearable.'

'Away from you is hell, I mean it.' Graham blushed with sincerity. 'I mean it. Don't go for too long, Frederick.'

'We'll write. I'll return soon. I promise.'

'I can't live again in that blackened room.'

'You mustn't. You are so lovely in the light.'

Graham snuggled into his chest blinded by his own past: an amiable child admitting the big cock until disgusted (Dad dropped me for my little brother), of repulsing adolescence, abandoning studies, wretchedly breaking away from home and fleeing to New York, joining its marginal life, of turfing his torturer Philip out, and now, beginning to become himself unshackled by guilt or convention, finding a sane place in the everyday, finding admiration, latterly love. Graham knew his new "nakedness" depended on Frederick's armour of care. Maybe it seemed flimsy but it was effective. He'd never dared love destructive fathers, any fathers. But he'd sought an enabling love, like Frederick's, all his life having been trapped in the cavern of sex at twelve dreaming of consolation, not dismemberment. And now with Frederick leaving he shivered again. Graham blinked. 'Not long. You promised.' He felt small and bruised.

The evening meal was extravagant and great fun. It was launched by Vernon.

'Guys, we've been thinking. As you know I must re-calk the boat - two day's work. I should go and collect our wine from Boothbay Harbour as well. So, what to do? Palmer had the brilliant idea of offering you the old banger. You could see Bath, John's and Muscongus bays on route to the winery, some of the places you'd miss if you come back. Stay with our friends and return with the wine, we have a feast, we sleep it off and I'll take you to the airport. What do you think?'

Graham's cheek trembled. 'All that, and return?'

'Vernon hugged him. 'You'd save the day.'

Palmer sipped his wine. 'The car's ancient, but presumably Frederick, you know about old Buicks?'

'I dreamed of driving one as a kid.'

'Vernon grinned. 'So, there we are. A perfect plan. Guys, I promise you a kingly farewell feast. I'm a bit tearful saying goodbye so I may just drop you off at the airport. Anyway, you've gotta return.'

Palmer nodded. 'Anytime, come hell or highwater.'

'Gee, I'm hungry.' Graham teasingly pulled Vernon to the kitchen, bruised by dreams which kicked and slapped him into a laughter and lust overwhelming bad memories. It was wonderful.

Vernon braised the lobster portions, blushing at the lad's gladness. It mirrored his own. 'I'll get my guitar out and play for you, after.' he said, decorating each plate with garnish before they carried them into the firelit room.

They feasted. Vernon tuned and played an English madrigal, singing the top line, filling in the other voices with the guitar. 'It's from *Samuel*, book two, about king David facing the death of Absalom. The terrible sadness of love and loss and betrayal:

> *The king went up to the chamber over the gate, and wept;*
> *and as he went thus he said, "O my son Absalom, my son,*
> *my son Absalom! would God I had died for thee.*
> *O Absalom my son, my son!"*

Graham paled. The song echoed his own life time of grief which seldom surfaced. Happiness now allowed his eyes to water.

Frederick traced the tear line. 'No one mourned the death of a twelve year old until now. They're my tears too.'

Palmer patted his arm. 'Grief is too often hugged rather than abandoned. Vernon taught me that when first we became lovers. Being here for us (you too?) washes some of it away. You remind me of much I'd forgotten, Graham. No wonder we've grown to love you.'

The finishing apricot liqueur was a bridge between food and love, which richly carried them all into sleep.

'Apart from the heavy steering and only doing a mile per gallon, the Buick's been grand.' Frederick said, swinging his legs out at the Boothbay Winery's rear outbuilding where the B&B guest suite had been prepared for them.

Graham winced. 'Good idea your leaving the brute facing down hill. Cranking it is hard yakka. I'd rather kick over a bike any day.'

'Cheaper than the gym.' Frederick smiled. 'Keeps your lovely body fit for any work.'

They left the car under a stand of evergreen firs and spruce, the remnants of an ancient forest into which buildings now intruded, walked down the slope and towards the main port along a long spindly wooden footbridge. Out to sea, shoals of sails graced the dimpled water. They watched a big schooner and an elegant sloop drifting (that's what it looked like) with well filled sails like swans among more diminutive ducks.

'Let's be tourists today.' Frederick said.

Leaning on the rail of the bustling wharf watching the crowd watching the boats, Graham put an arm round his friend. 'You drive well.'

'Your navigation was spot on.'

'Frederick, I do love you, in spite of my blistered hands and an aching back.'

Frederick guffawed. 'Complaint number one hundred. I only put up with it because you're so lovely.' his eyes twinkled. 'In bed.'

'Sex, sex, sex. That's all you think of.'

'That's your fault Your excitement is infectious. Come on, let's find the narrow gauge steam train to the village. Hey, there's its whistle, like the donkey engine I had as a boy.'

They sat in the last carriage. As there was no one to watch, hands strayed over knees and straining phalluses. There and back without a break. Engaged in the oldest game in the world, the shed of antiques in Railway Village was of little interest to them. Anyway, by then they were hungry.

They ate in a lobster/fish market on the quay, sharing a long table with a motley group the same age as Graham. Three girls from Cornell University were nearest, talking incessantly, 'Yes, we're on holiday, we're all studying microbiology, all in the swimming team and all Lambda's.' They chortled. 'Julia's interested in geology, Zoe in Indian history and Barbara's interested in hunky guys.' they added (looking serenely at Graham).

Everyone started singing. Frederick decided it was going to be a long evening. He thrust a fifty dollar bill into Graham's fist, whispered 'I'll see you later.' and left, chased by ribald hoots of 'Sure your little boy'll be safe?' He strolled across the long footbridge, the emerging stars promising a silent holy summer night. He paused half way, his back was stiff. It was tiresome. 'Trying to keep up with one of Barbara's "hunky guys" I suppose.' he said to himself. 'Graham's shy yet sure when tackled, socially or in bed. It's so winning. I'd dearly love to stay with him in New York for ever and ever. I wonder if our love could last that long?'

An old woman sidled past. 'Sorry to be nosy, but don't you know that love has its seasons. It blazes for a while like the New England fall. Then rots imperceptibly away. My last novel says as much. You should know this at your age.'

'First sign of madness.' Frederick murmured embarressedly.

'It's the stillness. Sometimes we talk to leaven it. We must. I talk to myself a lot now I'm alone.' She pushed a food wrapper into the water with her stick. 'Well, I'll say good night. "Flights of angels" too.' and shambled on soon lost in the gloom.

It's a heavenly night, Frederick thought. "And flights of angels, sing thee to thy rest", Hamlet's death. Surely she doesn't mean death, rather, flights of angels singing in so gentle a night? He turned away from the darkness of ocean towards the lights of Boothbay twinkling through the trees. 'Oh, I don't know.' he said aloud. 'This silence is golden.'

He strolled on, past the Winery lights and into the dusky sighing old trees under which their room sheltered. He clambered up the stairs, undressed and slipped into bed, leaving a dim lamp under a bedside table for Graham. He lay comfortably, angels' whispers wooing him to sleep.

Graham joined the crowd of young which descended on the Harbour Inn for its bright lights (allowing mutual appraisal) and one expensive drink (for a bit of class); then they wandered away from the water to a snug walled garden the Cornell girls had frequented on a previous holiday.

'There's a new creep running it, but the garden's unchanged.' they announced, returning with a tray of drinks. 'He growled at us, saying "These are Christian premises" (whatever that means). We're not welcome here. Pity!'

Graham went in for the next round. The barman looked angry. Graham blushed. 'Can I have . . .'

'Out. We don't serve perverts.' the barman growled.

'Cool it Sid. He's with them students.' one of the drinkers at the bar said. 'Anyway, who's the pervert, you tinkering with your kids or what?'

'Mind yer mouth.' the barman grated.

'He fucks little boys.' someone said softly.

Graham blanched. He eyed the barman. 'Do you?'

'I said, mind yer mouth.' The barman lifted up the bar counter, stepped out threateningly and pushed Graham towards the door.

Graham had seen that wild light in his father's eyes.

'Leave it, Sid. The lad's done nothing wrong, even the preacher knows that.'

Something snapped in Graham's head. All the terrible years of shame and hurt were screaming, his old self and his new were screaming,

'Never. Never. Never!' He blindly struck out at his tormentor, fists flailing, then, held together in one mighty upward punch which cracked the barman's chin, lifting him off the floor as Graham kneed him cruelly in the groin, punched his stomach as a fist came flying out grazed his cheek, punching him so he tripped on the carpet and stumbled backwards.

The barman was griping Graham's tee shirt, Graham fell, pulling the man with him. Falling on his back, legs up in life-long placatory position, pain filling him.

Graham bent his knees, straightening them as he landed, flinging the body behind him. There was a crash as the man wrecked a sturdy timber screen. A grunt. Blood. Vomit. Splinters. Graham in fury rolled over and struggled towards the mess of wood and body intent on killing, of ending his putrid torment, overwhelmed by revenge. Three stolid fishermen dragged him away, one wiping his bloody nose, the others holding him until his spasm of rage passed.

'Easy, son. You're a typhoon. He had it coming, I told 'im before. Listen, you'd best go before the police arrive. We all saw it was not you started it. Best go all the same. You students have brains and brawn and real guts. It's the best fight I ever seen. OK?'

Graham nodded. Shakily he went to the garden door where the students were huddling distrait. The white faced Cornell girls, shepherded him away. Zoe saw him home, kissed him outside the Winery and whispered. 'I'd stay if I could. Have a hot shower, an aspirin and go to bed. We'll never ever go back there. God, you belted him. I thought you'd kill him. What a creep, as evil as gays. Imagine doing those vile things to little boys. He should be locked-up. Good night Graham. God bless, and sleep well.'

Graham crawled unsteadily up the steps and stumbled into the dimly lit room, unsteadily showered, swallowed two aspirins and fell like a corpse beside Frederick spasms wracking him.

Vile and evil: gays like us, fathers like mine. All locked up together in one vomit filled cell. Is that what the world wants? Is that what Frederick and I are? Can't I escape that black room which imprisoned me all my life? Is there no other future?

Battered by such torments, he fell, down, down into the depthless well of sleep.

He was woken by the ministrations of Frederick and Norah from the Winery, a trained nurse who carefully inspected him, declaring nothing was broken under his heavy bruising. Frederick anointed him with Arnica, pushed a very strong suppository into his anus and watched over him until the pain was masked.

'If you're well enough, let's leave this afternoon? Get back to Palmer's Place early evening and recuperate there?'

Graham's faint smile pulled him into repairing sleep.

Palmer and Vernon had telephoned the Winery. They were waiting. Palmer picked Graham up and carried him into the living room where the fire crackled, shooed cats off the sofa and ever so gently lowered him onto soft upholstery to the accompanying hoots of Butch the diva parrot.

Vernon backed the car up to the basement door for unloading the wine, then rushed in panting for tea. 'So, you made it. No more wood chopping, lots of rest, swimming and eating wholesome food. Even Butch agrees.' he smiled at the puffy face and stroked Graham's arm concernedly. 'For an angel, you look awful.'

Palmer stood, back to the fire. 'I hear Boothbay Harbour has a hero, one named Graham. Champion of abused kids, wronged students and gays; night-reveller, trouble-maker who, like a god, descended on the port, sorted out their number one creep and vanished. The Chamber of Commerce has revoked Sid's license, the police closed him down and the real Christians feel vindicated yet fearful their precious village will be shunned by tourists. No one at the Winery let on. We've enough troubles. Anyway, you did nothing wrong, defending yourself against a venal bully, as all the fishermen and students proclaim. My lad, it's great to have you back. The spirits of this place will protect you and heal the wounds disfiguring your beauty. Vernon's right as usual. Loll around, eat, drink, bathe and be merry.'

Frederick glanced through the window. Seasonal fog had descended. A grey blanket shrouded the trees hiding the beach and the cove, closing in like a protective hand. No one heard the laughter cloaking concern or the ribald stories, saw the flush of feelings, the dissolution of pain or the friendship warming everything throughout the house. It was a swirling mist carrying its own end of summer cure.

*

LATE AUTUMN IN NEW YORK. The first snow, shivering upward between ranks of gaunt buildings, tugged by scooping winds taking the last leaves up as well, hovering uncertainly like lost souls, the last stricken spirits of summer making it too cold to dawdle.

Graham dallied with a bourbon in the Met bar. It had become a habit after work, reminding him of first meeting Frederick and all that had followed. The drink softened his ache or diffused his awareness, he was not clear which. Christmas was coming, but not Frederick who lamented in a recent letter he had to spend it in hospital. "Bloody doctors and tests and more tests. All I want is to come over for you." he had written. Graham sighed. One drink couldn't salve his ache, couldn't fill the emptiness gnawing him.

'Oh, you're staff, I see your name plate. Tell me, is the box office open?'

Graham looked dully up. A well dressed woman hovered over his table, smiling but ruffled.

Graham nodded. 'We close at eight, half an hour after the performance begins.'

'Shit. I don't get away from the office until then. Oh it *is* trying.' She grimaced and sat down. 'Graham, is it?'

He looked at her, at his name tag and nodded again.

'You look sad. Let's have a drink. What's yours?'

'Bourbon. No more thanks.'

She was gone, tripping through the empty bar, dancing to the counter and returning with two glasses of golden liquid with ice bobbing and crackling, and a tired smile. 'There we are. I'm Fiona. Here's to "absent friends".

Graham's face fell. He stared blankly at the table.

Fiona put a tentative hand over his. 'I am sorry, Graham. Sometimes absence makes the heart grow fonder.'

'He can't come for Christmas. He's in hospital.'

'And, fondness?'

'Love.' he whispered.

'Your lover?'

He trembled, near tears, remembering his touch, his passion, his curiosity and the shining armour he'd bequeathed to Graham during their summer holiday in Maine.

Fiona was startled by the intensity. 'You're too young to die of love.' she murmured, gently squeezing his hand.

'Frederick said. "Live first".'

'The best advice.'

'Alone?'

'I try Graham. But not sure it's possible.' Fiona studied his face awash with pain. He's like a little boy struggling with giants, she thought, suddenly aware she often felt the same.

He drank the bourbon she'd brought. 'I said no, but thanks.' He struggled back into the present. 'You want a ticket to what performance?'

Fiona blinked. 'Ah, I wanted two for the Puccini on January eighteenth.'

'There's not much left. Only the expensive ones.'

'Shit, I left it too late.' she said under her breath.

'I could reserve two for you if you'll pick them up.'

'Could you? Let me give you cash now. Will three hundred do? Here you are.'

'It's too much.'

'Postage?'

'I can't put the change in the envelope.'

'Then, keep it for me.'

'Fiona.' (She was startled by the caress in her name). 'I'd rather not, um, you know. It's far too much.'

'Listen, it's only money. Who cares? It'd not bankrupt me even if you scarpered.'

'Wish I could.' he said gloomily.

Searching for barbs to hold him which his fragile charm and preoccupation overrode, she parried, 'Where would you go? Home?'

'Home! Never. But with no education I can't quit, not in the Big Apple. I'm trapped behind bullet proof glass.'

'That's nonsense. My company is run by guys with no schooling but with loads of life experience and lashings of charm. Out there, skill and personality, *not* degrees count.'

'Nothing counts here.'

'Thanks for saying "Fiona". Then move, Graham.'

'The ads are for storemen, dishwashers, packers, cleaners, or people with degrees.'

'Can you ride a motorbike?'

'Yes. Had an old Harley~Davidson. Rebuilt it. Knew every nut and bolt, squeak and groan. Sold it to get here.'

Fiona's heart was thumping. She was suddenly nervous. She handed him her business card and scribbled "Tom" on the back. 'Ring Tom in the morning. He heads our despatch section. We have a team which picks up and delivers all over the city. Bikes and gear supplied. It'll get you out. Our company is not unique; we promote people of all qualities. We're innovative and successful. You may feel too old to buzz round NYC, but think of it as a start. Anyway, Tom is special. You'll like him. Calm, resourceful, skilled manager, loves a good story and good food.' she paused, Am I too pushy? she thought. 'Just an idea. Bin it.'

Graham looked up interested. She had a gentle face, a fine discretely sensuous body and a firm shyness which emboldened him. 'A no hoper like me?'

'A return of a favour.'

'Reserving tickets? Hardly.'

'Being honest and concerned.'

'Frederick and I put those first. He told . . .'

'He told you to feel and to think.'

'That too.'

'Why is he in hospital?'

'He won't say. Perhaps it's his back.'

'Come now, was he that good a lover?'

Graham almost smiled.

Fiona regretted the joke.

'There was something. Deep. I felt it massaging him.'

'So, you have a training.'

'Finished the course, couldn't afford the certificate. Frederick says my hands speak for me. He taught me to speak-up and not cower. He said I was a snail in a pretty, useless shell. And much more. We had such fun. I'd borrowed a mattress for Christmas and spoke to Vernon on the Maine coast, hoping . . .' he fell silent.

Fiona shivered. Has someone crossed my grave? she thought, It's easy to forget that gays are as crushed or elated as the rest of us. 'Cheer up, Graham. You're joining many others celebrating the Boy's birth alone.'

Graham read the card:

Fiona Pinkham B.Sc(Harvard), Dip MAA. FAIAA
Art Director
A P A Associates
1161 South Street, NYC.

He grinned. 'Wow. You're not just a pretty face.'

Fiona grimaced. 'Cut the male chauvinist jokes.'

'I'm serious, Fiona.'

She shivered again. The caress in his "Fiona" was unmistakable.

Believing him, she flushed like a girl but managed: 'And you do have a pretty shell.' Secretly undressing him she added, 'But I rather think it's a snake lingering there tempting innocent maidens with promises of tickets and small change. But seriously, keep the tickets for me. We'll find a way of meeting. Unless you are coming to see Tom, in which case you could deliver them in person.'

'I will ring in the morning. My shift here doesn't begin until one o'clock.'

It seemed to Fiona there was nothing else to say. They finished their drinks in silence. It revived her.

'Can I give you a lift? My car's in the basement. Where do you live?'

'In Washington Mews, near NYU.'

'Fine. My penthouse is close by on the northern tip of Stuyvesant Town overlooking the Brooklyn Bridge and across the water to Brooklyn. Daddy bought it for me after Dan walked out. That's a long story, probably as saddening as yours. He's still an absent friend after five years.'

Graham spied a tear. 'Your loved one?'

'More than anyone.'

'Crying after all this time?'

'Silly, isn't it.'

'Some love is forever.'

She nodded tearfully. 'What a pair of duffers we are. Come on, let's go. My hanky's too small for the two of us.'

Graham was stabbed by unaccustomed comfort What had Frederick said, " Let pain go. Share it."? He was so right. It was discomforting to find the world peopled by sadness. He followed her through the shimmering lobby and down into the bowels of the Lincoln Centre to a very smart white sports car, pristine snow flakes now running puddles, the interior wood-sheened, with white leather seats and matching wool carpets. No wonder she was a director. The car proclaimed success, power and wealth way beyond him. No wonder she didn't care about exorbitant tickets or the change. Like the diva "dragon" who'd tossed Frederick out of his seat, she could buy the whole bloody place, he thought glumly.

Fiona read his disquiet. 'It's only the box, not the chocolates.' She smiled him into the car.

It's perfect.' he murmured.

Fiona thrilled with the generosity of his admiration. It was any car to her, as common as her own body. Was the boy talking about the car, about her or about the match of machine and owner? She fumbled with the starter (which was unusual), dismayed by the pleasure she felt. 'By the way, have you eaten?'

'No. I've only just finished work.'

'Why don't we have a bite at *Gino's* on Washington Square Park, very near your flat. You know it? No? I've not been there for ages. Dan and I once used it a lot. Gino is a sort of god-father to me. Cuddly and attentive with a brilliant chef. Yes? Then no argument, it's on me. Dino will wet his Florentine pants when we show up. He's a love, so forgive his nonsense.'

The welcome stunned Graham. Gino called out all the staff who clustered round their table while he delightedly proclaimed, 'Signora Fiona, mia tesoro, mia piccolo amore, ah how wonderfilled like ar olden times. Ah, your smile still breakas my 'eart, and what a handsome friend, your Signorgraham, our neighbour, Luigi, Maria, si si, in the Mews, I will caring for everythings. Your menu, our delight. Luigi, pronto: Signora Fiona's wine, the spinaci ricotta, gambero con vedura, the olive bread; ah, and aqua minerale con gas. Maria, take these spare servings away. It must be my birthday. Ah, mia tesoro Signore, Signor, benvenuto!'

The succulent meal, the extravagant welcome, deep pile carpets, white linen, candle light shining wine glasses firstly richly ruby later flashing gold, sparkling in eyes softening sorrows until nothing intruded on their gentle pleasures.

Later when stumbling to the rear, Graham was hailed by diners in a far corner who whispered 'Royalty incognito, or Someone?'

'Um, family, I think.' he said cheerfully. In the toilet he laughingly forced his erection into his jeans. He'd forgotten about fun such as this. 'God, I want that job.' he whispered to the cherubs voyeuring from the cornice. Their smiles buoyed him. His arousal warned her to stop drinking.

'*A poco a poco.*' she murmured. Eaves-dropping, Gino beamed. He was an acute host. Maybe this time his treasure would find happiness. Maria's frown indicated success was in the air. Gino proffered liqueurs on the house.

The clocks were striking thirteen (or so it seemed) when they parted demurely at her car. The white perfection purred from the curb. No lights, Fiona waving. He watched her go, his princess, his treasure (he blushed). He wandered home through brightly painted streets every window whispering, 'Tomorrow, and tomorrow, and tomorrow.'

'My tomorrow.' his call ricocheted off stony walls chasing the eddying snow up into the grey velvet darkness. He fell asleep, his head on Frederick's lap, with Vernon's hand searching his leg, a tent in his pyjamas. That particular bewitching joy was all he sought.

In the morning he telephoned. Tom was glad. When could he drop by? Now? Why not! Graham took the subway to the Fulton Street stop and walked to South Street. He waited in reception. A slight, pale, bright eyed man held his hand gently in intangible greetings. 'Graham? Great to meet you. I'm Tom. Come on down to the engine room.'

The atmosphere was easy, almost carefree. Tom benignly sanctioned the silliness of his two young riders who greeted Graham with winks and firm handshakes as he went into the glass walled office for the interview.

They talked mostly about Maine lobsters and sauces and accompanying vegetables and garnish, straying into life, love and frustrations and, finally, motor bikes. Tom grew delighted with another Harley~Davidson enthusiast, who knew far more of every nut and piston. He liked the boy. Fiona was right, Graham was honest. Tom valued that first. Secondly he surely was gay? (Tom discretely was, as some of the firm's directors were, baring Fiona). Thirdly, Graham knew his stuff, unlike the silly pair revving up outside. Graham was serious fun, and much more than handsome. Tom was keen to try him out.

They agreed a trial two months on generous temporary wages, a negotiated staff contract afterwards, his wage the bottom line of a permanent salary. Graham was pleased. He'd resign from the Met at once; start as soon as possible. The letter of intent from APAA, a formality both knew.

Tom was surprised by the lad's enthusiasm. If he's like this about biking, what's he like in bed? he thought fondly giving him a generous slice of onion and cheese pie he'd cooked last evening for his Beloved (the top director) saying, 'You'd best put skates on. Don't be late for the last day, eh?'

Graham laughed. 'Leave as a good boy. Is that your bike? Oh, it's like mine. Let's fix it up after work? Thanks a million for the pie.'

The carriage Graham rode to the Lincoln Centre was covered in graffiti which danced and shimmered over every surface, saying

HOORAY HIP HIP HOORAY. Almost best of all, the Met grudgingly agreed to his leaving at the end of the week, paying him his remaining salary, and no curtain calls. Gino's *putti* had indeed blessed him. So had Fiona. Oh, shit (as she would say), the tickets. I've not reserved them. I'll do it, ring this afternoon, drop them at her office, he decided.

Fiona was happy Graham had been offered a job. Happier he'd reserved tickets, happier still when he agreed to deliver them home and stay for a drink, then worried he'd not find her flat as perfect as the car. A happiness whose cause eluded her, yet marked her with blushes and sudden smiles and a breathlessness she'd not experienced since a girl.

She was angry. 'He's not even twenty. Here I am, over thirty, mooning about like a love-sick cow. Anyway, he's gay. I must pull myself together.' She said to herself, rushing home well beforehand to change her dress, brush her hair and touch alluring scent here and there, rejuvenate the flowers and pull two pizzas from the freezer, tempting him to stay. She had set the stage. It was the best she could do.

All the windows of Brooklyn shone with the last sunlight filtered by a gauze of snow clouds, a host of reflections brightening her spacious crows nest flat, licking her walls highlighting paintings, showing the tremble in her hand as she answered the door-TV to let her opera boy inside. He was early. Was it a sign she mattered to him? At last he entered, to be bathed in reflected orange light, as mysterious as the moon, as perfect as any dream. They stood quietly watching life die in myriad rectangular eyes, leaving the murky water as grey as death, the bridges, sharp scratches on its steely surface already furred by eddies of snow. He turned and smiled shyly. 'Thanks for the job. I love your flat.'

He left late, saying he'd walk home. She took his hand, went to the door and kissed his eloquent lips, feeling desire firming, feeling herself accepting it. She capped his bulging fly. 'I knew you weren't a snail.'

'It's been nice.' he said huskily pulling away and retreating.

'Let's do it again?'

'I'd like that.' And he was gone, in a blur of the lift falling ground-ward to the crisp snow-snarled city.

Fiona musingly cleared away, aware the dusky emptiness of the flat was invading her. 'He's like a dream just beyond reach.' she said. 'His body shows itself, its hunger, its firmness of which he seems unaware, yet a shyness holds him back. Does he have regrets too? Can one so young know betrayal, despair? Is he a reflection of my own chagrin? It's fascinating - Kaa, the snake hypnotising the monkey banderlog until they walk into his jaws. It's his through-and-through beauty I long to embrace, a boyishness, untrammelled by what follows. Yet shyness protects both the naive and the injured. What has this man Frederick done to him? There's too much love to indicate brutality, plus a dreamy gentleness. Why does he love so deeply? Perhaps it's father/son stuff. Most sons grow up. I wish this one would.'

She groaned. 'Stop meddling, Fiona. Let the boy alone. Shit, what's going on? I get him a job, have him over, wine and dine him, pant for his attentions, want to be eaten? It's as rash as my giving up Daddy's ambitions of a science career for one of my own.

'Well, here I am. Made it. Going to blow it if I don't stop this nonsense. And glad I don't care. Very glad. Shit, do I love him?'

She hurried to bed, and danced with the angels all night.

It grew into a harsh winter. Christmas was approaching judging by the first Santas reddening store windows and prancing through the snow.

Graham was enjoying APAA, although the icy streets were chilly and dangerous for motorbikes. Warming himself in Tom's office, he was presented with a slim document setting out a permanent appointment.

Tom grimaced. 'Sorry about the salary. It's the highest of your grade. I'll try to push some petty cash your way to supplement it for the repairs and management you've taken on. Jees, Graham, I don't know how I coped before. I'm harrying admin about wages. My section is not well paid. But it will be.'

Graham grinned. 'It's fun though. The lads are wild and willing. Tougher than me. I hate the cold.'

Tom nodded. 'Thanks for your own wild willingness. You should look around. You're too good for this position. Everyone agrees. Get some management experience and then come back.'

'Now we've finished your bike.'

'True but unfair. By the way, take it on a special delivery to Gem Productions. Insist on seeing Etienne. He's interested in you. One of us. Park in their basement. My treasure should be safe there.'

'Trying to get rid of me?'

'Securing you a permanent future here, dear boy.'

'Tom, you've been great. Friend and boss.'

'Move on but come back often.' Tom shivered with pleasure.

Gem productions was a prestigious organisation, located at the west end of Rector Street overlooking Battery Park and the South Ferry terminal; a trend setter in Advertising and Marketing. The girl at the front desk sniffed and pointed to the lifts saying to Graham. 'Fifteenth floor, turn right, fourth door on the corridor. He says to come up.' Her sneer communicating disbelief that leather clad trash had any place in so important a director's day.

Etienne was tall, thin and gay. 'Are you clad, under all that?' He pointed to the snow spattered bike wear.

Graham nodded.

Etienne solicitously helped him out and inclined his head to where Graham might leave it, appraising his tight jeans and sloppy jumper with interest. 'Tom raves about you. No wonder his Carl is jumpy. Get a natty suit. The position is for a junior staff administrator. Assessing, coordinating, balancing project teams, keeping the peace and high productivity. Can you start end of January?'

Graham was nonplussed. 'Here? Um, later?'

'Not later than mid March. Start at twice your present salary. After induction, three times. We value climbers. Our sort do, did Tom tell you?'

'He said you'd brief me.'

'Just have dear boy. Ring your acceptance by the end of next week. I'll confirm by return.' Etienne handed Graham a business card. 'We want one of our own. We're the best. You have to match that. Came by Bike?'

'On Tom's revamped Harley~Davidson.'

'My, my. We are privileged.'

'He thought style might help.'

'No. It's mainly your face. No wonder he loves you. Can you kit-up outside?'

Graham felt dismissed. He shook hands, picked up his heap of leathers and left. It was a fantastic offer. Money. Position. But a smug unconcern made him uneasy.

He reported back to Tom who advised, 'Take it.'

Unconvinced, Graham nodded. I'll discuss it with Fiona, he thought.

Their weekly trysts had grown into nearly an infatuation. Fiona was rather more than a woman with whom he shared private thoughts, she was the only person in his life. Her attentiveness stirred him to deepening trust. They were intimate without commitment. He was finding Frederick's absence made her proximity tantalising. 'If only she'd take me to bed.' he whispered frequently to his pillow.

Frederick had opened a can of sex worms; Graham now wanted what he'd denied all his life, to express feelings, to make love. 'No wonder guys cruise.' he also whispered. His pillow remained mute.

Fiona was sanguine. 'Tom's probably right. Go for a while. Then come back to us.'

'I'm happy now: the Company, Tom, you, being out and about. It's fun.'

'Aren't you coasting, Graham?'

'Do you mean, wasting my time?'

'Waiting about, without direction.'

He frowned. He was dallying. Wanting more from her. Far more. Maybe she didn't fancy him, maybe their friendship was limited. God I want her, he thought.

Fiona caught the flicker of desire. Perhaps he doesn't know how to proceed, she thought. She'd prepared a feast for them. Served it in candle light. Plied him with wine. Part of his preoccupation was about Frederick who'd not written for some time. But the rest? She longed for him to take her and kiss her deeply, desire her body as well as her company, fill an ache she hid even from herself in the rush and bustle of her work.

They were both coasting, she admitted to herself. Waiting for what? For loneliness to implode? For old age to ease longing, to force patience? Her lust for him seemed one-sided. That was not enough to carry them anywhere. She couldn't trust him or herself. She had to do something. Fiona looked at his lithe young body lapped in candle light, watched his able hands at work, saw him relax in feasting, his lips, sought so often with small response, bare his teeth in his wry smile. She drained her glass. 'Graham, please stay tonight.'

He looked pleased and uncertain.

'Sometimes I get lonely.'

His cheek trembled. 'In your bed?'

'If you want.'

He stood, went round the table, put his arms around her and whispered into her fragrant bob of boyish hair. 'More than anything.'

Her heart thumped. 'Now?'

'Better still.'

The feast abandoned, they skipped to bed, lingering over bare flesh, soft cavities and, eventually into groins until she could wait no longer and pulled him in. Power thrilled in her. His arching body hovering over hers its pulsing phallus storming her deeps until, with an excruciating rush, both climaxed. Her cloud of sweaty contentment stopped drifting when Graham opened his eyes and said. 'Let's have desert now.' She tenderly kissed him.

The days of December melted away, unlike the snow which settled and grew a crusty top making the city into an ice rink. Some days Fiona left her car and went by subway. She was interested in Graham's reports of Gem Productions and of matters 'below stairs' in APAA, guiltily aware she was snooping just like her father who made a point of being the first to know of scandals, successes and collapses in the business community. She was alarmed by an increasingly imperceptible distance. 'Is the boy in Graham being swamped?' she begun asking herself. But their love-making developed such wild delights she soon forgot.

Her billionaire father presented her with a huge bank draft (in lieu of his shopping for a personal Christmas present). She bought the small unit adjoining hers and tentatively offered it to Graham cajoling him, 'We both need neighbours as friends, need separate lives (disingenuously, she blushed); need space to develop; we like sharing (he nodded); and you could save some money against hard times - isn't that good financial sense?'

'It's too much, Fiona. But let me think about it.' he murmured.

Then she caressed him all over, her exploration still a delight after joyous weeks. She knew many of his hungers now, even his anus. Knew how godlike he became when aroused, and how utterly she lost herself in the flurry of their climaxes and the peace growing afterwards.

This time she almost overplayed her hand. He bubbled over before she let him in. She savoured cleaning up and stroking desire into him. It was a rapturous ending.

Afterwards she lay on her side looking into the brown warm pools of his eyes. She licked his long dark lashes. 'That's where I drown.' she whispered.

He snuggled up and tongued a nipple round and round. Cupping the breast with a tenderness which displayed love beyond words. 'If I live there, can I still visit like this?'

Fiona sighed contentedly. 'Oh, my Graham, Didn't I tell you? That's the one condition: you must.'

Fiona extricated herself from her traditional family Christmas saying she was spending it with friends. She took Graham shopping for food, drink and decorations which, between bouts of hearty love-making, were eventually hung. To her delighted horror, she realised she depended on his calm sense leavening her willful impetuosity. One day she put his clothes in the machine with her washing. Handing him another robe she smiled. 'We look like a married couple in our matching dressing gowns. But no slippers and pipe.'

He grinned. His robe opened.

She glimpsed pubic hair and creamy flesh. 'But it doesn't matter. Look, there's my better half.'

He pulled her into his arms. She held the flaccid power sure of Graham's delight not in boasting, she'd learned, but appealing for acknowledgement. Such a sweet little boy discovering what he carries between his legs, she fondly thought, He is growing up, I feel it.

Then, the leaving party in the basement of APAA. Most of the 'above stairs' staff drifted down to say good luck, sad he was leaving, glad he would return; surprised that the reclusive Tom had prepared so fantastic a spread, shocked by his extravagant fondness for the boy. Everyone declared it was the best xmas party that year, possibly for all time. Fiona and Graham lingered and helped clear up. She was embarrassed by Tom and Graham's farewell kiss. She'd not seen passion between men. But the wine, her expectations of her own Christmas and a nascent love without conditions prompted her to smile fondly, kiss Tom (which she'd never done) and gently order Graham to open the garage doors so she could drive home. He sat silent beside her. Sad, happy, triumphant. 'Tom's the best. I wouldn't go unless he'd told me.' he said softly.

She pulled up for Williamsburg Bridge traffic. 'Tom loves you.'

'And why not? Love's like that.'

'I don't trust mine.'

'Nor mine. But I'm learning.'

'Dear Graham, your love is fine and beautiful. It tells me not to compete or control, simply let it in where it frolics and nestles in my heart.' She drove along the snow blinded avenue. 'I thought of Frederick when Tom kissed you. Did you? Yes? His love sounded true. Was it?'

He nodded, watching flecks hit and melt on the windscreen. 'He doesn't write. I'll check Washington Mews now I'm free between jobs.'

Supper was delayed until other pressing hunger was satisfied.

Lying tiredly in her arms Graham murmured. 'They all think I'm gay.'

'Well, aren't you?'

'I've never really known. Frederick says the boy in me died when I was twelve. I'll tell you about it one day. He found him alive, only needing attention to tempt him into the open - I told you, "a snail in a shell". He let me be twelve again. His love is extraordinary.'

'I love your boy and the man.' She blanched. 'Can I tell you, it's rude? (he nodded). 'Dan was cut. A naked giant. Heartless, demanding, fecund. But lacking the beauty of yours: its sloppy beret, the gleaming purple nob underneath, the unblemished stem which swells and lengthens responding to the slightest thing, even my longing.'

Graham guffawed. 'Nothing slight about that raging.'

She kissed him silent. 'Yours fills me. It's far more than physical. I can't explain how much it takes or the flood I'm carried on. I know your need to show it; that's the boy seeking recognition. The man plays it better than anyone I've known. Its power and beauty centre me. At last the giddy whirlwind stills. I am frightened by everything we do, it's magnificent. I die every time, then live again. I'm not in control any more. It's that irresistible boy-man. Don't hurt me when you go.'

He lay listening to her heart beating, looked up into her face. 'Let me go, and I'll come back. I promise.'

They lay for a long time holding a new reality.

Carols on Christmas eve in the Metropolitan Museum, Upper East Side overlooking Central Park whetted appetites. Fiona bought a CD of the choir as a last present for Graham. He found a large jar of brandy plums in the Museum shop and hid it in his coat. They dined afterwards in the Museum cafe, filled with remnants of the choir, a motley collection of arty music lovers sprinkled with a few fashion conscious regular patrons. Her radiant face reflected his. Finished, they sat sipping coffee waiting for the bill, too engrossed to be aware of keen or softening glances in their direction until surprised by the waiter who announced their bill had been settled by another who wished them both a very merry xmas. They looked around. It seemed as if everyone was smiling.

They took the subway home She stripped and fell ravenously upon him. It was soon over. Still smiling, they fell entwined into sleep.

The morning was dusk-grey with obliterating snow. He left to collect oddments for his new flat from his old digs in Washington Mews.

She saw him off. 'Father Christmas at twelve, then feasting, then a rugged-up walk in East River Park, then naked high jinks until midnight.' she whispered.

Graham grinned. 'What about the other way round?'

Fiona was solemn. 'Don't you care about tradition?'

'Sure, but love comes first.'

'Not at Christmas, you yummy reindeer.' She hummed the carol:

> *Oh, come all ye faithful,*
> *Joyful and triumphant',*
> *Come ye, oh come ye*
> *to Bethlehem.*

On the way to the kitchen to finish the sauce for the turkey steaks she looked in at their tree sparkling with a hundred tiny lights topped by an angel. She pressed her firming stomach. The doctor had said mid summer. Was it her present or his? Was it to be worshiped by shepherds and lowing cattle, a manger of happiness bursting from her womb, or was it shame to be denied and crucified?

Snow was whirling in the unsettled air beyond the windows. The day was closing in. 'Maybe no walk in the park.' she said quietly. 'That should please him.' she giggled. 'Our first Christmas. A happy one. At last.' She sat on the couch where he'd slept at the beginning. Cried a smidgen of happiness so as not to burst. Rose gladly and wafted back to the kitchen.

He did not return. She waited until it was too dark to be angry or to cry, and ventured (with a spare key) into his flat. It was dark. Abandoned. She returned to her own filled with accusing tinsel and sat in the dim glow from the tree.

Emptied, almost asleep, she heard a faint knock at the door. She struggled up and angrily flung it open.

A ghostly Graham stood swaying before her, wild eyed, blue lipped, soaked to the bone from wandering snowy streets. He croaked, 'He's dead.' and collapsed

With superhuman strength Fiona dragged him inside, stripped him and carried him to bed, lay with him until his shivering diminished, the weeping started and the awful truth sobbed out.

When she dared leave him, she rummaged in his sodden pockets, finding the fragile damp letters, the one, his unsuspecting last, the final one finished by his nurse which concluded:

I am sorry to tell you Frederick passed away this morning.
A combination of morphine and deterioration of the cancer in his
spine. He spoke of you fondly to the end, and wanted you to know his
life was graced by yours, and that you MUST go on laughing and
ploughing the wilderness for its treasures, all of which you deserve.
He asked me to say you should forgive but not forget. And
that all the love you'd shared would tide you over for ever . . . he said
other things I can't remember. I was upset, you understand.
He was such a fine man. I am so very sorry . .

Fiona wept. 'It's worse than Dan walking out. At least he lives somewhere, the bastard. This is total death.' She flattened out the crinkled sheets and laid them on a heater. Went back to him like a sleepwalker, trying to tackle loss and grief, and searching frantically for any minute grain of hope.

She hurried to the kitchen and warmed some milk with sweet chocolate and, holding his lolling head, poured some down his throat. He slumped like a corpse unaware of her tending, eyes unseeing unsleeping. In a paroxysm of determination, she remembered her own breakdown; the pills, the care, blank sleep which unravelled grief so eventually she could begin again. That was five years ago. PILLS screamed her addled brain. She found them and slipped one into Graham's unresponsive mouth. She stripped and slipped in to hold his chilly form. She would stay them both all night, she decided fiercely.

She woke to find him gone. Frantic she rushed through the flat, finding him crouched naked by the radiator re-reading the letters. She crawled to him and pulled him into a crazed embrace. 'My darling. My darling. Let me help you. Come.'

Obediently he took her hand back to bed, and into a tearful review of memories of events and feelings, of loss and old joy, the clew which might lead him to her from the darkest labyrinth ever experienced.

Fortunately everything stopped for Christmas so there was time to mope and to share, time for tears, despair and the possibilities of hope. Enough time to consult her doctor and form a plan to seek relief.

Fiona decided to take Graham to her family's hideaway by a forested lake, a couple of hours drive to the north. The doctor urged fresh air, wood cutting and snowy outings fuelled by wholesome food. Armed thus, and with the latest drugs, she rang her partners saying she had to be away from the office for several weeks. She loaded her car with quilts and warm clothes, put the untouched christmas dinner in the freezer for happier times and resolutely set off.

They followed the Hudson River before turning off into a less populous landscape where fewer roads had been cleared of snow. Their spirits brightened. Fiona stopped at a straggle of buildings, the nearest settlement to the family hut. She left her sports car at the local garage, replacing it with a 4WD kept there for the family. The garage was run by Jean and her two sons, Glen 18, and Art 14.

Jean beamed. 'Dear Fiona, what a real xmas treat. Glen's away. Only Art to help you move in.'

The boy looked serene.

Fiona smiled slightly. 'Art knows everything, and he's turning into such a handsome hunk. I'll borrow him and return him before dusk.'

Art grinned. He spied Graham slumped in the low white car and raised an eyebrow.

Fiona sighed. 'Graham's just lost his best friend. We've come to find some peace of mind.'

Jean shook her head sadly. 'Best place, my dear. Art, put those boxes of stores in the wagon, get your jacket and get goin.' She squeezed Fiona's hand after accepting a small wad of dollar bills. 'Not much to do just now. That's why Glen's away. Lean times my dear. Thank you.' She looked sternly at her youngest busy with packing. 'Fix up with Art. He's at too loose an end just now, so do make use of him. Guess it's his age. No father, no boundaries. But he is fond of you.'

Fiona wanly smiled. 'And very handy. I hope he'll help Graham. The sudden news of Frederick's death was a terrible shock. I thought he'd crack up.'

Jean patted her hand. 'Men need each other, Art's just realising. "Leave them alone and they'll come home wagging their tails behind them" as the song goes. Mind how you go. The snow's drifting. It's a harsh winter. But not the first. Cheer up Miss Fiona, there's magic in our woods.'

'Thanks, Jean.'

'Dear, remember, first get the stove lit to warm the house; then the open fire; and get Art cutting more wood. Glen left plenty under the deck; then turn the water on; otherwise, it's ready for you. Enjoy!' She waved them off.

It was not easy, skidding between drifts, trying to follow a track obliterated by drifting snow. Only the gap in the trees, an unreliable ley line guided them, and Art, who knew the forest like the back of his hand.

Fiona drove skillfully. The three squeezed into the front seat. Graham was warmed by the boy's proximity, the boy was responsive. Was it a small inner thaw? Fiona felt Graham "going" to Art. But she remembered his promise to come back to her. It is odd. But probably essential, she thought uneasily.

They slithered to a halt behind the shack. Art jumped down, grabbed a spade and dug a track to the door, then cleared a way to the carport and to the white topped pile of fire wood.

Graham and Fiona carried everything into the silent chilly hut. She lit the large stove, scooped snow into a big black kettle and put it sizzling onto the hob. Then lit the fire facing the living space while Graham and Art struggled out to the wood heap for more logs.

Fiona watched them sawing up more. Clouds of breath, reddening hands and faces, feet stamping, expletives as snow found ways into boots and cuffs, Art's puppy joyfulness enticing Graham to manfully face private questions about Frederick's death, and to see beyond his pain into a living world.

Fiona felt a lightness, the first respite since Christmas day. She filled hot water bottles for the bed from the singing kettle, set out mugs and muffins for the labouring men and felt glad. They were alone in a white clad land. The iced-over lake, the bare sugar maples and thicker clad furs and pines, the spoor of animals and birds proclaimed the season's solidity.

She called them in for tea. They sat round the open fire, thawing out, saying little. Comfortable, awed by being secure in so vast a frozen wilderness.

Art looked slyly at Fiona. 'There's still a heap to do. Do you really want to take me back? Please Fiona, um, can't I stay?'

She winced. 'Do what you can, Art. Thanks. But I'll take you and get back here in the last light.'

Graham looked perplexed. 'Because he's only a boy?'

'That too.' she said carefully.

'Because I'll tell. Because you sleep together and shouldn't be like this. Because it's sinful.' Art growled.

Fiona was rattled. 'It is not wrong to comfort a good friend, and to be free.'

Art was crestfallen. 'I know that. And I'd never tell.'

She angrily shook her head. 'You don't know how destructive gossip is. My parents would fall on me like a ton of bricks, the village would titter when I was shopping. There'd be unkind stories put about. It's taken me years to break free of all that. I will not be ruled again. Art, you don't understand. Privacy is the only effective weapon against the manipulative divas.'

'I do things I don't even tell my brother. Of course I'll shut my trap.' he blushed deeply. For his body led him astray, his dreams too. What he wanted troubled him as he explored himself and his friends in the summer freedom of the woods. Maybe it was wrong, but it was marvellous. Some one had told him, 'There can't be a heaven without sin' and (as the song goes) "You can't have one without the other."

Graham, poisoned by years of silence looked into the curling flames. 'Fiona, can't we trust Art?'

Fiona was stern. 'Never open your trap?'

'Never.'

'Keep our secrets, honour between friends?'

'Always.'

Graham put his mug down. 'Forever is a long time. Fiona's right Art. Our being here is a sacred act. I don't know about you, but I desperately need friends just now.'

Art was shocked how near to tears Graham was. 'I'm sorry about your best friend's death. I hoped by staying I could help.' He was silenced by a tightening in his own chest. Behind Graham's mourning lay love, that undiscovered thicket he'd only dreamed of, never dared mention.

Fiona took Graham's hand. 'So, shall I put a hot bottle in the other bed?'

He nodded.

Art blushed with wild delight. This was better than any dream. 'I really promise. For ever and ever.' He grinned. 'Fiona, will you ring Mum and tell her?'

The chores done, food prepared, a meal eaten, Art had wine and got the giggles, and Fiona taught them an old English round which chimed warmly in the dark chill world:

> *Hey ho, nobody at home,*
> *eat nor drink nor money have I none.*

Still I will be ha ha ha happy.
Hey ho . . .

Then, shyly, they all went to bed.

Art lay singing to himself, 'Hey ho, still I will be happy . . .', listening for a long time, in vain, to hear what humping sounded like, his head happily spinning, his hand comforting his erection. In an interlude he was struck by the thought, Graham's love is for a man. What sort of love is that? So, why's he with Fiona? and, wrestling with the paradox, he slept long and as deeply as any young boy.

The others, exhausted by the escape journey, fell like stones into eiderdowns, lightly locked together.

In the morning Art brought steaming mugs of tea and stood looking at them, curious and aroused until shivering gratefully he crept in beside Graham who'd opened the bedding for him.

He shone with pleasure. 'I rekindled the stove. It's snowing hard. I'll bring in more wood later and clear the drifts from the doors and put a heater under the car. I think we're stuck here. I'm sorry.'

Fiona laughed. 'No you're not.'

Graham grinned and squeezed his leg. 'I'm sorry it's not harder. Then we'd have to stay for ever.'

Fiona eyed him. 'You forgot your pill.'

'I'm all right. You and Art are better medicine.'

'Graham, please have one. It'll keep things steady.'

'My darling, I feel better. If I get squiffy I'll pop a pill. Promise.'

Art was wide eyed, "darling" meant love. Graham was hard to fathom. 'I was squiffy last night.'

Fiona ruffled his hair. 'Dear Art, if you don't behave, I'll lock you out like a naughty dog.'

Graham sniggered. 'It's not naughty dogs' or brass monkeys' weather, so look out, Art.'

Fiona looked severe. 'You too.' her face softened. 'Dear one, it is awful that life goes on. But there's no alternative. Art and I have broad shoulders so cry on them occasionally. That's also medicine.'

Art greedily looked away from her breasts swelling out her pyjamas. 'Do you know about Frederick?'

'Of course.'

'Aren't you worried?'

'Love is precious. I don't mind sharing him.'

'Um, with a man?'

'Like you?'

Art blushed. How could she possibly know about him, or his shenanigans in the woods?

She looked kindly, saw his distress and relented. 'I'd only be worried if you hurt each other, or me. But I trust you. Both of you, Art.'

Art saw an OK green light, not condemnation. He thrilled with relief, rolled out of bed vainly trying to mask his arousal and bounded away to dress, singing 'Hey ho, I'm happy happy happy . . .'

Fiona kissed Graham, feeling down his leg and into his crotch. 'I hope it doesn't snow for long. I want you so much. Any way you want.'

He rolled onto his stomach. She slid a finger down over his rectum. 'Do you miss him there?'

'Yes. Everywhere.'

She lay beside him and wept with a mixture of relief that despair was shrinking, and Graham was imperceptibly returning to her, challenging her doubts about whether they could share some sort of life. She snuffled. 'I'm happy really. I miss *you* everywhere. Isn't that silly?'

'It's why I came back.'

'Are you happy here?'

'Nearly all the time. It's weird, the three of us, like a family. The family neither Art nor I have. Is it some kind of fix which thrills us both and is effective because you embrace it too? How can happiness be you, me and a boy? Now, that's silly.'

'It's being away from rules and pushy folk. Being, what you call "naked". I think, being ourselves is a form of healing. Darling, the "fix" thrills me too. It's a mix of temptations and joy and adventure and shyness - or something like that, eh?'

'Exactly.' He kissed her. 'I've never fancied boys. Yet I want Art to be close. Am I fourteen again? The times I never had which Frederick said I must experience before moving on? He'd approve of all this I know. Art uncovers another me. I'm sure it's not strange for him. He tempts me to be wild, boy-wild, which touches wounded bits of me. Do you mind that I need you both?'

'Graham, I'm so really happy to have you back. How could I mind?'

'Sharing's easier said than done.'

'No my dear. No. I do understand having you is sharing. I treasure that.'

'Your love is very special, Fiona.'

'You must remember so is yours.'

'I can't support like you do.'

'You've given me everything and the will to keep it.'

'In spite of the divas?'

'They can trample and kick and scream. With you, I am stronger than they are.'

'That's also why I'm here.'

'A triangular couple.'

'A couple can't be a triangle.' Art stood, his arms full of snowy logs.

Fiona laughed. 'Dear Art (You've always been that, you know). Aren't we three a happy triangle?' He nodded vigorously. 'And Graham and I make a couple. It's a big lovely mess. But it works and it's for ever and ever.'

Struggling against tenderness, Art's face fell. 'Um, we are a sort of family.' He went and placed the logs in a bin beside the fireplace, hiding his confusion. His fleeting image was of a baby in a bier with his mother and his father, watched over by lowing cattle, lit by a bright star. Art was as poor as Jesus, as anonymous, yet at that moment filled with a million stars. Years later he admitted it was love, furthermore it didn't dim.

What capped his happiness was his mother telephoning and Fiona's response: 'Art, a trouble? Certainly not. He's one of the family. We couldn't do without him.'

It snowed, on and off, for a week. On bright days Art and Graham sawed firewood, occasionally balancing on the deck rail to pee into the snow drifts, yellow streams boring into the earth itself, they decided. Art was impressed with Graham's manly member and its flow, yet basked in praise of his forestry skills. One day, walking along the verge of the lake they saw a heron land and slide along the ice. Stock still they watched the ungainly bundle right itself and become an elegant bird.

'He's late, going south.' whispered Art, leaning back against Graham so he would hear.

Graham put his arms around the boy with a rush of pleasure. 'Glad you stayed?'

Art drowned in deep brown eyes. 'You bet. Do you think I'm trouble?'

'It's great, the three of us. Sorry about my moods.'

Art was enamoured, uneasy about his erection. 'There's nothing to be sorry about Graham. Um, did you um love Frederick? You don't have to say.'

'Yes. I'm so empty without him. Fiona and you have made it bearable. I was trying to explain to her - it's not having a broken heart but a dead one. He was a part of me.'

Art wanted to be a part, wanted to be bound by such love-power, wanted this mysterious heron-moment to last. When Graham kissed his chapped lips Art knew it was important to be beside a frozen lake, feet deep in snow, whiteness blinding him. It was a new happiness heavy with seriousness, more than a game. He had landed just then but found himself skidding out of control. But Graham held him until he knew the fragile ice of feeling would hold, so they could separate, he with the elegant inelegance of adolescence, both trudge back to Fiona's welcome.

The three regularly ventured into the silent woods. Struggling through drifts, shaking trees for snow showers, snow-balling until, with tingling fingers and faces, they bounded back inside to the fire.

Although his voice was unsteady, Art enjoyed singing in Fiona's round. It was an intricate song - three separate yet identical melodies forming a rich whole. Sometimes he sang. 'hey ho, hey ho' rhythmically over and over again , a sort of drone. The harmony thrilled him. Not only was he a part of it, but it was their triumphant anthem to the season, mixing Christmas, wilderness and love. There is a star shining on me, he thought gladly.

Then it was time for Art to go. The snow settled, their food ran low and Art, outside the blossoming intimacy of Graham and Fiona, felt an outsider. Fiona drove him back to the garage where she pressed $100 into his hand.

Art shook his head. 'You don't owe me anything.'

His vehemence struck Fiona. 'Art, you were hired. You did so much, even helping me with Graham, making it such a happy time, becoming a very dear friend. We don't pay for friendship with money - that's for chopping and clearing, starting up the house. You have our love, as we have yours. Don't confuse the two.'

'No, Fiona.'

'Dear Art, isn't friendship about sharing?'

'Of course.'

'Then, let me share our money as well as our love. It's nothing compared to your contribution.'

He was doubtful.

'I can't buy your love. You exchanged it for ours. Forever and ever, remember?'

He nodded.

'Take it.' She pushed a wad of notes deep into his trouser pocket near the warmth of his crotch, an additional bulge.

The pleasures of desire, love and high jinks in the icicled forest bubbled through him. He smiled, pleasure spiralling with regret, desire and triumph. 'Thanks.'

His mother was intrigued how gruff and happy Art was. 'They've bewitched you.' she proffered.

He grinned. 'The Snow Queen enchanted us with her snowy spells.' (Fiona had said that, but it sounded true).

Jean looked at her little boy. The icy air had roughened his face. Was there a shadow of a mustache on his upper lip? Was he more solid, manly?

Jean was relieved it had gone so well. Their livelihood was tied to the Pinkham family. Fiona had always lifted her spirits. Now it was Art's turn. It's unusual that growing up brings happiness, yet Art seems older and more settled, she thought gratefully.

Fiona returned with enough provisions for a couple of weeks. She dared stay away from the office longer. The hut was quiet. A fire burned. Graham basked on a mattress in front. She tip toed over and wriggled up his long relaxed legs and removed his clothes before her own.

'I missed you.' he said smiling.

'You are lovely by firelight.' she murmured caressing him, dwelling on areas of greatest pleasure until he lay on his back licked by flickering light. Gaunt, she thought, yet utterly beautiful, mirroring his response. She knelt over his phallus and lowered herself. Filled and shimmering, she moved up and down in delicious rhythm watching his face as his ecstasy flared. He stiffened and yearned so deeply she cried out. They climaxed at the same moment, lay before the dancing fire, content.

Fiona kissed him. 'Did you miss me that way?'

'Yes. Being wanted that way.'

'Love is wanting.'

They lay watching the fire die. Graham flung more wood on. She watched him bend, firelight spilling between his legs throwing his dangling sex into haloed relief. His powerful thighs drove such delight into her. She wanted to tell him. But an urgency in his voice as he snuggled waylaid her.

'Let's stay here, Fiona.'

'For more?'

'Yes. To use all the Snow Queen's spells up.'

He suckled her breast. Was it moist, or was it spittal? He plunged his tongue in paring her labia. She groaned, knelt before him as a boy opening her buttocks in invitation. Seething with homoerotic desire he fingered her weeping vagina and deeply thrust from behind. She climaxing he thrusting on and on with mounting lust.

Graham gasped. 'I'm nearly there.'

She cried. 'Oh my darling. Come, darling, come!'

'NOW.'

Storms filled her. Everything burst.

He lay exhausted cradling her. Fiona cried softly, unbelievingly. The Snow Queen's spells had broken the thrall of Frederick's death and carried them into an enchanted future. Vague but wonderful. For a split second they had become one person one joy one future. She loved him unreservedly, her motley magician who'd put a rabbit in her hat, melted her icy resistance and touched her with his wand so she knew, finally, they belonged together. But to dream this was one thing, telling him would be fraught. She dozed patiently in his arms.

The mattress remained. Their coupling, deeply urgent, burst in them for a couple of days and nights. Graham needed to shoot out everything: his loss, his longing, his love. Fiona longed to be his receptacle, matching his ardour. Each Titanic moment swamped them. Their bodies provoked by dreams of unity, foundered. Exhausted they reconnected to reality: tending fires, preparing meals, venturing out into the pristine wilderness, finding other pleasures. But sooner or later, with chilled feet and frozen faces, they were driven back to the hut, the fire and to nakedness. It was as if they'd crept into each other, sheltering, toying with the unspoken histories of their lives.

Graham admitted his early rape and told her how Frederick had drawn off the veil of silence, repression and shame, encouraging him to be himself - both passive and active, a receiver and giver - recalling his joyful holiday in Maine which had begun to make a man of him.

She confided the innocence of her infatuation with Dan, her dreams (more adolescent than adult) of being wife and mother, of deep divisions in her rigid family which haunted her as a child and woman.

He nodded, remembering her obstinacy over Art staying on.

She'd grown up dreaming rather than appraising, never seeing the incongruity of her relationships, such as that one.

'Like me and my ex, Philip. I fell for his tortuous sexuality, always the oppressed, exploited without regard.' he said.

'Much the same as me.' she mused.

He looked grave. 'Do you have dreams now of turning me into an ordinary guy playing trains with my son, making my daughter dolls houses?'

'Yes. Because you are ordinary as well as fabulous.'

'A father, me? Wanting to kiss Art, and more?'

'Is there more?'

'No.'

'Why not?'

'Because we're happy as it is - as it must be I guess.'

'Because it's pure. And it's love. Not what the world labels it. Graham, you mustn't be tainted by those sick values. I know your love. I'd die for it. So would Art. It's perfect, gentle, unshakable. We'd let you do anything to us because you use us with care. It's the "trust" we all agreed on as a triangle.

'It's filled us both with new courage and new demands. That's the power spurting out of you. The broken bits of your heart we harbour until you want them back. You fuck me, kiss Art. Different people, the same deep effect. One day after playing trains and dolls houses you might lie with him (he'll be a man by then) and, as you promised, come home for dinner, more love and dolls houses. Your appetite is oceanic. You need all of us. And we need you, don't you see?'

He blinked back a tear. 'Shame is hard to deal with.'

'Here, with me and the Snow Queen?'

'Even here.

'Isn't it lessened by telling?'

'Yes.'

'Let's promise to always talk. Face shame, share desire, enjoy sharing?'

'I tried to fuck everything out of me. Shame stayed.'

'We'll verbally fuck it out, and enjoy the other.'

'What I love about you, Fiona, is how you take everything from me and turn it into presents.'

'Darling, they are. Your smallest smile lights me up.'

'When you touch me - specially down there - I burst.'

'I know. It's amazing. It feeds my own lust.'

'Will you always forgive me and caress me?'

'Not always. But stay, and I'll caress you till you burst'

'Aren't we sick? A director and a gay planning to make babies?'

'Discussing our longing, making life out of our dreams is not sick.'

'No?'

'No. It's Snow Queen business. It's real life. Using what we are, making what we are able to. Some is new, some, patched and mended. But isn't that life?'.

'Fiona, with you it could be.'

'Do you mean it?'

'I mean it. Sometimes I wake in the night frantic you've left. I put out an arm and find you. That's all I need. Then I can sleep again.

'Darling Graham, your passions are so extreme. Of course I'm beside you.'

'I need reassurance.'

'I'd flip (I nearly did on Christmas day) when I looked and couldn't find you.'

'And you say I'm extreme.'

'OK, OK. We both are.'

Much was unravelled. Yet much remained unsaid, some simply forgotten. Some of it crucial. Willy nilly it would taint the future.

Such words cocooned them as they packed up and left, changed cars at Jean's garage, and spun back to the Big Apple.

A slight emptiness of future haunted them. Somehow the frantic bustle of the city, ambition, acquisition, even the enjoyment of the many concerts exhibitions and shops couldn't exclude longing. The small dark echo of Snow Queen enticements challenged their days now.

Fiona rushed back to ACAA and was quickly submerged in all its machinations. Her work and business relations were firmer, clearer and more focused. Everyone welcomed her, even the few nigglers. 'Where had she been? Was her friend all right? Had life returned to its equilibrium?' many fondly asked. She nodded in her usual quiet non-committal way. 'Yes, everything is fine.'

But her close associates noticed a preoccupation usually covered by a minute soft private smile. Perhaps Fiona did have something on her mind. But she was back in fine form, that mattered most.

Graham, with several weeks before starting his new job, tried not to mope. He visited Carlos, Fiona's father's dapper tailor who cheerfully measured and ran appraising hands over him in the secluded fitting area of his shop in Little Italy, lisping complements about his handsome new client, his dazzling prospects surely echoing Signor Pinkham's majestic status, and dwelling on his daughter's perfection, bringing extra shine to this gorgeous boy.

'You and the Signora Pinkham are special friends?' Carlos whispered conspiritorially.

'Neighbours and friends, yes.' Graham blushed.

'Ah.' Carlos beamed. 'Special private. I say no word.'

'Thank you.'

'Your secrets safe.' Carlos tightened the measure round Graham's hips and winked. 'A little more show for her pleasure, just here. The trouser falling free down legs and breaking on your shoes. Ah, splendidamente. You come with your friend, Saturday for final fitting and I show you shoes shirts sox per un principe, her prince si?'

Graham's penis swelled. He wanted Saturday morning with her in bed.

As if reading his thoughts, Carlos murmured 'Late morning. I reserve a space for her car.' He eyed the young man, longing to caress him, to rescue a smile from his clouded features, to eat him up as surely as the Pinkhams would. More delicious dressed or undressed? He pondered the moody power of Graham's crotch delighting in both prospects then graciously escorted him out.

With little in his flat, Graham gravitated next door. Fiona's was filled with books pictures music and films, all unknown to him. He liked her books on Greek art, seeing himself in many of the bodies. Greek men and boys are unselfconscious and beautiful, he thought, remembering in Palmer's Place where he'd proudly displayed himself for the first time. 'They look like their gods.' he said, aware his god-ness was nascent yet aroused by a caress. Then he longed for her touch and for her desire. Longed to be a raging god breaking inside her, making storms of delight to blow away insecurity.

One afternoon he watched Shakespeare's *Macbeth*, recalling

Frederick's mention of witches and ambition. Graham thought the tale grim. 'The Macbeths are modern managers, without respect or care'. he mused. 'But are they like me, driven by fantasy rather than being objective? Here I am acting like a prince - trendy apartment, smart clothes, social connections - acting the dream-image rather than being the hick I am without a cent in my pocket or a brain in my head'. Graham thought the final deception of Birnam Wood coming to Dunsinane Hill and of his beheading by Macduff of strange birth, was real enough. 'Like Macbeth, when I meet the illusion in my life, I'll tumble too.' he said sadly.

He prepared supper most nights. Fiona ate tiredly, pottered around the flat and fell into bed too sleepy to respond to him. On Friday she hurried back with a meal and took him to bed. Saturday morning - his dream - she accepted his storm, lapping up his ardour, filling with delight until they could lie replete and confess the week's doings. She told him of her frenetic work, the demands of staff and directors, of imperious clients, the challenges each commission brought.

Graham mentioned the godlike Greeks, Macbeth's deluding witches, of his borrowed image: all her accoutrements of life-style, glamour and wealth, a tempting nightmare hiding his real self yearning for the Snow Queen life in enchanted woods with her, not the NYC version of a rich girl promoting a hick. Yet this too was a mask for his loneliness. He cried for loss of his inner god, for loss of Frederick, for missing the joy found in the icy forest, for diminishing hope which neither money nor power could sustain. Such weekends countered his darker thoughts.

Fiona kissed his sex awake. With godlike power he took her. They rocked and sweated towards release, freeing him in diverse ways. Eventually, smiling, she hugged him. 'Did you miss me all the time?'

He nodded. Healed. His hair brushed her breasts.

She ran her fingers around his sculpted ears. 'I missed you with the same craziness. Come on, I'll soap my Greek god in the shower, dress him, then, clad in Carlos' glad rags, I'll take him to the Metropolitan Museum of Art where he can meet his brothers and sisters who, without Carlos' clothes, display your beauty. But darling one, I do not want you naked on a pedestal or your sexy bum raked by spotlights.'

He snuggled, his heart slowing, more alive, breathing more quietly.

Fiona pushed him to arms length. 'Graham, all the books and

music and art can be yours. All the great dreams are there for anyone who cares about them, as you (and I) do. They are our immortality. The ageless spirit of mankind which the woods whisper about. It's not a question of privilege but of right. You deserve their flux as much as anyone. It's the strength you need.'

They drove down town, parked in the spot reserved for them and were feted by Carlos, who, dazzled by her money and Graham's youthful looks, tended them with passion.

The boot full of clothes, they drove to Upper East Side and the museum, sauntered through the new Classical galleries and the American portraits and drawings, then lunched.

Fiona looked enquiringly at Graham.

He grinned. 'Hey, this is real porn. I wanted to touch them where you fondle me.'

She laughed. 'It's odd. We allow nakedness only here. Is the real thing dangerous?'

Graham nodded. I used to think sharing was losing it. When my dad saw my butt he took it. Frederick gave it back with my cock. Frederick looked at me as I look at the statues. Admiration lust love worship. Yes, all that. You're right. I am more dangerous now I'm naked. Much happier.'

'More complete.'

'Yes Fiona.'

'Boy and girl. Active and passive. Gay and straight. A fuller man.'

'Dangerously wanting everything.'

'Exactly Graham. The real thing.'

'Really?'

'I think so.' She pushed her plate away. 'Tell me, I can see your description of Hiram Power's *Fisher Boy* as being a girlish Art with his manly hands by our lake in summer, but why is the woman in JG Brown's *Meditation* like me?'

'Your boyish face, your short hair, your strong nose, your succulent breasts peeping through the dress, the way you slump wanting me to push inside. And a sadness - are you thinking about something you can't tell anyone?'

She looked adoringly at him eyes brimming. 'I love you more and more. Shit, I try to control it. It floods me.'

'I'm glad you understand. With me, there are things I hold back. It's a lifetime of bruising. I don't know how to be naked with you yet without swamping you Fiona, without losing myself.'

'Darling, I want so much, it hurts. I wouldn't have it any other way. My happiness, my sense of coming home to you, the god who ravishes me, gifting inner peace. Are we finding a new sort of love? Something in real time? Graham, whatever it is, it matters.'

'I know.'

'Do you see now what I was telling you? Literature, art are keys to our dreams, our inner selves. Naked bodies, studies of trees, penises, rocks and oceans; all sacred; all essential although little allowed outside?'

'And our right to it?'

'Absolutely.'

'I hurt with love for you too, Fiona.'

'Now?'

'Less pain after sharing this morning: the sex, the shower, breakfast. Then the clothes, the museum, lunch with you. Perfect. I'm sorry about Christmas, I flipped.'

'Graham, we managed it together. Let's have Christmas another time.'

'When there's a bright star in the east.'

'When there's something to celebrate.'

'Can we visit the sculpture again before we go?'

'Perving on tits and bums?'

'Got to see them somewhere.'

'A turn-on?'

'Yes.'

'Will it keep till we get home?'

'If you drive very fast, one hand on the wheel the other busy between my legs.'

So, Saturday passed in a dream.

The days settled. Graham explored Fiona's books. She dashed home to be with him and began to share her favourite novels pictures and poems. She spurred on his delving into Shakespeare, suggesting *Twelfth Night* which concerned their own preoccupations with gender, image, love and word-play, extended by acting out Romeo and Juliet, avowing frankness and avoiding a double death. They made the exchanges in the play their own. New tenderness developed. The plays piled up beside the bed, dipped into between bouts of love making.

Fiona watched Graham grow, glad how plenteously he

143

responded to words and pictures and (to her surprise) how rich his attentions were becoming. 'You can see my own fascination with words and images. They represent the unsayables, the dark brilliance behind dreams. I'm not artistic enough to paint or write so I took on advertising instead. Selling is demeaning but it's great fun creating a campaign.' she murmured between kisses.

Graham, luxuriating in her caresses, grinned. 'Remember *Twelfth Night* ? I felt like Viola/Cesario with Orsino during our early meetings, unable to express my feelings for you, caught in the prison garb of gayness, of inferiority and shyness.'

She kissed the tip of his glans. 'It was difficult for you.'

He glowed. 'Yes. Rape had stripped my rights.'

She cupped the vulnerable softness of his testicles. 'Yet you filled me like no other.'

'You made me feel I could do anything.'

'Did I? It was better than a dream. It still is.'

'In exposing hidden bits you ignited my power.'

'The statues, plays, paintings?' She rolled his foreskin.

'Are mirrors reflecting myself . . Ah!' (he came).

Her mouth filled with his warm velvet balm. Soft as his thoughts, his eyes, his testicles. Shifting in the release of his essence, an icy shard implanted by former agony, melted. She swallowed. 'I like your taste.'

He combed her hair with his fingers. 'I love you taking me. No wonder Romeo couldn't leave Juliet.'

Her face fell. 'But Graham, you mustn't die.'

He relaxedly lay watching the weak winter sunshine clarifying the misted city. 'I don't want to.' He rolled over and kissed her rapturous mouth.

Eventually one morning, a dirty-old-man raincoat hiding his modish new suit, he presented himself at Gem Productions. The receptionist said flatly, 'Wait. I'll see if you're expected.'

Like a butterfly from its cocoon, Graham slipped out of his coat and stood watching the water, toned a chill February grey, contemptuously curl its lips at ferries plying to New Jersey.

The receptionist eying the sexy apparition with awe apologetically received Etienne's response: 'He works here. Give him a company lapel pin and send him up.' She timorously left her buzzing bleeping winking desk and solicitously pinned one to the perfectly cut lapel of a perfectly scrumptious young man.

Graham looked at her in surprise. Was she fawning? He grinned and bounded to the lifts.

Etienne's eyes glinted. He proprietarily pulled back the suit coat to inspect the label, keenly aware of the tight tummy and the youthful aroma. He blinked. 'Did I really suggest Carlos? You look, er fetching to say the least.'

Graham recognised the glint from Greenwich Village gay bars. He's undressing me, he thought uneasily. 'The best I could do.' he grinned and stepped away.

Etienne tiger-smiled. 'Tom was right. Your best is sumptuous. You've the style I'm looking for. Sit down Graham and I'll tell you what I want you to do.' To hide his lusty admiration Etienne pressed his intercom button asking his secretary to bring the envelope marked "Confidential". He wanted this gorgeous boy nearby. His property, in his team. This flash decision excited him.

He gave Graham the pages of a draft paper on restructuring. Etienne was fly. 'I need to keep a finger on this. There is an older scheme and I hope this will consolidate it. That's what I want you to find out. I want your opinion as an insider/outsider. And, Graham, no one, not a soul, must know what we're up to. OK?'

Graham nodded.

Etienne gazed at him. 'There's a desk in my secretary's annex for you. Pop in to my office whenever. Report only to me. It will serve as an introduction to the company. This afternoon I'll take you down to Personnel for induction into your other responsibilities. We'll be in touch. Let's discuss the report over lunch.'

Graham looked doubtful.

'It's first thoughts I want. And to get to know you.'

Etienne gently took his arm and shepherded him out, returning to his empty desk, glad the network had singled out such a juicy peach for him.

Etienne took Graham to a bijou restaurant catering for discrete rendezvous. Graham wondered if he was approved of: his face probably; his morning's work probably not. For Etienne seemed disappointed in Graham's remarks that the report was only a summary of the team and the basic approach to the task, and without any conclusions.

Etienne sipped his red wine. 'That's what I gathered. I wondered if there were coded messages in the text.'

Graham regarded the cold glint in his eyes. 'It seems straight forward. They decided excellence should influence their deliberations.'

Etienne looked severe. 'Nothing else?'

Graham was defensive. "Only my impression after a morning trawling through it.'

Etienne relaxed. 'Thank you Graham. It's mine after several evenings. Eat up. Then I'll tell you what we do next.'

Graham had ordered lobster thermidor with a mixture of pleasure and pain.

Etienne raised an eyebrow. 'Not to your taste?'

'No no. Um, I've had better.'

Etienne was intrigued by the shadows flitting across the boy's handsome face. Salaciously he probed. Graham told him of his Maine holiday with Frederick, and the charmed evenings at Palmer's Place.

Etienne noticed the catch in his voice. 'Frederick?'

'A dear friend.'

'Very special?'

'Very.'

Etienne never let silence stop him. 'Still together?'

Graham looked blindly away. 'He's dead.'

'When my present partner lost the love of his life I caught him on the rebound.'

'I wanted to die.'

Etienne was uncomfortable with searing sincerity. It threatened his bubble of wealth-tinged appearances. He had dealt with pain in others by remaining uninfected. This occasion was no exception. He took the boy's beautiful hand and said gently. 'I'm truly sorry. But my dear, there is life after death. You must come to dinner sometime and meet Ed. I take it someone saved your life?'

Graham nodded. He cried. In his inner dark he saw Frederick and Fiona. Both had saved him. Right now he was in desperate need of them. He longed for the grandeur of the Maine coast, the silence of snow, their life-giving arms. He wanted his glass ticket office bowl to protect him, until, with a start, he acknowledged the present predicament. He remembered Carlos' quip: "Wear your clothes like a proud toreador and outwit the bulls of life." He blew his nose and dared a glance at his steely boss. 'Thanks Etienne. Tell me what you'd like next.'

Etienne ached with admiration. This spunky boy must be

devastating in bed, he thought letting go the captive hand. He relented. 'Finish your lobster. I'll fill you in during desert.' although you're sweet enough for the two of us, he thought. He blinked. Had he spoken aloud? The boy was regarding him with so curious a mix of gladness and pain - like a repulsed lover - that Etienne forgot who was in charge and why; forgot office affairs and Wall Street scandals in a flood of tenderness he'd not experienced for years.

The treasures in this prized-open box disturbing him were all the abandoned bits of himself, but alive and kicking. Graham's reputation was indeed well founded. He would fondly exploit the boy, maybe bequeath him a part of Gem Productions if he could bed him. It was a devious and challenging plan from which everyone benefited.

He watched Graham eat. Able hands deftly dealing with rubbery lobster drenching bits in creamy sauce (thick and warm as his cum, Etienne imagined), sensual lips dripping with cream, eyes shaded by cascading locks, deep and brown and girlishly demure; and rest of this blooming body he'd avidly studied in the office, its lithe succulence belying virginity pleasantly aroused Etienne. In a haze of admiration he finished his desert and embarked on coffee before managing to outline his latest plans: to add Graham to the cabal working on restructuring and so keep an eye on its deliberations, in order to be forewarned.

'You see Graham, I need time to digest the recommendations before the directors meet.'

Graham didn't see but nodded.

Etienne sipped his cognac. 'I'd like to keep you near. Temporarily with my secretary. How are you getting along with Mavis?'

'She mothers me. She's sweet.'

'Good. Then stay there. No harm in being seen as Management, or as my protege. Report only to me. When the time comes I'll move you and adjust your salary. You've done well this morning. You will be rewarded.'

After lunch Etienne introduced Graham to a production team working on the promotion of a new perfume range. There were pictures of flutes grand houses and bewigged gentry on the walls.

Bruce, the leader, warmly shook hands. Anna and Cathy smiled. Amory nodded distractedly.

Etienne regally announced, 'Graham will be half-time on the FG project from now, conferring with me regularly on management issues, plus a position on the restructuring committee, meeting today at 4PM. Bruce or someone take him to room 7071.' Abruptly he left.

Cathy giggled. 'Gee gee, our 'G' at last. We only need an 'F' now to complete the picture.'

Graham was nonplussed.

Bruce groaned. 'Horses for courses Cath dear. Come over Graham, I'll explain the campaign. FG is a new line of perfume and accessories. It's great to have you on board. A surprise bonus. No one told me you were coming. Good, you can help us keep our fillies in order (Cathy and Anna cheerfully grimaced.) Anyway, don't forget we have Felicity as our 'F'. Where is she?'

Anna grinned. 'With Felicity, we'll keep the cock and bulls in order.'

Graham laughed. It was suddenly lighter after a morning heavy with invisible threat. He took his jacket off and hung it over the back of a chair. 'So, tell a dumbo what's the connection between flutes, palaces , wigs and FG?'

Amory's face cleared. 'We don't know who chose FG. Are they initials of the GM's wife? Who cares. Anyway, we began looking for connections, for associations, nudging the scent starved shoppers' memories and came up with Frederick the Great. He was a flautist prince of the eighteenth century. Knew the great Bach and Telemann and Bach's son Carl Philipp Emanuel. It's early days, so any bright ideas, Graham, would be devoured with gratitude.' He stopped. 'Anything wrong, Graham?'

Graham's face was ashen. That Etienne, after the lunch time confession, had deliberately tossed him into hell, was devastating. "You'll be rewarded" he'd promised. Rather, hollow careless cruelty.

Graham's jaw tightened. He'd be a fearless toreador with only his rapier in the abandoned bull ring. He was no Macbeth confused by witches' babble. He would fight. "Lay on Macduff and cursed be him . . ." he said angrily.

'Eh?' Amory said.

Graham took the deepest breath before diving into hell. 'I was telling Etienne over lunch, my dearest friend died at Christmas. His name was Frederick. And here I am.'

Cathy left her computer, wide-eyed. 'He's brutal.'

Graham nodded.

Brian put an arm round his trembling shoulders. 'Let's make it

In Memoriam, Graham.'

'We'll make him your king.' Anna said tearfully.

Graham looked at them all and relented. 'The only things I know about Frederick the Great are that his mentor was JJ Quantz, the most famous flautist of the day, and that JS Bach wrote his Musical Offering based on one of Frederick's own themes. He was king of Prussia with a glittering court of musicians. (so Fiona's CD stated). Thanks Bruce. Actually an *In Memoriam* might help me put him to bed.' He gulped. 'I'm glad to be here. Hope I can help. Very glad.'

'Sorry I'm late.' A delicate energetic girl entered. A pert nose, ample breasts and a boyish body. Sparkling blue eyes regarded them. 'Hello. I don't think we've met. I'm Felicity Corhart.' She smiled at Graham. 'I was thinking about shepherds.' she said. 'The first pipers. Dancing sheep, rolling in the hay. All that kind of stuff.'

Graham warming to her joyfulness said:

> *When shepherds pipe on oaten straws*
> *And merry larks are ploughmen's clocks,*
> *When turtles tread, and rooks and daws*
> *And maidens bleach their summer smocks . . .*

'Must be Shakespeare.' Felicity said. 'Daddy would know. Is it?'

'Yes. The song ends *Love's Labour's Lost*.' Graham murmured.

Amory beamed. 'I like "oaten straws". Felicity, draw some straws spouting FG scent into a horn of plenty.'

Bruce looked around him triumphantly. 'Marvellous: shepherds' pipes, oaten straws, musical offerings. Wow, what a brain storming! And let's add more private memories, Graham's scent of sadness and maidens mourning the passing of summer. Amory, look out Quantz's music for a theme tune. Anna, check Prussia - soldiers, Chopin, Graham's "talented court". Felicity, you were late so get us all tea.'

'Oh, Bruce, always thirsting for more.' Felicity roundly laughed.

Graham went with her. 'Let me help.'

Unaware of his recent pain, she smiled: not simpering over his good looks. A friendly, Fionaish smile.

Graham watched her. She was in the bull ring with him, careless of danger, busying herself making six cups of tea. He gladdened.

Graham relished working on the FG project. The others realised he'd been thrown in at the deep end and, finding him clever and imaginative, eased him into the skills necessary to deal with computer-based work. He had a keen eye - probably from studying paintings with Fiona - so Felicity, the team's graphic artist, consulted him.

She told him of the Golden Mean. He grew excited over this Greek measure to which humans and plants relate. He liked the notion of everything growing up in golden ways. Felicity was charmed by his enthusiasm, arranging a trip to the Metropolitan Museum of Art, 'researching' (she announced) Classical themes for the FG images.

At the museum, some of Graham's reticence fell away. His lascivious enthusiasms stirred her. Whistles blew as she touched succulent marble buttocks. Flustered attendants descended growling cautions. Smiling, she skipped out of the gallery, taking him to the cafe 'To review progress' (as she put it).

Felicity laughed. 'You're right. Bare bodies must be caressed. Let's put a FG spray in one hand, the other, questing as we wanted to.' She swam in his warm brown eyes. 'Even the stiff old gays in Gem Productions will sit up.'

Graham looked sheepish. 'Can we get away with it? Fiona says nakedness is only possible in art galleries.'

Tantalising glimpses are acceptable. Anyway, Bruce knows the rules.' She eyed him carefully. 'Is Fiona your partner?'

'Yes.'

'Do you mind me asking?'

'No, Felicity. You need to know if we're friends.'

'You mean, so I don't haul you into bed?'

'So our friendship isn't over-complicated.'

'I wouldn't do that, anyway. Unless we both wanted.'

She saw a tremor in his cheek and recalled mention of Frederick. 'You loved Frederick, didn't you.'

He nodded dejectedly.

'Dear Graham, I won't hurt you. Not ever. I'm glad you can love. It's the true partner of nakedness.'

Graham was surprised. 'Yes, perhaps it is. It makes sense Felicity. Do you know, I've struggled to be naked ever since,' He hesitated. 'Ever since I was a boy, always feeling ashamed. Frederick and Fiona let me show myself. Saw me as myself. Yes, you're right, it's bound up with love.'

Felicity thrilled with pleasure. 'There's a lot of nakedness which doesn't involve sex. Let's agree our friendship contains some of that.'

The struggle in his face confounded her. Perhaps lust confused him. She accepted it more easily. Is he running away from something in his past? she wondered. She already liked him immensely. She wanted to caress him like the statues, feel his chamois skin, dribble FG scent over it and float away on an aromatic cloud. But she was careful as his warnings signalled.

Their friendship grew.

Work at Gem Productions threw them together. In addition to the FG project each sat on the Restructuring committee where work was guarded and opinions often obtuse. Graham had the suspicion there were other spies, as snippets of gossip surfaced in Etienne's *tête-à-têtes*. No wonder people were careful.

He admired Felicity's candour. Her thoughts and conclusions were manna for serious debate. In emulating her he inadvertently became the group's spokesperson until Sue, the middle aged chair would consult him about items in the minutes. Mavis enjoyed the frisson of her crowded secretarial annex. Etienne was gratified by the proximity of the work. 'Our young man brings the mountain to Mohammed.' he murmured to Mavis who nodded smiling uncomprehendingly.

Felicity and Graham often lunched together. Either sharing sandwiches over work in the FG project room or in Battery Park. Toni, manning the kiosk there, watched out for them on sunny days. He chuckled disbelievingly when they told him, 'No, we're not students but executives in a big company, look, in that building over there.'

'The tea's on the house.' he'd say.

They would stroll away with arms length intimacy, Toni fondly whispering, 'Do they know how fetching they are? Ah, what beautiful babies they'd make.' Turning heads in the queue with lewd grins and increasing appetites.

'Beautiful and good for business.' a burly gardener remarked.

Graham treated Felicity to lunch on her birthday. Basking in a wine tinged haze she blurted out, 'I'm going home to Ithaca next week-end. Would you like to come Graham? Daddy's at the university. We have a big house just off campus. Simon, my little brother, and I had a playroom which now has a spare bed you could use. Wouldn't it be fun?'

He longed to go. 'I'm not sure.'

'I'd like you to come. It's nothing grand. Jeans and jumpers and a toothbrush.'

'Pyjamas, surely?'

Felicity guffawed. 'Oo yes. Better not shock Mummy. Although Simon parades his nakedness often enough. You'll like him; Daddy too. He's a professor of Literature and loves Shakespeare. Simon's twelve. He'll grill you about our sex life and insist you play football with him. Fob him off. We could listen to *The Musical Offering*, some Telemann, Quantz and get out books on Greek art, and moon about outside. Graham, wouldn't it be nice - away from here - lunch in the park but all weekend?'

'I would like that.'

'Is it Fiona?'

'I should ask. We usually spend weekends together.'

'Only weekends?'

'During the week we're rather bombed out.'

'Will she disapprove?'

'No. She knows about you and pleased we're friends.'

'Then she won't mind. Ask her before I ring home.'

He raised his glass. 'Happy birthday, Felicity.'

'Oh Graham, you're the only one in New York who knows.' She smiled happily and squeezed his hand.

Fiona was touched he had asked about the weekend. 'We've independent lives, dear one. You look so excited of course you should go. Perhaps they'll be another family for you. Anyway, Felicity will take care of you, I'm sure. Let's dig out an overnight bag. Careful your suit doesn't get crushed.'

He gratefully kissed her. She hoped this was the prelude to a storm of thanks later. She idly wondered what Felicity's motives were in taking him home. It's an agony watching him grow up, she thought, tucking a CD of Shakespeare's songs in his bag for Professor Corhart and a pre-release bottle of scent designed at APAA for Mrs Corhart. 'And get the boy a soccer shirt in the airport.' she said smiling. 'Be your charming self, and remember, since Felicity likes you, they certainly will. Be careful, my pet, you're still mourning. Come back to me in one piece.'

He nodded, secretly vowing great care.

Their aeroplane was dwarfed by NYC Airport. A flea of a plane in amongst the pterodactyl big bellied intercontinental ones. But well suited to the tiny Ithaca airport. In the diminutive lobby, Felicity waved and hurried towards her mother in a bulky duffel coat and bright head scarf, accompanied by a beaming boy his red and white track suit visible under his hooded jacket.

'Mummy, Simon,this is Graham . . . supper and hot drinks sound marvellous. The ride here was OK. It's been a tough week. Mummy, you'd not approve, but Simon would: we've been reviewing nude Greek tits and bums like in Daddy's art books. You silly boy, do you think Gem Productions is a nudist colony?' She laughed.

Simon sniggered, Graham smiled. Mrs. Corhart was not amused.

'Mummy, it's fine art. The stuff in galleries.'

'Well leave it there.' her mother snapped. 'It's a cold evening, let's get you home. Welcome Graham. Eric, my husband and Simon are looking forward to football and Shakespeare. I guess you'll sort that out.' She smiled at him thinking, What a handsome boy Felicity's found for a change. She followed her prancing son to an ancient Volvo. Simon directed Graham to the front passenger seat and fell with a giggle into the back with his sister.

'You two, behave.' Mrs. Corhart said unconvincingly.

Graham thought the high jinks a loving teasing frolic. He wanted to join, but turned dutifully away. 'Mrs Corhart, is Cornell an interesting campus?'

'Interesting, Graham? Steep, better for skiing than walking.'

'Oh, I meant talks and ideas, all that university stuff.'

'I suppose I don't mind it. They are able students. Not as colourful these days.'

'I met some Cornell students from micro biology last summer in Maine.'

'The sciences attract the brains, Eric - Professor Corhart - tells me. He complains Arts freshers don't know the difference between (Now, what did he say?) between a hypotenuse and a hyperbole.'

Graham grinned. 'They're types of Indian and African hippopotamus, aren't they?'

She laughed.

Simon and Felicity froze. Rarely did their mother laugh. They secretly blessed Graham. It could become a fun weekend.

Traipsing up the back steps into the house Mrs. Corhart smiled at Graham. 'I've made a bed for you in the children's' old playroom. Simon, show him where.'

Simon eagerly took Graham into a large airy room and shyly watched him change into tee shirt jeans and smart warm jumper. He looks great, no wonder Sis fancies him, the boy thought.

'Oh, here. I got this for you.' Graham handed him an airport bag.

'Wow.' the boy breathed. 'A shirt saying "Pelé 10" The best footballer ever.' Excitedly he pulled off his clothes, glad to be seen, and donned the shirt; leaping up heading an imaginary ball. 'Gee, thanks. It's fab.' He looked winningly at Graham. 'Pelé's my hero. My friend at school has films of him. He'll be mad with envy. You can hang your suit in my cupboard if you like. Come on, I'll show you.'

He liked Graham. It was more than the shirt or making Mummy laugh, he seemed more available in jeans and jumper; like the woodsmen adventurers Simon hero-worshiped. Graham was real out of his suit of city armour, the well built man Simon wanted to be.

Simon's admiration was not lost on either of them. Candid and appraising, they smiled for one another. Dribbling an imaginary ball the boy led Graham to supper.

'Professor Corhart's eyes twinkled. 'So, you've joined a water polo team, son?'

Simon snorted. 'Edson Arantes do somethingorother is the greatest footballer.'

' . . . do Nascimento, alias Pelé.' his father said gently.

Simon's eyes widened. 'How do you know?'

'I saw him play.'

Simon was doubtful. 'No.'

'In Italy. Brazil vs Madrid. Pelé was unbelievable.'

'Dad, I didn't know you liked football.'

'When I was your age it was all I dreamed of. But, too young for girls too slow a player, I settled for books.' He smiled at his open mouthed son. 'Graham, we're all speechless (and that's seldom). Such appropriate presents: the first footballer, the first scent, the first playwright. Generous and unexpected. Thank you. Let me give you and Felicity more wine.'

Simon was rubbing his eyes by the end of the meal resisting leaving for bed until Graham intervened. 'Teeth, pyjamas and bed and I'll tell you a story.'

Simon grinned. 'Count to a hundred then come and see.' He scampered to the bathroom.

Graham found him by his bed naked but for his Pelé shirt.

'I'll keep it on.'

'The pros. air it between games to freshen up. Let's put yours on the peg behind your door.'

Simon raised his arms dutifully, stood naked graceful and undismayed. Graham blushed at his beauty. 'You could be a Greek.' he murmured retrieving pyjamas from under the boy's pillow.

Simon was emboldened by Graham's interest. Pelé fire licked his body. He shimmeyed into his pyjamas and dived under the duvet. 'Is it a football story?'

'No. But it's about someone who adores football and likes adventures. A boy almost as beautiful as you, Simon. Shall I tell you?'

The boy's smile blazed. He nodded.

Once upon a time a boy playing in the garden kicked his ball high high in the air (almost up to the moon). It fell in a thicket nearby.

The boy scrambled and wriggled and squirmed and twisted in and in and in, right through the tangled mass towards a pale glimmer he thought was his ball.

Twigs ripped his Pelé shirt, scratched his bare legs and face. Rough stones cut his knees and hands. He lay still and sore and bleeding. As his breathing settled he felt better if a bit lost.

A growly pleasant voice said. 'Hello, Simon. By my furry ears, you are a headstrong fellow. That was a great kick. Your football pulling down fluffy clouds and bumping my head. Why didn't you ask me to roll your ball out rather than making such a bloody mess?'

The boy gulped - it was rude to say "bloody mess" but luckily no one was about. He looked at his damaged hands and legs and understood and giggled and felt better, if nervous. For who was addressing him? In a clearing at the centre of the thicket, caught in cloudy fluff, sat an elderly raccoon rubbing his head and holding the boy's ball and smiling from ear to fury ear. He leaned forward and pulled the boy up and dabbed his wounds with a large leathery leaf until the scars disappeared. He offered the boy a soothing draught of sugary maple sap which made his eyes shine as brightly as his teeth, so recently cleaned. In fact, the boy felt stronger and faster and taller than ever. The raccoon tut tutted over his torn Pelé shirt and brusqly ordered a host of spiders to get busy and spin threads and repair the gashes. The boy, who didn't particularly like spiders crawling over him, giggled as, with all the spinning and weaving and mending, they tickled him.

'I think I should go.' the boy said.

'Finish your drink and I'll show you out.' said the raccoon.

The boy gulped the rest of the maple sap, and as he said 'Thank you', the thicket sprang back making a path down which the boy strode (as if going from dressing room to pitch). Soon, he stood in the open.

'Hey, Simon, want your ball?'

He turned. The ball was rolling towards him. He moved like lightening and kicked it into play.

'What are you up to?' his mother cried. 'Keep away from those thickets. There's many a ball lost in them.'

'Yes Mum, and finding them leaves you in a bloody mess.'

His mother frowned until realising it was not bad language but a true description of how knees and arms could get. But she groaned all the same. 'Come in now. It's getting late. Time for bed.'

'Yes Mum.' the boy said resignedly. He heard a low raccoon-like chuckle from the thicket. 'Sleep well, Simon. With sleep, you'll play even better tomorrow.'

The boy grinned. His new friend was quite right. And do you know, for the very first time, he skipped cheerfully inside?

After a breathing moment Graham bent and kissed the flawless forehead through its luxurious curls. Simon's arms emerged from the covers. He wrapped them round Graham's neck. 'I like having new friends.'

Graham blinked. 'So do I.' he said softly, and stole back to the others.

Felicity glanced up from the table. 'You've usurped my job as baby sitter, Graham. Your magic is better than all my coaxing.'

Graham smiled. 'Simon's as sweet and gentle as you and almost as beautiful.'

Felicity's heart raced. Unintentional though it might have been, the message thrilled her. But not as beautiful as you, she thought.

Professor Corhart chuckled. 'Margaret calls you "our snake charmer." Her little darling can wriggle out of anything except, it seems, your promise of a story. You see, my dears, we need stories even in this age of digital images. Come Graham. Let's leave our pretty ladies to clear up. I'll show you my story books.'

After the men left, her mother slyly eyed Felicity. 'Fond of him?'

Felicity sighed. 'Lots Mummy. He charmed Simon like he does the cruel queens in the office. He's different with me. But who is the real person? It scares me sometimes.'

'How well do you, er, know him?'

'I think I know him quite well - we spend a lot of time together. Yet I don't know anything. He's a special friend, one without a shadow.

He needs yet doesn't need me, and I'd trust him with my life.'

'So, you're serious. Are you, er, intimate?'

Felicity parried (as Graham would). 'Mummy that's private. But I like him immensely.'

Margaret Corhart nodded. 'We all do, darling. And that's a good start.'

Professor Corhart subtly probed his daughter's relationship to this handsome young man in the rich, parent-neutral arena of literature.

Graham's preoccupation with sexuality surfaced in their discussion about *Twelfth Night*:

'You ask whether it's a play about appearances - a girl dressed as a boy, the Fool actually a wise man, the responsible Steward a bumbler.' Graham said. 'But music and love are the first words spoken. Furthermore, love is threaded through the text like a musical theme. (he and Fiona had agreed).'

The professor nodded.

'It's clear that Count Orsino loves Cesario his new page boy; that Viola loves Orsino; that Olivier loves Cesario (Viola disguised); that Antonio loves Sebastian. Surely Cesario, putting on "women's weeds", is a subterfuge cloaking the fuller nature of Orsino's love for an attentive boy?' Graham was intense. 'Olivier's love for a girlish boy is resolved only by wedding her twin brother. The complexities of Olivier's and Orsino's love remain. It's a changing of appearances not a fundamental alteration that make the matches acceptable. In that sense you are right.'

The professor stabbed a finger on the last page. 'Feste's final song is about the cycle of life from a tiny boy to a death bed, "For the rain it raineth every day", our distress has always existed. Yes, Graham. It seems Shakespeare would include the various aspects of love in this cycle. So, what is your point?'

'He seems to be saying love is a bundle of emotions. That a man loves the boy in a woman as a woman loves the girl in a man. Does love embrace both masculine and feminine, and as reflections of ourselves?'

The professor looked up. 'That we're blinder than love to its variety. Yes, *Twelfth Night* queries our obsession with appearances. Orsino and Olivier were in love with an image of a boy (spurred by hidden qualities), Malvolio didn't see through the Fool, or know himself. So, what about your loves, Graham?'

Graham studied the kindly face. 'I'm like Shakespeare, I think.'

'So you like the Simon bit of Felicity and the Felicity in Simon.'

'Um, yes.'

'Well, I must say, it's a rich unusual love.'

'Scorned by many.'

'The many who also scorn peace and abhor ideas.'

'Daddy dear, peace and ideas should be put to bed now. Poor Graham came for a rest not a lecture.'

Her father wrinkled his nose. 'No rest for the wicked, Felicity dear.'

'Daddy, he's not that bad a snake charmer.'

'Felicity, Graham's bright, entertaining and lecturing me on love and Shakespeare. By all means, take him to bed.'

'Daddy, we're friends.'

'Yes, my dear. Old enough to decide such things. Graham, I'll dig out Athol Fugard's play *The Road to Mecca*, concerned with love, friendship and time. It ponders whether the quality of friendship (or love) is dependent on the length of the relationship. He's yours, Felicity. Good night my dears.'

Felicity shyly took Graham's hand. They drifted through the darkened house and into the garden. He looked up. 'The stars involve so many stories I don't know.'

'Did Daddy grill you about us?'

'In a thoughtful way, yes.'

'I told Mummy to mind her own business. I hate meddling.'

He pulled her into a close hug and touched her nose with his. 'You're lucky they care.'

She kissed him yearningly, fully, a lingering sally, savouring his thrill of desire yet demurely abandoning him at his bedroom door for her simple and familiar bed.

Graham woke suddenly. Sunlight sheened the garden, flooding the room. Simon stood waiting in his shorts and Pelé shirt. 'Can we play before breakfast?'

Graham rolled out of bed and, conscious of the boy's interest, donned shorts and a tee shirt. They carried their shoes so as not to clump around and wake the others. They tip toed into a chorus of birds and dewy grass. The sun was unusually hot.

They kicked the ball about, tiring. Graham kicked high. Simon leapt up and headed the ball into the swimming pool. Grinning complicitly he stripped and jumped in. Graham followed. The water was very cold but they frolicked and frothed and snorted and threw the ball about, soon climbing out with chattering teeth to huddle in the sun where Felicity came, camera and towels in hand.

The boys dried each other, got excited. Felicity snapped them, reassuring her little brother. 'The Greeks are naked and proud like you. Beautiful as gods. Not afraid of friendship.'

Simon was elated. His gods were naked or in football shirts. It was a perfect start to the day. After breakfast he pedalled over to his friends, bringing them back for fun in the garden, far too busy to be interested in Graham and Felicity sharing a hammock under the trees.

Felicity spoke about growing up, of Halloween, of having girl friends staying over, of summer swim parties, barbecues and of water fights with her brother. Stories punctuated by her tracing Graham's eye brows with curious fingers, and listening to the thump of his heart. His long legs entwined with hers, the bulge in his shorts craving caress - his favourite, she learned. His hand cupping her breast - it was hers. Intimacy, reaffirming weeks of friendship, stoked up longing. Talk dried as bodies took over.

Graham hurried inside to urinate. Mrs. Corhart inveigled him into helping with lunch preparations. His tasks completed, she trapped him with questions about his friendship with Felicity. He was shocked by the suspicion she had watched them talking in the hammock and disapproved. Questions, questions, hidden judgements, all buzzed like aggressive wasps stinging him. He fell apart.

'Listen, Mrs. Corhart, don't accuse me of being sly and deceitful, treating Felicity as a sort of sex toy. I never would. We're friends. We told you. It's not like that.

'I know most people are casual and callous over sex. I've never been. It's been a struggle to escape my rape as a boy Simon's age. Grim. Hopeless. You can't know the guilt, the agony of years of nightmares. The terrible loss.' He was sweating. 'I like Felicity very much as a dear friend, not a sexual toy. Why should we be ashamed of anything? It's not what you think. It's not.' He couldn't see clearly. The world whirled. His head spun as Mrs. Corhart fled the kitchen.

Graham cried a little. In anger. In regret not wanting a row. He wanted to abandon his shadows. Was there no escape? In the chaos of his perplexity Fiona whispered, "Take care my beautiful Graham and come back safely to me." With all his strength, gained from the love she and

Frederick had bestowed on him, he pulled himself together. Perhaps her problem is worse than mine, he thought timidly going in search of her.

She was hunched on the sofa in the empty living room. She gazed at him in horror as he stammered. 'I'm so so sorry Mrs. Corhart. I'm really happy here with you all. You are right to worry. Of course Felicity is precious to you. To me too.' He fell silent. She was so distrait he sat beside her anxious to prevent another collapse.

Mrs. Corhart swallowed. Weakly she shook her head and croaked. 'To both of us. Of course she is. I've never told anyone I was brutally raped by my first boyfriend. I know how you feel. One's soul destroyed. All sense of self one's hopes gone, just as you told me. The evil is everywhere and nowhere. That I expected it from you makes me deeply ashamed. My daughter's trusted friend, her joy - I see it in her face, Simon's too. What can I say. How can you ever forgive me?' Too stricken to weep she took his hand, a last straw.

But they didn't drown. Finally she managed to say. 'Can you forgive me?'

Graham squeezed her hand.

'Graham?'

'Yes. There's nothing to forgive. It was a glimpse of hell. We can cope, eh?'

She nodded cried blew her nose and struggled to her feet. 'I keep a curtain across the window, hell frightens me.'

He grimaced. 'The world's not much comfort.'

'A curtain in front helps.'

'Friends help more Mrs Corhart.'

'I'm glad for you.'

'Friends like you and your family.'

'Oh, Graham. The children dote on you. We all do.'

'Your care matters, Mrs. Corhart. To them and me.'

'Thank you dear.'

They walked back to the kitchen arm in arm. It was then she realised how impossibly complicated her children's' lives were.

He was stunned to find he loved Felicity, and Fiona; that Professor Corhart had shrewdly suggested Fugard's play because it told him both were enriching.

Over lunch the family plotted a grand candle-lit feast as Felicity's delayed birthday supper. Offered the Volvo, Graham agreed to assist present-shopping by Simon, a self-appointed, enthusiastic guide to Ithaca.

Felicity, with intimations of the earlier row, saw the beaming pair off, glad for them both. 'Si needs a big brother, Graham hungers for admiration, he's stunning when he's happy.' she said to herself as she tripped inside to gently shoo her father to his study then help her mother.

Gratified by Graham's interest, Simon guided them through the streets of delicate original clap-board buildings. They parked opposite one, now a chic shoe shop where Simon selected sandals to go with the summer dress from her parents. The boy's face fell on hearing the price. He was grateful when the "rich executive from the Big Apple" helped him out. He was more grateful still receiving sox with Brazil coloured tops and a pair of stretch boxers - the support Pelé surely had? To the amusement of the proprietor Simon left the shop wearing everything, and clutching a bag with his old sox and underpants and a tee shirt he'd surreptitiously added which said "Catch Me" for Graham and Felicity. They bought a Brazilian flag for his bedroom wall. On the way to the car, a homely cafe enticed them in for muffins and hot chocolate where the boy unburdened himself about larks with friends on their bikes; of peeping at a girl in the bath, sharing ribald laughter; of the rich variety of the seasons in his garden, adding, 'In spring, beyond the thickets, there's a tiny stream with tadpoles. That wasn't in my story.'

Graham chuckled. 'The story was a summer story.'

Simon grinned. 'We only see raccoons in winter.'

'They hide in the thickets with all the lost balls.'

Simon was edgy. 'When I was little, we used to hide there and take it in turns to have twigs poked into our bottoms. Don't tell!'

'Simon, I have such secrets. But the thicket in our story had a raccoon who liked you very much and admired your ball skills.'

Simon sighed. 'You're clever. And Felicity.'

Graham wanted to kiss the frown from his fresh face. 'Look at your dad. He was too young for girls and turned to books because he was too slow a footballer. Aren't you better than that?'

The boy nodded. 'Do you and Felicity . .you know . . do it?'

Graham was baffled by the common interest of the family. 'Simon, each of us does it with others. Felicity and I decided to be friends, And that's how it is.'

'Don't you like her that way?'

'I like her every way.'

'I thought so. Anyway, I'm glad you're friends.'

'Are we friends too?'

'Oh yes. I wouldn't talk like this to just anybody.'

Graham was almost tearful. The boy offered himself in the same way he'd once presented his butt to others, offering the treasures of his body. Whereas Simon offered his secrets in trust. It was innocent, beautiful and deeply touching.

The boy yearned to exchange secrets, that's why he asked intimate questions - secrets like seeds, given and harboured. A love so pure Graham ached with appreciation. How could he explain to Simon they were lovers? Yet the fiery joy in the boy dancing back to the car was confirmation, if any were needed.

Arriving home, the shopping bags were upended, the sandals secreted away with the other presents, and the smelly sox and underpants lobbed into the laundry basket.

'The tee shirt's for you two.' Simon said diffidently.

Felicity giggled. 'It's too small for both of us.'

'No. Take it in turns. Here, open it.'

She read, "Catch Me" and grinned. 'I like that.' Then turned it over. "If you can". She guffawed. 'That's him.' Pulling Graham's shirt off she spied a livid graze on his shoulder. 'Ugh, that looks nasty.'

'I dived to save the game. One of Pelé's fast curling deliveries. Me and the tree headed it over the bar. The tree got a yellow card.' Graham said.

Simon chortled.

'Simon, be an angel, get the bruise cream from the cupboard.' Felicity said.

Simon ran like the wind, watched her squeeze a white worm onto her finger and tenderly anoint the bruise spreading the surplus over chest and nipple, carefully ease the "Catch Me - If you Can" tee shirt over his head smoothing it over Graham's naked torso, saw a flicker of lust pass between them and secretly acknowledged they liked each other in every way. It was not so much a thought but his pounding feet proclaiming it as he dashed to his room to pin the Brazilian flag on his wall in a world which sang for him.

The party was a success. Everyone wallowed in delights. Wine winked in glasses, candle light glowed on skin and danced in eyes. Conversation was good humoured pointed yet placatory, as tasty as the food. When Felicity donned her dress and sandals there was a momentary hush. Simon spoke for them all. 'Sis, you look stunning.' The party brought each of them unexpected gifts. By the end, everyone felt stunned and stunning and floated cheerfully to bed.

Graham woke with a start. Unusually restless, he lay for a time hoping the nocturnal shadows in the garden would lull him back to sleep. But to no avail. He rose and padded to the kitchen, opened the fridge and, light blinded, found a carton of milk. He took a tumbler off the sink and filled it, in the gloom, to overflowing, hurriedly sucking before drinking properly. There was movement at his elbow. 'I can't sleep either.' Felicity whispered. Thrilled, he turned and offered her a sip. Breath mingled. She willed herself into his arms.

Hastily he pulled the cord of his pyjama pants, lifted her nighty and edged his erection between her thighs. She lifted her hips admitting him. They yearned for each other. She reached behind to steady them, found the box of cherry liqueurs he'd brought her from Ithaca and popped one into his mouth. 'It's the last one. It's yours.' she whispered. He thrust deeply. She kissed him fervently.

'Take it.' Graham murmured pushing the sticky chocolate ball into her mouth.

Felicity gasped and gurgled, smearing his lips with chocolate saliva.

He leaned back and pushed urgently holding her against the bench.

'Ah.' Felicity trembled. 'I've swallowed it.'

Sweet longing melted him.

'Graham, let's go to your room. No one will hear us there.'

He broke free, his body screaming for more. She led him through the sleeping house and into the old playroom bathed in moonlight, secure behind the firmly shut door and fell with him onto the lukewarm bed.

He lay for an endless delicious moment lashed by her frantic caresses his body burnt by lust until, unable to delay, he rolled her over, pushed her on her back and plunged in, in, in, in.

She cried softly, so pitifully he stayed his thrusting.

'Graham I came.'

'Hold onto it and come again.'

'I can't.'

Try. Stay with me, Felicity. Stay!'

He held himself over her tensing his buttocks swelling his phallus panting slightly, urging her response.

Felicity shivered as an enveloping softness filled her. It was sweeter than chocolate, more pungent than liqueur, an essence she knew only in dreams, a beauty so utterly undeniable she shimmered as orgasm fed orgasm until she burst, wave upon wave. All the beauty, energy and mystery of the world shook her. She was lost in herself, barely aware of Graham as a person or his phallus as an object. She seemed a part of his pulsing as he was wracked by hers.

Vaguely she knew he'd begun his final dance. His pace quickened. His flesh eagerly seeking her centre. Felicity lifted her belaboured hips offering everything. With an overwhelming lunge he burst. Her delicious storms gradually waned. He lay emptied beside her. In wonder she turned into him. Together they slept.

When he woke she was gone.

As Graham was leaving Professor Corhart handed him a CD of music from Frederick the Great's court.

'To remind you of us.' he said warmly shaking hands.

'You have to come back.' Simon said hugging him in the airport.

Mrs. Corhart kissed him and smiled. 'My son speaks for us all. Keep an eye on my little girl. Thank you for, everything.'

It was an extended journey, the plane calling at a clutch of places en route. Felicity took his hand into her lap. He watched an imperceptible regret tinge her face. 'Felicity, it was so good. Everything. Did you mind?'

Her eyes blazed. 'Graham, I loved what we did. All of it. I didn't know love was so unbelievably wonderful or that you could want so much or that I did. I've never been so fulfiled: feasting, larks in the garden, music and art and even Daddy's bloody Shakespeare, and crowned by our love making. I guess it's how you are.'

'Never, never like that. You are ferocious, demanding, holding the wildest riches, so happy and so beautiful.'

Hardly needing confirmation, her hand strayed onto his firming fly. 'Graham let's stay in touch.'

'Friends for always.'

'What did Mummy say to you?'

'We struggled and shared sadness and agreed you were precious.'

'Her sadness or yours?'

'Both.'

Felicity watched the landscape below slip away, a growing separation from home. She felt his erection soften.

Graham pressed her hand. 'You're lucky there's love in your family.'

She felt his twinge of pain. 'Do you miss yours?'

'No. They betrayed me. I was salvaged by two dearest friends. One is dead. I live with the other.'

The silence of his pain frightened her. She was comforted by the hope she might help him.

When Graham arrived back he found Fiona reading on her bed. She looked at him and smiled her precious small smile of welcome which had always drawn him to her. He blushed.

She instantly understood the firmness of his stance, the lightness of step, the warmth inside. She loved him again for his life and fortitude.

He lay beside her watching her read until he caught her straying eye. She put the book down and snuggled into him.

'Happy?'

'Fantastic.'

'New friends?'

'Amazing people, all of them.'

'Love?'

'I love Simon. He's a young Art but gentler more boyish more joyful. We had good times together. He's passionate and pure. What I long for.'

'But you were gentle with him?'

'Wildness between boys. Willful and sexless. Is that all right?'

'Anything done with love is. You know that.'

'It was heady being so admired. I felt like a god.'

'My dear, you've returned looking like one.'

Graham took her hand and slid it into his crotch.

'And Felicity looked after you?'

He was silent. She stroked his hair with her free hand.

'She was quite amazing. Um, we made love.'

'Compensating for Simon'

'That too. An unavoidable storm.'

'What you wanted?'

'Oh yes. No guilt no doubts.'

Fiona felt the after-surge of love-making and wondered if he wanted to go.

'I love her, Fiona, like I love you. She burns me up whereas you bring me to the boil.' He kissed her

Fiona shivered. 'Are you boiling now?'

He nodded and raised his hips so she could pull his jeans down and slide her fingers under his balls. It wasn't long before he slid inside her, moved with ecstatic sureness which shimmered in her, then came in a rush of glory and collapse.

Her misty eyes raked his languorous body. 'So, you're staying?'

'With you? Can I?'

'You don't need to ask.'

'I don't know what you want.'

'Do you want to be here?'

'Of course. You are this is my home.'

'Exactly. Do you feel disloyal?'

'I suppose so.'

'Graham, you felt different. I want that too, want a partner who strays into storms (male and female) and who carries them back to me like you've just done. How can you possibly believe it's disloyal to extend your love? Was it disloyal to love Simon and make love to his sister? No. Of course not. Each act enriches the others.' She dared more. 'You will ask yourself each time, 'Is this the love I want to hold onto?' Your heart must be answered first. Life should be a great adventure in love. I missed out until I met you. Now it's begun. It keeps me buzzing all the time. You must adventure too, dear one. If afterwards you come home willingly, then that's perfect.'

'I don't want to cruise again.'

'Willy nilly you'll confront unavoidable storms, and the question, "Where do I belong?"'

'Do you ask yourself that?'

'Yes. And my answer is, I belong with Graham.'

'I'm not as constant as you.'

'Tush. Your breasts are not as big as mine, your hair as long, your voice as high. Each brings complementary qualities to the relationship - a balancing.'

He nodded. 'A marriage.'

She forced a tiny pause. 'Well, a private union which marriage publicly confirms.'

'Aren't I more like a son?'

'I love you as son, husband, father, love-chick, baby, god. Nothing's cut and dried, Graham. Your sexuality for instance.'

'A shifty *Twelfth Night* reality.'

'My dearest, "If music be the food of love, play on." Play all the parts in the adventure, and love love love.'

'I love you Fiona. I thought of you there. I want to tell you.'

'I'm glad. I love you more every day. I've had a lovely weekend, knowing, after everything was done, you'd be here with me with your appetite for all sorts of stories and sex and songs and an obsession with nakedness I want to share. I've nursed the feeling none of this matters because it all matters when we share. See what a silly I am.'

'Professor Corhart showed me a way to home. We had good talks, often touching on love. He made me feel clever.'

'A good guy. Was it his way of loving you?'

'I guess so. Sharing passions, as you've said.' He gasped. 'You're right. Yes, I felt Simon and I made love (without sex, he's only a boy). But it was love we engaged in, a sweet innocent form lost to me.' He almost shook his head. 'Perhaps not so innocent. We watched each other undress, enjoying nakedness and physical intimacy, never straying into rape territory. What my father destroyed for me was the potency of hope - the dreams of growing up to become the gods I hero-worshiped. Oh dear. To lose ones heroes is to be gelded.'

'Perhaps you've come back with one or two more heroes.'

'Do you think so?'

'You seem more solid more potent, godlike.'

'Filling you with doubts and seeds and disloyalties.'

'Filling me with life because you're home. She kissed him and pulled him up. 'Come on, let's shower.'

She walked slowly to the bathroom. He followed, marvelling at the sinuous dance of buttocks, the back's nobility, the love caresses hidden in her mute hands, wondering why he'd ever imagined leaving her. She was so precious. How could he?

Graham found the office less oppressive. For one thing, he was happier in himself, happy his friendship with Felicity survived; secondly, he was becoming more useful, he grew more contented with the FG work.

He compared his team to the Corhart family: Bruce was often a busy, if more grounded Simon; Cathy and Amory combined into the mother; Anna was a surrogate father a role she shared with Bruce. Felicity and he were themselves busy with work and engrossed in a secret life. (They met occasionally for dinner, usually starting with thrilling love-making in her flat. Seemingly unaffected the following day. Only Cathy suspected anything was afoot).

Graham wondered if the group worked well because the leader's role was divided. At the final in-house presentation to staff and directors everyone said it was the best job currently in the office. Graham watched Bruce accept all the praise, gratified he acknowledged that everyone in the team was responsible. Perhaps Bruce was a good leader because he allowed the work to develop, rather than managing everything in the obsessive way senior staff such as Etienne did.

Felicity and Graham broached the idea in the restructuring committee because it seemed relevant to their investigations of achieving excellence.

'We gotta have strong leaders.' Abe said.

Murray nodded as usual, Caleb was non-committal. Ingrid and Felicity argued a more flexible leadership had clearly worked in the FG team. With Sue a sympathetic chair, and Graham solidly behind Felicity, the suggestion was included in the final report. Not only should leadership be flexible (task orientated as Sue put it) but project groups must be made up of skills relevant to the problem solving (building skill into a framework that focuses it, as Sue said).

Most of the office staff supported the recommendations, a coterie was against. Etienne grimly told Graham. 'It's too radical. Our gays won't work with women. Strong leaders are our best tradition, the basis of success. Our past is ignored at our peril.'

Graham was silent. How could Gem Productions stay the best if excellence were unregarded? he wondered after Etienne dismissed him.

Etienne felt betrayed. Graham was a gay fellow-traveller if his stance in committee was to be believed. 'The trouble with us gays is our perfidy.' he said to himself. 'After years of manoeuvring we've won the core of this company, and in one short report will lose the lot.' He stabbed his pencil into his blotter. 'So Graham, it's not love (ah your sweet body), it's war. But the divas will prevail. You and your friends will suffocate in the Aida pit of nonentity. The trumpets will only sound to acclaim *us*.'

He bided his time aware Graham had friends outside on whom Etienne depended. He adjusted his plan, alerted by reports that Tom from ACAA had called on Graham. 'Routine, it may seem, but it's a threatening reminder of the network's influence.' Etienne mulled.

The directors, for form's sake, invited Sue to meet them. Wanting moral support she asked the committee members to elect a representative to accompany her. The only serious contender was Graham. Sue approved.

The directors heard Sue's summary of the work in silence, responding along the lines of Etienne's comments.

Graham looked around. Etienne was absent. He felt vulnerable without his boss but spelled out the central concern about excellence and the structures directing work to that end. He spoke with passion, concluding. 'We at Gem Productions are proud of the Company's record and want to maintain our lead in the market. The staff supports the aims of the Report, a majority accepts the restructuring as necessary to achieve excellence and ensure our pre-eminence.'

Sue smiled at him. It was well put, she thought.

The chair looked icily at Graham. 'You ignore the traditions and character of the Company. But then, you joined us recently. We note the committee's views formed from the time you joined it, that despite warnings you have persisted in steam-rolling your mistaken views onto it. We don't need a revolution, only a little spit and polish. The view of the Board is unanimous. The report will not be implemented and we hope you will seek employment elsewhere.'

Sue was white faced. 'It was joint work, sack us all.'

Someone said. 'Your loyal service is appreciated.'

Another. 'The others were hoodwinked.'

The chairman waved them silent. 'Young man, you have an appointment with Etienne in fifteen minutes. See you keep it.' With a curt nod he dismissed them.

Sue and Graham collected their papers, rose unsteadily. As they left Graham said bitterly. 'As Feste puts it, "The whirligig of time brings in his revenges." I'm neither enemy nor fool.'

Outside the door Sue burst into tears. Graham put a fatherly arm round her and navigated to the tea room. 'Sue, you are a great chair, a dear thoughtful patient member of staff, my inspiration and many others'. Don't worry about me. Your predicament is much worse - with a family, needing the money security and all that.'

She nodded and slipped another sugar lump into her beaker. 'It's so wrong to blame you.'

Graham's cheek quivered. 'Yet I've felt for ages I'm caught up - a pawn - in someone else's game, one I don't understand. Well Sue dear, maybe it's over.' He left his papers on top of hers, manfully almost grinned and went to see Etienne.

The usually empty desk was strewn with photographs and papers. Etienne's grim face softened. 'I don't think you understand what's at stake. I am sorry. But the board is adamant. Is this how you spend your spare time?' He pointed at the pictures. 'We found them in your desk.'

They were Felicity's snaps of him and Simon horsing by the pool. Naked aroused glowing with love. His Pelé boy; his vivacious sister; his joy. An innocence and delight so completely out of place here; they seemed porn images, the illegality of love, the obscenity of his own experiences when twelve, more horrible because so completely innocent.

Graham felt sick. The game he was caught in involved sexual exploitation, power over youth and innocence. In the game it was expected the weak submitted, as he'd submitted to his father, as Simon was assumed to have submitted to him.

In this game he had been abused first by Etienne, then by the board. Now they were punishing him because he didn't submit. Graham shook with fury. Mrs. Corhart had been right to worry about Felicity. This lot cared for no one but themselves. It was shameless immoral and brutalising. With the pretensions stripped away Graham recognised it was not his game; in fact it was what he'd run from all his adult life. He glowered. 'It's not like that.' he said quietly with great intensity, shepherding the photos into a slim pile and slipping them into his pocket. 'You wanted to see me?'

Etienne nervously pushed a paper towards him. 'I have a generous cheque here in your name which I'll sign if you'll sign this letter.' The letter stated:

To the Board of Gem Productions:

Dear Sirs,
Further to our discussions today
I tender my resignation from
the end of this week.
Sincerely yours,

— — — — — — —

Even in the midst of his fury Graham was aware Etienne was sweating. 'You first.' he said.

Like a lamb Etienne signed the cheque, buying Graham out of the game. Then Graham signed. It was over.

But not quite. "The whirligig of time" wrought other changes. Felicity's disappointment there could be no art director without the restructuring was eclipsed by her anger over Graham's sacking. The photo incident enraged her further. 'I won't be ruled by nerds who know nothing about art or friendship.' she cried. And resigned on the spot. Other talent would follow.

Graham urged her to telephone APAA and ask about graphic design work. 'At least talk to Fiona Pinkham. She'd give you good advice.'

'Fiona Pinkham is one of the best.' Felicity said gratefully. 'You worked there, didn't you. Can I mention your name?'

Graham smiled. 'Yes. Anyway, she knows about you.'

Her eyes widened. 'Fiona - is she, she can't be your Fiona?'

He nodded. 'Nobody knows.'

'I can't see her. She'd chuck me out.'

'Never. Our love isn't ownership or so limiting.'

'But I've been fooling with her bloke.'

'Because we fell in love.'

'So?'

'So, of course we share work and play and love.'

'But you and she?'

'Also share. Are you upset by my loving Simon?'

'No.'

'You see, love grows in many directions.'

'Yes.' she said doubtfully.

'My love is for you and her and Simon. Eh?'

'And she feels the same?'

'Absolutely. She's clearer than I. Steadier.'

'Yes, that's what you need.' Felicity said thoughtfully.

'Ring her for me, will you?'

'For you, Graham?'

'Because I love you and think you'll be happy there.'

'I suppose she can only say no.'

'It's a tiny risk.'

Felicity sighed. 'I do love you, my friend without a shadow, very much.' She telephoned and was granted an appointment.

Firstly, Felicity was shown round APAA by one of the design staff before being ushered into an airy studio-office where tea and Fiona were waiting. It was so easy an exchange that Felicity forgot how probing an interview it was. She was relaxed and relieved by the end.

Fiona took her hand in farewell. 'It goes without saying I'm glad to meet you. I can say we'd like you to join us. With your talent you could easily get into one of the top famous agencies. So why us?'

Felicity blushed. She wanted to kiss her for her generosity and trust. 'Fame doesn't interest me. Your work inspired me at college. It still does. I'd love to be as good as you.'

Fiona grinned. 'Thank you my dear. And thanks for befriending Graham. He's too precious not to love. I'm glad you know that. I try to separate work from my private life. One is freer that way. Our friendship was impossibly fragile for so long - on both sides - that working on it out of the public gaze has become a habit.'

'Love needs its own secret place.'

'And its secret place at the moment contains us both, our man, your brother and one or two others. I feel it's big enough for all of us. Do you, Felicity?'

'Yes. And it's just happened.'

'I think so Felicity. Like a brilliant idea popping out.'

'A lovely thought. Our creativity tucked up with love.'

'Isn't love the first? Making love, making a family, making sculpture, making laughter, thinking anew?'

'Graham says love is a variety.'

'As scary as it's joyful, we should remember.'

'Is it scary, lacking words and images, joyful because afterwards we see again?'

'Yes, we do see again. But differently. I guess that's why we go on making all kinds of other things. Felicity, let's talk more, sometime. We share with difficulty but it's better than nothing, yes?'

Felicity nodded. Fiona is brilliant and wise, she thought. On an impulse she kissed her and hurried away through the thronging streets savouring their contracts.

Graham was unemployed. 'Such is life.' Fiona teased knowing Tom was already determinedly networking on his behalf. She was glad Graham was sanguine about change. Wanting the neutrality of wilderness, she tentatively suggested a week in the forest hut. He was over the moon.

'Let's take our Christmas dinner.' she murmured.

Graham laughed. 'You just want presents.'

'Of course. Wrapped ones and clouds of wee slimy ones which wriggle into me.'

'No death or sadness.'

'Would life and happy everafterness suit you?'

'What do you mean?'

'I'll tell you over our Christmas.'

'Tell me?'

'About life and happy ever after.'

'Another story?'

'The same one.'

'Fiona, I don't know what you're talking about, but I love stories. The best always begin "Once upon a time" and end, "They lived happily ever after." Is this one like that?'

'Yes.'

'Goody. Let's have lots of bedtime stories.'

'And Graham, there's lots of choice.'

'You mean I get to choose the story?'

'That's exactly right.'

'You won't push me round, bully, rape or abuse me?'

'I won't.'

'I'll cry for more. May I?'

'As much and as often as you like. I'll ring Jean. Let's leave straight after work. It'll be dark so the lovely Art will have to guide us through the woods. Is that all right, or do I have to rape you for a "yes"?'

'Perfect. But rape me anyway.'

Graham had never thought, let alone said such a thing. It meant two things to Fiona: firstly, that her leadership in and beyond bed was accepted; secondly, that he'd overcome his nightmare and self loathing enough to voice it. She ached with gratification.

Arriving at Jean's garage, they changed cars. Art drove them safely through the gloomy forest to the hut. He helped them unpack, then busied himself with fire, water and wood. Later, they all lingered companionably round the fire before creeping to bed.

Big brother Glen arrived in the morning with the balance of provisions and a saw. He and Art cut a mountain of wood and left for work at the garage.

The peace was a veil lifted. Fiona and Graham stood spellbound on the deck overlooking the shimmering lake. After the icy winter, life breathed anew: the shy green in trees, shoots from the earth, birds busy nest building, early forest flowers, gnats' ballet across the face of the water, the ebullience of frogs' spawn, the first nagging mosquitoes, spoor of rabbits and deer. The jubilant inevitability of spring was breathtaking. They rambled in the woods, came back, put wild flowers in vases and prepared their celebration.

He set the table while she busied herself with food. As dusk fell he lit the candles and gleefully viewed the presents. She brought the first course. He opened the champagne. They eagerly tore at wrappings between mouthfulls. Most of the presents were sensible - jumper, jeans, designer sunglasses, shirts for him; a scarf and carry-all bag plus a pert fluffy teddy bear which she greeted with smiling tears, which reminded him of her pointed promise of a story.

But the turkey and a flaming pudding intervened, and a couple of incoherent carols. Then he filled their glasses with the last of the bubbly, pushed back his chair. 'Story time.'

Fiona slowly sipped and hesitantly sipped again looking at him as if for the first time.

'Well?' he said softly.

'Love me Graham.' she whispered.

'I do.'

'I need you so much.'

'Just for now?'

'Always have. Can I tell you that?'

'I think I've known. I only came back from death because you were there.'

'Having you, kept me going through all those dark times.'

'Why do I matter?'

'You give me so much. You care.'

'So much. Mmm, so do you.'

'Is that what you want?'

'When you touch me, Fiona, it's a sort of prayer making me whole so I can go into you and afterwards walk free.'

'Only you deeply fill me. Your breathing penis, your sticky syrup banishing emptiness. That's what I must now tell you. You filled me with life that very first time. I couldn't tell you at Christmas. It's what I really want. Darling (don't be upset) I'm pregnant.'

'A baby? For ever and ever.'

'Do you want forever?'

'Baby? And me?' Graham gazed distractedly into the mist gathering over the darkening lake.

Fiona sat quite still. 'Yes, you and baby, and many babies, living happily ever after, if, if you want.'

He wasn't listening. 'A triangular family.'

'Lots of little triangles to love and enjoy like Art.'

'Can I love him too? And Felicity and?'

'As family. We both need families. And trust.'

'Me and you? Me?' Graham went round the table and put his head in her lap listening to her womb. 'Does he mind what I do to him?'

Fiona smiled through her tears. 'SHE (I had an ultra scan). She's upset when her Daddy doesn't wet her head. Darling Graham, can we call her Frederica?'

His silence contained a split second review of his whole life. 'Do you want to remember everything?'

'Yes, Graham. All your loves, all our life together. Frederica will have your eyes, your roguish smile, long lusty legs, my hunger . . .'

'Your breasts, your generosity, imagination and power. Fiona, let's live in the woods. All of us. Away from it all. City life makes me sick. I'm sort of raped every day, touched-up, pushed around. Minor abuse in small increments of my dad's. I want to be with you and our children, Art and his; expressing feelings, reading, singing, wood chopping, playing hide and seek with the kids, silently fishing.' He caught her eyes, far away, familiar, sparkling.

'NYC is a graveyard - a memorial to power and greed and pretensions. Let's use the recourses it gives us to make a whole life.' He turned his head to see her. 'When I push into you I'm looking for sexual relief (a bit), for the power you fill me with (a bit), feeling, for an instant, wholed (a bit), but mostly wanting to belong.

'Belonging in you, through you to the great womb of the world, one of the playful gods, a part of the wilderness. That's the belonging I yearn for and found here with you.'

Fiona's eyes danced. 'Can we make a house and some children beforehand?'

'We must.'

'Oh, darling Graham, then we've already begun.'

'So, let's get married.'

'That too. Only to exchange vows. No organs or veils. No pomp or receptions.'

'Then afterwards Fiona, a honeymoon like this one. We'll wet Frederica's head over and over and teach her songs and tell her about love.'

'Lie in a grassy hollow where, one day, you and Art will build our own house. Tell me, will we have a cat?'

'Only if it's furry like your vagina.'

'And thrashes its tail like your penis and mew mew mews for milk of belonging two or three times a day to remind us.'

'Oh, Fiona. Wonderful. But is it possible?'

'It is, Graham. But only if we dream it.' She smiled radiantly. 'I know, because all my other dreams have come true.'

*

Pedal Point

PIANO MUSIC floats like pollen through arching street trees: occasional bursts of sound, wafting thistle down, "silvery robbers", as children call them. The ample roadway is dappled by shadow. Generous margins, a footpath and nature strip from which the trees spring, marking a tidy variety of picket fences and numbered gates, the paths in front gardens leading to stout front doors of houses set in spacious lots unchanged from times more amiable than today. The piano tinkle also resists modernization; not only the rush of cars but the raucous bawling of electronic music and the twinkling glare of televisions in front living rooms.

Times change. Another urgency drives the world today. Yet change is hardly noticable in the calls of children hanging-out on the street, in laughter or a ball left in the gutter, a skipping rope on a grassy verge, a kite snagged in tree branches. As with sighs of wind, bird song at dawn or the mewl of an infant, we experience the continuity of the changeless; our pleasure in the universal grows with the gentleness of the ordinary moderating excesses of the new; the sheep inside the wolf.

Let's cross the road. Do as Mother told us. "Look left, right, left again. If clear, cross." Look! The music comes from that house. Comfortably unkempt with what estate agents call "Old World Charm." A dull brass plate proclaims. *M.E Bird, Ba.Mus. M.phil. Piano Lessons.* Years ago, many expectant artists had scuffed the path, pressed the bell and cleaned their dusty feet on the mat. Nowadays children romped or sidled in (depending how much practice they'd done) heedlessly treading the worn flowery carpet along the passage, entering the music room awash with piles of music, busts of musicians, chairs in remnant recital lines and some florid wooden music stands where their friends and the famous had played or sung solos accompanied by Edith Bird's piano or her assenting head. She spoke of Clara Schumann, Franz Liszt, Rachmininov, Solomon, Artur Schnabel with a piety overlooked by the kids. But they flocked to her because she loved music and them; she sensed their dreams, nodding without rebuke.

One afternoon her fluffy waggy toylike dog escaped. She saw him scurrying across the road. 'One of you left the gate ajar.' she scolded. Placing her gold rimmed spectacles on the piano she hurried outside. She heard an excited bark, the screech of rubber tyres and a lusty childish scream. Saw a boy tumbled on the carriageway, a car glide round the corner, swerve to a shuddering stop, her naughty Felix (named after Mendelssohn) panting aghast against the opposite fence. She blenched, turned and went inside to ring for help. She knew it was serious.

When she re-emerged to scold Felix, nod gratefully to a policeman making a way through the crowd for the ambulance men, she began to shake.

'Felix, I've told you before. Stay inside. Look at the trouble you've caused. Naughty, naughty boy. No biscuit for you this afternoon.'

She picked up the unrepentant bundle and stumbled back to her pupils, shakily latching the gate.

'Mavis. Sonia. Be careful. That road's a death trap. Now let's have the Clementi. Not too fast. Yes my dears. Yes. Let it sing.'

She looked absently over her glasses. The room filled with softening sunlight. Dust danced. She was a child, playing the Clementi duet with her wizened teacher, preparing it for her concert debut. Frilly dress, white sox, red shoes (a daring touch), her long shining hair held in a red bow out of the way for bowing. She remembered a posy of flowers the scent of applause, the warmth of smiles, her teacher's pride, her parents, so small and far away, smiling, smiling for her.

'Let it sing. It will if you let your fingers dance. Mavis, use the sustaining pedal where it's marked. Pedal, pedal! Give it form, yes, like that. Oh yes.' Edith Bird blinked back a tear.

'I'm sure the boy'll be all right.' Sonia said.

'My friend's cousin was killed last year.' Mavis whispered.

'Yes, my dears, of course. Now I think you should go.' Edith extracted their money scrunched up in fists and ushered them out. 'Three more lessons then the concert. It's coming-on.' She looked up and down the road. It was empty. 'All right. Off you go.'

She blinked. Went to the roadside and gingerly retrieved a scuffed and greasy pedal which spun stiffly on its axle. 'The poor boy. I'll keep it for him.' she murmured, straightened, wandered through her gate and into the house. 'I love these breath-held evenings.' she said to Felix who dolefully watched her drink her evening sherry and nibble biscuits now forbidden him. But only until her second glass.

*

Constable Sparrow was busy in his notebook when the ambulance he'd summoned arrived. The boy was now conscious, white with pain. Bleeding and groaning as they lifted him onto the stretcher. 'I'll interview him at the hospital.' he told the medics. 'After you've patched him up.'

The ambulance bell faded. Constable Sparrow took out a tape and sketched car and bike positions, distance from the kerb, skid marks. Everything. 'Finished, lads.' he nodded to two policemen who gathered up the pieces in an accident truck and trundled away.

The car driver looked anxious, maybe shifty. He didn't protest when asked to blow into a breathalyser. The constable was skeptical of the zero reading, even on the second try. The driver seemed a damned fool in his smart big limo, too plush to be decent. Yet the nurd seemed upset. 'You can get along now. Bring your papers to the Station tomorrow. We'll prepare a statement for signature. Drive carefully in residential areas, sir. Better contact your solicitor.'

The car bumped off the grass and purred away. Sparrow's partner, Sid, looked up from the radio in their panda car. 'Where's the old biddy who reported the accident? There's no sign of anyone.'

'Let's go, Sid. We've enough to nail that lying bastard. Let's deal with the kid. He should be cleaned-up by now. Hope the hospital contacted the parents. Foot to the floor, Clyde. Seven minutes is the record. Or was. Go man!' A squealing, smoking U-turn, flashing blue lights the panda car roared off towards the hospital. Constable Sparrow grinned. Being on duty was fun.

The next morning the driver visited the police station with his solicitor. Papers were inspected, statements made.

'I don't see this as a full statement. But if that's all your client wants to record, so be it.' growled the constable. 'The court will not be happy.'

Dismissed, they made their way to the hospital. The duty doctor was firm. 'No visitors. Only family. The boy's in for surgery later. We must maintain a stable condition.'

'Surgery?'

'A toe amputation. It can't be saved.'

'Poor lad'

A knot of people wafted down the corridor. A woman in tears,

179

her husband black with rage, a solicitor in attendance.

'My little Jack. How will he walk, play football, dance? What's to become of us?'

'I'll kill that bastard. Nothing is good enough for him. Typical. Rich, careless. He'll pay if it's the last thing. Darling, they've done all they could.'

'If I'm instructed to sue, I'll get . . .' the doors swung to, silencing despair, rage and retaliation. The driver paled. His solicitor sighed. 'The court should believe your story. All the same, I'll alert your insurance company. The attitude of the police is regrettable.'

'The boy had fallen off his bike.'

'I understand. But a damaged child will influence the court and blame meted out. Truth is often the first casualty these days, it needs ferreting out. Guardian Insurance don't pay lightly. Don't worry. Let's meet and review the case in a couple of weeks. Now, I must be off.'

The men are separated by a trolley with body, bottles of blood and anxious attendants. In the car park they part, wave and carefully drive away.

But the Insurance company was sanguine. 'Let's wait and see what the preliminary hearing turns-up.'

At the hearing the police were adamant. It was clear the car knocked the boy over. The car driver was fully responsible. There were no mitigating circumstances. Full insurance could be claimed. Only then, was Mister Duckworth brought in.

Barry Duckworth was plump. His mop of greying hair unruly from his worrying hands, a broad smile softening his pasty face. His neck-ties were bright. His dress immaculate, reflecting his receptivity. He was someone to whom one told even private thoughts. He seemed too benign to be calculating (which he was), too discreet to talk clearly (which he could). He had, his clients admitted, a nose for the weird logic underlying the truth. Odd for a man almost stupid, almost vague, an ordinary nondescript chap who never pranced or preached, never seemed right but usually was. Only his neck-ties were memorable, and his smile which lingered like Wonderland's Cheshire Cat.

The kids, hanging out in the street warmed to his gentle inquiries, agreed that the boy, Jack (and the killer-driver) deserved the truth, nothing but. They gossiped to him effortlessly. He noted Mavis' comment about Miss Bird's dog and her phone call that day, and a scruffy little boy who muttered about "bike-trouble with the Black Band" at his and

Jack's school,

'The Black Band are big boys who pick on us. They damage our bikes, let down tyres, loosen bits, that kind of thing. They had it in for Jack because he told his form master about them.' the boy admitted haltingly; encouraged by the man's attentive mien he broke the gang embargo as Jack had.

When broached with the school, Mister Duckworth heard the matter had been aired at a staff meeting, that the head had ruled "Boys will be boys, let's concentrate on their education." which contradicted his denial of the existence of any bullies in interview in his paneled office:

'Duckworth. If I unearthed such behavior, I'd sternly forbid it in my assembly mornings talk. That would put an end to the matter.'

'So, Headmaster, a stiff lecture would be effective?'

'Our policy is clear. Gangs are forbidden. That would end it.'

'Yet, if a boy was injured riding a damaged bicycle home?'

'Beyond school? That over-stretches our responsibility.'

'Does the care of children have limits?'

'No. Schools have limits in a caring society.'

'The duty of care is within your boundaries?'

'Exactly.'

'Out of sight, out of mind?'

'Beyond the fence, others become responsible: parents, police, council officers.'

'Thank you, Headmaster. By the way, there is evidence of a group calling themselves "Black Band" in the school. They bully boys and damage bicycles. It's general knowledge for pupils, not unknown to staff. A hidden threat to younger pupils, I gather.'

'This is a happy school. We top the university placement lists.'

'The league tables don't measure comfiness or distress.'

'The tables reflect the real situation. Our parents and boys know our tradition of excellence.'

'What an interesting discussion about evaluation. I often wonder about a new measure for skill, such as reliability, clarity of thought, leadership, honesty; universal human values. You see, Headmaster, your tables are really inscrutable.'

'What ministry are you from Doctor Duckworth?'

'Mister. Investigating an accident one of my clients' clients was involved in with one of your boys riding home. Trying to unravel the cause, or causes. A legal matter. But what interesting issues have been raised, Headmaster.'

'Here we are concerned with the development of our wards, fitting them for life. The great challenge facing them. The best start. This is our remit. I can't help with matters beyond the school. Try the police. Is that all?'

'I am dismissed! Thank you Headmaster.' Barry Duckworth rose and slipped away leaving only a faint smile hovering needling the uneasy head.

That gaudy tie. Certainly not a ministry man. How does he know so much about us? Ah, he listens to rumors, always rife, always hyperbole, the headmaster thought. He pressed the intercom. 'Miss Blair, come in, please. Tell me, what do we know of The Black Band, here in the school?'

To his discomfort, the smile hung about like a bad smell. Luckily Miss Blair didn't seem to notice.

*

Jack's parents grudgingly agreed to an interview with Duckworth since its outcome involved an insurance settlement. They softened with the concerned talk about the boy's future, his chances, their hopes, their pride in how well he was coping, gratified by the concern.

'The hospital say he's a plucky lad, sign of good parenting, I'd say.'

'We try.'

'Tell me, has Jack ever mentioned problems with his bicycle?'

'Someone tampering with it at school. I told him to tighten everything.'

'Did he?'

'He's a responsible boy. He would've checked.'

'Why do you say that?'

'He depends on it daily.'

'I don't understand.'

'It's his bike. He'd care for it.'

'He's your son.'

'Listen, Duckman, there're only a few nuts. Five minutes work. Are you implying we should hold his hand, wipe his arse? At his age? Put him in the pram and take him to school?'

'No, dear, Mister Duckman is asking if you checked.'

'He's big enough to care for his own things.'

'Duckworth. I was indeed.'

'I did not.'

'In spite of the risk?'

'Risk RISK? There's risk in crossing the road, Duckmansworth. Let's draw the line sensibly.'

'Injury. Death suggest a different "sensibly"?'

'Dear, don't get angry. Mister Duckworth is only asking. We've wondered much the same.'

'Yes, Mam. Whether the car driver was at fault, or whether young Jack's bicycle was at fault.'

'You would say that.'

'Isn't it the right question?'

'The police and the court are sure.'

'Based on partial evidence.'

'It'll do me.'

'If an innocent driver pays for others' oversights?'

'It's my son I'm thinking of.'

'Of course you are.' Duckworth paused. 'Justice interests me. Isn't it an edifice on which our nation rests? It must be firm and true. Partial justice is treacherous. Maybe Jack's future depends on justice? Think about it. The cost of an injustice is dire.' He cautiously rose. 'It was good of you to see me. Best wishes to you and Jack. I'll see myself out.' The colours of his neck-tie flickered in their minds long afterwards as teasing psychedelic questions.

*

Jack was guarded by his physiotherapist and a nurse who had led Duckworth to him in the trim and tidy garden of the nursing home where he was recuperating. Barry Duckworth pushed the crutches to the end of the stolid wooden seat and sat carefully beside the boy whose frail pain-drawn face reflected shock, maybe fear at the glimpse of death when his head hit the roadway.

They sat watching other patients, some swaddled and in wheel-chairs, some hobbling, others slumped on benches in the sun.

'That's Megan. She's lost a leg. She often cries with the pain in it although it's gone, poor thing.' Jack squinted into the sun, glad of the reassuring quiet of his visitor. 'Your tie matches those lilies.'

'So it does, Jack. Your face is as pale as those daisies. Maybe nurse could paint your lips yellow; then, you'd match.'

The boy half-smiled.' But, they've got all their petals. Look at those bees tickling them.'

The man nodded. '"The Pobble who has no toes had once as many as we . . ." Do you know Edward Lear's poem about how the Pobble lost his toes, swimming, ignoring his auntie's advice about caring for himself?'

Jack blinked and surveyed his bandaged leg. 'No, tell me?'

'The Pobble who has no toes
Had once as many as we;
When they said, 'Some day you may lose them all;'
He replied, 'Fish, fiddle de-dee!
And his aunt Jobiska made him drink
Lavender water tinged with pink.
For she said, 'The world in general knows
There's nothing so good for a Pobble's toes.

The Pobble who has no toes
Swam across the Bristol Channel.
But before he set out he wrapped his nose
In a piece of scarlet flannel.
For his aunt Jobiska said, 'No harm
Can come to his toes if his nose is warm
And it's perfectly known that a Pobble's toes
Are safe, provided he minds his nose.'

That's all I remember. Why not get the book? You'll enjoy *The Pobble, The Jumblies, The Dong with the Luminous Nose, The Owl and the Pussycat.* It'll take you mind of your toe.'

'Poor Pobble. All his toes? Like Megan. Did he cry?'

'Read the book.'

Jack straightened. 'I made a friend here. Daniel. His leg is full of metal pins. The staff say he's brave. He fell from a fair ground loop-the-loop, in pieces. He laughs a lot and is angry at missing school.'

'Are you his mirror: grim and glad to be absent?'

'How did you know?'

'It's in your daisy face. Tell me, what can you remember of your accident?' He stared the two attendants to silence.

The boy eyed the gravel path. 'Not much.'

'The little dog?'

'There *was* a dog. It barked at me, yes.' Jack shivered. 'Yes, it ran in front. I braked and skidded. Missed it I think. Something broke. My foot got trapped. The bike sort of folded up and I fell. I screamed in the ambulance.'

'The hospital said you were brave.'

'They talked low. Pretended nothing was wrong. I thought of something terrible.'

'What about the car?'

'Was there a car? I don't remember. No! The foot- brake. My loose pedal. I skidded across the road. No car. My bike; the dog; lots of trees. Nothing else. I think that's right.'

'So do I, Jack. You *are* brave. Hey, listen, you've another nine spills before you become a Pobble.'

'My nine toes to go.'

'Look after them, Jack. Here's my card. If you remember anything else, or can't get the book, let me know.' Barry Duckworth leaned forward and patted a slim pyjamad knee. 'Your bicycle is wrecked. I'll try to get another for you if you'll sign a paper saying what you told me. Yes? Good lad. All the best.' He rose and stiffly walked away shuffling ever so slightly. Pobble-like.

The physiotherapist sniffed. 'Not such a bad bloke, for a private dick. Awful tie. Shall we go in?'

Jack grinned. 'I'll try to walk.' Ignoring the crutches sprawling at the end of the seat he hop-hobbled across the grass. He shrugged the nurse away. 'I'm not a Pobble yet.'

*

Edith Bird was engrossed with a teenager's major and minor scales when the bell rang. A tousle haired man stood patiently at her door. He reminded her of a baritone she'd accompanied at a gallery concert during the war - such a handsome fellow with a fine rich voice. She agreed to speak to him about the accident between lessons, would he kindly wait in the hall.

Barry Duckworth nodded and smiled and carefully eased into an ancient chair. He was a boy again waiting for his piano lesson. The torture of scales, sharps flats and aching hands. He smiled broadly remembering he'd come for another reason, tucked his legs under the chair and disturbed a small fluffy dog. 'Ah, that's where you're hiding.' he said.

Felix wagged his tail, glad of company; he didn't like scales either. Later, during the chat, Felix snuffled scratching his floppy ears expectantly. Soon, he was sure, they would all go 'walkies' as his mistress called it, but was not over-surprised when the next pupil rang the bell as she was agreeing to attend the court hearing as main witness for the defence.

Duckworth closed the front gate firmly saying, 'Don't worry, Felix won't be arraigned.'

When the day came, Edith Bird was up at crack of dawn, ready for the court. 'Felix, I've told you. While I'm away, be a good boy. Oo, it's like the old days: a taxi for a recital or a broadcast.' She pulled her front door to and locked it. The lock was stiff. It was seldom used. The driver helped her latch the gate and showed her to the car. Big and plush, and like the one which almost ran the boy over.

She nodded her head in time to the music (the driver's music, certainly) and settled back for the once familiar trip to the city. Unmoving and sightless she remembered the grim bomb sites, piles of rubble, smoking houses, bemused people who intruded into her music: its speed, its fingering, its sense which she would shortly unleash in accents gentler than war.

This time it was different. The driver didn't have a peaked cap, nor was the ride rattly and uncomfortable. So many new buildings. Many shining cars, and the intent throng milling about heedless of any threat; like her own little darlings confidently trooping into her music room.

'It's better now.' she said.

'Mam?' said the driver.

'It was a war against the brutal and careless.'

'War?' he spied her in his mirror. 'Oh you mean that one. They promised us a land fit for heroes. Fat chance of that, Mam. It's a jungle fit for no one, if you ask me.'

She sighed. His flat cheerless voice. Intimations of truth and disappointment. 'It would be different if everyone embraced music.'

'It takes more than music to make heroes.'

'Care; it begins with a concern for sharps and flats, quavers and minims, *Allegro, Minuetto, piano, forte,* care for the smallest things (children, semiquavers, rests, the truth). Heroes need the invisible power of ideals. Don't you see?'

'You, a muso, Mam?'

'Used to be. I teach now.'

'Can I ask, why you're going to the court?'

'Oh yes. I saw an accident. Mister Duckworth - I'm sure he's a baritone - asked me to tell the judge what happened. It was Felix's doing in a way. I saw the poor boy on the road looking like death. I telephoned for help. Afterwards no one bothered. Someone in a car was blamed but it was not his fault. Mister Duckworth believes no one helped the boy with his bicycle. Felix knew and rushed over. Too late, the boy fell and cut off his foot.'

'The wrong guy was blamed?'

'No one looked. Mister Duckworth - he must be a musician - says attention to detail carries the truth. I'd say, allows a truthful performance. It's the same thing. You see, it's a musical attitude. That's what I mean.'

'Cool, Mam. Cool. I agree.'

'Of course you do. You know music. You care.'

'Thank you, Mam. I was told to drop you at the entrance portal. Someone's waiting for you. Here we are. Tell 'em Mam. Sing the truth. Bless you.' He jumped out, opened the door and helped her to the pavement. A black-gowned solicitor took her arm and ushered her through the collonade. They were swallowed up by the echoing entry hall.

*

Judge Swann sighed, saw his notes had tailed off and, with a pang, wondered if he'd nodded off. His court was sparsely filled. The policeman was still waffling on about skid marks, collision damage, all worthy and doubtless correct the preliminary hearing had agreed. But the defendant pleaded not guilty and Vogel was defending him. What else was there to say? he wondered, doodling a tilted pair of scales, scratching it out and setting a full stop after his last comment, "If the car knocked the bike over how could it also run over it without being damaged?"

He had inspected the hospital report which concluded, "The boy's concussion, a knock on the head, compatible with collision with a vehicle." But the police report failed to describe any car damage. 'Vogel had challenged these anomalies.' he said to himself and yawned. 'It's only a battle over money.' he muttered. The Clerk turned enquiringly. Judge Swann scowled at him.

Counsel for the prosecution was finishing, 'So you see, my lord, everything points to the boy seriously injured by the car. We ask for full compensation, costs and a charge of dangerous driving at your own discretion.'

'That damn fool clerk is still ogling me.' he muttered glancing at the man making sipping motions. Then Judge Swann nodded.

'The court will rise.'

The judge sighed, rose and acknowledged the courtroom, turned and slipped out for tea.

*

Mister Vogel waited in the barristers' tea room. He carefully rose, took the outstretched surprisingly firm hand of the old lady, bent and kissed it.

'Do sit down. Tea? Earl Grey. Milk, lemon?' She was too frail to withstand the rigours of the court. But the only hope. He glanced up. Her beady eyes sparkled. She seemed perfectly at home. It worried him.

'You must know Franz Schubert's song about a song thrush and a lover stealing its carolling, *Der Vogel*? He dreams of flying through the storm to her. Heine doubts love. It's flighty, he says, fragile as a bird.'

'Ah, my name. I have Dutch origins. The music, no. Here we are concerned with the solid reliabilities of truth and justice.'

Edith Bird neatly clinked her cup into its saucer. 'Truth and music are not flighty. The truth is the poor boy fell off his bicycle, that Felix guarded him while I telephoned for help.'

'After being hit by a car.'

'No car, it came later. There was no one then.'

'The police have a different scenario.'

'How could they know?'

'Indeed.'

She rummaged in her handbag and produced a pedal. 'The bicycle broke. The poor wee mite couldn't ride without his pedal so he crashed. Felix tried to stop him. What a terrible sight.'

'You were there?'

'I saw it and rushed out. I found the pedal afterwards. I'd like to give it back.'

The solicitor frowned. 'The court will want it.'

'How can the boy ride without it?'

'His wrecked bike is in the possession of the court: police evidence. By the time he can, I hope someone gives him another.'

Mister Vogel grinned. 'Dear lady, you're a magician. Keep it for the judge. What you saw and that pedal fit the evidence and confirm our case. Tell his honour what you saw, and later, what you found. Don't be put off by the nit-picking throng.'

'Concentrate on the music. An early lesson.'

The solicitor shuffled to his feet. 'Five minutes ladies and gentlemen.'

'Mister Vogel rose, gathered his papers and waited for the old lady to join them. 'Just time to wash our hands.' he murmured.

'Essential before a performance.' Miss Bird said. Smiling they followed her into the lobby.

*

It was a long time since tea. Judge Swann sipped his water. Vogel was in form, trouncing police evidence, demolishing everything and only then, producing the only witness whose clarity belied her fragility and whose dignity charmed them all. Vogel reminded him, as always, of Schubert's carolling. Pity no one loved German these days. They lost more than the war, he ruminated. The term "German culture" was equivalent to a curse now. Ever since the war, when Dame Myra Hess risked Bach in her recitals. Piano and voice, ah, what wisdom resounded then. He sat up suddenly. Vogel was leading her (the prosecution dumb), no, prodding her, to reach into her handbag and produce the boy's pedal which no car could have dislodged. Trump card. He cut across the hush. 'Miss Bird, Edith Bird, the gifted pianist?'

'The old lady drew herself up grandly. 'Yes, your honour.'

'Collaborator of Myra Hess, the Griller and Busch quartets, Kathleen Ferrier?'

'Yes.'

'Edith Bird, I wept, many of us did during the war, when you played such beauty and hope into us. Today I welcome you to my court. It's an honour. Ladies and gentlemen, the siren who seduced us to remember the angels within our enemy. Angels such as Bach and Schubert, the other Mozart, Felix Mendelssohn. The savage breast was stilled for a moment in the carnage. And here you are, again making us see more clearly. I salute you!'

Miss Bird cocked her head towards the lined, bewigged face and smiled. 'Musicians are the secret enemy, telling of a nobler brotherhood than conflict, tuning ears to the sacred, defusing hatred. You see, you wept and survived. I wish all the armies could've. We'd have a better world, don't you agree?'

The clerk winced, looked at his assistant and shuddered. Was the old lady in charge? Swann was loosing his marbles. What would the papers say? Laughing stock, all of us. He was tempted to grab the judges's gavel and bang "silence in court". He shrank into his chair. It was outrageous! He shoved his bafflement away and listened. They were discussing music (nothing whatever to do with justice), the role of the performer to tease out veracity by attention to detail. (Swann remarked on a lack of such attention by the police in this instance); she wittered on about "the bigger picture" which details make-up, "testing interpretations with the heart" (what a load of old cobblers); a sequential logic of form and content which led from the start to the conclusion. "In my beginning is my ending" his honour had muttered and wagged his silly head. The clerk was struck by her pronouncement that a performance was similar to a judicial hearing in its mix of detail, sense and conclusion. When Vogel produced reports about school and home it suddenly did make sense. All of it. Yes, details and the bigger picture. Then, thank goodness, the old bat was discharged and a "not guilty" judgement pronounced with criticism of police, school and parenting. Crisis over. But what a performance.

'Funny thing though. It was a classic trial.' he told his colleagues later. 'Even the papers thought so.'

*

After the piano students' concert the seniors took their special guest past the site of his accident and to Miss Bird's party.

'Now, Jack, You sit here and keep an eye on Felix. He's trying to make amends.' Miss Bird said gaily.

The children milled around, dressed to kill in their performing clothes and beautifully behaved. Someone brought Jack a cool glass of pink cordial, an egg and tuna sandwich and a small cup cake. He was doubly content, first, being there in such a warm glow, secondly because soon he was going away.

One of the girls bounced in from the garden saying, 'Jack, let's see if you like butter.' She brandished a fist of buttercups under his yellowed chin. 'Yes, see you really do.'

He grinned. 'Almost as much as my new bike.'

Felix licked his hand (for another scrap of food) and Miss Bird looked severe. 'My dear, just be careful. Felix won't always be around to guard you.'

The door bell began to ring as parents arrived to ferry children home. Finally Jack, Felix and Miss Bird waited easily in the quiet music room.

'I never allow food in here. Only on very special occasions with a special guest. I hope you enjoyed our concert. The children certainly enjoyed having you. Music is medicine you know.'

'Thanks, Miss Bird. My own concert. I'm happy, really. They're terribly good, aren't they.'

'So often our gifts are invisible. We must ferret them out before they're trampled on.'

'Thank you for the party. You know about the Pobble?'

'With no toes. Yes, My friend Percy Grainger set it to music. I've got it here somewhere.'

Jack nodded thoughtfully. 'Mister Duckworth told me about it. It made me smile and want to walk. The ending is like your party :

The Pobble who had no toes
Was placed in a friendly bark,
And they rowed him back, and carried him up
To his Aunt Jobiska's Park.
And she made him a feast at his earnest wish
Of eggs and buttercups fried with fish;

And she said, "It's a fact the whole world knows,
That Pobbles are happier without their toes."

'Fish, eggs, buttercups and happiness made your party.'

'Could I be your Aunt Jobiska? Well, no wonder Felix is glued to you. He also enjoys buttercups and fish, and special boys. Now, let's see where Percy's little piece is. You'll enjoy it. He was a brilliant wild ragamuffin, a friend of my fiancé killed in the war. But no talk of death today. My, Jack, you scared me, flat out on the bloodied road. You MUST be very careful. You need your toes.'

'It's all right. I'm leaving, going to Daniel's school in the country. The teachers are friends and you don't have to go to every class if you've something worth doing. I was in hospital with Daniel. He says he can't cough now because all the bits of bone inside might choke him. He's great. He plays the oboe. He and I and Pete Uccello will be room mates. I'll be safe there.'

'It sounds a terrible accident, worse than yours. Music makes him brave, I'm sure.'

'I want to play guitar.'

'And sing?'

'Yes. Maybe about Pobbles and Jumblies and rock and roll.'

Edith Bird turned in triumph. 'Here's the manuscript in the elegant Grainger hand. I'll play it. Listen Jack.' She donned her gold-rimmed glasses, sat at the grand piano. The faded room filled with laughter and bells, fog horns, cat-calls and the tide running, sloshing and heaving the Pobble about the Bristol Channel. Her soft dry voice - was it Aunt Jobiska? - sang the words. Everything danced.

Afterwards they sat in silence watching the shadows rumba in the garden and the dust jig in bands of sunlight in the room.

'Wow! What fun. But it was sad and happy?'

'How well you listen, Jack. Music *is* sad and happy and majestic. The sounds in dreams, the food of life. Songs link the richness of our feelings to words making them less arid. My dear, of course you must play. And sing. All Pobbles and non-Pobbles must. It keeps darkness at bay.'

'What I saw lying on the road.'

Edith Bird trembled with the many darknesses she had faced in her long eventful life. The shrilling doorbell brought her back.

Jack started. 'That'll be Dad. He agreed to fetch me.'

She smiled and patted his knee. 'Safer than riding home eh? You'd better let him in my child.'

*

Sea Music

OUR ORCHESTRA CLUB took us away for a three week's vacation music making in a school near the sea on the South Downs. Performing all day and often into the night, we perfected another language. Polishing our technique by playing, playing until fingers and arms worked better, until everything grew - colours, taste, dreams. We discovered melodies in the sighs of wind, in deep breathing and laughter, in the din of the dining room, the creak of trees, in whispering grass and the scratch of pencils.

Someone told me "Music is the food of love." I hoped it was true. I was glad the world was such a rich playground. Susan, with whom I shared a desk in the first violins, grinned. 'There's love about. Not just the luvy-duvy sort. You know.' Walking to meals under gnarled trees, a moment on the high board before diving through the whippy wind into the clear swimming pool, sitting on the grass writing home, sometimes at moments in rehearsal I ached. Was that love? For I felt lapped by music.

A caretaker lived in a cottage by the main gates. He watered the grounds, maintained the pool as well as locking up the school grounds every night. Sometimes he sat at the back of the hall watching us play, afterwards drifting away without a word, the wind teasing his grey hair, a pensive smile lighting his face with the same glow as ours.

One day Susan and I rehearsed a concerto for two violins with string orchestra by Vivaldi, I saw the man was rapt, sharing my dreams. I played for him, watching his face suffuse with music. My music. Our music. I knew he ached too.

Afterwards he sidled over to where we were packing our instruments away saying how much he'd enjoyed it.

I was gladdened. 'Do you like string music?'

He pursed his lips. 'Yes. Their raucous body song.'

I shivered. 'Do you play violin?'

'No, flute, "Mother magic, cradle of the world." as one poet put it.' he murmured.

Susan giggled. 'That doesn't make sense.'

I shook my head not sure what to say, feeling something private and important lay in his words. '"Mother magic?"'

He smiled gently. 'Crooning *and* dreaming and . .'

Then I wanted to trust him with the nascent dreams nestling in music making me restless. His eyes danced. I blushed. Had he understood my thoughts? Would he snigger, as grown-ups do, at the silliness of a fifteen year old?

But he smiled winningly. 'Would you like to hear the sea crooning and dreaming?'

I uncertainly nodded.

'Is there time after your lunch today?'

'All right.' I stammered.

'Meet you at the main gate at one thirty.' He shyly touched my arm. 'Heaving water in airy space, the fragile gulls, the tenacious cliff plants are another symphony.' He drew back (as I would). 'The wind is full of the whispers it carries from far away. I love the wilderness of water and sky and the crumbling resistant shore.' His eyes shone deep into me.

Susan grinned at me. 'My, you look happy.' After he'd gone she frowned. 'Are you sure about him?'

I nodded.

'He's got a crush on you, the dirty old man. He's easy to outrun. And, mind the sharks.' She clipped her case shut and rushed away to a lesson. I found a practice room and played scales and excersises until lunch time.

It was a blustery day. The beach was deserted. Marking one extremity a band of rock stretched into the sea and disappeared. We stumbled to where it dipped into the waves. Wind-blown spume drove us back for shelter in a cleft in the rocky cliff. I shivered. The man pointed to a gull balancing on the breeze. 'It braves the chill in its search for food.' I looked up swimming in the clouded blue and stumbled, falling back into him. He very gently drew me into his warmth.

'My name's Tyl.' he said into my flying hair.

'I'm Natasha.'

'Wanting to fly like that gull?'

'No, I like it here.'

Tyl's hands slid up my thighs to the hem of my shorts. His warmth filled me with sea dreams. I pressed into him feeling pressure from his crotch reminding me of the thrill of playing him Vivaldi. Something too deep to know stirred.

'Sorry about that.'

'It's the raucous song of your body violin.'

He laughed and hugged me. It was perfect. I looked down for his straying hands. My skin glowed. When I looked up the gull had gone. Waves burst on the rocks. Clouds fluffed above the restless sea. Everything sparkled. High above us in the cliff small land birds bustled and chivied in the bushes, telling of the grass and trees behind the wildness of the coast.

'The smell of grass is what the wind carries.' I said softly. 'The scent of its dream.'

He squeezed my leg. '"Cradle of the world." Our cradle.'

I wanted him to be my cradle rocking with music and waves, rocking the ache away. I felt him wanting me. It was wonderful.

He nibbled my ear lobe. 'There's a beach beyond the rocks round the point. Let's look for shells.'

He let go my hand as we reached the distant sand. We treasure-hunted like gulls, like children, like the best friends we had become, filled with salt and glee in a timeless wilderness whose riches echoed in my music for the rest of that sparkling day.

I woke suddenly. The shadowy dormitory was bathed in moonlight. Hurriedly I pulled a track-suit over my nighty and tiptoed through the breathing ranks, out onto the landing and down stairs into the moon lit garden. I ran across the grass, my feet tingling with dew, slipped through the hedge marking the front drive and stole along to Tyl's cottage - a shadowed face in the dusky light.

'Natasha!' his only word on opening the door. He dowsed the light and led me into the living room. Soon an invigorated fire danced.

'Natasha, it's the middle of the night.'

'Oh. Do you mind?'

'Of course not. It's only that . . .'

'I know.'

'It's dangerous.'

'Not with you.'

'Yes, Natasha.'

'I had to see you. No one knows.' I flopped on the couch the fire hot on my face. He hovered naked but for scanty pyjama shorts, his outline like a fire-etched god, worrying over me.

'Oh, my dear, my dear.'

'I'll stay for a bit. May I?'

He sat heavily beside me as aware of his ballooning shorts as I. When I touched his bare shoulder he shivered and placed my hand on his pulsing sex.

'It's dangerous.' He groaned. His thrill when I held it invaded me. It responded, like my violin, tensing with unimagined music.

'See, it's your dribbling flute.'

'Ah, Natasha, please.'

I drew back, pushed his shorts down, pulled off my track suit. The white of my nighty flickered with firelight. With my hand around his sex, he knelt and kissed me. Slowly, tracing my eyes, my nose my lips. Exploring with his tongue which sang the same urgency as his cock until it burst. He fell on me with a groan, a moment of stillness like the end of a lingering cadence in a complicated sonata.

'Tyl, your heart's racing.'

'Natasha, I love you.'

Then I knew our music was the food of love; I was almost whole. As his heart and breathing settled I waited for the next movement. He found the hem of my nighty and lifted it up to my tummy. 'It's my nighty. I was asleep.'

'Ah, my angel.' His hand slid up my inner thigh and capped my pubic hair. Fingers strayed into my vagina finding songs in my silence. Ocean songs which grew and burst so I moaned lustily. His tongue searched, melting my pleading. I ripped off my nighty to press into his nakedness.

'Natasha?'

'Tyl, everything.'

'I need a condom.'

'Got one?'

He rolled off the couch, the fire flickering over his pearly skin his want wonderfully evident as he hurried out. I lay wallowing in delight.

When he knelt over me, his sex magnified by the condom cruelly gleaming like a bank robber masked in a stocking, a minute stab of fear stilled me. Then it was too late. I was invaded: a twinge of pain, paroxysms of pleasure, the thrashing ocean, waves breaking on and on and on.

With a drowning shout I clutched at my precious straw as he whimpered. 'Natasha, my Natasha.' as we fell down down into delightful deeps ending our music. Yet our song seemed never ending.

The fire died. We snuggled. Moon light joined us.

I stirred. 'We made music.'

'You played beautifully, Natasha.'

'My *Tremolo* bowing bursting your penis.'

'Yuk, for you?'

'Warm velvet. And your dying sighs. No, Tyl. And you bowed me far better.'

'Natasha we should've kissed. Only kissed.'

'Shhh. It was perfect. Don't spoil it.'

'It was.'

'Tyl, you filled me with real dreams. The first real time.'

'Incredible, Natasha, you took all of me. Everything your violin promised and your eyes proclaimed. Such gifts! It hurts.'

'I was thinking that. Tyl, why does love hurt so?'

'Deep experience consists of ecstasy and pain.'

'That's why music makes me cry.'

'Making love doesn't, it seems.'

'Making love . . . it's pure dreaming.' His tenderness was itself another dream.

Fumbling in the dark they dressed. He took her through the silent moonlit garden towards the gothic blackness of the clock-towered dormitory building, found the door where reluctantly they parted.

They contrived to make love daily. Fleeting release lightened the pleasure but deepening passion drove them to find more prolonged richer moments.

What involved them was Natasha's flowering. Tyl told her she was a flower. She said she was opening because he watered and tended her. He saw she was as deeply touched as he, they became engrossed.

His joy grew from a fascination with her gradually emerging inner mysteries. The deeper he ventured the richer her (and his) flowering. Naturally, deeper excitation led to wilder orgasms. But it was more than simply lust. Something of their inner fire escaped enhancing the every-day: his care of the school grounds, her music making; his patience, her sureness. Her teachers praised the growing power and sensitivity of her playing. Her growing talent was impossible to ignore. It was extraordinary.

The lovers gradually realized their exploration of lust was decisive. He had asked so often, 'Are you all right?' Eventually another answer glimmered.

Early in the last week, instead of meeting him, Natasha walked into the harbour town and bought a thick exercise book. 'To remember all we do for after I go away.' she told him. 'You can't see. It's private.'

Tyl grinned and nuzzled her left breast sensing her strumming heart. 'Private? I know what's written inside. We've drawn all our dark secrets out every night.'

Natasha blushed. 'Actually, my diary's written to you. There's no one else. But you couldn't read my scrawl.'

They decided to take advantage of a group bonfire. She would slip away to the little bonfire in his living room where they could dally.

And so it was. She sneaked away and, with a thumping heart, slipped into his cottage. He'd pulled the curtains, laid a mattress in front of the fire and hung an iron pot of cocoa in the chimney.

They sprawled basking by the fire. In spite of agreeing to loiter they soon undressed. She pawed him teasing shivers from his flesh, intruding into the most intimate places, finding scents and visions with tongue and fingers.

Tyl arched longingly. 'Natasha, Natasha. Fantastic. Oh yes. Oh my darling one, if you go on I'll COME.'

She savored his juice, transfixed by the rush of his need, delighting in enticement and his sheepish nod in answer to her gleeful whisper, 'All right?'

Then she wanted him to tease her open. She glowed when his light fingers and tongue made ripples break inside. Her need of him consumed them. Yet with a mischievous grin, he proposed a cocoa break. Natasha lay quivering, eyeing his erection, his strong back and able hands his muscular hairy legs. The delay was exquisite; the cocoa, nectar.

Smacking her lips, she pushed the empty mugs away and trailed her finger nails along his inner thighs, over his balls into his pubic hair without touching the rearing stalk, over the edges of his tummy feeling its lascivious shudder, then up his torso over his taut chest and into arm pits' fluff. She licked one and then the other ear lobe, drawing her pubis over his, sinking down onto full penetration, feeling a deepening flush, the tremors of a new longing shared with the most trusted person in the world. Flushed with slivers of lightning, she could do no more. The depth and intensity continued as they turned. She lay under him now, in one huge 'O'.

'Stay, Tyl. Yes, like that. Yes.'

He hung over her, embedded, pulsing. Gradually she released herself. Washed by the primal sea, she lost her body, her secrets, her voice. Cries gargled from her mouth, dreams pealing with the immensity of union. It was the nothing of her beginning. Of his. The invisible centre of life. He stayed her, stayed with her. Holding. Winkling out endless majesty, homing in on a speck which grew and burst, gladdening everything. At the end Tyl rolled off and slept. Natasha, buoyed by diminishing flickers of orgasm, drifted into tranquil sleep.

She woke at dawn. There he was, lying like a baby beside her. So ordinary, so precious she cried.

He opened an eye. 'Dear one, I thought only music made you weep?'

'Oh Tyl. And you, us and our music.'

'It was the best night?'

'Of my life.' She hugged him.

'Who are you, slip of a girl, bringing paradise?'

'Who are you, old leather thing, showing me the way? We must go back there before I go home.'

He embraced all of her. 'Now we know the road, surely we can return?'

'Will you take me Tyl?'

'Darling, darling. Of course.' He sighed. 'Now, you must go. It's light. We can't be caught together. You'd better go alone.'

She hummed the *Teddy Bears' Picnic*. 'Mm. All night. Wow!'

He watched her dress. 'Waking to find you here was a miracle.'

'Why me, Tyl?'

'You're stunning. I knew you cared.'

'You care for me like no one else.'

'Go, dear one so you can come again.'

'I'm so happy. Are you?'

'Bursting.'

'Me too. Is your flute leaking?'

'Bursting. I told you.'

'Then play a hornpipe and I'll dance to bed.' She threw him a ravishing smile, skipped up the drive and vanished through the hedge.

Tyl pottered, removing the mattress and cocoa mugs, retrieving the condom. He held it between finger and thumb, its creased fragile skin oozing long elastic strands.

'What an ugly end to so much joy.' he muttered dropping it into the bin.

The prospect of parting made them ravenous. Joy masked anxiety. Their unhindered wildness of coupling - Natasha's rite of passage, Tyl suggested, through roles of girl, woman, boy, animal returning to woman - was as demanding as her music making. As inspiring. Transforming her with a conviction that their power to sustain daily life had the same inevitability as the mess of musical polyphony reaching a glorious final cadence. Their last day convinced her of this.

First a triumphant concert, then a victory dinner and Natasha's two prizes, for 'Most Improved Student' and 'Outstanding Chamber Musician', followed by an all-night bonfire (for most: she surreptitiously left early).

Natasha let herself in. The cottage was silent and dark. Tyl must be locking up, she thought. She gleefully made tea and stumbled with it into the bedroom, pulled off her bulky clothes and slipped into his bed delighting in nakedly bathing in his scents. She pulled the duvet around her and happily sipped tea. So, where is he? she thought.

He found her there. She kissed his dew-cool face, poured his tea and undressed him. Fiercely he took her and erupted. She held her softening man tenderly. They slept. Woke. Drank chilly tea and began a long languorous caress until, with unbearable longing, she pulled him in. Their consummation carried them on a flood of sea music into each other's dreaming bodies to a dawn of smiling tears and contentment.

The earliest blackbirds were trilling when she opened the door and demurely kissed him goodbye.

'So many prizes, but yours is the best. Not a book-token or certificate. But something lasting for ever.'

'Natasha, write to me?'

'I promise, Tyl.'

'Off you go, my angel.'

The dewy garden, filling with light, was chorused in bird song. Natasha slipped up the stairs and into the sleeping dormitory. Some of the beds were empty. She grinned, undressed, pulled on her chilly nighty and wriggled into her unrumpled bed bubbling with the thought,

I'm not the only one. With the gong for breakfast, normality reigned.

After breakfast we packed. Then the bus arrived and sat outside the clock tower. Susan promised to keep me a seat. While all the others had a final coffee I ran to his cottage.

Out of breath I gasped, 'I had to see you.'

He was drinking tea. 'Dearest.' He kissed me I wept.

'Here, have a cuppa.' I set it down and made him hug me. I felt the pressure of his erection and found soft reassuring flavours in his mouth. My heart settled. He took our mugs in his strong hand. 'Come, I'll walk you to the bus.'

We sauntered down the drive to where it was waiting at the gate for stragglers. We stood noisily sipping tea.

'I'd better go.'

'Here, give me your mug.' His face in my hair, he whispered, 'Natasha, I do love you.'

'Forever, forever' echoed through my body. I daren't look back. I clambered aboard and slumped beside Susan. She cried (for us both).

'What a holiday, Susan.'

'It's all right for you.' she sobbed softly. 'Where were you last night?'

'At the bonfire. Susan?'

'After that. You were later than me.'

'Oh . . . were you with Jan the hunky oboe tutor?'

'Natasha, it was not all fun. Don't tell! In his room at first it was great. He's awesome naked. He squirted jelly into me and all over, you know, um, a condom calling me darling and all that. He hurt moving about. It was gross, even though he was happy. I didn't want, not like that.'

I held her hand. 'One day someone *will* love you, Susan. You're a fabulous person. You know that.'

Maybe I was once. Now I'm damaged goods.'

'Susan, you're sexy and clever. So he's a slob. But at least now you know what you want. Eh?'

She slowly nodded, looking at me in wonder. 'That dinosaur loves you, doesn't he. And do you? Mm? You lucky thing.'

The bus rushed us homeward. We were silenced.

Natasha was surprised by the social workers and police women. They invaded the house. Talk of rape and sodomy and extreme abuse worried her. 'Of whom?' she asked. 'You.' was the shocking answer. 'By that evil caretaker now in custody. How could they employ a man like him in a school? It's beyond comprehension.'

Natasha collapsed.

'We're here to help.' they all said.

'It's not like that.' Natasha sobbed.

'Your parents gave us your diary. It'll be all right. No one can hurt you now.' they said.

"Hurt, parents, diary, sodomy, abuse, diary, rape, custody, evil": the words screamed in her head. Reeling, her protests ignored, Natasha fell into blackness, a depthless yawning death. She called to him; all that came out was a croak: Our sea music, our music. Oh my Tyl, I never told you I love you. We sang about so much, about everything. In this terrible silence I'll remember our songs. There's nothing else. Nothing. Until we meet.

She stormed out of home vowing never to see her betrayer-parents again. She stayed with an aunt when away from boarding school. Life was a nightmare from which she escaped into music, both for its comfort and the strength it gave her, engaging with Tyl in the wild wonderful wayward dreams he had shown her. Music, the only solace.

One day all the papers trumpeted the demise of a paedophile who had died in custody during his trial. Although reaping his "Just Deserts", the police were castigated for poor supervision. The man had lain dead in his cell all night. He had been poorly after a stroke during "robust police questioning" some months earlier when he protested innocence in the face of terrible abuse documented by one of his victims. "Leave it to the courts to punish" the papers smugly demanded. "Procedures were primitive", they thundered calling for a public enquiry.

Tyl was dead. It was her fault. Natasha went berserk. Heavily sedated, she was confined in a mental hospital. The darkness engulfing her thinned one day when a new acuitive doctor played her a CD of a Vivaldi concerto for two violins. She twitched with a spasm of pain. He looked at her keenly saying he was an amateur violinist and would she play with him, that her instrument was in a locker in Admin. She cried for the first time in a very very long time before reluctantly agreeing.

He brought along some Tartini duets. They tuned and played.

'You're terrible.' Natasha said flatly.

'I'm sorry. I guess that's why I'm a psychiatrist.' he said. 'Please play some *real* music.'

'*Real* music?'

He nodded carefully, anxiously.

The violin bit into Natasha's chin. The slim tensed bow arched from her hand. The word *tremolo* intruded. She shook her head, too distrait to properly remember Tyl's magic phallus. With a sigh she haltingly began the *Prelude* of Bach's solo *Partita in E major*. It's joy burst the bubble of her depression, filling the bleak institutional space with life. She managed the first half, began the repeat and was swamped by despair.

The doctor put a wary arm round her. 'It speaks for us all.'

'Does it?'

'Who does it speak for?'

'For Tyl.'

'For you?'

'I don't know.'

'Natasha, It's a dream to me. But more to you?'

'Yes.'

'More than a dream?'

'All lost.'

'There's such joy and majesty and triumph.'

'Yes.'

'Your joy, majesty and triumph?'

'His. Our sea music.'

The doctor said, looking at her and way beyond:

> '*The sea is calm tonight.*
> *The tide is full, the moon lies fair*
> *Upon the straits; . . .*
> *The sea of faith*
> *Was once, too, at the full,*
> *and round earth's shore*
> *Lay like the folds of a bright girdle furled.*
> *But now I only hear*
> *Its melancholy, long, withdrawing roar . . .*
> *Ah love, let us be true*
> *To one another! for the world, which seems*

To lie before us like a land of dreams,
So various, so beautiful, so new,
hath really neither joy, nor love, nor light,
Nor certitude, nor peace, nor help for pain . . .

Matthew Arnold's *Dover Beach.'*   He paused, studying her stricken face.

Natasha blenched. 'Tyl knew there was no help, yet made the world into lullabies: "Mother magic, cradle of the world". Such perfectly beautiful dreams.'

The doctor waited. 'Tyl was the man in court?'

'Yes.'

'But Natasha, didn't he hurt you?'

'Hurt? He taught me sea music.'

'Yes, that's what you're saying.'

'I never said "I love you". I never told him.'

'Perhaps he knew.'

She nodded and nodded again. 'Perhaps. Yes.' She wilted. 'He said he knew what I wrote in my diary.'

The doctor started. 'The one the police used? Tell me, where is that diary?'

'I dunno. Parents?'

'I think you should have it back.'

'So do I.'

'I'll prepare a Compulsory Acquisition Form addressed to them, if you sign it.'

'No parents. No signature.'

'We'll read every word on the Form beforehand. You're only giving permission for me to get it for you.'

She looked stony.

'Natasha, please. First the diary, then I'll get you out of here somehow. You shouldn't be here.'

'I know. *They* should be. Tyl knew it wasn't teddy bears in the woods but monsters like parents, police, social workers, judges. The monsters in control.'

The doctor's cheek trembled. 'The monsters inside you?'

'No. The ones outside.'

'Like me?'

She trembled. 'Yes.' she whispered.

He risked: 'Play more mother magic?'

'I can't. I need Tyl's flute. Awash with tears, she collapsed on a sofa, longing for his cradling; the ache in her emptiness, unbearable.

The doctor waited hoping some of the loss she bore would wash out. Eventually she lay deathly still. He patted her shoulder. 'Play, Natasha.'

Natasha struggled up and began again. The *Prelude* grew from tentative scratching to triumphant glory. She finished white faced but calm.

The doctor whistled in admiration. 'Well done! That was awesome.' A tear glinted on his cheek. 'Maybe you could play another movement tomorrow?'

She almost nodded.

The doctor relaxed. 'You need to talk Natasha. Talking and playing keeps monsters at bay.'

'Turn them into bears.'

'No, my dear. Monsters are monstrous and best kept out.'

'I do that.'

'It seems to me you keep everybody out, which silences you.'

'So would you if you were dead.'

'Your monsters tell you, you're dead. But Natasha, you really played just now. You can't be dead, can you?'

'Most of the time.'

'Let's talk about that tomorrow.'

'Maybe.'

Natasha idled out into the grounds and walked unseeing across paths and lawns. Her violin had just spoken about forgotten things that once mattered. Was there any more to say? she wondered.

A blackbird bounded across the grass, its chest puffed out, its golden bill open in song, its beady eyes watching for monsters or worms.

Natasha sat. Grass tickled her palms. Clouds fluffed beyond leafy branches. High in a slip stream a couple of gulls floated. "They bear the chill seeking food." Tyl had said. She blinked. She leant hungrily back seeking a rocky cleft and a cushioning friend, and for a moment forgot her pain.

Natasha was seen by the doctor daily. Although grim encounters, she grew relieved to see him. His kindly firmness, her tears, the agonizing silences, lightened her. She regularly played for him, surprised by his appreciation and by rediscovering feelings of skill.

One day she was summoned to his office. Alarmed, she sat in a chair confronting his desk. He looked strained. She steeled herself for bad news.

'Hello, Natasha. I got you tea. Is that OK?'

She nodded suspiciously.

He opened a drawer. 'I received your diary last week and checked one or two matters you'd talked of. I'm sorry, but I needed to understand.'

She sat up electrified, stared at the dog-eared book full of Tyl, and filled with sea music. This confirmed there were some friendly monsters out there. She reached eagerly across the desk and snatched it.

The doctor studied her wistful smile. 'There's a passage I've marked with a red flash. Would you be very brave and read it aloud?'

Nervously she opened at the page and haltingly read:

Dog Wednesday: A terrible day. We were both so busy. We only met during my personal time slot in the gym store, safe from everything. We lay on a heap of mats. I undressed him, finding the goo in his pocket. Let him undress me slowly kissing my clothes off. We were bursting. Both really keen. I knelt. He kissed everywhere private and pushed his tongue into my bottom. It was wild. He poked gooey fingers in until my ring softened then he mounted me like a dog. Weird, him inside me like that!

Stretching, I thought I'd burst. When it hurt he stopped but soon was right in. It was exciting. It was the first time he'd been inside with nothing on. He said it was disturbing and thrilling, much better than doing it when at school. (We both laughed, "Boys will be boys, or puppy dogs!").

I went down on one shoulder and reached behind for his balls, my face in the smelly mat. He cried out like anything, moved very fast and pressed in and in, and whoosh, out it all came. I felt the splash.

His fingers played in my vagina. I lost count of everything. I felt it shrink and plop out like shit.

It was a bit disgusting. But he was right, it was thrilling. His excitement was extraordinary. Imagine, finding a wild animal under our skins? Another person.

He was so tender afterwards, I cried. We lay for ages without a word. I was a bit shaky going to the toilet.

He IS right: our bodies are animals, our minds make the difference.
Making silky beauty out of piggy ugliness when our lust is trans-
formed by love.
Like music, we must let our bodies run free, guide them with minds
and feelings so the Savage sings rather than grunts and fucks up.
It was terrible, parting. He wanted more too.

Through the troubled silence, the doctor said, 'Is that exactly what you wrote?'

'Yes.' she muttered.

'Every word?'

She scowled. 'Yes, I told you.'

'How would you describe it's mood, or its feelings?'

'Dunno. Tender, wild, trusting, scary, disgusting; two become four, two humans, two animals, four sets of feelings.'

'Thank you, Natasha. You have great courage.' He paused. 'I agree, it matches what you describe. Perhaps not four sets of feelings. Four creatures, yes, but the humans share feelings?'

'Maybe the animals do as well.'

'I see what you mean. So, maybe two humans, two animals and two sets of feelings?'

Natasha was silent, moved by memories of sharing within the complexities of difference. She sipped her tea, then looked up. 'Can you see why he mattered? Putting myself together with him was such a wild adventure.'

The doctor nodded. Picked up another paper. 'Listen to the police report on that:

One Wednesday he took me to the gym and ripped off my clothes. He
lubricated my anus and stuck it in. It hurt. He pushed my face into
the smelly mats stifling my screams. He poked in and in and then
pushed me away. I was shaking. It was painful on the toilet trying to
empty myself. He said afterwards I was perfect. Better than the boys
he fucked. He let me go although wanting more.

Natasha gasped. 'No wonder he died.'

The doctor clenched his fist. 'Natasha, remember we agreed he knew how you felt and what you wrote. I'm sure he did.'

She cowered in her chair, 'He loved me.'

'Your diary tells us that.'

'He told me.'

'He understood you Natasha. He knew *you* didn't betray him. How could you?'

'Never, never, never.'

'Exactly.'

'They killed him. They plotted and lied. I hate them. HATE THEM.' she shouted.

'Natasha, listen to me. Tell me, would Tyl want you to be out of here?'

'Yes he would.'

'Now, pay attention until I finish. Firstly, you broke the law, whether we accept it or not, it states that sexual relations with minors are forbidden; but secondly, however one judges that, it does not justify how it was dealt with; thirdly, as a sort of bargain, to right your confinement, I've got you an interview for a music school: a "Tuition & Accommodation" bursary, a chance for your sea music. He'd like that, wouldn't he?' The doctor was shaking. He'd risked so much, fighting her case with pleading manoeuvres. Could he tempt her away from this wholly inappropriate custody and out of her depression? He sat in mute agony.

'Tyl loved my music. He listened and cared. He wanted only to kiss. But I wanted the Everything he gave me. The dreams, the joy, the terror and animal shadow in music (in ourselves). He showed me adventure was possible. I could be a woman, a man, a boy, girl, bird, animal - all the bits came alive. You don't understand.'

The doctor's face trembled in his effort to deal with so passionate and disturbing an inner drive. 'Natasha, I am trying to help you. I offer this chance. Only you can say yes and move on.'

'You're getting rid of me.'

'If you accept, I'll accompany you to the audition. In any event, while you remain here, our work will continue. Yes, you're right. I am getting rid of you so you can live again: play and, I hope, love, dream, and be the remarkable girl hidden now within so much distress.'

She bit her nails. She spoke softly. 'Tyl said I was remarkable. I don't feel it. It was his love.'

'And more. It is you, acting that out in your music and in life.'

She chewed her ragged nails. 'I got two prizes. Did I tell you? For best player and for making progress.'

The doctor managed a smile. 'Lucky you. I'm sure you deserved them. In life there are few prizes, but now you have a chance both to progress and to star. Or, more of the same, eh? Do you want time to think it over?'

'For a monster you're quite nice.'

He laughed. Her drawn face blazed with youthful beauty. Sunshine and silence filled the room. It is very hard to handle hope.

'Would the E *major Partita* do?'

'Natasha, you know better than I.'

'I like the hurrying struggle to get to the end. The song, the skipping, its crazy youngness.'

'Sounds like you.'

'Oh yes. And Tyl.'

'And all of us my dear. Also, I found you a teacher. She's at the school. That's some help. Can you face a stranger?'

'Only another nice monster.'

'Can you let her in? That would be progress.'

'Do they all know about me?'

'I mentioned your talent. Since the teacher is coming here I had to tell her as well as the director, but nothing I've not told you already. My report about you will have two sections: a short professional comment, and a more general bit which you'll certainly see beforehand.'

'What's his name?'

'Mrs. Mamsey.'

'A meddling Mrs.'

'A very fine teacher. Shall I ring her and confirm an appointment?'

'She'll make me play boring scales.'

'Probably. Helping you.'

'You sound like Tyl.' she grinned.

The doctor picked up the phone. She watched him arranging her lesson. What were they saying? Then he retorted, 'I'll find a private room, yes, we'll need a music stand. Uha. Thank you. Goodbye.'

He bent down for a carrier bag under his desk. 'My daughter (who knows about these things) chose you a dress. Please don't be offended. Please Natasha. Prison jeans won't do for an audition. If it's awful we can change it.' He proffered the bag.

Natasha sniffed and pulled out a white cotton dress printed with huge red flowers. Impetuously she stripped to her knickers and shimmeyed into the dress, buttoned-up and tightened the belt. 'It's nice.' She stood shyly trying to catch her reflection in the glass of the door and moving her bowing arm testing the comfort of the sleeves.

The doctor's jaw dropped. 'Natasha, it's . . .'

She stood flushed before him, her shapely body suddenly visible, fire in her eyes, head on one side as if listening.

He blinked. 'It's . . .'

She laughed. 'You, lost for words? So you like it.'

'Very much.'

'Um, I can't pay.'

'It's a present. Clothes can be armor. You still need some, let's admit that.'

'I know. Um, thanks.' She fled down the corridor, into the garden, skipping over the grass.

'Hey, Natasha.' The doctor caught up with her. 'Your jeans and tee shirt.'

She bundled them under an arm, grinned and pranced on. 'See you later.'

When she reached the ward, neither inmates nor staff recognized her. It's better than armor, she mused. It makes me invisible. 'If only I can escape.' she whispered to the bickering sparrows, too busy with small worries to consider such a big one.

The audition started badly. Questions, comments: talk talk dumbed her. An elderly man asked kindly, 'Why do you want to study music?'

Natasha gently thwacked the bow against her leg. 'Um, music is,' Their silence seared. Tyl was touching her leg. 'Music is mother magic cradling the world.'

'Tell us why you chose Bach.'

'The *Prelude* is a shout of joy, lots of singing which makes me smile. Mrs. Mamsey says Pablo Casals began each day playing Bach. He thought it better than scales. I'm not sure she agrees.'

They laughed. Not *at* her. It was an easy going pleasure. Shadows lifted. Apprehensive she had no music they suggested she begin.

She closed her eyes. Stood in her white nighty in his cottage and played for him. His eyes glowed with lusty understanding. He was dancing to the bowing, to the strings of sound which vibrated deep within until, with a triumphant shout, he came as the *Prelude* ended. He longed for more. She played the following graver dances. Sweetly, huskily, rocking, cradling, banishing chill air with well-fed songs until the *Partita* finished. When she looked up, startled tear-bright eyes regarded her. Mrs Mamsey was smiling.

The elderly man said huskily. 'Well played, Natasha. You have a lot to learn, yet I feel we've little to teach you. What you said earlier about music, we all search for, and a few reach. You have more than talent, it's a gift. Mrs. Mamsey is quite right.'

Everyone nodded.

'You may take it, an invitation to join the Gold Hill School of Music will reach you shortly. We hope you accept.'

She was free! They let her go. Outside she told the nervous doctor whose frown vanished. They perched in the school canteen, relieved when the cacophony died with the students rushing away to classes.

'You know, I feel I've been here before. In another life.' she said dreamily. 'Anyway, I escaped.'

'Natasha, I'm proud of you.' was all he said.

'You know. The bloody sparrows told you my dream. I thought they only talked about food and sex. Hey, "the food of love". They were right-on. Here I am.'

Twelfth Night William Shakespeare. Get a student ticket and see the play!' He smiled warmly.

Then, she decided he really cared.

The faculty of the Gold Hill School of Music calmly accepted Natasha was weird and brilliant. Mrs. Mamsey, aware of her "difficulties growing up" as the doctor put it, patiently defended her star pupil's late delivery of written work, her disinterest in theory and history, and skepticism about most of the music she was expected to play. 'Given time and space, she'll develop.' everyone hoped. Perplexed by her disinterest in much of the every-day, the staff pushed her to fill a concert slot in the Wigmore Hall. It was short notice, yet Natasha was extraordinary enough to excite audiences. 'The interaction will be good for her.' tutors agreed.

The concert was a triumph. At the end, the delighted audience settled as Natasha, abandoned by her admiring accompanist, stepped forward for an encore.

She stood dazzled by spot lights and applause. '*Prelude* to Bach's solo *Partita in E major*.' she said shyly. She stood, stock still. Head cocked waiting for bird song, a message, encouragement? No one was sure. In the breathless hush she began a stream of notes at break-neck speed. Old timers shook their heads in critical disbelief then gasped at the clarity of articulation carried by the ebb and flow of waves of cadential lines shaping sense into waterfall after waterfall. Everything sounded as if for the first time, warm full-throated alive. Some wept in joyous disbelief. Then it was over. Natasha waited in the ecstatic hush unsure if they'd clap, if she should go, unsure because Bach's musical journey was unfinished. A enraptured young man rose and said very softly but perfectly audibly, 'Play the next movement!'

Natasha nodded and played. Played movement after movement to the very end.

Drumming feet and cheers followed her into the greenroom. She was glad it was over. Glad, when the throng, full of praise and jostling for autographs, retreated. Glad to stow her violin in its shabby case and to sit quietly, reconnecting to her longing for Tyl, which still echoed. She looked down over her dress - the one from the doctor she'd dyed dark blue for the formality of the concert. The red flowers were now regal purple in a night-blue sky, too somber for a nighty but matching her present mood. There was a timid tap at the door.

'Coming.' Natasha called.

The door opened admitting the young man, his untidy mop of hair at odds with his immaculate clothes.

'Have they all gone?' he murmured. 'Do you mind, um, if I . . ?'

She shook her head.

'I love you, your playing. It says what I want to say but can't.' He sighed. 'I suppose they all say that.'

'Only you really listened.' she said softly, aware of his sensitive face, his able hands and, was it longing flickering through his trim body, awakening her own?

'My name is Daniel.'

'Friend of lions.'

He grinned. 'Natasha, your music tells me more about dreams than lions.'

'Thank you Daniel. Listen, I must dash. Missed the coach back to college. And I'm famished.'

'Let's have coffee. No. My flat's close by. I'll make you supper and order a cab.'

'One of those quick cuppasoup suppers then I'll get a bus. Cabs cost the earth.'

'A proper supper to keep your eyes bright. My family has a taxi account. No need to pay. I won't hurt you Natasha, I promise.'

'I trust you.'

'It's all right then?'

'Yes Daniel.'

'Can I help you on with your coat?'

'I don't have one.'

'I'll carry your violin.'

'Brill. Let's get out of here.'

It was his parents' town flat at the top of a bulky Art Deco building. Under-used, palatial, impersonal, with deep carpets, expensive furnishings, walls hung with giant paintings, niches with spot-lit sculptures and glossy books on low tables. Natasha examined the paintings while Daniel busied himself in the kitchen before calling her to eat. He'd lit two candelabra. A wine bottle poked from a cooler. Crockery and cutlery gleamed.

Daniel grinned. 'It's Jamie Oliver's liver and bacon with fresh sage, onions and mashed spuds. The best fare for busy violinists. It's the only wine in the cooler. I hope white suits a virtuoso.'

'Me? Shut up Daniel, don't talk rubbish. But the food's brill.'

He was suddenly serious. 'Rubbish? Well, I think you're fantastic. You make your instrument speak. In the silence throttling me, that really is medicine magic.'

Her cheek twitched. '"Mother magic, cradle of the world". I'm sorry Daniel. I thought I was the only one throttled by silence.'

Natasha ate and drank everything. Ordered to the living room while he cleared-up, she lay briefly on the couch to let her head clear. It had been a demanding day.

Daniel found her fast asleep. He watched dreams flit across her face and flutter her eye lids. Very carefully he removed her shoes, covered her with a blanket then switched off the lamp. He couched watching her, his heart racing, sweating with tenderness. 'I love you Natasha.' he butterfly whispered, and crept away jubilant and disturbed to his bed.

Something beyond Daniel's deep sleep moved. He opened his eyes. It was morning. Natasha was inexpertly trying to cover his nakedness with his sheet.

She grinned. 'Tit for tat. I bet you spied on me last night. Daniel, you should've woken me.'

Jubilant, he pulled up the sheet. 'Why? Do you want to go home?'

'Is it all right?

'No one will ever know I slept near an angel.'

'A rather crumpled one, I'm afraid. Look at my dress.'

'Shut your eyes.' Daniel leapt out of bed and pulled on boxer shorts. Natasha eyed him with pleasurable regret. He rummaged in a chest of drawers and flung a roomy white tee shirt, as-new jeans, a yellow and a red button-up shirt. 'Shower and put these on, choose your colour. I'll get the one-hour dry cleaners to clean and press your frock while we have breakfast.'

'Wear your clothes?'

'Of course.'

'I don't want to be a Daniel.'

'Nor I. Too much competition. Shower? Come.'

He gladly took her hand and led her to the spacious shiny bathroom, carefully undid the buttons and belt and over dramatically shut his eyes. 'Slip the dress off. There's a bath robe behind the door.' But he couldn't help peeping. His heart leapt seeing her fecund breasts, her trim body, its greatest mystery hidden by neat pants.

She smiled. 'Now, out you go peeping pervert.'

Red faced he fled to call the porter for the dry cleaning mission, then hurriedly dressed to cloak his own excitement, prepared breakfast choking with happiness.

Natasha emerged with dripping hair, deliciously dressed in his clothes. He took a towel and rubbed her hair dry, savoring how easily she lay against him accepting his arousal and his ministrations, yet unresponsive.

She capped his bulging fly. 'Daniel, not that. I'm sorry.' she said gently.

'Is, is there someone else?'

'Yes.' she whispered.

He held her lightly, appalled by tears on her cheeks, unable to help her or himself.

'Tyl is dead because I loved him.'

'Dead?'

'They killed him.'

'Is that what's in your music?'

'Yes.'

'Natasha, let's be friends. I'd die if you left.'

'Dear Daniel. Of course. Can we? But you mustn't die.'

'Best friends.'

She surveyed her boyish clothes. 'Two Daniels?'

'I'm not sure which is me.'

'I know. *You* care.' She lifted her face and kissed affirmation onto his lips. She disentangled herself, surprised by his solid fragrance and her pleasure.

'Coffee or tea?'

'Coffee.'

I'll make us *cappuccinos*.'

'Yummy.'

'Juice, muesli, fresh bread in half an hour.' He looked her up and down. 'Let's wait for the bread machine. There's a shoe shop down on the corner. Let's get some matching trainers for you. Then we'll eat?'

'Daniel, I'm broke. Skint.'

'I'm not. Let's go. Come on Natasha, it'll be fun.'

It was fun, being with him, sharing his excitement in so small an adventure. That's what ordinary things became with him. Her scruples melted under his boyish enthusiasm. She accepted his final argument that money is like music: it's to be played. Every note. Not saved up; that sort of mean-minded silence was terrible.

She returned for breakfast to the yeasty smell of ripe bread, and sporting yellow trainers, another black (performance) pair nestling in a fashionable carrier bag with the shoes she'd borrowed for the concert. She refused a red pair and the red shirt saying it was all too much, and she'd been tricked into thinking it temporary. But she burst with pleasure.

He demurred. For his current delight was more than enough.

Breakfast ended with crisp apples. Daniel laughed as Natasha turned hers over and over suspiciously inspecting its freckles and imperfections.

'No worms. They're not windfalls, I leave those for blackbirds. I picked them yesterday from the top of the tree. Have a bite. It'll keep the doctor away.'

It was delicious. She gazed at his radiant face with curiosity. 'I thought you lived here.'

'Oh no. This is the Wrinklies' city pad. I only use it when they're away. I bought a derelict barn in the countryside during my fallow year before starting architecture at Uni. I've been rebuilding ever since. Now it's done. I've made myself a studio with a roomy store/garage at one end. The rest is much as I found it but weather proof, lined and with a new mezzanine floor over part. I ran out of ideas. You see, it's surplus. Crying out for a use.'

'A barn with an apple tree.'

'A small grove of fruit trees, a nascent herb garden and some ancient forest trees, far older than the building. He gripped her arm. 'Come and see for yourself.'

'There's no time this term. Although working, I might come for a day in the holidays. Could I, in about six weeks?'

'The journey takes half a day. You need . . .' He stopped and stared at her. 'Natasha, it'll be perfect for music. A couple of new windows in the south, a northerly one facing the long view over the valley, radiators on the heating circuit, some tiling and a chair or two. And your bed. YES.' He danced round her. 'Bring your violin. Live there during the holiday. Play and study there. It's separate, beside my studio. We could both work and then meet up for meals like now. You MUST come.'

His joy invaded her. 'I suppose I could play apple and pear music to the blackbirds.'

'Yes, and we'll tramp the woods and fields and ride into the village. Be together. What fun.'

She looked doubtful.

'Natasha, trust me.'

She sighed. 'I'm not sure it's enough for you.'

'Enough?' He stopped romping to look searchingly at her. 'It would be,' he said very slowly, 'a dream come true.' He jigged again when she smiled. 'Let's telephone and book your ticket. Oh, Natasha, are you as happy as I am?'

She laughed. 'What a puppy dog you are, Daniel. Do you think it really could be a dream come true?'

'Trust me.' he said quietly and firmly.

Daniel met the train. Outside the tiny station he led her to the bikes: his mud spattered, hers clean and shiny new. He unwound a strap from his waist and fed it into the handle of her violin case and lassoed his head. 'It's safer. I know the way. Your bag will fit into the small carrier off the handlebars. Oo Natasha, here you are at last.'

They cycled out of the station forecourt to the main road, through a country village, soon turning off into lanes snaking between hedgerows, through fields of cattle and sheep. The afternoon light licked the forested tops of hills. Lip shadows kissed trimmed edges of the lane in places where it twisted and turned away from the sun. The only sound mingling with the braying of livestock and a multitude of bird song, was Natasha's panting as she manfully tried to keep up. Finally they free-wheeled down a long gentle incline, past a ramble of farm buildings, through a new gate, down a crisp gravel path to his barn. Its bulk and serenity were imposing. The two were greeted by a plump severe looking woman who straightened, brushed a stray lock of hair off her face and smiled.

Daniel dismounted. 'Mrs. Munro, this is Natasha.'

The woman nodded. 'Hello my dear. So, the goddess exists. It's been "Natasha's floor, Natasha's bed, Natasha's windows, Natasha's kitchen" for weeks. Now Danny, if you look after her half as well as you have her music place, she'll thrive here. Dear boy, the kettle's singing. I'm done. Got to go. Arthur's arriving from boarding school this evening, so it's house full. There's eggs and milk and vegies in both fridges. Your supper is in the Aga; before you eat, give it an hour on the top shelf. Oh yes, Mary got you cider, got you BOTH cider, Danny. I switched the bread machine and the heating on and gave Natasha's floor its hundredth coat of wax. Looks like a still lake you could swim across.' She scrutinized the girl. 'Well Natasha, welcome to you. I'll send our Arthur over in the morning with hot scones. You look done in. A cuppa and a nap should do the trick, I hope you'll like it here my dear. We probably know too much about you. Danny is a terrible gossip. Our Arthur will insist you play. He's learning the violin rather unenthusiastically. We're just up the track. Pop in any time. Danny'll show you.' Mrs. Munro strode away up the drive and vanished beyond the gate.

Daniel shook his head. 'She's a pet. Looks after the place and spoils me terribly.'

Natasha grinned. 'So, you're Danny the drunk. You might have warned me.'

Danny grunted. 'She and Mary (her daughter) count the weekly wine bottles. They believe alcoholics drink wine. Decent folks' tipple is cider or beer. Coming inside?'

Natasha stood stock still filling with peace, birdsong the scents of wax and wood and varnish, standing close enough to catch his spicy sweaty scent (Tyl's under arms). 'Daniel, your barn is very very beautiful.

You *are* a good architect. Because you feel deeply, I can see you do. It's the same with music. Such an old building and made so alive, a virtuoso performance. It's perfect here. Just as you said.'

He gently took her arm. 'This is your own house. Mine's beside you. We'll have tea there. Then you should slip in here and take a nap. No one will disturb you, sleeping or practising.' (He blushed remembering her mischievous grin trying to cover his nakedness six weeks earlier). 'If you like I'll show you around. Come and get me. Otherwise, I won't bother you. We're friends, so, some duets, some solo work. Are you as happy as I?'

She nodded, put her small bag beside her violin case on a couch-bed in the living room, kissed his cheek still chill from cycling and went with him into his serene spacious light-filled studio.

Mrs Munro had left a plate of biscuits still warm which made the tea delicious.

Quite suddenly Natasha felt secure. Was it the soft glow of wood and terracotta, the gleaming brass and paint work, the lovingly worked spaces hand-made to hold precious things, a mood - just beyond reach - of sure delight?

Now, and for the first time since Tyl had died, she felt she belonged.

She lazily sipped tea and munched as he talked about his architectural practice and his ideals, until he said. 'Enough about me, what about you; do you think you can work here?'

'Oh certainly. I'm learning the second solo sonata by Ysaye. It's a battle between life and death. It's impossibly difficult. But as a sort of farewell and memorial to Tyl, flowers on his grave and (I hope) my going on, it's all my life just now. This wise old barn will help me I'm sure. You too. It's good of you to put up with me. No one else could.'

He watched agony flit across her face. At last she smiled at him. He flushed with relief. Maybe there could be a place for him in her "going on". Maybe? That, capped all his dreams.

The shrill outrage of a blackbird disturbed scoffing wind-fall apples was the only reminder of a darker world beyond the peaceful barn. They settled easily into a routine of early work before sharing breakfast, then, longer separate work sessions until lunch and a kip, afterwards, getting out: usually rambling through fields and woods, or sometimes cycling to the village.

They visited the Munro farm along the rise, Natasha, charmed by the shy children (Arthur 14, Mary 18) who clearly doted on Daniel.

Helping Mrs Munro with scones and tea, Natasha said. 'Daniel is lucky being loved by you all.'

'He spent a lot of time with us at first. Alienated from his filthy-rich parents, he somehow needed us. He's been so supportive during our many difficulties. Not just money. He's become another son.' Mrs Munro stopped buttering scones. 'Can I be nosy Natasha? What about you and him?'

Natasha winced (still in thrall to her love of Tyl). 'Um, he's my closest friend. The only one. We're not intimate, if that's what you mean. We both want it that way.'

'He loves you my dear.'

'He's a fantastic friend. This is a fantastic place.'

'I'm glad you're happy. He lights up every time he mentions you. Always has.'

'You know Mrs Munro, he gives me so much and without conditions.'

'Yes, Natasha. That's his special way. Now dear, watch the kettle while I take the food in.'

Natasha gazed out of the window at cows straggling to the milking shed, and reviewed her first days: the chest of drawers with clothes for her including the red shirt and the matching trainers refused on their first morning after the concert; green wellington boots for the swampy fields below the barn; warm jumpers which made her sexy he told her; blue thermal underwear and sox donned on the chilly evenings as if they were athletic skiers or ravishing dancers; and an ornate wooden two-faced music stand he'd found in a junk shop, cleaned repaired and polished, a resting place for the hugely demanding Ysaye solo sonata, its empty side inviting another to share other music making. There were flowers on the low table in the sitting area, a shelf of his favorite books. She acknowledged Daniel had made a beautiful music studio, thinking about her at every turn. He was so endearing.

The kettle boiled.

Natasha filled the big tea pot to the brim and carried it into the next room where Mrs Munro was saying, ' . . . Oh, you mustn't leave her alone while you're away. Our Arthur will sleep over. I'll bring her a hot pot when I come over to clean.'

Natasha caught her eye. 'It's quite safe. But I don't want you alone in the barn when Danny's away. Arthur, you don't mind, do you? Maybe Natasha will play for you, bring some enthusiasm to your practising. Two violinists, as thick as thieves, as they say.'

Arthur nodded. His soft grey eyes lost behind a wild thatch of hair. 'I'd like that. Get away from Sis and her farmyard chatter.'

Mary pretended severity. 'Great! The peace of term time you pimply creep.'

Their mother shook her head. 'Shush, children. Natasha's not used to our bear pit.'

Daniel grinned. 'Listen Arthur, you behave. What *could* two violinists get up to?'

'We'll tango.' Arthur murmured glancing shyly at Natasha.

Natasha was a trifle put out. She had looked forward to a couple of days on her own. But, imbibing their kindliness she smiled. 'Yes, we'll dance and sing and play duets, and Arthur must advise me about Ysaye; he's so so impossible.'

'Me?'

'Not you, Ysaye.'

Daniel saw Arthur colour with pleasure. Was he the sort of boy Natasha liked? he thought uneasily. He sipped his tea. 'You know Mrs M, Natasha makes as good a cuppa as you.'

'Of course. She loves you as good as me.'

Daniel's mood lightened. Mrs M was so often right.

Natasha kept to the easy routine in Daniels' absence. She returned from a stroll through a deepening chilly dusk to find Arthur's violin case and tooth brush on the step. The boy waved from the top of the apple tree, jumped down pockets bulging and gambolled over. 'Mum told me you like apples. Here you are.'

Natasha laughed. 'The worms are packed with vitamins.'

Arthur swept up his meagre possessions and bounded inside. 'No wonder your nose is blackbird yellow.' he stopped. 'Natasha, I'll go if you want.'

'Put your things on my bed. Arthur, I'm glad you're here. Night's a grim black tree sometimes.'

He looked at her, pleasure-desire-relief on his face. 'Black trees black birds and blushing apples to tempt you.'

Natasha was startled by his eloquence. She grappled with his inference. 'It was Eve gave the apple to Adam. Then they discovered good and evil.'

Arthur was emboldened. 'They grew ashamed about what they did, and were kicked out of Eden.'

Natasha eyed the boy. '"Good *and* evil". All the good in my life is here.'

Her introspective preoccupation spurred Arthur. 'Is this really your bed? Don't you share with Danny?'

'No, we're friends.'

'But don't you want . . . you know . . .want.' he was silenced by his own tumultuous adolescent aspirations.

'Yes.' she whispered. 'All the time. But just now I can't.' Natasha trembled. 'Daniel is too precious. No more Arthur, please.'

Arthur's head swam. Behind their every-day masks they each knew shame, shared the same agony. Now he knew. At last, here was someone with his struggle. He was swept by a deep tenderness. He sat expectantly on her bed as she showered. He was next, a shrunken set of Daniel's thermals across his knees, like the ones she'd don. They were twins. Violinists, apple lovers in a complicated Eden of shared angst. He bubbled with relief and pleasure.

Later, he stepped tentatively from the bathroom. 'I'm a bit rude. You can see everything.'

She savored his manly form. 'Your cock, my breasts. Why not show them? Or shall we put on big tee shirts and be medieval page boys?'

Arthur shook his head. Although preoccupied by his revealing display and her keen glances, he knew deep down they were already dressed for paradise.

Natasha guessed his youthful thoughts. For she sought a segment of desire not completely adult. Rather, an embrace of sameness with difference she'd explored with Tyl when she was a similar age as this wayward gentle boy. She savored the boy's girlish reflection of herself. It was a tentative step towards becoming a fuller person. Similarly, Arthur sought the girl in her boyish reflection of himself as a way into adult sexuality, experiencing less anxiety and deeper pleasure than familiarly groping at school. Unconsecrated, each sensing balancing delights.

It was an immensely pleasurable evening, being childish adults, talking and talking, eating and drinking, laughter, nervousness; a host of satisfactions. He sleepily stumbled up the stairs to bed on the mezzanine overlooking the music studio and lay listening to her preparations for sleeping until she dowsed the lamp. The grim black trees had vanished.

Sweet velvety night cushioned their rest. Adding shelter to their holiday. When Natasha returned, The Gold Hill School of Music seemed more benign. She needed her new well of happiness to balance her disquiets: her struggles with Tyl and Ysaye were disorientating. She was a girl again overwhelmed by technical demands and flailing emotions. Mrs Mamsey, equally frustrated by her star pupil's refusal to seriously attend to her other work (including forthcoming exams), suggested Natasha consult Vladimir Godanov, a virtuoso violinist who'd flown in for recording sessions and concerts and several master classes at the School.

Vladimir looked askance at the tense drawn student, tom-boyish in jeans and a sloppy jumper, and her impossible proposal of playing an Ysaye sonata. 'There are only a dozen players in the world who'd tackle it.' he muttered in his thick Russian accent. Furthermore he was skeptical about the slim list of problems about which she wanted to consult him.

Unenthusiastically he told Natasha to start at the beginning, wondering how to kindly advise dropping the project. He sighed and waited while she drew her bow over a block of rosin, tuned and, without opening her music, began.

He was stunned by the life she tore from her violin, the fragments of Bach's third *Partita* and the *Dies irae* which rang, cries of joy and pain in terrible conflict - all the extremes of his native land (where peeing on a clay urinal was tinkling song).

This slip of an unkempt girl touches my soul, he thought, and looked at her carefully for the first time. She played on unawares until stumbling, she stopped. 'You see, it's there.' Natasha said embarassedly.

'My dear, who cares.' he said thoughtfully and took up his violin. 'My tomcat, my fingers arch over the neck. Only those fingers making notes touch it. It's easier to play and allows the instrument to sing. Position is everything. Try!'

He played the beginning of the sonata. Natasha nodded. It not only sang, it sounded neater. She tried again. Both engrossed, they worked on. He, demonstrating double stopping postures and bowing, she, rapt, following his every move. They tired.

'Go and practise. I'll see you tomorrow.'

'Brill. You've been great. You don't know how much I appreciate it.' She packed up and slipped away.

He sat staring sightless out of the window, shaking his head. 'In this cacophony, where did she come from?' He laughed. 'This grubby angel's been to hell. She's wonderful.'

Vladimir's grubby angel worked until she ached, sought his help until he suggested she leave Ysaye for a while to concentrate on tone by playing Bach with him.

'Bach's shadow falls on everything, and we will play the Master together.' He thrust music of a D Minor double concerto at her. 'Play with me tomorrow. Remember, tone before notes. I'll bring my accompanist.'

The last movement was canonic - both players having the same melody a few notes apart. Its complexity forced Natasha to find a fuller richer tone matching his until the two sounded as one. She was sweating and trembling with exertion. Only then did he relent, saying, 'Your playing reaches into my soul, Natasha. There's nothing more to say.' He kissed her, handed her two tickets for his next concert and dismissed her. 'I don't know what hell you come from, but hell-fire and joy make music worthwhile.'

She was exhausted, glad. He knew about hell-fire and joy. They shared it. She was elated, more convinced than ever she had to play this celebration of, and farewell to Tyl, now, while she still remembered everything as it was; not fogged by memory or the distortions of police or parents. She *would* play the sonata as her end of year exam. There couldn't possibly be opposition.

But there was opposition. The piece was not on the list, and beyond any student's skill; it involved no accompanist which the School thought a vital part of training; finally, the examiners announced, undergraduate students such as Natasha, had no authority to make changes. (Otherwise, what was the point of taught course work?).

Natasha sat outside the examination room for much of the day, patiently weathering frowns and queries about an absent accompanist, protected by her burning conviction that playing Ysaye was essential both in her personal journey and for her musical development.

Only Mrs Mamsey's advocacy persuaded the examiners to relent. At the end of the day they agreed to hear Natasha play only the first movement. Summoned, she entered the room, unpacked her violin, ran the bow over a rosin block and carefully tuned.

'Retune! Your A's not 440.' someone said.

'Is a common pitch necessary for a solo?' Natasha murmured. 'I found a slightly lower pitch helps the sound so much that I tune down a little, nearer to Bach's pitch.' What a silly battle, she thought, It's the music which counts, Vladimir would agree.

'Let's leave the subject of pitch and old music, shall we?' Mrs Mamsey said, depressed with the probable outcome.

Natasha waited for the *soto voce* exchanges to cease, for a silence to fill. One or two of the panel raised eyebrows, thinking the student too nervous to continue.

'Proceed.' one said wearily.

'I'm waiting for you.' Natasha said.

'Natasha, please begin.' Mrs Mamsey said trying to smile.

Natasha stood firmly on two feet, closed her eyes and lifted her bow. Her left hand was already shaking for the vibrato of the first notes.

The cheerful Bachian theme, filled with centuries of song, burst. Then the threatening furor of the most ancient *Dies irae* savagely intruded. Theme and counter theme battled it out in a rush of life balancing a breakneck stream of death. Full raucous irrepressible. With a firm brush of her bow it finished.

Shocked silence greeted the second, slow movement: sweet delicate melancholy. The bow slightly angled now, the sound thinner, an ordinary melody stripped of sentiment. That so fresh a player could express such hopeless desolation unnerved the jurors. Spellbound, they jettisoned judgement, unbelievingly heard two violins yet seeing only one slight crumpled girl double stopping. Such deep longing. Mrs Mamsey nodded, recalling the tortured girl she'd first met in the mental asylum. Then the movement's end. Bare wrath. A base note holding on to the everyday, an eloquent mirror of Natasha's state of mind since that first lesson.

Natasha paused and put her bow down. Still unchallenged, the third movement danced out jerky and plucked, skeletons far more scary than Saint-Saéns's *Carnival of Animals,* the Devil and his mate cruelly mimicking the jocund opening. Other's plaintive themes shyly intruded, but wrath held them all in thrall, with touches of nobility bringing tears as life was remembered and dismissed. Silence. Then, the last movement: a frenzy of struggle and terror, the fine threads drawing us all to the final only certainty. Such sadness, a longing to escape. It was magnificent. Ending with fevered cries, a resolution of sorts, with the last two chords savagely proclaiming "The End".

'Goodbye Tyl.' Natasha whispered in tears. Blindly she thrust her violin into its case. Blindly she sought, in a cruel silence, the distant door and left the room. It was over. No one heard her cries. No one cared. They never had. She fled through the tunnelled corridors of the School and out into the dragon streets, hurrying to the only refuge she had. Such a long tortuous journey to the small country station, tramping the rough lanes oblivious of birdsong and breeze, running away from the agonies of the past towards her secluded space in the barn.

A car pulled up. 'Hey, Natasha, want a lift? Home early for the holidays are ye? No one to meet thee? You can drop off at the Munro farm. Hop in, lass.'

Eventually she alighted, stood dazedly in the empty lane. There was a wild shout. Arthur came running. 'Natasha, oh, Natasha.'

'Arthur, what are you doing here?'

'I ran away from school. Can't take it anymore. At sixteen, they can't keep me there. I want to be a farmer, you know that. Mum and Dad's furious. I'm in the dog house.'

'You too. Dear Arthur.'

'Here, Natasha, give me your things. I'll take you home. You know Danny's away, do you? I'll have to look after you until the end of next week. Anyway, I'm not welcome at the farm just now. Come on!'

When they got in Natasha wilted and burst into tears. 'I ran away too. I played the Ysaye sonata. They hated it. I failed. All my dreams crashed. There's nothing anymore'

Arthur hugged her until she stopped shaking. 'We'll have a cuppa. And then you'll play it for me. Fuck all schools. How could you fail? That's for me. You're really clever.'

Tea soothed them. Then Natasha played the whole sonata. Arthur sat still as a headstone until it was over. Then he rose and gently took her violin from her, packed it away and drew her down , music still echoing in his ears, down onto her bed. He was untamed, tentative; fired by all they had ever shared, her vulnerability (and his), her incredible eloquence, her beauty. Many realisations.

'Natasha, you told me of our lives. Only the best player in the world can make music speak like that.' He kissed her hungrily.

'Arthur, do you really want me?'

'More than anything in the world.'

'All right then. Do you have a condom?'

'Of course. That's what fob pockets are for.'

'Dear wild gentle Arthur,. My bringer of apples.'

They lay naked in amazed exploration. She warmed to his youthful eagerness. He erupted as she caressed his burning skin.

'It's better that way.' she whispered. 'Now you'll last longer.'

But he quickly finished and lay panting beside her.

She stroked his soft cheek. 'Happy?'

'God, I love you Natasha.'

'My dear lovely boy, you mustn't.'

He kissed her mouth silencing it, suspecting she was right, half aware each had crossed a shadowy line and now faced the future.

They were perched like two birds on the back step dappled by late afternoon shadows when Mary found them. 'Natasha? Arthur, so there you are.'

'Hi sis. We've both run away from school, and all the better for that. Don't be cross.'

'No one's cross anymore. Dad decided he needs you here. Mum had a little cry. I think she's glad I'm staying and you're back here.'

Arthur grinned. Aren't they worried we'll *both* roll in the hay?'

Mary coloured. 'Arthur, that's enough. Dear bro. Your jokes are also serious. It's like the song:

> *Teenagers squeezed into jeans do it.*
> *Even half-baked Boston beans do it.*
> *Let's do it, let's fall in love.*

'Well, it's better than what we did at school.' Arthur blushed.

Mary was more intrigued by Natasha's trembling smile, 'Natasha?'

Natasha's face fell. Then it all tumbled out: the huge struggle to master the sonata, the determination to play it, the yawning silence, her despair in the examination room, and then flight.

Arthur hugged her. 'But we don't care now, do we.'

Natasha eased into his embrace. 'Mary, he's been such a good friend, dispensing his usual magic drying up my tears, bringing smiles.'

'Now Arthur.' May said fondly. 'Go up and make your peace and get your night things. We can't leave her alone tonight.' She smiled uncertainly at Natasha. 'I'm so glad you've come back to us. It's been a long time.'

Arthur happily leapt up and bounded away. Easing into family life and comforting Natasha was suddenly everything.

Mary sat gingerly down. 'Natasha, I want to tell you before the others do. I'm pregnant. They think it's a married man. And I don't tell. But you should know. I dearly love him. He is - sort of - married. Well, in ways that matter.'

'Mary?' Natasha was shocked. 'Are you happy?'

'Very, very. It happened. A wonderful surprise.'

'Don't you want to live with him?'

'I do, in a way.'

'So, he's in the village?'

'Um, sort of.'

'So you see him. That must be hard.'

'Not at all. It's always been that way.'

'Dearest Mary. You do look happy my lovely sister. Tell me, how can I help?'

'Be here as often as you can for me. And for him.'

'Mary?'

'You and Arthur have run away, coming to where you belong.'

Natasha saw pain and joy battling in Mary's gentle face. 'Belong? Do I? I don't belong anywhere. "For me and for him" You mean . . . Do you mean Daniel?'

Fearfully Mary nodded. 'You're angry. I know he loves you and waits for you. He and I are old friends, nothing more. I know that. Try to understand. You and I are sisters. I don't know anything else. All your loves (I've seen it in your eyes) and his baby. We're all nearby. I suppose you can't understand.'

Natasha was stunned. It was all true. Their intertwined lives, the sense of family. Daniel's devotion (was it really love?), then, her's and Arthur's escapes to be at home, to be together, to find (dare she admit it?) love. Tenderly she pulled Mary to her. They were crying the same fierce joy Natasha had tackled in her hymn of farewell to Tyl and in everything she played and had begun again to feel.

'Dearest Mary, of course I understand. You speak of sea music, the only truths. Dear sister, I know you love him. You always have, and me. It's why I came. For you, for Arthur. For him. For all of you and this bewitching place. I need all of you, especially you, to help me see properly. The world blinds me.'

She gazed at the apple tree. 'Nothing's altered. We share every-thing, because we always have. It's like chamber music. Although the focus changes we all contribute to the richness. If someone drops out everyone is the poorer. You've been amazing - all of you - coaxing a dead snail out of its shell. You were right, telling Arthur to be here. I don't ever want to be alone again. I want to be with you. Yes. That's why I'm here.'

She rocked Mary. 'His baby, wow!'

'Our baby, Natasha.'

'Lucky baby, so many mothers and fathers.'

'Danny's designing a flat in our hay loft for baby and me.'

'Does he know?'

'I'm not sure. He doesn't need to.'

'Our secret then?'

Mary nodded. 'Mum looks suspiciously at all the married men around, never thinking of Danny.'

'Don't you want him?'

'Yes, but not that way. You see, he's never been mine that way.'

'He doesn't seem to be anyone's. He's always loved Arthur. I wondered if he prefers boys.'

Mary shook her head resolutely. 'Yes, he loves Arthur. And he's waiting for you.'

'I don't know why.'

'One day you'll know.'

'Do you think people are like places? We grow into a place; can we grow into people in the same way?'

Mary smiled. 'But *we* feel. It takes time for us to realize that.'

'A life time.'

'It depends how carefully you look into yourself.'

'It's too dark to see anything.' said Arthur cheerfully joining them. 'Sis, you're to go home and bring a big hot pot over. Mum's cooking our supper. Come on Natasha and help me put these vegetables away.' He waved Mary up the slope. His smile matched the light he lit on the way to the larder. 'My fob pocket's bursting.' He nuzzled her cheek.

'Does Daniel love me?'

'Of course he does.'

'Oh. He'd be upset then.'

'At first. But I won't steal you.'

'Dear Arthur, I know that.'

'So does he. We share here.'

'Music of our bodies.'

'And love. And everything.'

'Is that what you escaped for?'

'Of course. It's what I've always wanted.'

'I think I understand.'

'I love you, Natasha. That too.'

'Dearest Arthur. You sound so fierce and manly.'

'Oo I am. GRRRR!'

'Arthur Bear growling in my bed hugging me.'

'Your life. For ever and ever.'

'How can you be all right?'

'If the future's like today.'

'Arthur, you growl about such important things.'

'Being here. With you. Being happy. Is there anything else?' He was radiant.

She pressed his swelling fly. 'Thank you for being here. Tonight you must help me come. Push my pain out. Show me happiness.' She kissed his astonished mouth pushing it into a smile which lit his whole body and warmed her.

As days passed her preoccupations with exams and the hectic city faded. The quiet calm of the barn soothed her. Gradually Natasha settled into its routine, working, resting punctuated by visits from the various Munros, and straying over fields and woods. Arthur worked the farm, arriving early evenings hungry for tea and sex, the urgency of his love-making settling as satiety grew, until stoically he withdrew because Daniel was expected.

Natasha wondered whether Daniel was the external world coming to torment her, or her dear friend returning home. She saw him walking springingly through the gate wheeling his bicycle, his wild mop of hair haloing a soft generous face, his fine hands and trim form radiating its usual fullness. Her doubts evaporated.

But he looked stern. She brushed her blouse down dusting off Arthur's joy, and waited for a rebuke.

'Mary met me on the road. She told me they failed you. I don't believe it. Natasha, you're brilliant.'

She gave a little cry of relief of welcome blowing away a remnant of fear. 'It doesn't matter. I'm here. If you'll let me stay.'

'Permission to stay? Nonsense. This is your home Natasha. But how could they? All your work. Such extraordinary playing. It's not right. I'll telephone Mrs Mamsey.'

'Let's have a cuppa, Daniel? She pulled off his back pack unhitched a couple of plastic bags from the handlebars and led him inside. Soon the kettle was singing, the tea brewing in a large golden brown teapot. She watched him drink. Hands round the mug, steam in his face, his shapely lips taking in the nectar.

'I don't believe it.'

His preoccupation with a dead exam, a pointless judgement ruffled her until resignedly she said. 'Then ring her.'

He returned perplexed. 'Natasha, you baffled them. Mrs Mamsey said it was agreed eventually they had to award you 100%. "For the most outstanding playing they'd ever judged." It's a first. You're a star. But they are insisting you abide by the curriculum next year. What on earth were you thinking of, blundering off without a word to anyone?'

'Tyl and you.'

'Tyl?'

'I was saying goodbye.'

'And me?'

'Wishing you would be here.'

'Dear one, I'm so sorry. But I gather Arthur and Mary mucked in.'

'They were wonderful.'

'My dear, I'm done in. Two weeks of meetings, pressures and sleeping in strange beds. I must rest. We're eating at the Munros tonight so needn't make anything here, thank goodness. I'm knackered.' He shook his head. Natasha, I'm sorry.'

Without a word she took his hand and led him to his bed, crouched and removed his shoes, then his outer clothes. Her heart skipped as she pulled back the bedding so he could lie. He was solid, dependable, still fighting for her, always supportive. She covered him. Watched him sleep thinking, so this *is* home. She wanted to thank him. It would have to wait.

The next morning they breakfasted under the apple tree. It was bright and still. The bleat of sheep drifted up the bird-sung valley. She couldn't wait.

'Hug me Daniel.'

His strong arms wrapped her into his solid body. He smelt pungent - work, trains, smoke, countryside. Natasha shut her eyes, nestling there but not expectant. Somehow he knew, certainly his penis did. She felt its urgency of their first morning. But it was different now. She was free. All the treasures he'd showered on her softened her self-deprivation just as Arthur's youthful lust had unlocked her. She nestled, this was home. Shyly she lifted her face to his. 'Daniel, all this time. Was it love?'

'Of course.'

'Arthur and Mary said "of course". Tell me, was it my last visit?'

'No. From the beginning. There was a girl playing at the Wigmore Hall. I was instantly smitten. When she stayed the night and I found she was an angel, nothing else mattered again.'

'I was locked away.'

'I knew, one day, I'd find the key.'

'There isn't one anymore. Yes there is. It's you.'

A smart low-cut sports car rolled through the gate down the gravel drive and stopped at the garage. A dapper man jumped out and waved. He had a straw boater rakishly over one eye and sported a big bow tie.

'I say, sorry to intrude.' he called with decorum. 'This is the barn of the Munro farm? I'm looking for Natasha. Are you by any chance . . .?'

They scrambled to their feet and nodded.

'What luck. How-do-you-do. I'm Nathan de Villiers.' He shook hands. 'Call me Nathan.'

Daniel freed himself. 'I'm Daniel. Coffee? I'll get you a mug.'

Natasha waited, trapped in Nathan's clammy hand, confronting his brow beaded with anxiety.

'Vladimir Godanov raves about you. My dear girl, you're our only hope. He's the draw-card of my little summer festival in St Brides at Birdlip. Can you, I mean, drop everything, er, and join him? It's you or nothing. Not an easy man, even for a virtuoso. But adamant. Know what I mean. What do you say?'

He was as doubtful as she. Silence. Daniel strode out with a steaming mug.

'I can't play in public. I've been sick. Even now there are nightmares.'

Daniel put his arm round her. 'You played the Wigmore Hall.'

'That was to you and a few others.'

Nathan, driven by desperation, bleated. 'The Wigmore, eh? Why, dear girl, The Birdlip audience is smaller, certainly not much bigger, all gentle music lovers, many, now friends. Of course, Daniel would be my guest. I beg you with all my trembling heart, reconsider! An emergency calls for a very special solution. Vladimir says you're the only possibility. Is it silence, or, with you, heavenly music?' He set his trembling mug down. 'You see, the quartet was ravaged when the first violin broke his arm last week. So we found a flautist for flute quartets, plus my wife Angela supporting them. Disaster averted until the second violin was felled by glandular fever. Our first concert is next weekend.

'My subscribers are lovely, not the usual snotty nosed bitchy lot. Far from it. So you see . . .' He tailed off, stood dejectedly as the apple tree shivered and grinned in a silence fresh with shadows and light.

Daniel very gently shook Natasha free of entwined tension. 'I like Birdlip. It's a small sleepy village: stone houses, stone walls marking fields, tall rather noble stands of trees (probably remnants of an ancient wood), a cosy pub and rather steep lanes. I've never been into the church but it's squat, rather like your studio. I had a job near there last year. Natasha, I'll come with you, naturally. There's no examination panel. No rules but yours and Vladimir's. Surely dream rather than nightmare?'

Nathan saw the struggle. He gulped, stepped back and uncharacteristically held his breath.

Natasha spat coffee grounds back into her mug. 'You want me to go?'

Daniel blinked. 'Come across the abyss to me, to all of us Natasha. Isn't it time to leave darkness and to join us?'

'That's what I've been trying to tell you.'

Daniel blinked back a tear and limply hugged her.

Nathan beamed and pushed his luck: 'Can you come now? I'll take you.' Natasha looked doubtful. 'Both of you.'

'Give us an hour.' Daniel said kissing her mouth against protest.

Her heart was racing. So was his. For at long last she'd said yes.

The car ride to Birdlip was exhilarating. Nathan drove nonstop recklessly well. They suddenly drew up at the rehearsal hall in the village.

When Natasha appeared Vladimir stopped in mid phrase letting out a Red Army whoop. 'Ladies and gentlemen, here is my little tom cat, we change everything. No Mozart. Natasha and I will play the double concerto in D Minor by Maestro Bach. Chamber music, let me think. Mozart flute quartets, trio sonatas by Tartini or Vivaldi, Madam de Villiers has agreed; some Schumann, Rawsthorne, Prokofiev. Da, da!

'Natasha and I will prepare. We work well, her cat to my dog. Just you see. Now, Nathan, for you is cheer up. Your programme printers will use the wee night folk and everything will be spick-span ready.

The leader grinned. 'Excuse me Vladimir, "tom cat"? Do you mean tom boy?'

'Ah, they tell me tell me. Yet your English needs more animals, like Mother Russian. But say after she plays whether I'm right. My little tom cat looks sweet and furry but her purring is full of claws and dancing and the spirits of Music. Never mind the words. Let's get started.' He rummaged in his battered leather music carrier, handed out sheets to the orchestra, a score to the conductor and grinned when a second music stand was positioned opposite his.' Only for rehearsals. We know it like the backs of our bows (you English say "paws").

The conductor, used to virtuoso bedlam, smiled. He opened the score, looked at all the players, lifted his baton for the new start.

Nathan cowered at the back of the hall near despair, until the strong fierce song of the violins and gutsy support of the orchestral strings, carried him in delighted disbelief to heights he often longed for. Finally he cried. It was going to be all right. Already it was wonderful.

Now there were to be rehearsals all day. After enjoying a couple of breathlessly brilliant hours, Daniel and Nathan left them to it and sloped off to the Pub. Nathan ordered the first round and booked them the only free room. Out of the tweedy shirt sleeved scrum, emerged a local councillor who hailed Daniel warmly.

Nathan excitedly plied them both with another round latching on to the man. 'I've seen your name on letters. Nice to clap eyes on you, what! May I be so bold as to beg a little more assistance? Vladimir and the musicians want a stage in the hall, like the chancel in the church, for better sound and sight-lines. Is there any chance at all, Councillor Ayrton?'

Daniel chipped in. 'Why don't I do a sketch and speak to Mike Manscotti. His joinery shop would do it. He's honest, did a brilliant job for me at *Hare Grove?*'

Councillor Ayrton, aware all the local B&B's were booked, the local pubs and restaurants busy, was tempted by this tangible improvement which could carry his name. He chuckled and nodded to Daniel. 'I'll stick my neck out. You are a great team. You've got a week and £3,000.'

Nathan swallowed in disbelief. 'Daniel, that elegant barn is your own work?'

'Yes.'

'My gracious, it's frozen music. You and Natasha are a pair of miracles. But there's nothing left for architectural fees.'

'No worries. I'd be glad to help the festival, Natasha also, and my friends round abouts who made *Hare Grove* such a pleasure, including Councillor Ayrton who helped with permissions. I owe him.'

The councillor smirked.

Nathan blinked. That slip of a girl, and now Daniel - two unlikely looking virtuosi. Well, music delivered unexpected gifts, he thought. 'Two shy wild flowers blooming in the cow-pat countryside' he said to himself, trying not to look too dazed. Was his festival shaping up to be the best ever?

Daniel was pleased to have something to do. Nathan cheerfully drove him to the joiners where he listened uncomprehending to talk about grand piano loads, mortise and tenon joints, stressed skin and portability, noting the sense in pieces which fitted together yet were light enough for Fred, the caretaker, to erect and cart away to store.

Mike the joiner sighed. Another emergency, he thought. I'd say no to anyone else, but Daniel is OK, and the money would tide them over the holidays. 'Now you listen to me Dan, me boy. The money'll pay for everything including fixing any cock-ups and transportation, AND (because I bet you're doing it for naught) something for you. People think ideas are free, coming from thin air. Oh, there is one condition: six complementary tickets to hear your girl and the Russian. Old Mrs Cooper was in this morning for her revamped trousseau chest. She was ravin'. People's sayin your girl's an angel. No wonder you keeps her to y'self.' Mike grinned. 'Agreed? Well, we best make a start.'

Of course it wasn't straight forward. They expected that. The joiners wearily called it a day at ten o'clock that night. Mike drove Daniel back to the pub and bought them night-cap ciders, quite soon clapping his big hand on Daniels' shoulder and saying, 'G'night, Dan. Great start. Probably do with you in the mornin before we begin cutting. Find out when we've access to the hall, will yer?'

'Mike, an amazing night. Shit, I forgot steps.'

'Wondered if you'd forgotten. I've got an idea. Let's speak in the morning.' Mike chuckled driving away quietly through the darkened village. He knew these two heads were better than one.

Daniel followed the signs up stair after stair to room 21. It was a crooked space right under the roof. Natasha had left a dim light burning and put his pyjamas on the pillow. She was curled up like a mouse at one side of a giant bed. ONE bed! He gasped. There, his angel slept. There beside her, space for him. He crouched down to watch her. Daniel was astounded. Asleep in his bed lay the fragile angel he'd tended since stricken by her so, so long ago; delirious times of waiting until now, when she'd zoomed through the abyss and was bravely facing her innermost monsters and tackling performances whose quality already made many gasp. He shivered in disbelief. 'Our bed.' he whispered. 'Oh, my Natasha there you are, dreaming. I never want to wake.' He undressed, donned pyjamas, switched off the light and slipped gingerly into bed. She was softly breathing. He nestled closer. Her warmth invaded his sleep all night.

They were woken by Vladimir who stumbled in bubbling about music and waving reams of it. His excitement blotting out their reluctance. He and Natasha poured over scores until another knock on the door heralded two flushed daughters of the house bearing breakfast trays.

Vladimir leapt up, a will-o'-the-wisp in his one-piece night suit, and left with a cheerful 'See you in an hour for a run through my little dumpling.'

Natasha sighed and felt for Daniel's erection. 'Tell your huge hungry man, soon.'

They ate. She showered and left. Daniel's mobile tinkled. The distant site foreman was adamant. Soil collapse was serious. The engineer was coming. 'OK, I'm busy this morning but I'll drop in later this afternoon. No, I'm not at home. So it will take time to get to site. Maybe Mike Manscotti (remember him at *Hare Grove*?) will drive me over.' Daniel grimaced. Another long day.

After he and Mike had checked dimensions in the hall, Daniel took Natasha aside. 'Dear one, there's a crisis on my *Firtree Grange* job. I can't get back here tonight. I want time with you. Is that so impossible?'

Natasha buried her head in his chest. 'I miss you all the time. It's silly, I know. Of course you must go and make beautiful buildings. But Saturday's the opening of the festival. Even though Vladimir and Nathan are so supportive, I'm scared. I hate crowds. I'm here because of you. Don't be away. I'm a mess, Daniel.' She shut her eyes for a moment, leaning into the encircling warmth of his body. 'Music and you and my life are a terrible tangle. I'm sorry.'

Daniel flushed with tenderness. 'My Natasha, I need your wonderful tangle too. I *will* be back on Friday come hell or high water.'

She was crying. Was it with pain, relief or delight in his response?

'I say, is there a problem? Anything I can do?' Nathan sidled over anxiously.

Daniel explained.

Nathan put a reassuring hand on Natasha's arm. 'Fret not dear girl, I'll pick him up from his barn tomorrow afternoon and whisk him here in one piece if that's . . .' He was ravished by her smile. (It matched his response to her playing). 'Anything for you.' he cried gaily.

Vladimir felt a twinge of jealousy in spite of his nightly jaunts with a lusty farm boy in the woods beyond the pub. Natasha's was a need not as lightly met as his. 'Being in the top league compensates.' he wryly told himself. 'Natasha needs the lift to a realization she *is* extraordinarily good.' Vladimir grinned. It was fun telling her this with music.

That afternoon, Mick and his team threw everyone out of the hall and installed Daniel's stage and the afterthought-steps.

Natasha and Vladimir were ferried to Nathan's house to join his pianist wife, Angela, in rehearsing a clutch of chamber music destined for a late night slot in the hall. The combination of Natasha's playing and Daniel's new stage had persuaded Vladimir to add some one-work performances after the evening's concert following a short break for refreshments.

'I'll take a collection for the musicians.' Nathan crooned, elated at the growth of his festival. There had been favorable newspaper reports of the preliminary rehearsals of the revamped programme. He thought it prudent not too show Natasha who was already flighty enough. His favorite was:

> THE BIRDLIP SUMMER FESTIVAL *is shaping up to be a premier music event. Vladimir Godanov has found a partner as brilliant as he. Natasha Cunnington, whom we heard first in a fine recital at the Wigmore Hall, is Vladimir's protege, and a student at the Gold Hill School of Music. Her last minute stand-in is felicitous. Their partner ship in the Bach double concerto, and a variety of string chamber music is already breathtaking in rehearsals.*
> *With so many fine players, this year's festival promises to be an especially treasured event.*
> *The festival director, Nathan de Villiers says a few tickets are left.*

Vladimir coaxed sparkling playing from everyone. On Friday evening Natasha stumbled wearily up the crooked flights of stairs to her room under the roof. She pushed open the door, saw in the dusky light a supine figure on the bed. She dropped her violin case on a chair and flung herself onto Daniel. 'Oo, goody, you're back.' She wriggled into his embrace delighting in his arousal and exchanging fervent kisses. 'Have you got a rain bonnet for that?'

'Now? Really? Oh yes. Arthur emptied his fob pocket last night and told me to look in the pub loo. It has an endless supply, if you've got lots of gold coins.' Daniel chuckled.

'Dearest Arthur. What would we do without him.'

Daniel struggled free, locked the door and stripped, returning to Natasha. With trembling hands he helped her undress. They lay, exploring with tentative hands and lips. She took his phallus in her hand. 'What a monster. And all mine.'

He flushed. 'I can't help it.'

'You can. What's yours is mine. It's fantastic.'

'Don't tease.' His cheek quivered.

'I'm not.' she said resolutely.

'They used to strip me at school, hold me down and bring me off chanting "For a horse you don't shoot much".'

'Daniel, it's beautiful. Look, it wants me.' She bent, pushed back its cloak of skin and kissed the gleaming helmet.

Daniel groaned and ejaculated.

Natasha held the softening flesh tenderly regarding his bashful face. 'A tiny rehearsal. It will dance in me next. Deep riches. Was that all right?'

He nodded, his ardor rekindling.

'I'm glad you're not gay. I wasn't sure.'

'Nor was I. It was difficult waiting, wondering if I could, if you, if you . . . Oh, Natasha I really love you.'

'Dearest, dearest Daniel. Come on. Oh, it's now, it's . . .' Natasha gasped as a huge fist filled her with pleasure, way beyond words.

Seas broke over her. Music boomed. Like the thirsting earth she opened and was engulfed by tides of majesty. Vaguely she felt Daniel's frenetic finish, a faint suffocated whimper as he rolled off to lie blissfully close. Drifting as she drifted, singing islands swimming on a sea of delight, wafting to sleep, to wake, to find each other with new tenderness, so that she wept for joy.

'I hurt you. Oh, my darling, I'm sorry.'

'No, no. Complete. Such glory; Daniel, how?'

He grinned. 'The same for me.'

'The same for me.' Natasha kissed him.

'I never thought anything could be that good.'

Natasha sat up. 'Um, do you mind if I call you Danny? All the people who truly love you use that name?'

Daniel was wide eyed. 'You want?'

'To be in your family. Free to love and work, living together . . . you know.'

'Everything, Natasha?'

'Everything Daniel. Music, apples, houses, babies. Sharing and sometimes separate.'

'Yes, Natasha.'

'Wow, a big yes Daniel, er Danny - my shadow my sunshine.'

He smiled in wonder. 'It's always been yes.'

'My wildness?'

'Is most precious.'

'Lots of music and love will tame me. Your sea music carried me here.'

Daniel swam in her eyes. 'I'm glad you're a mermaid and not an angel. Mermaids are slippery and wet and fabulously sexy, as well as singing like angels. Natasha, I want all of you.'

'Oh, Danny, so do I.'

They drifted in each other's arms, farther and farther from the everyday into oceanic realms whispering 'Forever.' 'Forever.'

The summer day had gently faded. Daniel reached behind and switched on his bedside lamp.

Natasha shivered at the rhythmic play of ribs on his stretched skin. She glowed. 'Danny, are you hungry?'

'Yes.'

'I'm famished. Let's go down for food.'

They dressed each other. Then, hand in hand, stepped down the ancient creaking stairs.

At the bottom, dazzled, they paused. Everything looked wonderfully different.

*

Choices

TOM LEANT COMFORTABLY upon a coppice gate. Frozen mud cracked under his heel. It's the sound of twigs breaking, he thought. He mused on increments of sadness burnishing soft hope into the leather hardness of a dutiful son, or a man of the world. Yet his youthful core still buoyed daring, delighted in the unimaginable, shone with ambiguity, cloaking doubt with shyness and brightening his vista.

'I'd like to show that Peruvian boy my frosty world.' His whisper hung like bird song in the chilly dusk. 'Is it as beautiful in the Andes?' Those gypsy eyes had flashed . . . messages of, of what? Hunger? Gratitude? Friendship? It echoed Tom's boarding school predicament the previous years. (Even then, an unruly child aching for connections). 'He's not for you.' he murmured. 'An assistant stage hand's below the interest of a child star.' Tom punched the gate until frosty dandruff spewed off its rails. He grinned. 'It's better these days, being in work, except for the dreary train journeys.'

But memories were arousing. He pressed longingly against the icy bars, turned and looked back along the rough path. Old man's beard clung to bare branches standing sentinel. Everywhere the grass was white. An animal had hungrily limped from tuft to tuft; proclaimed by the chewed stems and uneven wandering tracks, ending in despair or satiation? he wondered. The sky was lost in grey. Snow flakes floated down preluding a silent night. His meandering footsteps had fused with the frozen ruts of the track used in summer by hay carts and hikers. Now, the wizened world had frozen. Although chilled, Tom's ears burned.

'It's the cold. They're not talking about me. No one overheard what I want.' He sighed. 'The trees don't object, the introspective darkling world doesn't see or hear, or care.' he said retracing his steps, content seeping away as he approached the house.

He met his earlier tracks where they turned. 'Everything's balding, losing even memories. Too decrepit, too cold. Abandoned.'

A holly bush by the porch nodded, its blood berries affirming a cruel winter. Tom stamped snow from his boots, pushed open the door and entered.

A dim hush. Everyone gone, the abandoned clutter memorials to the past. Tom started. Beady eyes glared at him. 'It's only Sis's ancient teddy.' He shivered. 'It's unsettling, like the railway terminal. People couldn't mask its limbo. They might as well've not been there. Like now. My ache is independent of crowds. We passengers are as aimless as fallen snow flakes.' He sighed, and reread the note:

> *Darling,*
> *Your father is taking me to the theatre. We'll stay with Aunty Emma tonight and Saturday, returning Sunday evening. Hope your production is coming along. Remember, we'd love to see it when it opens.*
> *Your supper is in the microwave. I put other meals in fridge/freezer. Don't forget to feed Fluffy.*
> *Have a good weekend.*
> *Love,*
> *Mum.*

'Fluffy would hate Euston station: nowhere to sit, no comfort; the huge concourse filled with a muddle of stalls squeezing folk into formless left-over spaces, unable to view the electronic time tables or the platforms, debarred from the sky, abandoned by themselves. Its space erodes richness. A hellish reinforcement to education, the law, politics and religion. How faceless can we become? How empty? Hey, our play tackles that.'

Tom looked into the microwave. There, a bowl filled with Mum's famous sauce. A bag of pasta lay on the kitchen table, a saucepan of water sat on the cooker. Tom shook his head in thankful disbelief.

'As if I'd starve.'

A bell shrilled. Tom drifted to the door.

'Tess, what on earth?'

'Hi Tom. The ford of your driveway is treacherous. Can I?'

Tom grinned, stood back, glimpsed an icing sugared car in the yard and let the snow-flecked girl slip inside. 'I was about to have supper. Stay Tess?'

'So early? Parents?'

'Away for the weekend.'

'Oh! Shall I cook?'

'Mom's left a mountain of grub.'

Tess blushed. 'I'd like to Tom. Um, but it's snowing.'

'I'll get you onto the road. Don't worry. Here, let's have your coat.' Tom helped with buttons and sleeves and her head scarf. The fragrance of her hair startled him. 'Tess, you bring winter with a whiff of spring.'

Tess smiled archly, shook her hair free to cascade over her shoulders and lightly kissed Tom's cheek. 'I bear invitations to my twenty first, next summer. We'll feast in the Lock House pub, then cruise the canals in a long boat, drinking and dancing all night, to your band I hope. So you *must* come. Can you?

Tom's cheek burned. 'Me, and the *Madpies*?'

'Yes, all of you. Daddy's agreed to pay.'

'What do you want for a present?'

'Nothing. It's an official gig. You're enough.' Tess surveyed the trim slight form of her childhood playmate who'd accompanied her romps through woods and meadows, swimming, harvesting, talking and dreaming, who, in spite of boarding school, she thought, remained a bright-eyed boy rather than greying into respectable adulthood like most of her friends. 'It's not like the old days: you in theatre work, me at Uni. I miss you.' her cheek trembled.

'Me?' Tom guffawed. 'Our gate's bereft this winter. I was there today.'

'Does it have a white hat and gloves? And does it miss me?' Tom's wan smile warmed her.

'Of course. It wants to show you its finery and provoke a poem about hat and gloves.'

Tess almost frowned. 'It remembers our first kiss.'

'I thought you'd forgotten.'

'Nothing, Tom. What fun.'

'The *Madpies* and I, only if you stay.'

'Promise to get me out of here?'

'Promise.' Tom took her hand and led her into the kitchen. 'You deal with the cooking, I'll light the fire. Let's eat on our laps?'

'Firelight?'

'And candles.'

'Romantic.'

'Our coppice gate agrees.'

Tess looked earnestly into his warm brown eyes. 'Fun. Is that what you remember too, Tom?'

'Something special; like you, Tess.' His yearning flared. She's still so alive so terribly articulate, he thought happily. He leaped away brandishing a box of matches. Catching his erection under the band of his underpants he then bent and lit the fire, stood back watching grotesque shadows erotically challenge the staid livingroom, dancing to the music in his heart amplified by clatter from the kitchen. 'What fun.' Tom glanced at Teddy whose eyes twinkled in agreement.

Tom bounded to the kitchen. 'Let's open the wine. There's more where this comes from. Cheers, Tess.'

'Cheers, Tom.'

Their glasses touched pealing pleasure.

Tess clumsily stacked the empty plates which glinted in the fire light. She stretched out and giggled. 'I'm squiffy.'

'Me too.'

'*You* don't have to drive.' She ran her eyes down his sprawling body savoring its muscular undulations, intregued by his ballooning fly. She brushed the bulge whose yearning reflected her own. It had lightly pressed against her when they were kids, and during their long kiss by the gate. Once again she yearned.

Those carefree times remained. The fire had uncovered them. She wanted to give them voice challenging the silence of separation yet his tenderness, shy privacy, his tense beauty were evasions. Was he gay? Probably, he was with theatre folk. But he wanted her she found when he stretched for her, pressed her lips and kissed, lingering gently hungry, releasing her longings and daydreams urgently throbbing through her. Tess was in a whirl. Is it the wine? she wondered. The firelight, his bursting beauty, all those long summers wandering gleeful in shadowy woods, simmering in hot dry grass, growing up together? Does Tom feel the same?

He unzipped. She explored his hidden warmth, his treasure his longing. His anguished face proclaimed the ecstasy bubbling from him cloaking an inner power which had driven him to her defenseless, he gasped. 'Oh, Tess, so good. Oh sorry. God, I'm sorry. We should've stopped.'

'It happened. Both of us wanted it. Has anyone told you how

fantastic you look, coming?'

'No. We zipped up and turned away.'

'Boys?'

He nodded. 'Do you mind?'

Tess shook her head and hugged him. He hid his face in her breasts whispering. 'Better than any dream.'

Holding him unresisting, Tess agreed. A long ago summer after splashing in the stony stream they had lain like this, scantily clad, jubilant, at peace. It seemed nothing much had changed.

Tess stood up and dutifully carried the dishes to the kitchen. He was still lying on the floor when she spoke.

'Tom. Time to go. Be a love and guide me to the road. It's scary in the dark.'

He lay motionless.

'Tom, you promised.'

'I know. All right, I'm coming.' Grudgingly he rose, pulled his pants on and followed her to the coat stand in the hall. As she rugged up he drew her close and kissed her. Longing and gratitude mingled. He struggled into a top coat and opened the door, drawing back as a flurry of snow swept his face.

'Let's first look at the track. It looks bad Tess. Come on.' He pulled out a torch. They fronted the silence of falling snow skidding down to the icy ford where he stopped her. 'It's impassable. We're snowed in. You'll have to stay.'

Tess skipped up the mushy slope after him. They bounded into the house awash with a perfect dream. Tidying up forgotten, they scurried to his bed, nimbly abandoning clothes finding endless pleasures in their bodies and in talk. Finally grey dawn nudged them asleep. The whole world slept under a chill white blanket.

Tom woke to purring and a tongue raking his cheek. 'Fluffy you slept with us wicked pussy. Hungry? Golly its midday.' Tom yawned, rolled out of bed, flung back the curtains and padded to the kitchen escorted by an engratiating cat. Fluffy gobbled while the kettle sang. Tom hurriedly made tea and scuttled through the chilly house to bed. Tess smiled over her mug. 'The snow's blinding in the sun, everything's sparkling.'

'They get it from your eyes.'

'Do they? It's your doing Tom.'

'It was fantastic Tess.' He pushed against her. She caressed the wand which had filled her. Tom groaned, stiffened and wet her thigh.

'That's for the tea.' Tess studied his fallen face. It's as if Tom's on a desert island, so alone he thirsts, she thought. She snuggled down with him enjoying his bashful ease in a luxury of skin.

While Tess prepared brunch Tom inspected the front drive.

'It's not only snowed in, but the water over the ford's frozen so no one can come or go. Let's ring our folks. They'll have to stay put. It's an impasse.'

He grinned jubilantly as Tess danced round the kitchen waving a wooden spoon in time to her impromptu song,

> *Snow snow crispy snow,*
> *lots to do and nowhere to go.*
> *Lots to do with you with you,*
> *frisking and fucking, Tu-whit tu-woo!*

Tess grabbed his arm.They fell into a loose embrace. Lifting her head she swam in his eyes. 'Tom, there's a Shakespeare song:

> *When icicles hang by the wall,*
> *And Dick the shepherd blows his nail,*
> *And Tom bears logs into the hall,*
> *And milk comes frozen home in pail;*
> *When blood is nipped, and ways be foul,*
> *Then nightly sings the staring owl:*
> *Tu-whit, tu-whoo! - a merry note,*
> *While greasy Joan doth keel the pot.*

'So full of winter and of life. You bear logs, I'll keel the pot. We'll find a way to our gate and then we'll kiss and coo with the merry owl. Tom, I love you.'

'Is it Christmas: so many presents? Wild and wonderful Tess, never grow up.'

'And you?'

'Hungry and happy. You give me life.'

'I'm full of yours.'

A wondering kiss sealed their dream.

After a snack they ventured out, through the white-hung garden into a dazzling landscape.

'It's new and tidy, scarred by few feet - us, a few birds and a fossicking hare' carolled Tess.

Tom burst with happiness. 'I'm hungry and new.'

'That's how you look.'

'Thanks, Tess. For staying. For letting me . . .'

'Being here again.'

'Like the old days. You're right, Tess.'

'It's the same place but we've changed.'

'No we haven't. Just the same after we strip off: clothes, convention, oldies' clutter.'

'Tom, our needs are different.'

'You hold mine.'

'So do you. I think you always have.'

'It didn't seem much then did it Tess?'

'Children don't dwell on choice. We didn't weigh need or response.'

Tom squinted into the brightness. 'Perhaps being together is enough.'

'I want to share.'

'You always have.'

'I suppose I have. But now it's different. I'm glad you're the first Tom. Now, as when we were kids.'

They had reached the coppice gate. She stopped and turned to him.

Tom felt her yearning. He slid a hand into her jumper, found a breast and pressed a nipple. Tess melted into him until lips touched lips, mouths opened and tongues explored. Tom held her up awash with lust: hers, his, hers, and everything sparkled yes, yes, yes.

'Before we go back, let's make angels. I'll show you how.' Tess skipped off the path into deeper snow and flung herself on her back, opened and closed her legs and arms, then carefully got up. 'Look, an angel.' she said smiling. 'Now it's your turn. Go on Tom.'

After brushing each other down they leant on the gate and admired their guardian angels until Tess stirred.

'I'll go back and ring Mummy. She'll be wondering. Shall I make us tea?'

'The smallest cup. I can't wait any longer.'

'I'll put you on your back and make angels with you, my man Friday.' Ambling away Tess chuckled. 'Then you must tell me if you've a tiny bit which loves me Tom.'

He watched her prance away. 'Tess's laughter adds to the beauty here.' he murmured.

The naked trees were elegantly etched on the delicate blue sky fleeced with orange clouds cushioning the waning sun drawing long purple shadows from every rill. Ice-stiff grass glowed. The snow blushed slightly gold. Rooks wafted home, specs high in the clear air. A faint skirl of sparrows entwined with the remnants of Tess's laughter. 'Don't squabble, lads, Tess and I'll put crumbs on the bird table and keel the ice off your water bowl.' He called.

A thrush fluted its evening song enchanting the gleaming desolation, stirring the young man.

'It's our song. I do feel new. Hungry too, as hearts beat as breath pants, as thrushes sing perfection into the world. Oh, Tess.' Tom skipped and skidded along the track. 'What's new is the feeling I'm going home.'

Readers might now wish to read Thomas Hardy's poem *The Darkling Thrush*.

The Defender

THE EXPLOSION blew off the mountain top crushing drilling machines and the pipeline, burying every bit of gear and equipment under a mess of immovable rock. Nothing was left (the police said) neither blueprints nor evidence incriminating a single terrorist. Suspicions would soon fall, it was rumoured, on townsfolk and on those in the valley nearby. But with no evidence and no witnesses, our glee was untarnished.

But who knew about the top secret drilling through the mountain, threatening every local both in town and on the land? Probably very smart skilled persons from the town; for the valley dwellers, peaceful if unconventional, were all accounted for. So, who? One of us, or outsiders? Was terrorism harboured in the country town, did it lurk in the distant city or, like historic Bushrangers, skulk in the Bush beyond?

The place was crawling with strangers (mostly police, we guessed). Everyone was edgy. Too much ferreting, yet sharing our question, "who?" but not our delight the Bush, the town and everyone who lived there had been saved by an irremedial act.

A lone tree stood sturdy high, frothing at the fierce sun, shaking out shadows to dance like a swirling skirt around its foot. A wiry handsome young man rested against its dappled trunk pensively studying the valley sprawling below him. An unruly river holding in a loose caress virgin forest, contoured fields of wheat with olives, an untidy scatter of huge boulders, grassland and clumps of trees sheltering a variety of houses looking almost as natural as the rocky outcrops. This bewitching day, pealing songs of birds mixed with distant calls of children gambolling between rocks and water, naked bodies gleaming with sun and river, as dazzling as their cheerful shouts.

The man stirred. 'Soon my own kid will join them. Beloved, all of them; ah innocence, we're so damaged in growing-up.' The man looked up through the shimmering branches. 'Clouds, always different yet constant, the same for millennia. The blazing blue of the sky filled with fluffy dreams and promises while here on the ground, despair and ugliness. I can't laugh like a child anymore. How long will they?'

He pulled up his shorts fumbled and peed onto the leaf litter, shook his penis dry and sighed. 'Only Kirsty, already swelling, makes me forget about separateness. Her caress, my delight, finds the child in me. She calls it a magic stick. It *is* with her. Then, clouds, river, trees contain me, shoot me far into paradise. We are gleaming new yet terribly ancient like the rocks. Old bodies fresh with love. Is that it? Kirsty says I'm a wild man. Maybe it's true. Hidden behind clothes, language, customs I embrace the unthinkable, the immeasurable. Is that what she means? Yet I've always tried to be dutiful.'

He pulled the foreskin off his glans. 'Softest skin cloaking a wild one-eyed face. Jo, our worldly doctor neighbour, says it's the root of beauty - felt and seen. How much does she know about mine? She wants it. So do I; that secret has long been told but I can't damage this paradise. I mustn't for all our sakes. And our baby, our children who'll soon enough scramble down to the river finding joy and companionship, the love of clouds, rocks and each other, as we did. They'll be gods and goddesses in their time, and long after I'm gone.' He let his shorts leg fall down his muscled thigh, demure, decent, eying ants too busy with the damp to be aware of a new shadow fallen on them.

'G'day Luke. Not at work today? I wish you'd play footy with me.' A stout ten year old stood eagerly jigging, a brown leather lozenge in the crook of one sunbronzed arm, quizzically admiring his hero, defender of the Town's Juniors with the best scores over three seasons. 'I practised as you said. But my drop kick is still bad. Will you?'

Luke watching eagerness flicker over the soft young face, melted with trusting grey eyes dancing for him, and the dawning promise of a fit beautiful body visible through brief shorts and a thin tee shirt. He swallowed his pleasure. 'G'day Nestor. Not now Mate. I've things to do at home. Later maybe. Practice a bit more, can you?'

The boy spied the damp leaves, grinned pushed his shorts up and weed on the same spot in unconscious trust mimicking Luke, toying with a thrill of intimacy. 'OK. If you promise to play later. I'll tell my little brother Timi who's swimming now. Kim might come if he's over his mood: Gran says being fourteen is difficult and Timi's better off being a fish. PLEASE Luke! We'll be in the orchard. Gran will give us tea, she's baking today so it should be yummy. Anyway, she wants to see you she said. Will you? Please?'

Luke's loneliness imploded. 'No. Yes. Maybe. Oh Nestor, I'm . . ' his voice tailed off.

The boy looked up and lightly nodded. 'Play with us. We'll cheer you up. So will Gran.' Nestor had no qualms about the human condition. Either he or Bunyip (central figure in their bedtime stories) smoothed away sadness. That was the magic in the valley some called caring which he considered a normal part of every day.

Luke flushed. He so wanted the intimacy of a hug, of losing himself in this youth, of finding trust and hope and love, in abandoning doubt and guilt. But messing about with boys and a ball was not enough to assuage his emptiness. Another bigger game was worrying him. One without umpires or coaching or applause. If only there were rules, if only . . . Luke bent and wiped stray urine off a youthful golden calf. 'All right Nestor. Footy and tea later.'

The boy grinned. Now he shared peeing *and* football with his hero. The valley had heard. Gleefully he drop-kicked, the ball spinning up into the air, then dashed after it along the track towards his house glad Bunyip had brought such happiness.

Luke watched him go with a twinge of pleasure. Nestor had remarkable understanding: first befriending (admiring was more accurate), then nakedly declaring it; marrying him and Kirsten by the river very early on before marriage had been broached, then haunting their house when they eventually moved in, curious about home-making and love making, involved with everything. Luke, aware of his shyness, had not "explored" his body (as Kim had described their engagement); Kim, Nestor's mature precocious older brother, was careless of social risk. Luke longed to be the same.

He meandered back to his own house loathe to continue repairing the ground recently churned by his builders installing the new pre-fabricated wing. He wandered inside for a glass of water, sat in the gloom studying the pictures Adam had given them of a week-end after Mary's and his joint wedding and baptism of their baby, Jason. Mary was Luke's big sister, Jason his nephew. What a cheerful time: a crowd of children wearing nothing but smiles lingering on the flat swimming rock by the river, plus a huddle of dogs and a few grown-ups, including him and Kirsten, not yet ready to swim. Luke grimaced. 'Freedom, joy and innocence.' he muttered. 'For how long?'

'Forever. Forever. Forever.' The gnarled trees overhanging the house whispered softly brushing the corrugated iron roof. A dog whined in assent scratching the outer flywire door. Nick and his attentive bitch wanted work to begin, wanted a drink from the empty trough beside the tank, wanted to gambol and to guard a busy master whom they often chased as he rode his motorbike back from town and along the rough valley track who fed, watered and played with their puppies and welcomed them all onto his verandah as if they owned it, for which they responded with occasional rabbits caught in the bush, and once, a snake, plus the chewed shoes and messes incontinent puppies sometimes leave.

Luke pulled off his shirt and stumped outside, grabbed a mattock and strode to the piles of earth and rocks. He glanced approvingly at the area already shaped and, after filling the dogs' water trough, continued the back breaking work of preparing the garden. Kirsten was away in the distant city for a few days giving him time to dig fruit tree holes, flower beds, a levelled lawn and mounds as they had devotedly talked over. He was changed by their new house, the prospects of a family, a sumptuous wife. She would reward him in various ways he hungered for. The dogs lolled in the shade panting and contented. For them, nothing was out of place.

The shadows lengthened. Luke squinted at the dimming sun, stood his tools against the verandah edge, pulled on a tee shirt and followed the dogs down the track to what was called "The Green" ringed by the houses and pavilions of the original family where three grey-eyed brothers excitedly waved and scampered towards him. Luke's spirits rose. He loved football, doted on these three rascals who boisterously defined his own sexuality, thought and enthusiasms, each a unique reflection of life in the valley, and a special friend. In diffuse ways they too endowed him with magic as Kirsten did.

He fondly mused over the saying, "The child is father to the man". His feelings confirmed this. A second truth lay in their involvement with personal skill rather than a preoccupation with competition. It was a cheerful balance which Luke took to his training sessions in the country town beyond the valley. In spite of their down-playing of competition, defence was effective and winning easier. He wondered if the intense connection between player and game which skill wrought was the cause. They played footy like they played music, striving for the sharing of a perfect performance; enjoying the sweaty struggle, the physicality and experiencing power. Unabashed, the boys had adopted Luke as the perfect 'footballer uncle-brother'. Endowing him with a prowess effecting all their efforts. Deepening enjoyment and love.

A frail old woman watched fondly from her verandah until seeing Timi, the youngest, flag waved a scarf and called 'tea's up!' She loved the scramble of shapely male bodies, heaving breath, sweaty faces and eagerness as they fell sprawling at her feet laughingly calling for her cookies and drinks. She had always intensely nurtured sharing. It gladdened her to find it, particularly with her grandchildren and in her extended family of which Luke and Kirsten had become a part.

Luke often reminded her of Tim her late husband. Whereas Tim had always embraced everything fearlessly, Luke, even as a grubby small boy, nervously outfaced risk. He had, since the explosion, seemed unusually withdrawn. A lifetime with Tim had taught her how complex and fragile sensitive men were; now he was gone she wanted to support this fine young man. She'd talked it over in her mind with Tim who encouraged her.

After the three boys scampered away to baths, supper, a story and bed, Sophie placed a feeble hand on Luke's firm shoulder and looked carefully at him. 'My dear, peace and quiet now my sweet grandsons have gone home, they do love football with you; by the way, I asked Miranda for our old crib, the one Jo, Adam, she, all my children - and hers - first slept in. I thought, maybe? Kirsten might need it sometime soon. Am I interfering?'

Luke flushed slightly, disabled by the intimacy. 'Um, yes. I suppose we've never said anything.'

'I cleaned it up with help from Kim who worked with a will, bless him. Anyway, it's ready. If you need it?'

'Kirsty says it's due in five months. Did she tell you?'

'No dear. Just intuition. The valley provides signs. I am a silly parrot reading too much into them. Yet I can still help somewhat. Tell me, does my Jo know?'

'No one yet.'

'We need a doctor. She's brilliant and is very fond of both of you, so confide in her, because she's family and a doctor like her father, my own dear Tim. And another thing . . .'

'The children?'

'No Luke, you. My most secret thoughts following the night thunder I heard and mentioned to no one, which turned out to be the explosion which saved us, that's what I wanted to share with you. Thoughts not requiring a reply. Rather, placing them in the silence of our beloved valley which together we might continue managing. Now listen: in this world of appearances, every act must have an actor, every team a leader. Well, as you know our leader is a mythic creature Tim called Bunyip. Much of what happens here is cloaked in dreams. You and Kirsten realize we are influenced by the invisible, most of it shared, bits remaining secret. That loving quality of this place is embedded in its history and in us.

'Only after Symph died and Will and Miranda settled here did any of us realise Symph, a quaint old bushman, had been guardian of the valley and ourselves. He (not we) supervised defence from marauders of this precious valley in our struggle to settle here and nurture it. Only after your brother Peter's wife died and he and Jo married did any of us remember his old house overgrown in the Bush which is now yours. See what I mean by invisibles?'

Luke shyly nodded.

'From another viewpoint, I am reminded of something Picasso said during his stint making clay sculptures, "To make a dove, first I must wring its neck." Within creation is embedded destruction; the two are paired. This invisible fact, above and beyond ordinary law, guides the making of everything. Creativity inevitably involves destruction just as love is linked to hate, happiness to pain. I see you understand. But I want to say to you that in following the one set of rules we must overlook the other, otherwise firstly, nothing is created and secondly, we go mad.'

She wiped a stray wisp of grey hair from her face and gently touched his arm. 'With Kim you each experienced your paired male and female selves. It could be misunderstood as an illegal grope. I, he and you knew it was a mutual exploration of masculine feelings of love. Yes, it was wild *and* wonderful. Scary *and* thrilling. Harmless, eh?'

Unclenching his fists he nodded.

'Most things done mutually with love are harmless. That is another essential mystery which doesn't need publicity, only deeper acknowledgement.' Gran paused. 'Sometimes we have to do terrible things in resisting evil. I am convinced - so is Tim - a law above the law contains the truest judgement. For instance, the collapsed mountain. It might be due to vandalism by strangers in an act to which we are not party (as the police seem to believe). Or it was an inspired act by our community to save its life, its well-being, its environment. A huge achievement. Judging an act such as this pushes us into another sphere, into Bunyip's universe where honour can be attached to criminality, as pain belongs with love, and where heroes are unknown but revered.'

She almost smiled at his tense face. 'Dear one, I don't know what happened. I don't need to. What I believe is the valley has another invisible champion who protects everything, fields, forest, river, rocks, all us folk, the whole town, the fecundity of our world and our future. No honour can be showered for this, only pride, admiration (like my grandsons grant you) and the greatest of invisibles, love. Surely these balance guilt and fear? Ask inside yourself! For it's your own very own conversation.

'Anyway, it's an old woman's considered thoughts as much as an expression of my deepest feelings. Now, I want you to go. Bless you for bringing so much joy to the boys, for ardently making a home amongst us, gracing the valley to which you surely belong. Shall I ask Nestor and Kim to bring you the crib tomorrow?'

Luke nodded; numbed and reeling he rose, went unsteadily away over the Green and along the dirt track snaking between clots of trees towards his house. The day had waned. He shivered chilled by early dew. The first faint stars wept in a darkening sky as they had the night, quite alone, he had used Adam's rejigged mobile phone to trigger the distant charges Bert and he had planted in the illegal drilling cavern containing machines and a plethora of pipe work. He thought no one had heard the thunderous explosion nor guessed how it happened. Even the dogs had slept while the world was blown away leaving his unbearable secret in this valley of love where such evil should not be allowed to shape the earth or to plant or to nurture, a gross extreme best obliterated. His impregnable youth was corroding. Now a curse was ripping out his guts and all his dreams were bleeding away.

Lights through the trees. Jo's family house. He needed warmth. Light. Healing. Something to still his dread. He stepped up onto the dusky verandah. Shadows milled. His hand and legs were licked by friendly dogs their rough coats grazed his bare skin. As usual, the door opened easily. The lights inside blinded him.

Jo was shocked by a youthful apparition of her husband years ago; her girlhood dream long before she had married him. But she knew it was Luke, knew he was troubled, wanted to hug his anxiety out until beauty and confidence returned. And suddenly understood the disquiet she'd watched over several weeks. With a flush of longing she dropped her book, rose and took him in her arms - a frail limp precious thing containing godlike majesty, everything she'd ever wanted.

Dazed, they swigged shots of whisky until their stomachs burned. And numb, yet terribly alert, they collapsed on the couch whispering endearments, searching for skin with fingers and lips. Abandoning clothes thoughts and caution they lay naked together burning with wordless hunger.

Jo caressed the slim muscled back its topography inspiring her whispers: 'Of course we love. Just as we love the valley, children, husbands and wives, family, yes, all of them. Each other. Oh Luke, each other. For always.'

He nodded again and again as she felt for his phallus and took it to the mouth of her vagina. His every nod drove it. On and on until they shimmered together. His body nodding and thrusting at pleasure. She gasping, responding, matching him: 'Luke - burst - *my* - mountain - Oh - I - know - it was - you - you - and - my - brother - and. - Burst, yes! Are you coming?'

Luke was panting, sweat running down his tensing skin smarting his eyes, slipping on her arching body, building, building glory, currents seething in dynamite. 'I'm nearly there.'

She spoke to him through the whirlwind. 'Come any time. I can . . . Ah, AH Luke, it - was - you - mountain - wasn't - it? Oh now NOW.'

Lost in the maelstrom he thrashed wildly and ejaculated, 'Yes, YES! Yesss.' collapsing on her washed-out body, empty sacks, flushed and ruined. 'Yesss . . .' bodies sharing love and the most terrible secret.

Overwhelmed, he lay as dead. Jo tenderly brushed matted hair off his sticky brow, reached up and kissed his neck and face. 'There, there. Let it go my darling. It's ours and nobody will ever know, never, while the river runs, the valley remains and our kids and our love. Never, never. Not even the trees will whisper. It's ended. We can go on.'

Blindly he saw the silver thread of the river dividing and joining the land, felt the surge of water easing with ageless inevitability towards the faceless immensity of the ocean. Secure, he drowned in her arms as life returned to normal.

*

IF you enjoyed these stories you may be interested
in buying two companion volumes:

Loukoumia :

FIFTEEN STORIES set in Greece from 800BC to the present day. The
earliest is *Goats and Stones* an ordinary man's odyssey set in Aulis where
the Greeks were delayed on their way to Troy, also *Song of Songs*, the
recording of Homer's two epics. *The Wine Dark Dance* is a semi-fictional
biography of a modern islander. In *Home from the War* a boy relives the
Odyssey, as, similarly in *Ship of Flowers*, a girl is enlivened by a story.
Persephone's Veil and *Azure* explore the influence of myth. Other stories
are set in modern times: *On the Smoking Road, Yiayia, Teddy, Shadows, The
Sailor, Oghams of Want, Repairs, A Cat with no Name*.

ISBN:0-9520851-9-4, 210x146mm, 203pp, PB, 2006. RRP:£11.50.

Outrageous Fortune :

THIRTEEN STORIES: *Tree Man* set in Victorian England, *First Kiss* in
contemporary Australia. Both *Plundered,* set in Greece, and *One Eyed* in
Europe post 1945, concern rape. *Down Some Road* describes contemporary
South Africa. *Beyond the Crib* is a tripartite story in medieval and present
day England. *Mirrors* is set in modern Italy, *Pause in Heaven,* in
Afghanistan, *Loss* in Iraq and Italy, *Intimate Letters* (after Janicek's string
quartet) is set in Australia. *Srebrenica* reflects on the Jugoslav war, *Only a
Skerrick* concerns three generations of Australians.

ISBN: 978-0-9552974-0-3, 210x146mm, 320pp, ill. PB 2007. RRP: £12.

** WRITE TO The Sicnarf Press (see address on verso of inner
title),
or e-mail to <francisoeser@hotmail.com>.
Quote reference SS1-3 ask for special discounts. **